Hidden Coven

The Complete Series
Books 1-5

Kim McDougall

CONTENTS

Book 1
INBORN MAGIC

Incantation

My will into fire. It was a simple spell. What could go wrong? I tilted my head, studying the three spell ingredients on the grass—an amethyst, a posy of fresh buttercups catching the last rays of sunlight, and a candle in a glass votive—all sitting with me inside a ring of salt.

I had no idea if that was right. This was a seat-of-the-pants adventure.

Damn, it's humid.

A proper witch left her hair long and loose for rituals. Mine hung like a damp towel around my neck. The grimoire suggested spells were best done sky-clad, but public nudity made me self-conscious. Even in my secluded backyard, I wore a long t-shirt and panties.

I peeled the shirt from my damp skin and rearranged the ingredients again, laying the flowers across the amethyst. Buttercups were a visual aid to represent heat and light. The crystal would bend my sympathetic magic to ignite the candle and POOF! I'd have fire.

Light into heat, heat into flame.

I frowned at the wilted flowers. Did withered buttercups retain their affinity with the sun? Would a carnelian stone be better than the amethyst for fire magic? Maybe. I dithered and I knew it.

This was the problem with independent learning. I had no one to ask about the finer details of spell weaving. The only decent instruction book I'd found was Miss Abernathy's Grimoire, an ancient, hand-written tome of dubious origin. Miss Abernathy said to "use a crystal attuned to your spirit and the cycle of seasons." What the hell did that mean? How could I tell if a stone was attuned to me, let alone the season?

I sighed. The afternoon wore on toward dusk. The amethyst would have to do. At least it had grounding properties. If nothing else, I could use some grounding. This whole process left me jumpy.

Carefully, I poured more salt on the circle around me to keep out bad spirits. Better not to chance it. Not that I expected demons to be interested in my lowly attempt at magic, but Miss Abernathy's first rule of conjuring was "try your best and prepare for the worst," one of her frequent and slightly patronizing platitudes.

The ground was warm and damp under me with the loamy smell of recent rain. I crossed my legs and stretched the kinks from my neck before closing my eyes and trying to relax. Turning my mind inward, I pushed away hundreds of fledgling thoughts vying for my attention. My connection to the ground evaporated as I tuned out the itch of grass on calves and thighs. Waves of light and shadow swirled across the canvas of my closed eyelids, splitting and melding like breakers on a beach.

This has to work.

The number of near-disasters and odd coincidences in my life came to a head last month. I could still feel the strain of my clenched fists while Charles, my cheating ex-boyfriend, choked and clawed at his throat. I hadn't touched him, but his eyes bulged, and his face turned red before realization made me stop. I had done that to him.

That fiasco spurred me to finally take up the reins of my education into the dark arts.

Wrong thoughts.

I shoved Charles aside and focused on the sensation of my body parts dropping away one by one. My toes disappeared first, then my calves. A light breeze prickled my sweaty skin, breaking my concentration.

Deep breath in. I began again.

Goodbye toes, calves, thighs, shoulders…

My mind floated in a whorl of light and dark, free but anchored to the secret well inside me—a space between my heart and my womb where I imagined all my memories, hopes and dreams were stored. I dipped into that well, drawing on the power I found there.

I opened my eyes. The last rays of sun glinted off the crystal.

"Ignis." My voice rang like a church bell heard two counties away.

The amethyst glowed, so dark purple it was nearly red. The rest of the world blurred and darkened as I looked down a long tunnel at the stone and posy.

Light into heat, heat into flame. Power of the sun into fire!

Something inside me broke, like the membrane around a yolk, spilling power through my veins.

"Ignis!" I shouted.

The amethyst gleamed.

The flowers blackened and smoked.

Light into heat, heat into flame!

The candle wick sparked. A giddy surge of power washed over me. It was amazing. Exhilarating! Every fiber of my body tingled with a brilliant intoxication. I held up fingers that glowed from within. I was the fading twilight, even as I bathed in the twilight. I was the power. Magic rushed through me, flooding my veins, bolstering me until I felt like a leaf tossed on the wind. I laughed with pure joy.

Then the wind became a tornado.

Magic turned livid. Light flared with a white-hot screech. Pain shot through me. The candle shattered in an explosion of wax and glass, slashing me with dozens of tiny blades. But the pain went much deeper. This new force bit my soul, tore a piece of me away, and shredded my power.

I tried to scream but heard only a desperate gurgle from my throat.

I couldn't move.

The magic I'd unleashed thrummed, drowning out all sound and thought. I tried to unlatch the razor-sharp tendrils biting into me, binding me to the magic. But they clung to my secret well. I'd laid open my sacred space, and it was now violated by power I couldn't control. I was caught, held tight in an invisible iron grip.

And it sucked my magic dry.

Frozen, I teetered back and hit the ground.

SALVATION

The pain of my face rubbing against the ground woke me. My body spasmed with cold that had nothing to do with the weather. My thoughts rolled like sludge. I tried to sit up but my arms and legs didn't respond. I breathed deep. At least my lungs worked.

Shards of glass littered the ground and clung to my skin and hair. A war drum pounded in my head. I felt a desperate need to blink, but couldn't force my eyelids shut.

How long had I been out? My limited view took in the back end of the yard, the fence and tall cottonwood tree now lost in shadow.

I tried to move my legs. Nothing. The effort left me shaking again.

The ground felt solid and rough under my bare legs. A whispering breeze chilled my damp skin. I could feel these sensations, but I couldn't move.

You are a strong, intelligent woman. You got yourself into this mess. You can get yourself out.

I tried to calm the panic tightening my chest by going through the spell's instructions again. What had Miss Abernathy said about such things? I'd read a quarter of the massive grimoire, written as it was in fine, cramped script, but I remembered that only advanced witches could affect permanent change. Most spells wore off over time.

I'd have to wait it out. Or someone would eventually find me. Tomorrow, when I didn't show up to open my shop, Danielle would come looking for me. Or she'd call my dad and he'd come. I wished I'd put on something more than a thin t-shirt and polka-dot underwear.

I was cold, but reason told me I wouldn't freeze to death, not in August in Pennsylvania. Unfortunately, reason had left me when the candle exploded. Fear replaced it.

A car door slammed. Feet crunched on my gravel driveway.

"Are you sure this is the place?" asked a deep voice. A woman answered too softly for me to understand.

I'd left my windows open and the doorbell chimed clearly through the house. I was torn between the need for help and wariness of the strangers. But surely, someone who wished me harm wouldn't ring the bell?

After a short wait, feet crunched on the gravel again.

Back here! Back here! I screamed in the silence of my mind, willing the pair not to leave. I couldn't be left alone again. I'd die here. I felt it with every beat of my heart. My body would shut down, bit by bit, and I would die.

The footsteps continued past the driveway to the back gate. The latch rattled and stuck. The deep voice swore. Tears blurred my eyes, and my heart pattered erratically. I feared the strangers at the gate, but I feared they'd walk away and leave me frozen and alone even more.

The gate swung open with a creak, and footsteps thumped as the couple ran toward me.

"Are you all right?" Her soft hands touched me, looking for injury. "Quinn! She's bleeding!"

An upside-down face appeared in my line of vision, giving me only an impression of long dark hair and big eyes.

"Can you move?" she asked. "Are you hurt? My name is Abilene. This is my brother, Quinn."

"Abi, give her some air. She's spell-locked. Look at the circle of salt." The deep voice reflected irritation. Suddenly, I was very conscious of my polka dot panties. Then the rest of his words sunk in.

Spell-locked?

"Your name is Barbara. Is that right?" Abilene said.

Bobbi, not Barbara. No one had called me Barbara in a long time. But how did these strangers know my name? Was it a coincidence they'd found me when I needed help? Or had they been looking for me?

"You're caught in a serious magical backlash," she said. "We're going to help you." They stepped back to confer. My senses were in hyper-drive and their whispers grated like sandpaper on a sunburn.

"We have to take her to Mom," Abilene said.

"No."

"Quinn, I can't do it on my own."

"It's not an option. She's a complete unknown."

"She's a novice. Look at the setup. Crystals for God's sake. She's a complete amateur. No way she's a threat."

Amateur? I would have taken offense, except she was right.

A long silence crept by before Quinn's face appeared in my line of sight. In the dark, I saw only the angular shadow of his chin and jaw.

"We're going to help you, but we can't do it here. I promise we mean you no harm. We have to take you to someone who can unlock your aether. Do you understand?"

I didn't understand, but he radiated calm authority. My fear and panic eased so suddenly, I wondered if they'd drugged me.

"I'm going to pick you up now." Strong arms supported me under shoulder and knee as I was hoisted up and held against a solid chest. Moments later he laid me gently in the back seat of a car.

"She's shivering," Abilene said.

"Her wellspring is dangerously dry," Quinn said in clipped tones. I heard the keys as he tossed them to Abilene. He slid into the seat beside me and snapped, "Drive."

Abilene drove too fast on the country roads, skidding around corners. Quinn covered me with a blanket. I shook violently. Was I having a seizure? He rubbed my arms and legs, then gave up trying to calm my shaking and pulled me bodily onto his lap. His warmth drenched me in comfort.

"Easy," he whispered, tucking my head under his chin and wrapping his arms around me. "It'll be all right."

Somehow, I believed him.

DETENTION

Time dragged by in a haze. An icy ball sat in my chest, radiating cold through my bones. I wanted to sleep, let the cold take me…

"Stay awake," said a gruff, male voice.

Someone shook me. Quinn. I could smell him—deep woods and male sweetness. I clung to the scent, the only sensation penetrating my fogged brain.

I was fading. That was okay—cold, but painless. I'd see my birth parents and sister again. It had been so long…I could hear her calling "Bobbi!" in her little girl voice…always yelling at me for teasing…

Hard hands jostled me. Voices murmured. We were moving again. I tried to tell them to let me go. My face thumped against Quinn's chest. Running. Hard footsteps. Stairs? Strange smells, clean but unfamiliar. A bed. Finally. I drifted…

"You've got yourself in a right pickle." The new voice vexed me. A woman. Something hot pressed to my lips, and liquid burned my throat. The drink jolted me back to life, reigniting the searing cold inside me.

Shadows flitted past my eyes. Hands probed, testing for a pulse and rubbing life back into my cold limbs.

"Barbara? Can you hear me?"

Bobbi! I wanted to scream. It seemed important. If I was going to die here, I wanted die with the right name.

"I'm Jane." Her hands pressed my stomach and moved upward, past my chest to my neck. She peered into my face, too close for me to see more than a smudge of nose and eyes.

"My daughter says you lit up the night with that spell you tried. You lost too much magic and your wellspring is locked tight. I'm going to fix you now. There may be some pain, but then you'll feel better."

She seemed familiar, like the few vague memories I had of my mother. Maybe it was her posture, or the faint scent of sage clinging to her clothes. Her hands returned to my stomach. The warm touch soothed until she slammed a fist into my chest. Shattering pain jolted through me. Then everything went black.

Again.

I woke to daylight streaming through a small window. I sat up and the memory of my ordeal hit me. Bandages covered the worst of the glass cuts on my arms. I tested the rest of my limbs. Hands working. Check. Toes pointing. Check. All seemed in order, and yet, I felt like a disjointed collection of badly used parts.

The roof slanted over my head as if I were in an attic, but the room was clean and airy. I wondered if I should wait for someone to come for me or get up and find my hosts.

My hands trembled. I lay back on the pillows, thinking about the series of bad decisions that brought me to this strange place. Learning magic wasn't like learning to write computer code or even like educating oneself in history or math. Magic couldn't be self-taught. Or it shouldn't be, I now realized. I owed someone a big thank-you for bringing me back from the edge of disaster. Time to find out who my saviors were.

I stood and waited out a touch of lightheadedness. Someone had changed my shirt and left a pair of cotton shorts folded on a chair and canvas runners on the floor below. I dressed, wishing I had a brush or even a bra. Without a mirror, I ran a hand through my tangled hair and opened the door.

In a hallway with staircases at either end, I passed several closed doors. Could one of them be a bathroom? I was past the point of needing one.

Indistinct voices filtered up from below. I peered over the landing. A man and a woman sat around a small table, drinking tea from earthenware cups.

"Abi says she's powerful," he said.

I recognized his voice from last night. Quinn. The memory of his arms holding me in the car and his soothing voice came back in a rush of…what? Embarrassment? Attraction? Apprehension? He sat with his back to me. I studied the strong lines of his shoulders and the dark hair that curled despite the short cut.

"We should keep her here," the woman said, "until we know more."

I remembered her name. Jane. The one who'd unlocked me. She must be some powerful witch if the others deferred to her.

She didn't look like a witch. A silver bob framed her lined face. She wore a printed dress with a knit sweater over her shoulders, despite the heat. Glasses hung from a chain around her neck. She looked like she'd be right at home baking cookies for a herd of grandchildren, except for her flat expression of distaste.

I looked around the room. The rustic decor had touches of floral and lace. Statues of the eternal gods—male and female—sat on a plain wooden altar next to candles and shallow bowls. Those would be filled with salt, water, and earth for castings. This was definitely a witch's house. I looked at the altar with greedy longing. Here, I could learn from real magic users.

Quinn shook his head. "She has to go. The sooner the better."

And I thought Quinn and I had hit it off.

"I'm telling you, she can help," Jane said.

"She's completely untrained!" Quinn thumped his mug on the table.

"If we don't welcome the untrained, then we have no purpose."

"Our purpose is to protect those who already live within the coven's ward."

"She can't leave." Jane's lips set in a firm line. "I won't let her."

Whoa, what?

Quinn leaned back in his chair. "You won't keep her here if she doesn't want to stay. I'm not even sure the ward will contain her. Abi can still sense the aether she let fly last night."

Damned right, you won't keep me.

Jane seemed to consider his words. "I won't let her leave. Not yet. I'll put a confusion spell on her, if I have to."

Was she serious? Could Jane really keep me here against my will? And why not? They obviously knew a whole lot more about magic than I did.

I had to get out. Looking for the door, my gaze lit on the altar again, and I wavered with indecision. I really wanted to know more about magic. On the other hand, a confusion spell didn't sound like something I wanted to learn about, at least not from the wrong side of the incantation.

Why couldn't Jane and Quinn be the good people they appeared to be? That would be so simple. But I heard my brother's admonishing voice in my head.

"You're too trusting." Ryan had warned me away from that cheating scum, Charles, and I hadn't listened. Ryan also said I only learned not to play with fire by getting burned. Maybe it was time to change that.

I inched away from the banister.

"Mother, you can't keep her against her will," Quinn said, his voice low and dangerous. "The Thirteen will never allow it."

"The Thirteen will do as I say. If I want her to stay, she'll stay."

I didn't know who the Thirteen were, but I wasn't sticking around to find out. Jane might have helped me last night, and I was grateful, but I wouldn't be anyone's prisoner. No way. No how.

I tiptoed down the back staircase, my need to flee at odds with my need to stay quiet. The stairs led to a rustic kitchen with a wood stove in the corner. The earthy scent of dried herbs hanging among the pots and pans filled the air. Not one modern appliance marred the old-fashioned room. No dishwasher, microwave or mixer.

I snuck out the door in hopes of walking to town or flagging down a passing car, but found no driveway or road, only a path snaking toward a garden. Flowering bushes mingled with herb plants in a wild tangle. Quickly, I lurched away from the house. I needed to hide before Quinn and Jane realized I'd skipped out.

The path led to a small shed. No, not a shed. An outhouse. I cracked open the door and the ripe scent confirmed it. Not one to look gift potties in the mouth, I slipped inside and relieved my bulging bladder.

Back on the path, I wondered where I was. How far had we driven last night? I had no way to know. No phone to call my father either. Nothing but my feet to get me home.

I tried to run, but my legs felt like rubber. I settled for a brisk walk. The path curved around an orchard of pear trees and came out…

…into a medieval town square.

DISORIENTATION

A cobblestone street swept in a circle around the square. At its center, a small fountain flowed over a pile of rocks into a pool. Cottages lined the outside edge of the road. Many had tiny gardens, walled to keep out rabbits and bursting with vegetables and herbs. The first people to catch my eye were dressed in homespun fashions that mimicked medieval-wear and added to my confusion.

A crazy thought nearly unhinged me.

Have I traveled back in time?

After last night, I was ready to believe anything. But no, some of the villagers were dressed in jeans and t-shirts. A few women wore long tie-dyed skirts and flowing hippie blouses. Not a time shift, but something was definitely off about this place.

Everyone engaged in purposeful activity. One woman, dressed like me in shorts and a t-shirt, knelt in her garden to pull weeds. A teen boy chopped wood. An older woman hung towels to dry on a clothesline. She smiled and nodded as I walked by her cottage. Several dogs ran through the square and a grey tabby cat watched all the activity with a lazy gaze from the top of a stone wall.

I headed toward the fountain, where a young woman with brilliantly blond hair filled a bucket from the pool. She offered me a wooden cup.

"Drink the gods' water, ya?" Her round cheery face eased my nerves.

"Thanks." I took the cup and drank. The water was crisp and cold. I hadn't realized how thirsty I was.

"My name is Olga. These are Olga's buns, ya?" She held out a basket of hot cross buns.

"I'm sorry, I have no money."

"No matter." The woman shoved a bun into my hand. Hesitantly, I took one and bit into the doughy sweetness.

"Delicious," I said, with a full mouth. Olga beamed.

"They are special good-morning treat. Pick-me-up buns," she winked. "You hungry, you thirsty, you come see Olga, ya?"

"Ya. I mean, yes."

Olga beamed again and moved on.

The food did revive me. I wondered if Olga laced her buns with caffeine or something more mystical, but I welcomed the boost.

I followed the road around a bend, munching my breakfast, and came upon a group of children sitting under a tree, listening to a man sing a silly song about a cat who kept coming back to the accompaniment of his guitar. I remembered it from a TV show I'd watched as a child.

"…Buuuuuut, the cat came back the very next day," the man sang and all the children laughed.

I hurried down the road that swung past more cottages and more people busy with morning chores. Another ten minutes of walking found me back in front of the fountain. Olga grinned and offered me another bun.

What the hell? Was there no way out of this place? My need to flee became palpable, a frantic bird caged in my chest. I followed the cobblestones again. Unease grew in me by the second.

I looked for any kind of intersection. Before I hit the main square again, I stopped, breathing heavily in the morning heat. Sweat trickled into the hollow of my back. The fountain square was just around the bend ahead. Jane's house would be to the left. I glanced down that path. No one was after me yet. I headed right, into the thick forest.

I had to find the main road.

Stealth wasn't my forte. I cracked branches, stumbled over roots and crushed wildflowers in a mad dash to get away. I left a trail a blind man could follow, but speed was my best defense.

Already thirsty, my head throbbed like the worst hangover I could remember. What had I done to myself last night? Obviously, the spell had backfired. And it hurt. A lot. I hoped I hadn't done any permanent damage.

I jogged until a stitch in my side left me gasping. Bending to relieve the pain, I sucked in air. A buzzing noise filled my ears, reminding me of the failed spell. Could I still be under its effects? I shook my head, but the noise remained. That was definitely magic. Someone was casting a spell nearby.

My legs burned with exertion, but thoughts of Jane's threat urged me on. I slowed to a walk, gulping air. The buzzing blended with another sound.

Rushing water. I scanned the trees, looking for the river. My body screamed for hydration. I stumbled on.

A thick fishy smell overlaid the forest scents. It had to be the Anneke River. I could follow it downstream all the way to Ashlet, where it ran through town. All the way home. Unless I was east of Ashlet. Then I could be wandering into more wilderness.

Indecision didn't stop me long. I could only think of getting to water. I blundered through greenery. The rushing sound increased but so did the buzzing.

The river flowed just ahead, and water glittered between leaves. I eased my pace. Something was wrong. I felt an odd pressure in my head, and the buzzing noise had grown too. I opened and closed my jaw, trying to pop my ears.

Moving forward, every step was an effort as if I moved through molasses. The air seemed to push against me. I pushed back, hands held wide in front of me. One painful step at a time, I forced myself forward.

I had to…get to…the river.

The buzzing sound screamed across my skin, raising the hairs in alarm. I couldn't stop. Every second in this place confirmed my need to run.

Just…a little…farther.

The ground sucked at my feet. The sky weighed on my head.

One step more. Water was only a leap away. Water meant freedom. And sweet, sweet hydration.

Something hit me from the side and I fell face-first into the brush.

Temptation

I hit the ground. Breath burst from my lungs. A large, hard body crushed me. I thrust my elbow into flesh and heard an "oof!" Kicking backward, I scrambled away, raking dirt and ripping nails.

"Barbara! Stop!" The voice rose in anger. My desperate mind took a minute to register it. Quinn.

He pulled me to a sitting position. My brain still fogged, I slapped away his hand. We stared at each other, neither blinking, neither moving, both of us struggling to catch our breath.

"Are you crazy or just stupid?" His voice echoed as if from far away. The buzzing bothered me like a swarm of gnats. He grabbed my hand and yanked me farther into the woods, away from the water's edge, until the sound dimmed.

We sat on a boulder and he thrust a bottle of water at me. I gulped, not caring that most of it spilled down my neck. I wiped my arm across my chin and, for the first time, I looked into the face of my savior—my would-be captor and now attacker.

He was angry. His brow pressed down, lips thinned in fury. Short, dark hair curled in the humid heat. A strong jaw and prominent cheek bones highlighted his almond-shaped eyes, so dark blue, they were almost black. It was an interesting face, one I could imagine fitting in anywhere in the world, though handsome enough to always stand out.

His chest heaved from the run and my eye was drawn to an iridescent beetle charm on a leather cord around his neck. It rose and fell, catching the light as he caught his breath. Had he run all the way from Jane's house to stop me? From what?

"Quinn, right?"

He nodded.

"What the hell was that?" I waved weakly toward the water. "And while you're at it, where the hell am I?"

"Barbara, right?" he said, mimicking my questioning style.

"Bobbi," I rasped. "Call me Bobbi, not Barbara."

"Bobbi, then." He crossed his arms and glared.

Away from that awful buzzing sound, my mind cleared. I froze. My hand clamped around the water bottle.

"Did you put a confusion spell on me?" My muscles shook with fatigue, but rage was a great motivator, urging me to run again. "Tell me now! What have you done to me?"

Quinn held out his hands. "I didn't do anything to you."

"Why'd you tackle me?"

"Because you were too stubborn to stop when you felt magic about to crush you." His eyes lashed me. "You did feel it, didn't you? That pressure?"

I nodded and he grunted as if I'd confirmed my incompetence.

"It's a ward, the boundary of coven lands. A protection covering the entire island. Any witch with a bit of sense would feel it and know to stay away."

A ward? Like an invisible barrier? It seemed impossible, but hadn't I been the one trying to conjure fire last night? How could I believe in one kind of magic and not the other? And I could feel it. The incessant buzzing pressed like opposing magnets.

"But you come and go. Doesn't it hurt you too?"

"No, I'm keyed to it. Like anyone who lives here. You're not. If you tried to cross, it would…" He frowned.

"It would kill me?" I could still feel the pressure of that awful magic squeezing the breath from me, even as it lured me into its trap.

"Maybe not. You're pretty tough." He smiled faintly. "But it would hurt like hell."

I glanced at the river. My stomach turned in knots.

"Seems drastic. What if a regular person," I didn't know the proper term, "stumbled on it. You could hurt someone."

Quinn shook his head. "The ward includes an obfuscation element too. A mundane would be turned away long before the ward could hurt them."

A million questions vied for my attention. I'd never felt so ignorant in my life. But I needed one thing out of the way first.

"I heard you this morning. Jane said she would keep me here. Against my will." I tried to push as much venom into those words as possible, to let him know I wouldn't be used so easily. He studied me. I crossed my arms over my thin t-shirt as much in defiance as to hide the fact that I wasn't wearing a bra.

"Am I a prisoner here?"

"Not at all." He raised an eyebrow. "I'll take you home as soon as you're ready. I give you my word. You shouldn't chance the ward alone, but I brought you through safely last night. I can do it again."

I wanted to trust him, but reason—with my brother's sardonic voice—urged me not to. Quinn noticed my hesitation and frowned.

"I won't let Jane or anyone else hurt you." Calm assurance flowed with his words, and my panic eased. Quinn wasn't so bad.

"I have a lot of questions."

"You can ask them." His tone implied he didn't need to answer.

"I'm not going anywhere until you tell me what's going on." It was a dangerous gamble. Quinn obviously wanted me gone and fast, but the longer I delayed leaving, the longer Jane might get her way.

"Fine." He leaned against a tree, a picture of ease. "Shoot."

I took a deep breath and tried to order my thoughts.

"What is this place?"

He leaned in. I jerked away, but he smiled, plucked a leaf from my hair and let it drop.

I hardened my frown. He wasn't going to charm his way out of answering my questions.

"This," he sighed and waved one hand at the trees, the village and the ward, "is the Hidden Coven." As if that explained everything.

"So, you're witches?"

Quinn gave me a pass for the dimwitted question. "So are you."

"Yeah, I got that part." Even if I was in sore need of training. "How did you find me? Last night, I mean. How did you know I needed help?"

"My sister, Abilene, is a sensate. She can sense magic in all its forms. And you gave off a pretty powerful surge. She was in Ashlet when she felt it. We found you by the residual aether. Abi said it was like a bright cloud around your house. That's how I tracked you this morning, too. I'm not as strong as Abi, but I can read a magic signature, and you're still humming with it."

I was a beacon of ignorance. Terrific.

"And my name? How did you know it?"

I expected more hocus-pocus, but he only shrugged and said, "Google."

I blinked. Could this day get any weirder?

"Jane is your mother, right?"

Quinn nodded.

"She said I need to stay. Why?"

Quinn chewed on that question for a long minute before answering. Was he trying to come up with a lie or only choosing his words carefully?

He finally huffed out a breath and said, "Jane wants you to stay for the same reason I want you gone." His eyes hardened. "The coven is in danger. It takes a lot of energy to protect us from our enemies. I think you're an unnecessary risk to our security. I don't like strangers. And I don't like surprises." He ran a hand through his short hair as if he was used to a longer cut. "But you're a very strong witch. Jane thinks you can help us…"

"I can't! I'm barely a witch at all. You saw. I can't even light a candle without blowing things up!" I held up my bandaged arms as proof.

"And that's why I want you gone. You're an unknown. A liability. It's my job to keep this coven safe and you do stupid things like tap your wellspring dry and blunder into wards."

"Gee, Quinn, why don't you tell me how you really feel?"

He closed his eyes and gripped his odd bug necklace as if he found solace or wisdom in the touch.

"I'd like to help you, but I can't risk it. Not now. I'm sorry."

"You don't get to decide."

I startled at the new voice. Jane stepped from the shadow of a tree. Instinctively, I took a step backward. Quinn didn't even turn to face Jane, as if he'd sensed her before she spoke.

"Mother, she's too dangerous."

I grunted back a hysterical laugh. Of all the witches standing in these woods, I was the least dangerous.

"Exactly why we can't let her go home without proper training." Jane strode up to Quinn. She stood no taller than his shoulder, but she stared into his face with determination. "She unleashed her aether. There is no turning back. What if Koro found an untrained witch with her power? She wouldn't stand a chance. And neither would we." I looked from the small pale woman to her tall fierce son.

"Who's Koro?" I asked.

Jane turned to me, but ignored my question. "Let us give you some basic training."

I narrowed my eyes. "No confusion spells?"

Jane's flat expression gave nothing away. "I won't force you, since my son objects so vehemently." She didn't look at him. Her steely gaze never left my face. "Please stay for a week. Let us teach you."

Magic boot camp. It seemed like a small price to pay to learn how to control my magic. But could I trust them?

"I have a business to run and family," I said. "They'll worry if I'm gone for long."

"I'm sure you can arrange your affairs," Jane said. "But before you decide there's something you should see."

DIVINATION

My energy waned. On the trek back to the village, I had to stop several times to rest. I felt as if someone had pulled a plug, and bits of me were swirling down the drain faster than I could catch them. Jane seemed impatient with my slow pace. She walked briskly, stopping to look back with a frown every time I paused for a breather.

"You ran your wellspring dry last night." Quinn helped me over a log blocking the path.

"My wellspring?" He'd mentioned this before but it still didn't make sense.

"The source of your aether."

"Could you speak mundane please?" I snapped. Exhaustion made me cranky.

"Every witch has magic deep within her. Call it a life force or even a soul." He touched the beetle at his neck. I wondered if he knew how often his hands strayed to it. "That's your aether. The wellspring is the vessel holding that power within you. Put simply, aether is pure magic. The wellspring is the cup that contains it."

"And all witches have this aether?" I asked.

"Everyone does. But not everyone can access it, not even all witches."

I remembered connecting to the amethyst, then the dreadful pulling sensation, as if my vital organs were being sucked from me.

"Is that what hurt when my spell went wrong? Did I somehow damage my wellspring?" I imagined a crystal goblet shattering, spilling my soul.

"You weren't properly grounded for that spell." Jane waited for us to catch up again. "Magic is greedy, and since you weren't connected with the earth's natural power, the spell pulled everything from you. Good thing your wellspring was so deep or you would have died before you severed the link."

I frowned. "I don't remember severing it."

"Well, you did. More proof of how strong you are." She seemed smug, as if my strength reflected more on her good judgment than my deeds.

I mulled it over as we broke through the last bit of brush before the village square. They kept saying I was a strong witch. I didn't feel strong. I felt scared, weak and vulnerable.

The village was even busier now. We passed an open-air kitchen where a young witch fed vegetables into a giant pot hanging over a fire-pit. Standing by a wooden chopping block, two more women kneaded dough. They smiled and nodded respectfully to Jane but waved flirtatiously at Quinn as we walked by. The people here were every shape, color and age. I heard several different languages spoken as we made our way toward the village center.

I wondered about the organization of witches on a global scale. How had this place existed without anyone knowing? Were there other covens? Other supernatural beings? My mind shied away from that. I wasn't ready for vampires or werewolves.

Olga still stood at her little cart by the spring. She handed me a cup of water with a wide smile, and I gulped it down.

"Have another cup," Jane said. "You'll feel better."

It did help. The coolness spread down my throat and tingled in that place I imagined as my wellspring.

Olga handed me another bun, took in my haggard appearance and piled a second one in my hand with a wink.

"Thank you." I took a bite and savored the cinnamon sweetness.

"Go easy on those," Quinn said.

"Do they really help with fatigue, or is that my imagination?"

"They'll give you a burst of energy all right, but in your state, you'll crash hard when they wear off."

I took another big bite. They were so good, I'd take my chances.

"Come with me," Jane said. She headed down a path no wider than a deer trail that I hadn't noticed on my first run through town. Quinn motioned for me to follow. Once in the trees, the path widened. A young man sat on a low wall blocking our way. When he saw us, he jumped off the wall and stood ram-rod straight.

"Morning, Karl," Quinn said. "Everything quiet?"

Before answering Quinn, Karl bowed to Jane.

"Good morning, Mistress." Jane returned the greeting with a nod, and he turned his attention to Quinn. "All's quiet, sir, but I just came on duty. Ben said that last night was rough. Siranda is unsettled."

An uneasy feeling settled in my gut. Why did they need a guard so close to town? Wasn't that what the giant invisible ward surrounding the entire coven was for? Or did the guard protect something hidden in the woods? And who was Siranda?

A long wail erupted from the trees and Karl grimaced. "She's about to start up again."

The sound continued for several heartbeats, a cry halfway between the howl of a wolf and the lament of a mourner. Power sizzled through the ground under my feet, similar to the buzzing of the ward, but less aggressive. I recognized that signature. Magic.

The wailing continued in a terrifying harmony.

We entered a clearing with two stone hills, typical of old tomb cairns. The ground encircling them was well-trodden. Several paths led away to cottages tucked between the trees. Guards sat by the opening to each cairn. More witches lounged on lawn chairs outside the cottages, but no one spoke to us.

We circled the first cairn until a small opening showed a hollow inside. Quinn nodded that I should go in, but he was tense and frowning. Clearly, he didn't want me here.

Jane pushed between us. "Come. Meet Siranda."

I ducked under the low arched doorway. My eyes took a moment to adjust to the darkness.

A wraith-thin woman with milky eyes huddled on a pile of rags. Mouth agape, drool running into her greasy hair, she broke into a wail that scraped along my nerves. Collar bones stuck out of her thin shirt as her body arched into the scream. Then she fell back against the rags, pointing a skeletal finger upward.

Pictographs glowed red in the dim light, covering the ceiling and walls. Slowly, a new drawing appeared at the tip of Siranda's outstretched finger—a stick figure hanging from gallows.

"She's a seer," Quinn whispered behind me. "We brought her from Romania when her coven kicked her out. Had this cairn brought with her stone by stone."

"Why'd they kick her out?" I asked.

"She foresaw the obliteration of the coven and called for the sacrifice of the matriarch's granddaughter." He looked at Siranda with a mixture of pity and unease. "I'll wait for you outside." He turned and left.

Jane shrugged. "Siranda's circumstances bother him. My son is a soft center covered in a hard shell."

"Like a Tootsie Pop," I said.

Jane smiled tightly. "And just as sweet."

I wasn't sure "sweet" was a word I'd use to describe Quinn. Serious, maybe. Reserved. Definitely sexy. But I supposed even baby scorpions were sweet to their mamas.

"Why don't you clean her up and clothe her properly?" I asked. I could understand Quinn's distaste. Siranda looked like a half-starved beggar.

Jane reached over and lightly touched Siranda's arm. The seer shrieked and threw herself against the wall.

"That's why."

Siranda muttered and tugged her hair. I turned my attention to the drawings that covered the walls.

"They're moving," I said. The stick figures jerked in repetitive motions. Amazing. They were all variants on the same theme. People tied to stakes, burning in fire, beheaded by swords, hung on gallows. Each of the victims wore a pointed hat.

"These are all witches."

"Yes," Jane said. "Witches dying horrible deaths. The return of the Inquisition. In her more lucid moments, Siranda speaks of this future. A flux is coming, a time when magic will be a driving force in our world again and it won't go well for us. Mundanes have a hard time believing in monsters. But witches? Witches are only a small step away from the devil and so from God. Much easier to believe in witches and blame us for all the evils in the world."

"You don't know it will be like that." My voice was quiet in the small space.

"Don't I? I know mundane courts of law will do nothing to protect us when magic starts to fly. So I will protect what is mine."

Jane's bland expression contradicted the fanatic conviction shining from her eyes. My argument bone tingled, and I wanted to stand up for the general goodness of humanity, but part of me knew she was right. Mob mentality often did rule. Now that I'd unlocked my magic, would the pitchfork wielding villagers come after me?

I moved across the room to study the undulating pictographs. They were mesmerizing. On the far side of the cave, a blackened scorch mark oozed across the ceiling, pushing the stick figures aside.

"What's that?" I asked.

Jane hesitated. "That is our worst nightmare. A demon who would see us all dead or enslaved." Her eyes blazed fierce fire. "Even now, he seeks to penetrate into the heart of the coven, to seize the power we control—if only he could find us."

"Koro?"

Jane nodded, her face grim.

The black shadow slithered toward us, stopping here and there, like a dog sniffing for a trail before moving on with the hunt. I had the uncomfortable feeling that it knew we were watching it.

"But who exactly is Koro?" My mind conjured up horrors best left in the pages of pulp fiction.

"None of your concern," Jane said abruptly, dividing the line between real witches and wannabes like me. But she was right, this wasn't my problem. I could go back to my world and leave all this craziness behind. Or could I? Could I go home and forget all I'd seen here? Could I give up magic, now that my wellspring had been opened?

Our voices had roused Siranda. She turned milky eyes on me and raised a finger.

"You!" Her mouth opened impossibly wide and she shrieked.

"You! You! You!" The sound cut like knives. She stood on crooked legs and raised clawed hands. Her mouth twisted with hate.

"You kill me!"

ℭPROTECTION

Siranda tore at her face. Red lines of blood scored her cheeks. She yanked hair and ripped her shirt. Her wail began again, loud, dreadful and shocking.

Jane pushed me outside. Two attendants rushed from a nearby cottage to deal with the seer's tantrum.

"What was that?" I gasped, glad for the bright light and fresh air.

You kill me. I shivered at the memory of her absolute hopelessness.

"She's prone to fits." Jane watched me curiously. "You shouldn't take offense. Most of what she says is gibberish. It's a difficult art to weed the truth from her ramblings."

Quinn wasn't as nonchalant as his mother. He frowned and glared at me. Goody, I'd broken his seer. Just one more reason for him to dislike me.

Jane marched past Quinn, stopping to say a quiet word.

"Are we done here?" I wanted to go home.

"No. Jane wants me to show you the core," Quinn said. "She wants you to truly understand our struggle before you make a decision to stay or go."

"What's the core?" I wrapped my arms tightly around my chest. I wasn't sure if I was ready for another lesson in Magic 101.

"It's best if I show you."

Thankfully, the path cut downward here. I couldn't manage an uphill climb, not even with Quinn at my back to steady me with a hand every time I stumbled.

Jane waited at the door of the second cairn.

"This is the core," Quinn said. Another attendant sat beside the arched doorway. She offered water from a cooler and I drank gratefully.

My head buzzed in that now familiar signal. I stood near great magical power.

"I don't want to go in there." I had no idea what waited inside, but instinct told me it wasn't good.

"I got you through the ward last night," he said. "I'll protect you from the worst of it." He held out a hand with a grim smile. "Don't let go."

With shaking fingers, I took his hand. It was strong and warm. A wave of comfort flooded through me. The man was a drug.

Jane entered the cairn without ducking. I stooped, took a step inside and stopped.

Holding onto Quinn like a lifeline, I let my eyes grow accustomed to the low light. On the path, I had sensed power coming off this place. Inside, there was no mistaking its weight. My chest constricted. I fought to steady my breath.

A man and a woman sat cross-legged on the stone floor, eyes closed, hands pressed to the ground and lips moving in a constant rhythm.

"They're vestals. Bond-mates to the core." Jane's dark eyes missed none of my reactions.

The vestals' words were unintelligible to me and filled the cave with a slithering, discordant incantation. Their haggard faces were lit by the giant… thing suspended in the middle of the room.

The core.

Shaped vaguely like an anatomically correct heart, the core pulsed with magic. Purple veins of power throbbed within its orange glow. Two veins, each as thick as my arm, reached from the heart to the vestals' heads, like dark umbilical cords, but the cords didn't support life. They drank it. I could feel the greedy flow of magic. The whole structure, shimmering and translucent, might have been a mirage, but I didn't want to touch it and find out.

I gripped Quinn's hand harder, wishing I could pull it inside me, wishing I could wrap his protection around that fragile space I was beginning to recognize as my wellspring.

Instead, the core's cunning magic crept inside me. I could taste it—sour and stinging like popping candy. Its scent burned my nostrils. The thumping beat drowned out all other sound.

Another vein separated from the core and reached for me. Its tentative probe wavered before my eyes. I knocked it aside, too horrified to scream.

My breathing stopped. I gagged. Choked. Fought for air.

Over the roar in my ears, I heard Quinn yell my name. I doubled over, sucking for breath. And my heart beat again. But it wasn't my own tempo. My treacherous organ beat to the tune of the core's pulsing song. I belonged to it.

And part of me welcomed the possession. The magic promised strength and euphoria.

With a tender prod, the purple vein kissed my cheek, seeking a connection.

"No!" I lurched out of the cave, breaking Quinn's grip and the grasp of the insidious heart. Outside, I ran into the trees, stumbling in my haste to be away from the cloying magic. My foot caught on a root. I fell and retched into the bushes until bile stung my throat.

Blood recoiled in my veins. The sky spun around me. I was painfully aware of my heart beating in frantic palpitations, but at least it was my own again. After a moment, I breathed deeply and lay back in the cool grass.

Quinn sat beside me and gently raised my head and shoulders into his lap.

"Are you all right?" He looked odd upside down. His bug necklace dangled in front of my nose.

I nodded, not trusting my voice.

"You're a sensate, like Abi. I'm sorry. I didn't expect you to attract the core so easily. If I'd known, I would have created a proper shield around you." He pulled a handkerchief from his pocket and wiped my lips. Lovely. I snatched the cloth and turned away.

I am a sexy, intelligent, woman. I closed my eyes and almost puked again. *I am beautiful and strong. Bodily functions are a part of my beauty.*

I rolled away from his grasp and pitched into the trees. If I had to throw up, I wanted a thick screen of foliage between us. I massaged my wounded pride and mopped sweat and saliva from my face.

That's when I saw the grave markers scattered among the trees. I turned slowly. My eyes darted from stone to stone, some almost hidden in the under-growth. Each had an engraved name, dates and symbol for the witch buried there.

Jane appeared beside me. She laid a hand on one of the gravestones.

"Sensate magic is a blessing and a curse." Her tone was accusing. "It's a powerful gift, but one that can cause you great harm if you leave it untrained. As you just saw." She waved a hand over her shoulder at the cairn. "Most vestals study for months before they can commune as easily with the core as you did."

"That was easy?"

"Easy for you. It takes months more to learn how to shield yourself enough to stay sane."

"Fun. Why do they do it?"

"The core is an engine of sorts. The elders who started this coven, the

Thirteen, conjured it over twenty years ago. It projects the ward and cloaking spell to keep this island hidden. Like all engines, it needs fuel. We're standing on a ley-line." She crouched and laid both hands flat on the ground in imitation of the vestals. "Can you feel it?" The question seemed simple, but her eyes were intense. Was she testing me?

I nodded.

"The core needs help to access the ley-line. The vestals act as conduits for the magic. They draw it from deep underground and feed the core. But as you felt, the core is hungry for magic. All magic. And unless you protect yourself, it can steal your aether too."

I stared at her in shock and splayed my hands across my stomach as if that could protect me from those hungry purple veins.

"My husband lies here." She stood and touched the stone again, a rough moon-shaped marker. I choked back a dozen questions. This place demanded a hushed reverence. "That would have been your fate, if you had given yourself to the core. We've lost too many witches to it."

I could feel the echo of the core's lure. It had been easy to succumb. These witches—this coven—kept poking holes in my perception of normal. Every time I was ready to believe in them, believe in their goals, they jabbed me with another injustice.

"What a waste." I couldn't keep the disgust from my tone.

Jane's placid expression darkened. "You couldn't understand. You think because you bungled into some raw power, you know what it's like to live with magic. Your ignorance is only outmatched by your arrogance."

Her words shot me and hit bone. I couldn't deny that I was ignorant, but Jane had the monopoly on arrogance.

"What my mother is trying to explain," Quinn said from behind me, "is that those witches sacrificed themselves. It's a sacred duty. A voluntary duty. The vestals live and die knowing they protect the rest of the coven."

I turned, counting the graves. Twenty-three sacrifices to their precious core. Too many.

Quinn placed a hand on his father's gravestone. How old had he been when his dad chose to sacrifice himself?

"Each of them knew the risks," he said.

"Hush, child. It's not her business." Quinn glared. Either he didn't like to be called child, or he disagreed with his mother's assessment.

"How many vestals are there?" I asked. The idea of being shackled to that core sickened me.

"Twelve right now," Quinn said quietly. "Though we have several more in training."

"And will they end up here too? Does the core devour them all?"

"Not all." He pointed at the graves. "They were well-trained volunteers. Many more have lived through their service to the core and retired in good health. The core isn't a killer. It's just a vessel, a giant battery funneling magic from the ley-line to the ward. Those who are strong enough to be a link in that chain survive. It's an honor to serve, and retired vestals are treated like heroes."

"Well, that's a relief," I said. "Do they get gold broomsticks?"

Jane scowled. I'd pissed her off and I didn't care. I was tired of being the emotional piñata. Information, sensations and forebodings overloaded my synapses. I needed time to process.

Jane, ever watchful, saw the quiet frustration on my face. She spoke a hushed word to Quinn and left, passing by the attendants who rushed in and out of Siranda's cairn. The seer was quiet, but the silence felt like the calm before a storm.

"What did she say?" I asked.

"She's going up to make lunch. You're welcome to join us." His tone gave no indication if he wanted me to or not.

I looked around at the graves. So much death. I didn't know if these fallen witches were brave or foolish.

I had no idea what motivated Jane to show me these things, but teaching me magic was only the tip of her plans. The way she watched me—like I was a chimpanzee that surprised everyone with full speech—made me nervous. And what did the coven need so badly to hide from? They had enemies; that was clear enough. But surely a group of trained witches could take on one man. What was it about Koro that scared them enough to sacrifice themselves guarding against the possibility of his attack?

Jane had called him a demon. That had to be hyperbole. Jane also thought the whole world sought to prosecute witches. How far of a leap was it from the Inquisition to demons? And where did the seer fit in?

"What happened to Siranda's coven?" I asked. "She foresaw their doom, right?"

Quinn nodded. "They died. Most of them anyway. The girl she called to sacrifice caught a mutated form of tuberculosis and passed it on to her entire coven. Their homes were burned by a neighboring village, but Siranda was already gone by then."

So, Siranda wasn't just white eyes and bluster.

And I was going to kill her.

I was no murderer. The only way I could be responsible for her death was through blundering incompetence, something I seemed to excel at lately. My chest ached from my battle with the core. Jane's revelations had done nothing to calm my fears. This place was dangerous. These people played with forces I couldn't begin to grasp.

But I couldn't go away knowing my ignorance could cause harm.

"Jane said she would train me. If I stay for a week, will I know enough to get through the ward myself?"

"Yes and no." Quinn narrowed his eyes. "We will train you, if that's what you want. But I won't let you come and go at will. I won't key you to the ward. And when you leave, you go blindfolded. You won't be able to come back."

"I see." I already figured Quinn wasn't the trusting sort, but this was a new level of paranoia.

His tone softened. "You have a gift. And we will teach you to use it. But we can't let our guard down. Not now."

"Because of Koro."

He nodded. I had a choice to make.

"Is there some place I can make a phone call?"

INTERSECTION

Coven Island was truly off the grid. No electricity, no running water. No Internet or cell phone connection. The little guy who wandered around asking "Can you hear me now?" never made it to this place.

"You should get a couple of bars out there," Quinn said, handing me his phone. We stood at the end of a stone jetty that cut into the river. The ward hummed like a high intensity electrical grid.

"Is that the Anneke River?" I asked. "No, never mind. You can't give away your secrets. I get it. My status is strictly need-to-know."

Quinn's stony expression said he didn't trust me. Well, the feeling was mutual. But I had made my decision. I was staying, at least for now. I didn't need to trust Quinn or Jane. I only needed to learn from them.

"How do I get through the ward?" I asked. Quinn had said it probably wouldn't kill me, but those weren't odds I could accept.

"I'll create a mini-ward around us, like a shield." He pulled me toward him. His grin was a bit feral. "Don't worry. I don't bite. Usually."

I answered him with a smile of my own, but the corners of my mouth wobbled. Quinn brought out a paradox of emotions. He could be soothing or unnerving. Right now, he made me nervous. For that matter, the giant invisible fence made me nervous. Not usually a jittery person, I had no outlet for these uncomfortable feelings.

Quinn pulled me tight against him, my back to his chest. He tensed in response to the touch. Good. He was uncomfortable too.

"I can't project the shield far, so you need to stay close." His voice rumbled beside my ear. He stood six inches taller than me, and I felt completely enveloped by his embrace. The nervous jumble in my gut morphed into something more slippery and nebulous.

With our left hands clasped tightly and wrapped around my middle,

Quinn worked his mojo. Raw power rolled off him like waves of heat off a summer road. The air shimmered and thickened. I was acutely aware of every inch of his body touching mine, from collar, to chest, to long thigh.

"Walk slowly," he said gruffly.

We shuffled down the gravel jetty. His knees bumped the back of my thighs with every step. We stumbled and my head knocked his chin. My ears popped and we broke through the coven's ward.

"You have to do this every time you leave the island?" I squirmed, wanting to shake out my arms, but Quinn held me fast.

"No. The ward is keyed to me. I only needed protection for you."

"Well…thanks." I didn't know what else to say. He'd been my white knight so many times, I'd lost track.

"I'd like to give you some privacy, but if I drop this ward, I'm not sure I'll be able to rekindle it." His voice sounded strained. The heat of the day seemed to melt us together. I dared not turn to look at him. I dared not move.

"That's okay. No private calls to make." I fiddled one-handed with the phone. He punched in the password to unlock it. I dialed my store first.

"The Woolery, how may I help you?" a cheery voice said.

"Hi Danielle, it's Bobbi. I won't be coming in today."

Quinn shifted. The button of his jeans grated against my back. I closed my eyes and tried to focus on the voice at the other end of the phone.

"Hey, boss. I kinda figured that. It's already past noon. Are you sick?"

I thought about saying yes. It would be a small lie. I felt crushed from my magic bombshell, but Danielle was a busybody. She'd want to bring me soup and muffins.

"No. I'm fine. I just had a family emergency, and I'll be out of town for a few days. Think you can hold the fort?"

Quinn's breath tousled my loose hair.

"Me? Hold the fort? You mean I'm in charge? Oh, wow! That's awesome!"

Awesome. Right.

"I'll be back on Monday. Don't burn down the shop before then." I tried to make it sound like a joke, but Danielle attracted disaster.

"Sure. No prob. Have fun. I mean, sorry about the family thing. Hope it works out."

"Thanks. Is Molly there? Can I speak to her?"

"Just a sec." I heard the phone clatter on the counter.

Molly McFadden ran the knitting bee that met at the shop three times a week. She'd been a friend of my mother's, and I'd known her all my life. She wasn't technically an employee, but she'd keep Danielle from getting in too much trouble. The family emergency excuse wouldn't fly with her because she was also my dad's new live-in girlfriend, a situation I was still getting used to. Molly knew my entire family consisted of my dad, my brother Ryan, and two sisters, who'd both moved out west and I almost never saw.

The brisk wind coming over the water zipped through my thin t-shirt. I shuddered and Quinn gripped me tighter.

"Bobbi? Are you okay?" Molly's voice came through a crackle of static.

"I've got a bad connection here," I said, already looking for an excuse to cut the conversation short. "I was supposed to help Dad with the goat fences this weekend. Tell him that I'll be there next week instead."

There was a long silence on the line.

"Are you in trouble?"

I sighed. I could actually hear Molly pursing her lips. The woman was damned perceptive.

"I'm fine, really." I didn't know how much to tell her, but she wouldn't be satisfied with half-truths. "Look, I'm just taking some time off. I'll tell you all about it when I get home. I promise." There. Maybe she'd think I'd met some guy and run away with him. She'd like that.

"Fine. Come for dinner on Sunday."

We said goodbye and hung up. I turned slightly, conscious of my body sliding against Quinn's. His slow smile tugged at some hidden girl parts that I hadn't thought about in a long time.

"You own a store?" he asked. I wondered how much of the conversation he'd heard.

"The Woolery on Main Street. In Ashlet," I clarified, in case we'd come farther than I thought last night.

"I know the place. There's usually a clutch of old hens inside, knitting and eating scones. Somehow, I can't picture you there." He cocked his head as if looking at me in a new light.

"We don't always knit. Sometimes we spin yarn."

He quirked up one eyebrow. It was a good look, cheeky and sexy at the same time.

"I like wool," I said lamely. The eyebrow stayed raised and I felt the need to justify. "My mother gave me a rescue sheep when I was eight. I fell in love with all things woolly." That would be my adopted mother, but I didn't get into specifics. Quinn had his secrets. I could have mine.

"I get it," he said. "Witches are often in tune with natural things—fibers, rocks, plants. And animals probably sense power in you too."

I shrugged. My palm was slick with sweat where it pressed against his.

"Here's the deal," I said. "I'll stay for a week, but I can't promise more. And no one is going to mess me up with confusion spells, got it?"

"A week," he confirmed. "No funny business."

"And I expect to learn some real magic."

"Agreed. Now I need to let go of this shield." His complexion had turned wan. His free hand snaked between us and groped for the bug charm. "Let's get you back to Jane's house for a rest. This evening we can talk more about your training."

I nodded and we stumbled back through the ward, an awkward eight-limbed beast. Somewhere in that shuffle, my fear and distrust chafed away. I was a witch, and this oddly seductive man was going to teach me everything he knew about magic.

VENERATION

We didn't make it to Jane's house. As soon as we stepped into the square, people surrounded Quinn, pestering him with questions about everything from a lame donkey to missing candles for the Lammas festival to a squabble between two women over a cat. Olga popped a couple of buns in our hands while Quinn doled out orders, advice and sympathy in equal measure.

"Sorry," he said, wiping crumbs from his hands. "I've got to take care of a few things. Go back to Jane's and rest. No one will bother you."

"I can help with the donkey."

Quinn frowned. Last night's trauma had faded like a nightmare upon waking, but my muscles ached as if I'd overdone it at the gym. The walk to the jetty and back had tired me. But I wouldn't sleep, not with so many new ideas spinning in my head. And I didn't want to hang around with Jane. Honestly, she scared me a bit.

"You shouldn't overdo it." His scowl was impressive.

"Really, I'm fine, and I'm pretty handy around a hoof. My father keeps a rescue ranch." He nodded reluctantly and handed me off to a young witch named Aidan.

"At least eat something," he called. I waved him off, shoving a bun in my mouth with a grin, and followed Aidan.

We headed down the one village street and turned off at a large weathered barn. With creamy skin and a pink button nose, Aidan was a boy in the last throes of childhood. His shoulders had yet to fill out and his hands seemed too big for his gangly arms. He wore a sullen, wary expression.

"Stubby's around back in the small pasture." He scuffed his shoe against the barn door, not meeting my eye. "I tried to put him on stall rest, but he won't stay alone in the barn. He's pretty sick. He'll probably die." He said those last words with such nonchalance that my heart went cold. I touched his sleeve and he raised his head. Aidan's gaze burned with sorrow. The expression was so raw, I took a step back.

"Well, let's see if we can't fix him up," I said with a smile I didn't feel. I knew what it was like to get overly attached to farm animals.

Stubby turned out to be a fat donkey with a black cross on his shoulders. He stood evenly on all fours as he grazed, but when I approached he hobbled sideways, clearly favoring his front right leg. I picked up the foot and the sour stench of thrush hit me.

"When was the last time someone picked out his feet?"

Aidan shrugged. "Dunno. I just help out when Bruce is away."

Typical. Most people get a donkey and never look at its feet, thinking because it doesn't have shoes, it doesn't need foot care. I didn't know who Bruce was, but I'd give him a talking to when he got back.

"Well, let's get him into the barn."

After much cajoling, begging and cursing, we managed to get Stubby into a stall where I picked out his feet. I sorted through supplies in the tack room but found no antiseptic wash. This village really was off the grid. I wouldn't find anything as handy as iodine here. I settled for old fashioned soap and water, but made a mental note to ask Quinn about getting proper supplies for the donkey. They must have some kind of first aid here.

Then I set about cleaning all the stalls so the infection didn't spread. Aidan sulked around the barn.

"Here." I put the handles of a wheelbarrow in his hands. "Why don't you muck out that stall?" He nodded, but when I looked up a few minutes later, he was gone. I didn't care. I'd grown up around rescue critters and enjoyed barn chores.

I knew I should be tired but my second wind had come in, and I coasted on Olga's magic treats and adrenaline. For the rest of the afternoon I tidied the tack room and barn, and then threw cracked corn in the yard for the chickens. I found cabbage and apples for the goats. Sweeping up hay and dust was like meditation. The gentle swap-swap of the broom lulled me.

It had been one hell of a twenty-four hours. Even though my fire spell had bombed, it had unlocked some secret part of me. My wellspring. The source of my aether.

Magic.

A hysterical laugh burbled up from my throat.

Light into heat, my ass. It turned out magic didn't follow the rules. It was rude, erratic and unfathomable. Spells, wards and covens—Quinn spoke of these unbelievable things with ease. I envied him. He'd been born to this life and knew from childhood that he had this power within—power to affect real change in the world. At almost thirty years old, would I ever be comfortable wielding my aether? Would my wellspring ever feel as integrated into my body as my heart and lungs?

Would I ever stop blundering into wards?

"You look like you've been dragged behind a horse," Quinn said from the doorway. My broom jerked to a stop. I followed his gaze down to my clothes. A smear of mud had dried across my shirt. The white shorts were green with donkey slobber.

"Came close to it." I leaned heavily on the broom. "Turns out Stubby is short for stubborn." The donkey glanced up from his stall, munching hay as if nothing could be farther from the truth.

"Here, I figured you'd want this." He handed me a bottle of water and I drank it down.

"So, when do I start learning magic?" I asked, putting away the broom. "Not that I mind taking care of the animals, but I've got a lot to learn in a few days."

"Tomorrow." He studied me with a small smile. "I wanted you to rest today, but I guess that didn't work out."

I shrugged. "Barn work is cathartic." And I did feel better. My muscles, cramped from the locked spell, had warmed and loosened. I felt like me again, only bone-weary tired.

"Well, let's get some real food in you before Olga's baked supplements wear off," he said. "And Jane's waiting."

That sounded ominous.

In the end, Jane had to wait a little longer. I found clean clothes in my room, but I had to shower off the grime before I put them on. I had done too much today. My legs were jelly and my stomach painfully empty. The need for food warred with the desire to hide in my room. I didn't have energy to spar with Jane, and the thought of seeing Quinn again set other conflicting emotions fluttering. Mostly, I wanted to sleep and forget them all for a few hours. I glanced longingly at my bed before heading out the door.

Argumentative voices reached me as I came down the stairs. Just what I needed. I almost turned back for my room when I recognized Abilene's soft tone. I hadn't thanked her yet for helping me. Jane cut her off, though too quietly for me to understand her words. Then came a man's voice I didn't recognize.

"Siranda is upset. You should have never brought in an outsider."

Quinn answered in a low rumble. He hadn't wanted me to meet Siranda either.

"I don't care!" The man's voice rose in exasperation. "Something's not right! She's unstable."

I didn't want to intrude on a private conversation, but Quinn had made it clear they all waited for me. I steeled myself and walked into the room, cutting off the conversation. All eyes turned to me.

"Hey, everyone." I flapped a hand in a wave. The upset man composed his expression. He pulled a hand through his hair in frustration. Dark curls fell across his forehead as he let go.

"Bobbi, this is Gavin," Quinn said. "He's the head of the vestals and my brother."

"Foster brother," Gavin said.

Abilene made a snorting noise. "Here we go."

"What? Can't have her wondering why one brother turned out with such an ugly mug." It had to be a family joke. I could see Quinn as a child, punching his brother's shoulder in retaliation for the insult. Adult Quinn only glared.

Gavin was shorter, with a slim build and an elfin face, but neither brother was ugly.

I held out a hand to shake Gavin's but he only nodded and moved to sit at the round wooden table. I thought I had made another enemy, but he winked at me and grinned.

"Don't worry about him," Abilene said. "Gavin doesn't touch other people, ever."

I could think of a few situations that would be made awkward by that phobia. Before I could comment, Jane brought in a platter of food.

Supper consisted of simple, whole foods: bread, raw vegetables, cheese (from the goats, I suspected) and cold meats. I was so hungry, my hands shook as I filled my plate. Quinn offered me wine, but I preferred the crisp spring water that Olga called gods' water.

"I hear you made quite an impression on my seer," Gavin said as he heaped sliced meat onto his plate. "You don't have plans to kill her, do you?"

Bread turned to paste in my mouth.

"Gavin, that's enough." Jane's reprimand cut like a whip. "We don't interrogate guests, at least, not until after dessert."

Gavin grinned.

I pretended to enjoy the family banter, but I was glad when the rest of the conversation centered on the daily workings of the coven, with no more talk about Siranda or the core. I fiddled with my napkin. The muscles in my legs tingled with the need to move. Exhaustion had come and gone, leaving me hyper-aware and fidgety. The room swayed. I watched my fists open and close as if they belonged to some other body.

I had the irresistible urge to run.

When Abilene started another story about someone I didn't know, I stood up, knocking my chair to the floor. Four startled faces jerked up at me.

"Just need some air," I mumbled and headed out to the back garden.

The evening was bathed in that peculiar silver glow, just after twilight. I ran like a giant monster tramping down the neat path. My feet seemed too big. Gauzy emotions mugged my brain. I found a clearing with a fountain dedicated to the pagan god and goddess, and sank before them. The goddess winked at me. It might have been a trick of light.

What was I doing here? The last twenty-four hours had been a hodgepodge of strange events, all linked, but seemingly random. Had I really gone from nearly dying last night to picking out donkey hooves this afternoon?

My skin buzzed. Muscles twitched. Night sounds echoed painfully in my head: whining crickets, wind chaffing leaves, and water murmuring.

"You okay?"

I jumped. Unlike me, Quinn moved through the trees like a forest cat.

"I'm fine." My reaction was immediate and insincere. "Just tired."

"You're more than tired." He sat in the grass beside me. "You shouldn't have worked so hard this afternoon."

I clasped my hands in my lap, trying to calm the tremors.

"I feel strange. She didn't…Jane, I mean. She hasn't done anything to me, has she?"

Quinn pressed his lips tight. "No."

"How can you be sure?"

"My mother's magic is as familiar to me as my own. I would know."

He didn't say Jane would never do such a thing. "Besides, she got what she wanted. You're staying."

"So, why do I feel like I'm drunk and hungover at the same time?" My voice cracked. I was scared. Really scared. I'd seen too much, done too much in such a short time. I felt like my spirit lagged behind my body, somehow out of phase with time.

Quinn laid a hand on my knee, warm and soothing. I gripped his fingers.

"Aether is energy, your life force, if you will. You depleted too much of your vital energy, and now you're paying for it. Here, drink this." He pulled a silver cup from behind the statue of the Lady and filled it from the fountain spring. I drank greedily. My stomach was both overfull and achingly hollow.

I felt a puff of magic from him, and Quinn lit a lantern sitting beside the fountain. The flame only heightened the shadows all around us.

"Frankly, I'm surprised you made it through the day. Your wellspring was dry when I found you last night. You're very strong." His eyes were in shadow, but I felt the weight of his gaze. "But completely draining your well could kill you."

An admonishment. I'd been careless again.

"So train me. Teach me how to use magic without killing myself."

He pulled away. "Tomorrow. You need to rest and replenish your strength." He tried to rise, but I grabbed his hand.

"No. Please stay. I can't possibly sleep like this. And I don't want to go inside just yet. I feel like…" I dragged a hand through my hair, not caring if I left it a tangled mess. "I feel like I'm about to break into a million pieces. Please, Quinn."

He took my measure. His gaze trailed from the fear in my eyes to the tremors under my skin, and he sighed. Poor guy. I was such a chore.

"We can draw some energy from the Lady, so you can sleep. Hold out your hands."

He turned my palms up. His hands, warm and smooth, cupped mine from below. Lantern light glinted off the beetle on his necklace.

"Normally, we'd consecrate a circle before starting any kind of magic training, but the god and goddess are deeply rooted in this ground. They won't let any harm come to you here."

I thought about the pain of my last attempted spell and my shoulders tightened. I tried to pull my hands away, but he caught them.

"Relax," he said. "This will help. Picture your wellspring. Do you have any feeling for it?"

I nodded, not trusting my voice. When I had tried to light the candle, magic had sprung from my inner depths. Now, I searched for that spot again.

"Focus on it. Don't try to touch it. Just be aware of that space inside you." His deep voice gave me shivers. He was a black silhouette sitting before me, broad at the shoulder and tapering to a slim waist and long legs that merged with the shadows.

I tried to block out my sense of the man, to focus on the energy inside me. My aether. Such a strange word. But magic by any other name was still magic.

"Close your eyes." His voice rumbled with hidden potential. The rest of the garden fell silent, as if the night creatures waited with hushed breath. "Feel your center. Imagine that same center in the heart of the earth. Dig deep for it. This is the Lady's wellspring. I will help you find it."

He turned my hands and pressed my palms to the ground. An instant connection tingled through my fingers. For a moment I was aware of the massive, awe-inspiring being that was the Earth. Then heat surged up my arms. I gasped when it hit my lungs.

"Don't fight it," he said. "Just let it flow into you."

The Lady's lifeblood sang in my veins.

"Good," Quinn said. "Now open your eyes." I did. A nimbus of light surrounded us.

"Can you see that?" I asked.

"Yes, that's the glow of your aether mingled with the Lady's. It's beautiful." His eyes held mine.

I laughed. Magic radiated through me like every soothing memory I had. I lay back, confident that the soft ground would catch me. The stars seemed brighter now. Crickets resumed their happy chatter.

Quinn leaned over me. The nimbus of light circled him too. His aether or mine? It didn't matter. My fingers, still tingling, reached up and caressed his skin, feeling velvet under the rough prickles of a new beard. I opened my mouth to speak about the wonders I saw, felt and heard. I never got the chance.

His lips covered mine, warm and eager. Magic jolted me again. His chest pressed me to the earth, connecting us both while his mouth opened enough to make me eager for more. His tongue brushed mine. A low sound growled from his throat. He broke away, tucking his nose into the soft hollow beneath my ear. He kissed the pulse in my neck.

"I wasn't expecting you," he whispered, hot against my skin. "Never saw you coming."

You never do. Not the real passions. Those hit with the force of an earthquake, sudden, terrifying and all-powerful.

I tilted my head up, wanting to taste him again, but he cleared his throat and moved away.

"That was a good start. We'll try again tomorrow," he said, "when you're feeling rested. Goodnight, Bobbi." And the forest cat disappeared into the trees as if he'd never been.

I lay against the Lady Earth, with the pungent smell of crushed grass the only evidence of a kiss I might have imagined.

CPROVOCATION

Iwoke tired and confused. I took several breaths before the events of the past days came back to me and I recognized the bed I lay in. Drinking from the Lady's well had eased the empty ache within me. I rose, ready and eager to take on magic again.

Jane had left a note with a basket of fruit and muffins for breakfast. I ate alone, wondering what I'd say to Quinn. In the harsh early light, our moments in the garden seemed like a dream, a fancy from my over-exhausted mind.

Why kiss me, then walk away as if it never happened? By the gods, I hoped he wasn't one of those tortured souls, longing for a past love and too wrapped up in his own problems to commit to a new relationship. I'd been there, done that and had the t-shirt to prove it.

And there was the kicker: hope. Through this entire nightmare, Quinn had reluctantly stood by me, and I'd begun to hope for more. I wanted to slap myself for falling for his charms. I should know better.

Abilene showed up after breakfast, bright-eyed and chatty.

"I'm going to teach you some basic magic this morning." She wore her dark hair pulled back in a ponytail and watched me with deep blue eyes only a shade lighter than her brother's.

"I thought Quinn was going to teach me."

"He had to go away for a few days." She must have seen my frown. "Don't worry. It's only coven security business. Siranda's been acting up, and he's gone to check on a lead from one of her visions. This happens all the time. It's usually nothing."

Or he was looking for an excuse to be away from the coven for the next week. That thought did nothing to boost my ego.

"I guess taking cues from a seer can be difficult," I said.

I never saw you coming, he'd said, as if I might have been one of Siranda's drawings.

Abilene nodded and set about clearing breakfast dishes from the table.

"We're going to try something really simple." She was full of brisk efficiency for the task ahead. "But first I'd like to fill in some of your background, so I know where to start." She pulled a notebook from her bag and sat poised to take notes.

"Are you a hereditary witch?"

"A what?"

"Do you come from a family of witches?"

"I don't know." I paused. "My whole family died when I was six. My aunt and uncle raised me," I paused again. "Not a real aunt and uncle. They aren't actually related to me."

I didn't want to get into the convoluted structure of my unorthodox family and, apart from expressing sympathies, Abilene didn't press for details.

"What level of spell-weaving have you mastered?"

"Level? I didn't realize we get badges for this sort of thing."

Abilene's pen stopped scratching notes. "Just tell me what spells you've succeeded at."

"Well, there was the light into flame disaster, though the grimoire left out the exploding glass part." My skin still burned from dozens of tiny cuts.

"What grimoire?"

"Miss Abernathy's."

She laughed. "That old bird? I'm surprised you didn't blow up more than a candle."

"I take it Miss Abernathy wasn't a true witch."

"Oh, she was a witch all right. She was also quite mad. I wouldn't trust anything she wrote down for posterity. She had a wicked sense of humor."

Well, that was a good waste of two-hundred dollars.

"Anything else?" Abilene asked.

"My brother, Ryan, calls me a coincidence magnet. Maybe I am."

"Brother?" Abilene looked up. "I thought you said they were all dead?"

"Emmett and Ellen Kennedy raised me, but I think of them as my parents, and their son, Ryan, is more like a brother than a cousin." The Kennedy's relationship to my birth parents was hazy even to me. Emmett only told me that my real father had been like a brother to him. And they had always treated me like one of their own. Some part of the lost child I'd been had recognized the need for family, and I'd been calling Ellen and Emmet "Mom and Dad" as long as I could remember. When Ellen died three years ago, I'd mourned the only mother I could remember.

Abilene nodded and made a note. "So, odd things happen a lot?"

"Just coincidences," I said with no real conviction. I had no convictions left. Every truth I had once known was up for grabs.

"Or maybe what you call coincidence, I call magic." Abilene put down her pen. "Tell me about these coincidences, and let me decide."

So I did. All my life, odd things happened to me or to others when I was around. Once, all the light bulbs in my house burned out at the same time. Two years ago, during the worst drought in Pennsylvania history, my garden bloomed brightly. When I was thirteen, Dillon Halbred kissed me, then told all his friends I was a slut who let him go "all the way." The next day, Dillon's hair mysteriously fell out. Doctors had no explanation for it.

"That was the first time I thought I might be a witch," I said.

"You cast a balding spell?"

"No, not really. I didn't know any spells. I sort of willed him bald. I wanted to humiliate him. And he was so proud of his wavy brown hair. Such a putz."

Abilene arched an eyebrow in an expression just like her brother's.

"Anything else?"

"Not for a long time. Then, last October something shook me awake in the middle of the night—an explosion." I remembered jumping out of bed and rushing to the window. The town of Ashlet lay twenty miles east; its lights lit the sky in a steady, reassuring glow. No fire.

"I couldn't explain it, but I rose the next morning feeling strangely vigorous."

Abilene nodded. "It's the flux. You felt a flare. It's a real aether boost."

"The flux? Jane mentioned that. It sounds like a plague or something."

"It's a shift in natural energies." Abilene drew a globe on her page. "All signs point to the reemergence of magic in the world. Ley-lines—like the one fueling the core—are swelling. Within a year, no one will be able to ignore the signs." On her globe, she added intersecting lines crossing land and sea.

"And that's why Jane is desperate to hide the coven?"

"It won't be an easy shift." A shadow covered Abilene's expression and she scratched out her doodle. "But we were talking about you. Any other coincidences?"

After that night and the strange explosion, the coincidences had multiplied. I told Abilene about Thanksgiving at my father's farm. My sister's annoying husband got drunk on one beer and passed out on the couch, leaving the rest of our family to enjoy dinner in peace. I had silently wished for exactly such a boon when Chris arrived with a bellowed greeting and squeezed me in a rib-cracking hug like he did every year.

Not all the coincidences were so benign.

"When I found out that my boyfriend, my ex-boyfriend," I corrected, "cheated on me, I went a bit off the rails."

"Messy breakup?"

"I choked him," I said. "Not on purpose. And I didn't actually touch him. I just remember I wanted him to shut up. I didn't want to hear any more of his lies. Then he turned red and started to choke." I looked up to find Abilene watching me, sympathy in her eyes.

"That scared you."

I nodded and flexed my fingers, remembering the strain of clenched fists. My anger had manifested and I'd hurt Charles. I'd also scared myself into action.

"That's when I found Mrs. Abernathy's grimoire."

Abilene looked thoughtful. "We know you're a sensate, but we'll have to test you for other abilities. Do you know anything about your personal aether?" Abilene asked.

"Quinn explained it."

I had to stop bringing my thoughts around to Quinn. Hopefully, the feel of his hands on my skin would burn off before he returned.

"Good. You've got a deep wellspring. When you tried the fire spell, I sensed aether burst from you all the way in town. I was on a really bad date, by the way. So, thanks for the excuse to leave."

"You're welcome." I smiled. I'd had my own share of bad dates.

"Okay, lay your hands palms up on the table." Abilene lit a candle and placed it to my left. A spicy scent wafted over me. Next, she vigorously rubbed scented oil into my palms.

"Rosemary oil," she said. "It's in the candle too. For purification. And it'll boost your psychic abilities. Now, close your eyes and find your aether. Nod when you think you have it."

I turned my sight inward. I was getting good at this. Each time, I could find my wellspring more quickly. Going with Quinn's description, I imagined it like a chalice, close to my heart. It should have been brimming, but it felt bone dry. All the magic I'd pulled from the earth last night was gone.

"Do you have it?"

I nodded.

"Now imagine your veins are straws sucking from that well."

That was a little harder. The straw imagery kept morphing into a chocolate milkshake. Abilene, with her super-sensate abilities, felt my struggle.

"Try something else. A cup, maybe, or a spoon, dipping into the well." After a short silence, she added. "Got it?"

I nodded. "Good. Now, drizzle the aether, like water over your stomach, up your arms and into your hands. It's warm, like your skin. Let it pool in the palm of your hands."

My fingers tingled. I opened my eyes, breaking the connection. My stomach dropped as if I were on a roller coaster. The tingling evaporated.

Abilene beamed a smile. Her hands hovered over mine.

"I think I felt something," I said, feeling oddly hollow. "But I lost it."

"That's okay. Holding onto the aether takes practice. But most witches take weeks learning to simply call it up. You're a natural connate."

"I thought I was a sensate." Witches were big on labels, and I was having trouble keeping track.

"You are. Sensates and seers are specialties. There are others too: soothers, kinetos, pyros, thaumaturges, alchemists. But all witches fall under one of two classes: connates and weavers. You're a connate, a witch with inborn magic."

"Don't all witches have inner magic? Isn't that what being a witch is all about?" I asked.

Abilene pursed her lips as if deciding how to simplify things for the newbie.

"No. Not all witches can access their wellspring. Weavers can't. They use spells, potions and charms, taking magic from the environment. Connates used to be much rarer and some people call them wizards or sorcerers. We prefer to keep it simple. All magic comes from the Lord and the Lady, regardless of your ability. But those of us with inborn magic are less rare than we used to be. The shift is coming. A time when magic will reign over other natural laws. It affects us all, but connates more than others."

"So that's why my...aether," that word still felt phony on my tongue, "has become more noticeable and unmanageable lately?"

"Yes." Abilene doodled in her book again and wouldn't look me in the eye. "If you keep going, untrained and all, there's no telling what will happen. That's why Mom asked you to stay."

I frowned. I had made the choice to stay but really, what other choice had there been? I had to learn to control magic before it controlled me.

"When I leave, will Quinn really force me to wear a blindfold so I can't find my way back?"

Abilene shrugged. "He's cautious."

"And not big on including outsiders, is he?"

"No, but having an untrained connate living close to the coven isn't good for any of us. Besides, I think he likes you." She held up her notebook, with a sly smile. She'd drawn the initials Q and B inside an arrow-pierced heart.

I wasn't touching that one with a ten-foot wand. Quinn's disappearance felt too much like rejection.

"Exactly how old are you?" I asked.

"Seventeen going on forty, as Mom says."

I hadn't realized she was so young. She had such a confident presence, I had assumed she was closer to my age.

"Anyway, Mom wants you to spend time with different witches." She packed up her tools and notes. "You can observe and practice tapping into your wellspring. I thought I'd start you off with Bella. She's the resident herbalist."

"Sure." Learning about the different uses for herbs sounded like a solid idea. Maybe I could find something to treat Stubby's thrush.

Shelves neatly stocked with hand-labeled jars, baskets and pouches lined the walls of Bella's cottage. It was an apothecary to make old Miss Abernathy jealous. While Bella finished crushing seeds in a mortar, I moved from shelf to shelf reading labels. I took a jar of purple sage and held it up.

"May I?" I asked. Bella nodded solemnly. I opened the jar and took a deep whiff. Sage always reminded me of my mother—my real mother, the one who was only a shadowy memory. The smell of sage brought her into sharp focus for an instant, and I heard the echo of her laugh before the impression faded.

Bella watched my reaction. Deep pouches hung below her eyes, giving her a baleful look. I smiled and closed the jar.

"What are we making today?" I hoped we could start with a healing potion. Bella handed me a bucket.

"There are slugs eating my lettuces."

I frowned, but she'd already turned back to grinding. Obviously, I needed to pay my dues before the old witch would deign to teach me. I spent the next hour battling insects and weeding the vegetable patch. At least I left with a salve for thrush made from aloe, goldenseal and grapeseed.

Next, I met Barry, the weaver. I told him about my wool shop, and he grunted in noncommittal approval.

"I read about spells that can be incanted through weaving. Can you show me how they work?"

"No."

Barry was not a man of many words, but he was a talented weaver. For an hour, I watched in mesmerized fascination as he wove an intricate fabric with a sunburst pattern. Magic hummed from his fingers, but I couldn't tell how he used it.

After lunch, Abilene sent me to the blacksmith. In the stifling heat from his forge, I watched him mend pots. Nothing magical there, just brute force and patience.

In the late afternoon, I finally headed to the barn to treat Stubby's feet. He wasn't in the pasture. A fallen down rail at the back end of the field showed his escape route.

In my short visit, I'd cautiously discovered that Coven Island wasn't really an island, but a wide peninsula jutting into the river on the east end. I was almost certain it was the Anneke River, which meant that the west side of the coven's ward butted up against Reacher State Park. If Quinn insisted on taking me home blindfolded, I had a good idea how to find my way back. Getting through the ward would be another matter.

But I had other worries. How far would the donkey roam? If he headed west, would the ward fry him like cured leather? Or would his thick donkey brain feel the invisible barrier and turn him back? Quinn hadn't told me how the ward affected animals, and I didn't want to risk it. I grabbed a lead line before jumping over the broken fence.

I felt like quite the tracker as I followed the distinct signs of trodden grass and broken branches, until I came to a rocky clearing and lost the trail. Several paths led away in different directions, but none showed hoof prints. Pines loomed overhead and coated the ground with dead needles that sprung back underfoot.

Stubby could have gone any way. I picked a direction at random. If I didn't find him within a few minutes, I'd head back for help.

Underneath the trees, shadows darkened my passage. I hurried through undergrowth, snagging my shirt on branches and stumbling over uneven ground.

A low howl sang through the trees. I stopped.

Wolves? Inside the ward? My first thought was for Stubby. A pack of wolves could easily take down a lame donkey. The howl rang again. A flock of blackbirds cawed, and I jumped as they took flight from a branch above my head.

The sound rose into a painful moan. Not wolves.

Siranda.

Up ahead, a cottage peeked through the trees. I'd walked halfway around the coven and come up to the cairns from the far side. Siranda's wail gained momentum, rising like the dirge of a banshee. A door slammed. People ran from the cottage. I hurried forward. The trees opened upon a crowd of witches.

The seer's wail was a siren call, but the onlookers' attention fixed on two men bringing the body of a young woman from the cairn that housed the core. They laid her on the ground.

"Who's taking over for her?" Gavin yelled. One of the gawkers jumped and ran inside to take up the fallen vestal's duty. There would be no respite to mourn the dead. The core must be linked to the ley-line at all times or the ward would fail.

Helplessness turned to anger in my heart. I marched over to Gavin and grabbed his arm. He stiffened.

"Can't you give them one minute to grieve before sending the next one off to die?" I said.

Gavin unhooked his arm from my grip with a grimace.

"If I could, I would let them all grieve." He pointed to the cairn. "But there is another witch inside. If she doesn't get help immediately, the core will overwhelm her too, and we'll have two funerals tomorrow."

I stared at the body lying on the ground. Young and pretty with curly blond hair, her face was relaxed in death. I thought of the core insinuating itself into my breathing, into the essence of my being. How easily it had conquered me. What strength did these witches have to fight such a force?

Another young witch pushed through the crowd and fell on the dead vestal.

"No!" She cried in great, gasping sobs and shook the dead girl. No one tried to stop her. The vestal was beyond help.

I recognized my barn helper, Aidan, in the crowd. His expression reflected the misery of his thoughts, and I wondered how many times he had witnessed this scene in his short life. Was that the source of the pain I'd seen in him?

It wasn't fair that the core took such a price. It wasn't fair that these young people bore the burden of security for the entire coven. It wasn't fair that the witches had to hide!

In that moment, I knew one week wouldn't be enough to learn the secrets of the coven. And I didn't want to leave until I understood what motivated Jane and her thirteen elders to hide at such a cost.

I turned away, unable to stomach any more.

Gavin stepped in front of me.

"There are things you don't know about," he said. "Things waiting out in the world to do worse than kill."

"You mean Koro."

His eyes widened.

Yes, I know some secrets.

"If he's so important, tell me about him. Then, if I bump into him, I'll know to run the other way."

Gavin's expression held none of the impish charm I'd seen last night. "If you meet him, it will be too late to run."

FRUITION

Being a witch sucked.

For the next three days, Abilene shuffled me around from witch to witch like an unruly kid no one wanted to babysit. In theory, that would have been a great way to observe and learn, but no one seemed inclined to teach me much.

In all fairness, the death of the vestal hung over the village like a mournful shadow. People went about their daily activities with little conversation. Only the children added a bit of cheer. Death didn't touch them, and they ran through town, screeching and laughing. I watched them as I filled my water bottle at the well.

How many of them will grow up to be vestals? How many will die to keep the core fed?

I kept to myself as I weeded gardens, hauled water and helped the weaver spin yarn. I spent more time at the barn with Stubby and the goats. I enjoyed that last chore, and helping Olga bake round cakes for the upcoming Lammas festival. She eyed my efforts dubiously. We packed the cakes in cloth-lined baskets and baked a batch of regular scones for Olga's afternoon rounds. These, we handed out to various workers, along with pitchers of cold spring water. This seemed to be Olga's main task, to keep the coven fed and hydrated. I began to look forward to her interruptions and the refreshing water. I didn't miss soda or the other sugary drinks I usually filled up on while trying to get through a day at the Woolery.

My days were filled with manual labor, and my untrained muscles screamed for bed each sundown. Despite the long hours and stiffness, I could get used to this life. But I learned no more magic.

I rarely saw Jane, which was a feat considering I stayed in her house. She left before I rose, and I often ate by myself before turning in early. I suspected she spent most of her time with the vestals at the core since that was the only place I actively avoided.

The funeral for the dead witch was a quiet affair. No one expected me to attend, but on Wednesday, the village square was even more somber than usual.

Twice, I tried to question those I shadowed about the core and the mysterious Koro who stalked the coven. My interrogations met with blank stares bordering on hostility and I gave up. I wondered if Jane had told them not to answer my questions. But why invite me to stay, then teach me no magic? My frustration grew by the day.

On Friday morning, Abilene whirled in, ready for her brief lesson. I could readily call up my aether, but every time I tried to hold onto it, the magic slipped through my fingers like water.

"Don't worry," she said, gathering up her bag and rushing out the door. "It'll happen."

"Wait. I need to know more…" But someone called to her from outside, and she was already heading for the door. It wasn't clear to me what role Abilene played in the coven, but she seemed to be Jane's right hand, and she rarely had a moment to spare. She smiled and promised to be back in the morning.

I sighed. I had one day left. Somehow, I didn't think I'd crack the mysteries of magic in that short time. I resolved to get some answers before the day's end, whether Jane, Abi or Gavin helped me or not.

I hadn't seen Quinn in five days. The memory of his kiss seemed like a hallucination.

I walked into the barn to check on Stubby (who had come home on his own from his little adventure) and found Aidan crouched in a corner. He didn't seem interested in barn chores. In fact, it looked as if he were hiding. Tears cut wet streaks through the dirt on his face.

"Hey," I said, startling him. "You okay?" He darted a glance behind me and relaxed when he saw we were alone.

"I'm fine." He wiped his dripping face with a bare arm.

I put my back to the rough wall and slid down until I sat beside him, my knees drawn to my chest like his.

"Can I help?"

Aidan shook his head.

I let a moment of silence go by and then another.

"You know, I'm pretty much a stranger here," I said. "I'll be gone in a couple of days. Sometimes it helps to talk to a stranger." I shied away from promising to keep any secrets. If he was in real trouble, I'd get him help whether he wanted it or not.

He stared at me from two hollow pits of grief. My heart ached for him.

"Just tell me." I prodded him with an elbow, and I thought he might.

Then he dropped his head and muttered, "No, no, no!"

He jumped to his feet. I reached out to grip his arm, but he threw me off and ran.

Well, that was dramatic. Probably an adolescent romance gone bad. I vividly remembered being that age and how emotions boiled over so easily. I didn't know Aidan well enough to meddle in his affairs, but I'd mention it to Abilene next time I saw her. The boy was definitely hurting.

A bonfire was planned for that evening to celebrate Lammas Day, a minor holiday on the witches' wheel of yearly festivals. I collected dead wood as I headed back to the house. Sunlight flickered through the trees in that buttery glow that only happens on hot summer days. Dinner would be the barbecue I smelled cooking all afternoon, but I couldn't wait. I'd been ravenously hungry all week. Abilene said I was refilling my wellspring. It took both physical and psychic energy.

I dumped my load of wood in the village square. After a quick wash at the well outside Jane's kitchen, I turned to head inside for a snack.

Quinn leaned against the wall beside the back door, eyes closed and arms folded across his chest. He wore dress pants and a rumpled shirt with a loosened tie, his suit coat draped over his arm. His pale complexion suggested he'd been recovering from an illness. Wherever he'd been, it looked like it was all business and he'd had quite enough of it.

He opened his eyes. "Hey."

"Uh, hi," I said. "You're back."

Good one, Captain Obvious.

"You've got another leaf in your hair." He reached over and plucked the foliage from my tangles.

"Right. I was hauling kindling for the bonfire."

"Is that tonight?" He rubbed his eyes.

"Yes. Will you be going?"

He nodded. "I should let you get ready. I only came to report to my mother."

I didn't ask what he needed to report about. He wouldn't tell me anyway.

"Listen," I said, "I need to talk to you. I've spent the whole week following half a dozen different witches, doing chores alongside them. Not that I mind the chores," I amended hastily. "It's just that I'm supposed to be learning to use my aether. And all I've done is pull weeds and muck stalls. I'm no more trained than before I came here. And tomorrow…" Tomorrow Quinn would blindfold me and take me home.

Quinn studied me for a long moment, until his gaze made me uncomfortable, and I shifted from foot to foot.

"Go sit," he said finally, pointing to the patio table and chairs set in the shade of the garden. He returned with a pitcher of water, two glasses and a pillar candle.

He poured the water.

"Drink." Taking off his tie, he undid the top button of his shirt. The bug necklace nestled against the hair curling on his chest.

I drank, hoping the cool water had the same effect as a cold shower.

"I've said it before but I don't think you realize how close you came to dying that night." He looked tired. I wondered how far Siranda's prophecies had taken him. "Mother and I both felt you needed time to replenish your aether."

He poured me another glass of water. "Drink some more."

"I'm fine, thanks."

"Drink it." His tone implied he would pinch my nose and force it down my throat if I refused again.

"Fine." I gulped the water and slammed the glass on the table. "Happy?" I glared at him and he smiled.

"Try the flame spell again," he said.

"But I don't have any of my tools. The amethyst, the circle…"

"Those things are for weavers. You're a connate. Your magic comes from within, not from props." His eyes held mine and I couldn't look away. "Find your aether and touch it to the wick."

"Sure," I grumped. "Easy-peasy." But I focused inward. Finding my aether was no problem now. Its fingers reached into every cell of my being. But when I turned my focus on the candle, I shivered with momentary panic. Could I survive the pain of being spelled-locked again?

Quinn saw me hesitate. "You're safe here. I promise. Just try it." Quinn was a paradox of comfort and suspicion. He flip-flopped between these two poles, drenching me with either calm assuredness or authoritarian dread. Right now, he had the comfort flowing full blast. With him beside me, I felt as if I could accomplish miracles.

And I did. The wick ignited with a gentle puff.

"That was incredible." Aether brimmed in my fingertips. Quinn watched me with something akin to desire in his eyes.

"You glow like a pixie when you cast." He looped a lock of my hair around a finger and rubbed it with his thumb.

"It was easy. Much easier than last time." My voice grated huskily.

"Gods' water." He nodded toward the pitcher. "You've been drinking it all week. It replenished you."

"Gods' water?" I had thought that was just Olga's odd phrasing.

"I told you that a ley-line runs under this island. That's what fuels the core. It also affects the water."

Olga's daily hydration rounds were more than a courtesy. She was responsible for keeping the aether flowing in the entire coven.

"The ley-line infuses the water with magic. It's one of the reasons Mother chose this site for the coven, and why our enemies are desperate to find us."

I thought of the inky shadow stalking Siranda's drawings and shivered.

"I never realized that something as simple as water could be so powerful."

"We're close to the gods here," he said.

Another reason I should stay. I hoped my eyes conveyed the words my lips couldn't.

I rose clumsily, pushing away my chair.

"I'd better wash up." I started to walk away, but he stopped me.

"Bobbi, will you come with me tonight, to the festival?"

I turned. The sun burst through the trees behind him, lighting his hair like dark fire. He looked almost shy. Or maybe reluctant.

"You mean like a date?"

"Like a date."

"A date would be nice," I said, pretending to be all cool about it. "I'll meet you there."

I ran up the stairs, took one look at my borrowed wardrobe and ran back down to find Abilene and a dress for the festival.

Manipulation

The murmur of voices lured me outside.

Freshly showered and wearing Abilene's summer dress, I found the entire coven standing in Jane's backyard. Well, not the entire coven. There were no children, but at least a hundred people had gathered quietly. Some were dressed in formal-wear, others in nothing more than a few gauzy scarves.

Jane stood by the altar to the gods, looking regal in a white robe. She carried a smooth wooden staff in one hand and a lit candle in the other. The last rays of sunlight caught her silver hair in an angelic halo. With eyes closed, she seemed lost in meditation as the assembled witches shuffled in and stood in a circle around the altar. Each carried an unlit candle.

Like her mother, Abilene wore a simple white robe. A basket hung on her arm. She smiled and gave me a thumbs-up when she saw my dress. It was cream silk covered in ruby red roses and a little too short for me. But it hugged my chest and flared prettily at the waist. I couldn't do much about the barely healed cuts across my chest and arms, but at least I'd taken off the bandages.

I looked for Quinn and found him as he saw me. His eyes widened, and he pushed through the crowd to my side.

"If you say something about how well I clean up, I'll punch you," I said.

"Well, it does make a nice change from donkey slobber and leaves in your hair." He grinned. I punched him.

At that moment, Abilene rang a bell three times and Quinn's face turned serious.

"The uninitiated aren't allowed inside the circle during the sabbat," he said. "Can you wait here?"

At first, I didn't know what circle he meant, but then I saw it, or rather felt it. Energy radiated from the ground in a wide swath around the altar.

"You go. I'll be fine."

A drum started to beat with the distinctive thrum of a Celtic bodhrán. No one moved. The pounding filled the air, blocking all other summer noises. We waited. Red light flickered through the trees and disappeared as the sun fell.

The hair on my arms stood up and I felt pressure in my ears, as if I stood near the ward again. Shadows turned purple as full dusk arrived. The drummer beat a last staccato and fell silent.

Jane's voice rang out, sharp and clear and full of power.

"Lord and Lady, I call on you to sanctify this circle, to join us in celebration of your power and our own as we build, stone by stone, a new temple of life in your honor."

She stepped behind the altar with her candle and lit a torch staked in the ground.

"Here is the tower in the East, a light for the life-giving sun." Her strong voice reached the far edge of the circle.

Abilene took a Lammas cake from the basket, broke it in four pieces and crumbled one on the ground.

They moved around the circle to the next torch.

"Here I light the South, the beacon of fire that kindles our power," Jane said. Abilene offered more Lammas cake to the earth.

I held my breath. I had read about sabbats but this was my first time as witness. It all seemed a little over the top to me—the candles, the white robes and the medieval invocations. But my new-found magic radar sensed great power here. No longer a collection of herbalists, gardeners and blacksmiths, these were witches in full command of their magic. My aether sang in response, and I desperately wanted to join the circle.

Jane lit the next two torches, invoking the gods' favor at each point. "Here I light the West, in honor of the gods' water that fills our well. Here I light the North where lies the rock of our foundation, the solid earth of the Lady." Abilene crumbled cake at each point.

Now Jane lit the last candle standing between the statues of the god and goddess, and invoked a final blessing.

"Lord and Lady, I invite you into our temple that you might bear witness to these rituals invoked in your honor. So mote it be."

The assembled witches repeated as one, "So mote it be."

The drum beat again. Nine witches, men and women dressed in gauzy robes, began a slow dance around the inner circle. As the beat sped up, so did the dance until they whirled in a frenzy nearly too fast for the eye to follow. I could feel the power—the aether—building like a child's top being wound tight before flight.

The dancers dropped to the ground with a sudden stillness. Jane strode to the circle's edge and sliced through the invisible barrier with an athame, a double-edged ceremonial knife. I felt power whoosh out this new door. The dancers stood and skipped through the opening. The rest of the witches followed, each lighting a candle from Jane's taper as they walked by.

Quinn handed me a lit candle, and we fell into the crowd heading for the town square. Here, all the collected firewood had been piled into a heap. Abilene lit the bonfire, and the witches stood in silent contemplation. Then, with some unknown consensus, the candles were snuffed and a cheer went up. The party had begun.

Olga, with a brigade of helpers, moved through the crowd offering goblets of wine and moon-shaped cakes. More instruments appeared and a space cleared for dancing. I didn't recognize any of the complicated reels, but I sipped my wine and watched with fascination as lines of dancers met and parted, bowing and spinning with carefree delight.

"Would you like to give it a try?" asked Quinn. "I can show you the steps. It's a basic reel."

"Maybe later." I smiled. "When the wine has a chance to loosen my feet. Right now, I'm just happy to be part of this." I let the thought trail off, not wanting to sound trite. For the first time in my life, I felt like I was part of something bigger than me. Something important. Something that didn't translate into words. At least not with Quinn standing there smiling with that damn eyebrow cocked and mocking me.

"I get it," he said, and the look in his eyes told me that he really did.

The music changed to a slow song with a throbbing beat. He took my goblet, set it aside and pulled me into the circle of dancers.

His hand held the small of my back. Mine rested on his chest. The fingers of our other hands entwined. Shyness suddenly overcame me. I'm not generally timid, but his heat, his scent…his aether overpowered me. I couldn't look at his face, and studied the iridescent necklace at his throat instead. The surface was smooth as resin. Up close, I could see a rainbow of color reflecting the firelight. My newly honed sensate perception felt magic coming off it in a subtle hum.

"Is that a real bug?" I touched it with one finger as if it might bite.

"Yes, it's a cockroach."

"A what?" I drew back slightly. "But it's so pretty."

"Exactly," he said. "I wear it partly to remind myself to look for beauty where I least expect it."

"Partly?" I raised my eyes. He watched me.

"It's also a throwback to my time spent down south in the islands. A bit of voodoo protection." He shrugged. "If nothing else, it drives my mother crazy."

"Jane doesn't believe in voodoo?"

"Oh, she believes. She just doesn't approve. Magic should be done her way or not at all."

"And you don't agree?" I thought of Jane's admonishment that I needed to be trained at all cost. Did that mean I could find tutors outside the coven— tutors who did things differently?

"I believe we are only on the cusp of discovering the real worth of magic, in all its forms."

His eyes fixed on mine and held them. We swayed to the music. Our bodies bumped together. My fingers jumped under the thrum of his heart, and my own breath responded. He surrounded my senses. The scent of him was heated summer skin with a tang of beeswax. And most of all, I sensed his aether circling mine, an embrace of passion and comfort all at once.

Quinn stepped back and a chill wind blew between us.

"I need to tell you something," he said, "about me. About my magic." The spell entwining us broke. He held me at arm's length, his grip tight on my shoulders.

"I told you about sensates, the kind of magic you and Abilene have. I have a particular magic too. I'm a soother."

A cold feeling pooled in my gut.

"A soother?"

"It's what makes me efficient at security. I can affect people's moods, make negotiations go smoothly or calm a crowd getting out of control."

Efficient. Smooth. Calm. He used such friendly, meek words for something so horrifying.

"You mean you manipulate people." Was this why I had been drawn to him? Why I had given myself over to his touch so completely in the garden? I hadn't come to the coven looking for romance, hadn't wanted romance, but had Quinn foisted it on me with no regard to my feelings? I felt betrayed. Trust in my own senses vanished.

"Please don't look at me like that. I don't do it to people I care about. It's a tool. A weapon against our enemies, that's all."

"What about that night…in the garden?" I asked. His pained expression told me everything.

"That was spill-over," he said. "You were scared, your wellspring nearly dry, and I was trying to stem your panic before you went off the rails. I just took it a little too far."

I was so angry, I wanted to hit him. How dare he control me?

"So, the cloud of desire I felt a moment ago, what was that? Pheromones?" I pushed his chest, and his hands fell away from my shoulders. I shoved him again. He didn't resist.

"That was…" he licked his lips as if the words had suddenly run dry, "unexpected. I can normally keep the soothing under control. But you affect me in ways I don't understand." His voice dipped to a husky whisper, nearly drowned out by the music. "I want to devour you, Bobbi, but I also want my aether to surround you like a bubble, to keep you from the rest of the world. To keep them from hurting you." His face was a mask of bitter anguish.

I didn't know who he expected to hurt me and I didn't care. I turned away. He reached for my arm, but I held up a hand to block him.

"I can't. I just…" I couldn't put into words how disgusted I felt. Jane had threatened to put a spell on me and I had run. But Quinn…Quinn had promised no harm would come to me. And I'd believed him. Good old Bobbi, the trusting dupe.

His handsome face was covered with stubble as if to drive home his rugged maleness, but a little lost boy looked at me from his eyes. He knew he'd done wrong and couldn't make amends.

My heart went out to him. I wanted to tell him that it was all right. I wanted to reach for him, but I stopped with my hand in the air between us. Was he soothing me again? How could I trust that my forgiveness was real? How could I ever trust him again?

"I'm not doing it now," he said, as if reading my thoughts. "I promise. I would never purposely try to sway your emotions. And I can teach you to recognize soother magic."

I shook my head. It was all too much.

The bonfire spiked with a thunderclap, and flames shot into the dark sky. Sparks rained down on us. I slapped at a cinder that burned through my dress. A shriek of pain came from somewhere inside the village. More screams sounded as panic mounted.

"What's going on?" I asked.

"I don't know." Quinn turned away, already looking for the source of the panic.

"He's here!" Someone yelled in the darkness. "Koro!" A woman stumbled by, knocking me to the ground, then scrambled to get away. Quinn pulled me to my feet. The night seemed darker, despite the blazing fire.

"You need to go," Quinn said. "Run to the ward and get through it, if you can."

I stared at him in shock. He kissed me hard.

"Go!" He shoved me towards the trees and ran in the other direction, into the middle of the screams.

Combustion

Flames plunged the village into chaos. I looked around, not knowing what to do. The ward would hurt me. If Quinn wanted me to go, a worse danger was coming.

Koro. The enemy nobody talked about. Was he here?

People ran in all directions with buckets, trying to extinguish dozens of fires burning through cottages. There was no order. Children cried. Someone screamed. The fires blazed too hot and my ears ached with a deep drone. Some kind of magic had invaded the village. I could taste it, like acid prickling the back of my throat.

A child wailed alone by a cottage. No one seemed to notice. I swallowed hard and moved toward her just as a man grabbed her in his arms and ran.

I stood alone in the chaos, undecided. Should I run? Magic pressed on me. All my senses screamed with its foulness. I couldn't leave. Not with the entire village under attack. I didn't know who had invaded or what they wanted. But I knew where they would strike.

The core.

I ran. The bonfire threw harsh shadows, and the flickering light confused my senses, until I turned the corner for the path leading to the cairns. Here, all was cool, dark and quiet. Too quiet. No one stood guard at the low wall. My eyes, blind from the glare of the fire, couldn't penetrate the gloom beyond. I skirted the wall and left the path. I wouldn't blunder into the clearing. A week in the coven had dampened my impetuousness.

Creeping through underbrush, I came to the vestal house from behind. One light shone in the window of the long cottage.

Floorboards creaked. Someone stepped onto the back porch, and a silhouette passed in front of the window. I knew that set of shoulders.

Quinn.

I stepped from the shadows. He spun and froze with a knife poised to strike. My heart pounded. Our eyes met. He motioned for me to be quiet and that he was going in. I nodded.

The screen door rasped. He stepped inside and stopped.

I crowded behind him. Nothing could have prepared me for the sight inside.

Bodies sprawled on couches and floor. Closest to the door a woman lay, her face contorted in fear that even death couldn't ease. Her hair was messed, as if she'd struggled. The stench of released bowels stung my nose. I gaped from face to face. Gorge rose in my throat. No blood marred the bodies, no bruising, but each pair of dead eyes reflected the horror in my heart.

Something had swept through the cottage, killing them quickly and painfully. Quinn moved from body to body, checking for life, but I knew he would find none. There was no aether left here.

Except...

A tiny spark tugged at my will. It didn't feel like any aether I'd sensed before, but it was definitely magic. Could someone still be alive? I couldn't pinpoint the source. My eyes swept the room. I wished I could control this sensate thing better. Stepping over a body, I moved into the heart of the cottage. Magic pulled at me. In the hallway leading to the kitchen, I found him.

Aidan. The teenaged barn hand sat with his back against the wall. I thought he must be the source of aether, but as I crouched, I knew he was gone. His eyes focused on nothing. I touched his neck. No pulse.

But there was magic here.

I glanced down at the thing Aidan clutched in his lap—a box of dull grey metal, lead or pewter, inscribed with runes.

It was open.

I peered into the blackness it held. Doom lived in that box. I could feel it as easily as I could feel the heat of fire.

"Quinn!" My voice strangled in my throat. Blackness swelled, a miasmic shadow of hate and fear. A shadow slipped from the box like black oil. It rose. It shaped. It manifested!

Seven feet tall, it loomed over me, body shifting and coiling like a diaphanous serpent. Yellow eyes bored out of an ancient face, craggy and twisted. Opening a massive jaw, it hissed. The sound ripped at my soul. Clawed hands circled my throat, its touch cold and hard, despite its ghostly translucence. I choked. My hands raked through it, but caught nothing.

It could touch me, but I couldn't touch it! My mind whirled with fear. I couldn't fight it!

Through the hazy mist, I saw Quinn launch an attack.

"Wraith!" he shouted, but his strikes had as little effect as mine. I struggled and kicked. The creature held me against the wall, its grip firm on my throat. A spiked tail rose above it and plunged down into my chest.

I gasped. The spike bit through skin, muscle and bone, leaving no mark as it struck my wellspring. Pain obliterated all thought. I felt it sucking. A repulsive face leered into mine. It drank. My aether slipped away with every sip.

My own foolishness had nearly depleted my wellspring once before. Now, this hideous creature would take my aether for its own, twisting all that was good and pure in me to its purposes. And when my wellspring was dry, I'd die.

No.

I pushed past the pain and looked into the creature. Really looked. I saw how it killed. Like a leech, it hooked into my aether with tiny barbs of magic, not unlike the tendrils that had reached for me from the core.

Abilene's lessons had taught me the shape of my aether, its boundaries and its depth. I reached for it.

With a push, I forced my aether outward. It surged. The creature flinched. I pressed on. Power flowed through my veins. My magic was my will. And my will would not be overcome. I shaped my aether into a blade and sheared the wraith from me.

It shrieked as its hold broke free. But I refused to let it run. My aether knife drove deep into its heart, pushing, digging, grinding until it found a wellspring.

Then I drank.

How do you like that, you bastard!

Magic flowed into me, murky shadows mixing with my own blue light. I thought the wraith's darkness would overpower me. The giddy lure of evil enticed me. All magic was alluring. The feeling of rapture could be addictive, and in that moment, I understood how the vestals let the core overwhelm them. It would be easy to give in.

But not today. Today, I wouldn't bumble into magic blindly. With a push of my will, I forced my aether to bloom. It circled the foul magic within me and snuffed out the darkness.

The wraith screamed and shattered into fragments of shadow that dissolved in the night.

I stood gasping before Quinn's astonished face.

"How the hells?" He shook his head. "Never mind. We have to go. There may be more."

He reached down and shut the grey box before more wraiths escaped.

"Hold this." He shoved it into my hands. I tried not to look at Aidan's dead face. There would be time later to understand and mourn.

A scream shook the night. We ran outside. Shrieks of pure terror echoed through the darkness. I stumbled after Quinn, up the path leading to the core, fearing what we would find, but more afraid not to go.

In the clearing between the cairns, six more wraiths writhed in the shadows.

CONNECTION

The guards were already dead. Fear marked their faces, fear at the shock of having their aether sucked away. The wraiths shifted. No legs broke the swirling mass of incorporeal shadow. They floated over the ground, huddling together like a pool of darkness. Waiting for what?

Another wraith pulled the last vestal from inside the core's house. The big witch fought the insubstantial grip of the monster. He thrashed and kicked but his blows had no effect.

"Can you…" The ground shook, cutting off Quinn's question. I grabbed his arm to ride out the wave.

The core. Without handlers, it was becoming unstable. Soon it wouldn't have enough power to fuel the ward. And when the ward fell, whatever was waiting outside—whoever had sent the wraiths—would have free rein inside the coven.

"Can you stop them?" Quinn whispered.

"No." I had little idea how I'd beaten the first one, but I knew I couldn't take on seven.

The last vestal's face went slack as the wraith reached into his heart and tore out his magic.

The night fell silent. Even Siranda was quiet. Had they killed her?

I edged around the clearing to get a look inside her cairn. Bad move. The wraiths turned as one mind. Yellow eyes glared at us from within black faces. Quinn gripped my hand, pulling me away, but it was too late. The wraiths came at us.

"Get back!" A light flared. Jane and Abilene appeared from the shadows. Jane wielded her staff that glowed eerily blue. She raised it above her head and light blazed. The wraiths recoiled, their insubstantial forms slinking together like one inky shadow.

"Get back!" Jane yelled again, but the monsters held their line. The ground shook, tossing me against Quinn.

"Give me the receptacle," Jane urged. I stared at her blankly and she grabbed the box from my hands. She opened it and I cringed, expecting more monsters to slip out. But the blue light from her staff bathed the box and I recognized that pure glow for what it was: Jane's aether, magic stronger and purer than any I'd ever sensed, and I understood why Jane was the high priestess of Hidden Coven.

"I call on you, spirits of darkness. Hear my call." Her voice rose with authority. "I call on you, specters of evil. I know your true name, Korlogorn, servants of KORORAETH!" My flesh crawled at the dark power in those names.

"I call you, Korlogorn. Come!" The wraiths shrank. The black misty bodies flowed toward the box and disappeared inside. An unearthly moan filled the night like the rumble of distant thunder. Jane slammed the box shut on the last wraith. Her staff winked out, leaving us in total darkness. She huffed out a breath and teetered sideways. Abilene caught her.

The moaning continued. It wasn't the wraiths, but the core groaning with the effort to connect to the ley-line without the help of vestals. Siranda answered the call with her own high-pitched cry.

"The core," Abilene said. "It's going to crash!" Behind her, other witches gathered, pale faces reflecting fear in the moonlight.

The buzzing sensation I felt near the ward washed over me. The sky pressed down, robbing me of oxygen. The ward was coming down, and Koro, the wraith master, would be free to attack the coven.

"Where are the other vestals?" Jane snapped.

"Dead." Quinn's face was grim. "There's no one left to connect to the core."

It took months of training to form a bond with the core. And months more to learn the restraint needed to keep your aether separate from the thirst of the machine.

But it called to me. Just like the first time I saw it, the core wanted me. I stumbled across the ground, tripping over a body. My heart beat erratically, trying to connect to the unnatural rhythm. I gasped, choked and fell into the cairn.

Above me the massive heart pulsed, purple and crimson. Thick coils reached, searching for me. I closed my eyes and waited for their bite.

Quinn jerked me back. Behind him, Jane and Abilene crowded in the doorway.

"No!" he said. "You can't do this. It will kill you."

"And if the ward fails?" I asked through gritted teeth. "How many more will die?" The pressure of the cracking ward pushed on my lungs. I needed the bite of the core to breathe again.

Quinn studied me. Seconds passed like falling stones. His tight brow softened. There was no other way. And he nodded.

"Remember how you drank from the Lady's well?" he said. "Connect the core to the ley-line the same way. I will help you, if I can."

My breath came quickly, in stilted gasps. The core wanted me. I reached my aether toward the coiling tentacles. They latched onto my head, throat and chest, wrapping me in need.

And they drank.

Just like the wraiths, they siphoned my wellspring, but I felt no darkness in the core's need. It was hungry in the way an infant cried for milk—a monstrous, inconsolable infant. My blood thrummed to its tune. My breath was no longer my own, but a slave to the core's need. I panicked. Power flowed from me at an alarming rate. I'd be dead long before I could figure out how to connect the core to the ley-line.

I fell. My hands scraped at the hard ground. In the garden, with Quinn as my guide, it had been easy to find the earth's lifeblood, but I couldn't reach it now.

The core pierced me with a thousand invisible needles, shredding my soul with its need for aether.

The room spun. The core drank. I couldn't think, could barely hold up my head. My wellspring drained and my heart slowed as the core consumed me. Its sucking breaths were long and languid as if it relished the last drops of my aether.

Oh, gods, it hurts.

I choked. My throat filled with bile.

A shock of magic jolted up my arm. Aether—soothing cool aether— washed through me. I recognized the taste of it.

Quinn.

His hand clamped mine. I forced my eyes up to his savage gaze. He was feeding me his aether. One bitterly delicious drop at a time, Quinn poured his soul into me.

I would not waste it.

Struggling against the pain and weakness in my limbs, I pressed my free hand to the earth. The ley-line ran directly under the cairn. I could feel its force, like a rushing current beneath my fingers. If I could reach it, the core would have its feast of magic, enough aether to fuel the ward and replenish mine. So close, yet I couldn't push through the rock separating me from this life-giving current.

Another jolt of magic surged through me. Abilene held Quinn's hand. Another jolt. A third witch held hers. We were a human chain of aether, souls linked arm in arm.

I pushed magic into the earth, shoving the insidious tentacles from the core with it.

Eat this!

My aether screamed as I flung myself through rock to the ley-line. I plunged into the pool, the ultimate source of the gods' water, and it bathed me in light, power and healing.

The core drank deeply. We were all one: me, the core, the ward, the ley-line and the chain of witches who had come to my aid. I could feel each life force and knew that even when I finally let the link drop, we would still be connected.

And outside this chain of united power, I felt Koro raging at his failure.

REVELATION

The Java Jump was quiet. From the street, I glanced through the window. I wanted to meet Quinn on neutral ground, and the café was three doors down from my Woolery.

He'd called me that morning, after a two-week silence. Two weeks since the meltdown at the coven. In the quiet afternoons, while I restocked shelves or filed paperwork, I could almost believe that extraordinary world of the Hidden Coven—and the striking Quinn Mason—didn't really exist. Almost.

He waited at one of the round tables, a cup of coffee before him. Out of place in this ordinary setting, his shoulders were too broad for the cramped space, and his long legs didn't fold neatly under the small table. The three-day stubble was back, and it looked good on him. He saw me through the window, and a slow smile spread across his face. My heart winced a little.

Air-conditioning hit me with welcome relief as I walked in.

"Hey," I said, sitting across from him.

"Hey." Luckily, the waitress saved us from more scintillating repartee. I ordered a cappuccino and Quinn asked for a refill of his black coffee. I knew he wasn't a cream-and-sugar guy.

I had a dozen questions about what had happened at the coven and what was still happening to me. The core had torn open my well of aether. I saw the whole world differently now. Every living thing was just a bundle of raw magic. Magic that I could taste, hear and smell. Magic I could plunder. It wasn't a mantle I wore comfortably.

I'd learned a few things before leaving the coven. Aidan had brought the wraiths inside the ward. His sister confirmed that he'd been acting out since their mother's death a few months before. She was a vestal, another casualty of the core, and Aidan had taken it badly. While in town, he'd been approached by someone with a plan to bring down the ward. For the good of the coven, he'd said. He'd given Aidan the box of wraiths, directing him to take out all the vestals and start fires in the village. Quinn suspected this contact was Koro's agent. Whether the agent expected Aidan to live through these tasks was unclear.

I had a hard time connecting the lanky teen who had helped me in the barn with the traitor and murderer.

Eighteen witches died in the attack, including all the vestals. I'd stayed linked to the core for over an hour while Jane and Gavin found the novice vestals and brought them to relieve me. I hoped they were well-trained enough to resist the lure of the core.

Siranda, the seer, had not been harmed, though she had drawn nothing but black shadows on her walls for days afterward.

All this, I'd learned before Quinn blindfolded me and drove me home.

Now, he watched me while I sorted questions in my head. The awkward silence perched like a third, very large guest at our table.

Well, this is fun.

"How's Abilene?" I asked at the same moment he said, "I miss you."

More awkward silence. I tried to smile but couldn't hold it steady. His hand covered mine for an instant, then he pulled away as the waitress shoved a cappuccino in front of me and refilled his coffee.

"Abilene's fine." He stared into his mug, gripping it with both hands. "What you did…that was very brave."

Brave or stupid, I wasn't sure which. At least he didn't call me reckless.

"What were those creatures that Aidan let loose?"

"The Korlogorn," Quinn said. "They were once witches that Koro enslaved and turned into wraiths. They are his assassins. No one has ever been able to kill one before. Even Jane can only banish them from this dimension."

I had killed a wraith. It seemed impossible, but at the time, I had simply known what to do. Drinking the creature's aether had seemed so simple…so natural. Quinn watched me as his words registered. Once again, I felt like a bug under a microscope.

"Are you ever going to tell me who Koro is?" We'd had this conversation before, and it hadn't gone well. Jane kept her secrets close, and as head of the coven's security, Quinn mostly agreed with this tactic.

"You can't keep me in the dark. Some big-bad failed to take the coven because I was rash enough to throw myself at the core. If he knows this, if Koro has other spies in the coven, I'm a sitting target. But I don't even know what he looks like."

Was he another witch? Something worse? Could he find me again?

"Koro is…" Quinn sighed and all the fight left him. "Koro is a demon. Or the closest thing to a demon that can survive in our world."

I sipped my cappuccino, digesting this. I'd need more caffeine.

"I don't know what he looks like," Quinn said. "Only Jane has seen him in his true form, and she won't talk about it. He can't manifest in this world. Not without some really messy magic."

"That's good then. He can't hurt us, unless…"

"Unless he finds a mortal agent to do his bidding. We think this is who approached Aidan."

"And if he'd tapped into the ley-line through the core, would that have been enough power to make him manifest?"

"Possibly. I think it takes more than power. There is a ritual, something about blood of the seed. The books are vague."

They always were. I wondered what Miss Abernathy had to say about demons.

"But he has a taste for aether," Quinn said. "He lusts for it. For years, we heard rumors about him attacking other covens and drinking the witches dry. Some he turns into the Korlogorn. Others he kills outright. I'm not sure which is the worse fate. That's why Jane insisted on the ward. But now he's found us."

"Will you move the coven?"

Quinn shook his head. "I don't know. It's no easy job to move all those families. And we have the ley-line. It might be time to stop hiding."

"Can you fight him?"

"Maybe." Quinn smiled sadly.

A new thought struck me cold.

"Is it possible Koro's agent was in Ashlet because of me? You said he's attracted to aether. Could he have sensed my magic?" I thought of all the times I'd let magic fly in recent months, oblivious to its effects on others. Had my recklessness led Koro to the coven?

"I asked Jane the same thing," Quinn said. "She was noncommittal."

No big surprise there. The more I thought about my week at the coven, the more I became convinced that Jane had a hidden agenda.

"Your mother confuses me. She obviously wants me trained, but I can't help feeling that she dislikes me. She completely avoided me at the coven." I wanted to say she feared me, but I wouldn't go that far. Not yet.

"My mother is complicated. She's not easy to get close to." I sensed an old hurt in his words. "Even Abilene doesn't know what motivates her. You shouldn't take offense."

I wouldn't, but I'd keep a wary eye on the high priestess.

"I need to make you a proposition," Quinn said. "With Jane's blessing, of course."

I saw the mischievous glint in his eye, and I half expected him to get down on one knee.

"We lost a lot of good witches in that battle. Mother wants to boost our ranks."

"So, you're what, recruiting?"

"Yes, you still need training. And I realize you can't leave your life here right away."

Right away?

"You want me to live on Coven Island?" How could I leave my shop and my family? What would I tell Dad? Already, Molly was asking pointed questions about my week away.

"Eventually. First, we need to train you, get you initiated. Then you can decide."

Finally, I would learn practical magic.

"Can I learn to protect myself? From Koro, I mean."

Quinn frowned. "That's our first priority." He didn't lie to me and say I had nothing to worry about. That was both reassuring and not.

"Abilene and I will take turns with the training," he said. "You're definitely a sensate, and she can help with that. I will focus more on combat and defensive magic."

"That doesn't sound ominous at all," I mumbled.

Quinn gripped my hand. His smile was true and warm, with just the hint of impudence. I looked into his eyes, so blue-black—my aether tingled. Oh, yeah, I wanted to train with this man. I wanted to do a whole lot of other things to him, but combat magic suggested some quality together-time.

"Is this your super soother magic at work?" I teased. I'd already forgiven him for using his magic on me. If the whole village hadn't erupted in chaos, I'd have forgiven him that night. I understood now, how unpredictable magic could be.

"No. I tried to tell you before…" Quinn sat back and let my hand drop. He looked so crushed, I felt bad for taunting him.

"When? Before we were nearly eaten by wraiths then sucked dry by the core? Good times."

His fierce eyes softened and he laughed, a deep, rich sound that rumbled right down to my toes. Suddenly, I wanted to make it my life's work to give this solemn man a reason to laugh again.

His face turned serious again. "I don't use magic in personal relationships. At least I try not to. But I wasn't ready for the connection I felt—I feel—with you. I lost control that night in the garden. But I promise never to soothe you again."

When I learned to detect soother magic, it would no longer be an issue between us. I wouldn't let it.

"I'd like to see where this will take us," Quinn said. "If you're willing."

I scooted my chair closer to his.

"If I kiss you now," I said, "it would be all my fault? No soothing?"

"Completely your fault."

Our lips met and held. I opened to him and tasted his tongue on mine, a tentative prod asking for more. I let him in. He pulled me toward him and my chair scraped loudly on the floor.

I sat back though everything inside me leaned toward him.

"So, when do you start teaching me magic?" I asked.

He grinned. "Right now."

Book 2

SOOTHED BY MAGIC

DETONATION

Mother nature forgot to switch on the autumn button.

I parked in the municipal lot three blocks from my shop. I didn't mind the walk as the day was clear, and a warm wind blew off the Anneke River. It matched the heat in my stomach as I thought of my date last night. New relationships are always good. That zing of electricity when your eyes meet his. The constant urge to touch, and the restraint that only heightens need.

Yes, I had it bad.

"Mama, look! A witch!" I froze. With my mind wandering, I'd been absently playing with my keys, pushing one along the ring using kinetic magic.

Crap! Abilene had warned me about practicing in public, but I tended to fidget with magic the way some people doodle while on the phone.

The little girl's shriek made me drop the keys. I bent, hoping the child's mother was too preoccupied to pay attention.

"She's a pretty witch," the mother said.

"No!" giggled the child. "She's ugly!"

Well, that was uncalled for.

Mother and child walked past me, pointing at the decorations tied to lampposts. With Halloween only days away, the streets of Ashlet were festooned with scarecrows, pumpkins and witches. Not real witches, but the cute pointy-hatted kind with green faces and warts. Those stereotypes should annoy me, but they didn't. The world wasn't ready for the reality of witches, magic and demons.

At Main Street, I turned right and spotted Gavin sitting on a bench in Bridge Park, a tiny green space that doubled as a town square.

I stopped. Seeing Gavin here was unexpected and it brought back a mixed bag of emotions I was still working through.

Gavin was the head of the vestals, a group of witches who dedicated their lives to keeping the Hidden Coven…well, hidden. Their efforts came at a great cost. The core—the engine fueling the protective spells around the coven—hungered for magic. Many vestals had died over the years when it overpowered them.

Last summer, the demon Koro used a confused teen to let a legion of wraiths loose inside the coven. They murdered every active vestal, leaving me and a few others to take up the reins and feed the core.

It nearly killed me, but I learned a lot about my aether, the life-force magic that pooled deep within me.

I hadn't seen Gavin since I left the coven over a month ago. He leaned forward, elbows resting on his knees and a cup of coffee dangling in his hands. The sun lit his face, showing off tired lines. Behind him, the Anneke River rushed under the bridge connecting the two sides of town like a Band-Aid. Trendy shops on one side, decaying homes built by the original residents of Ashlet on the other.

"Hey, Bobbi." Gavin looked up with troubled eyes. His smile was genuine, if sad.

"Hey, yourself." I sat beside him. "Nice to see you around these parts." I wanted to hug him or shake his hand. It's what you did when you met someone who had lived through a crisis with you, someone you considered a friend. But he'd only shrug me off. Gavin didn't like to be touched. So I sat awkwardly holding my purse in front of me like a shield and fidgeted with my keys. The wind swirled brown leaves around our feet.

Gavin gulped the rest of his coffee and tossed the cup into a waste bin. A large flower box sat beside the bench, filled with dead petunias that the town landscapers hadn't yet cleared away. He touched the dried husks one after another, not saying anything for a long time. And there was a lot to say. We'd fought demons together. It left a mark.

When he did speak, it wasn't what I expected.

"I'm mustering the courage to visit my mother. She's at Riverview."

Ah. Riverview Psychiatric Care Facility was an imposing building on the west end of town.

"I'm sorry. I didn't know." I shoved down the desire to pat his back.

"It's not a big secret. She's been there for years, since I was a toddler. That's when Jane took me in."

"We have something in common. I was raised by friends of my parents too." I'd never understood what motivated Ellen and Emmett Kennedy to take in a lost, scared child. I only knew that Emmett and my birth father had been friends before the fire that killed my parents and my younger sister. It seemed Jane had the same selflessness, though she hid it well.

"I always feel like I need to stockpile sunshine before I see her. That place is…dark," Gavin said.

Riverview hospital had been converted from an old manor house. It was only a few blocks from my shop and I often passed it on errands. From the outside, it seemed charming, with a gabled roof and wrap-around porch. Inside? I really had no idea. But some days I heard screaming.

Gavin dug his fingers into the dirt of the flower box. Aether burst from him and the dead plants unfurled, turned green and bloomed.

Wow. Gavin was a flora mage. I had no idea.

"Enough gloomy talk." He plucked a petunia and twirled it in his fingers. "What's new with you? I haven't seen you in weeks."

"I've been busy." I couldn't help the guilty rush of blood to my cheeks. "You know how it goes with new relationships. The first weeks are pretty intense. I guess we've been cocooning."

Gavin frowned. "I thought Quinn was away last week."

"Quinn? No." I laughed. "We had our moment, but it didn't work out. This is someone new. His name is William."

"Huh." It was neither a question nor an opinion. He looked at me for a long minute.

"What about your magic training?" he asked.

"William is taking over. He's super. I've learned more in the last week than I did all last month with Abilene."

"Huh."

That tone was beginning to irk me.

"Does Jane know?" he asked.

"Jane is not the boss of me." That came out too much like a whine. "I mean, she won't even let me know how to get to the coven." Actually it was Quinn who insisted that I be kept ignorant of the coven's exact location. When I left, he made me wear a blindfold and I still hadn't forgiven him.

Thoughts of Quinn brought a brief unexpected pang to my chest, not exactly guilt. Remorse, maybe. But it was gone as quickly as it came.

"William says I should be progressing much faster." That was true. Since meeting William, I realized my aether wings had been hobbled by the coven's restrictive policies. William cut the cords for me. I held up my key chain with a grin and showed Gavin how I could pass the keys one by one with pure aether.

"Impressive." He didn't look impressed.

"Are you okay?"

"Yeah, sure. I should go see my mother and get back to the coven. Something I need to check on." He rose, and handed me the blooming petunia that had been a dry husk only moments ago.

"Next time you visit your mother…" I suddenly felt shy. I didn't know Gavin well, but he seemed to need a friend. "I mean, if you'd like company. I'm always around."

He smiled. "I might take you up on that." He paused, considering. "This new friend of yours, does he have a last name?"

For some reason, I didn't want to tell Gavin William's last name. I fought through the unreasonable tangle of my tongue. "Fain. His name is William Fain." The words hurt my chest as I spoke them and I had a wild urge to beg Gavin to forget them.

Gavin smiled and the odd feeling passed.

ᴄDISRUPTION

The bell above the door jangled. Molly McFadden looked up from her knitting and winced. Dottie Benson stormed through the door, wearing her trademark floppy hat. In houndstooth print, for God's sake. She spotted Bobbi, sorting the day's receipts. Already out of breath, she puffed up her chest, hiked up her massive bag of knitting, and made a bee-line for Bobbi.

She dropped her bag on the counter, scattering receipts.

Molly sighed. This wasn't going to go well. She turned back to her needles. Bobbi could handle herself.

"Miss Cole, I'm disappointed that you would sell such an inferior product. Look at this mess!" Dottie dumped a tangled lump of hand-dyed, artisan silk blended yarn on the counter. Bobbi frowned and tried to save her carefully sorted receipts.

"I warned you this wool was difficult to work with, Mrs. Benson." Bobbi spoke in her reasonable shopkeeper's tone, but you couldn't tell Dottie anything.

"Don't treat me like an amateur, girl!" Crows thought Mrs. Benson's voice was shrill. "I've been knitting since before you were born. I know poor quality yarn when I see it."

"I'm just suggesting that a less delicate wool might suit your purposes better." Bobbi had made the same suggestion the week before when Dottie insisted on buying the damned silk wool in the first place. Her sausage-like fingers were ill suited to delicate work.

"I paid good money for this!" It had been expensive, but she paid as much for the yarn as she did for scolding rights. She continued her tirade, touching on every unhappy moment she'd experienced in the shop.

The old cow's husband had gone deaf years ago. Some said it was voluntary.

Her rant gathered momentum. She moved onto the ills of social media and how this youth culture was destroying the arts. Yes, it was a mighty leap, but one Dottie made with flourish. Eventually, she'd wear herself out. Then Bobbi would credit her account and she'd buy some other equally unsuitable yarn.

"Why is everything today made fast and cheap? What happened to good old fashioned job satisfaction? I swear, you young people…"

Bobbi nodded in the right places and made vague noises. Her knuckles were white around the pen in her hand. She watched Dottie with a flat, flinty gaze.

Molly tried to keep her knitting even. No point in ruining a perfectly good hat over a Dottie Benson tirade.

"Are you even listening to me?"

Bobbi refocused on Dottie's face. It had gone a rich shade of crimson, the bags under her eyes a deep purple. More of a burnt plum. It would be a nice color for a baby hat.

"I swear, you young people have no respect!" The old nag worked herself into a good lather now.

"Mrs. Benson I'm sure we can work out some kind of exchange…"

"Exchange? I want a full refund! In fact, you should be paying me for wasting my time!"

"I can't do that." Bobbi's voice was as calm as a lead pipe. In the dining room, with Colonel Mustard.

"We'll see what the ladies at the crafters' guild think of this!" Dottie shoved the tangled mess of hand-dyed, artisan silk into her bag. "You think I'm a bothersome old woman." She poked Bobbi with a fat finger. Yep, she went there. Bobbi's eyes darkened. "But I have some influence in this town. You'll see!"

She headed out as fast as her orthopedic shoes would allow, stopping to yank the door handle. The door stuck. She yanked harder. A basket tipped off the top shelf, almost braining Dottie and spilling skeins of Icelandic wool on her head and across the floor.

Wasn't that a neat coincidence.

Dottie glowered and kicked the basket before leaving. The bell on the door rang merrily.

"Well, that was bracing," Molly said.

Bobbi shook her head and picked up the basket with shaking fingers.

"Do you think she'll really go to the crafters' guild and complain?" she asked. Ashlet was a small town. The Woolery's entire customer base centered on the guild of ladies who put on craft fairs every season.

"Most certainly. Last week she tried to get everyone to boycott Vincent's

Market because her can of corned beef was dented. Don't worry. Dottie squawks, but nobody listens."

Taking the basket, Molly gathered spilled wool and eyed Bobbi.

Had the falling basket been a coincidence? Funny how such serendipitous things happened with regularity around here. Molly had sworn to keep Bobbi's family legacy a secret, but secrets had a way of betraying themselves. Sometimes at the worst possible moments.

After Bobbi's disappearance last summer, Molly had called Jane, not a call she'd wanted to make. Jane and Molly had a history. An ancient history. They hadn't spoken in nearly twenty years, and time had not dimmed their animosity. But for Bobbi's sake, she made the call. Of course, the coven wasn't accessible by normal communication means. So she'd left a message and waited for a reply.

Quinn answered her, but he was reluctant to tell Molly what happened at the coven. He said only that Bobbi was learning to master her aether. He suggested Molly should speak to her.

Whatever had happened, it left scars. Bobbi didn't want to discuss it, but Molly kept trying.

"That was some trick, dumping the basket on Dottie's head," she said. Bobbi flushed and looked away. "Did you do it on purpose?"

Bobbi shook her head, then nodded. "I don't know. I guess so. I'm not really comfortable talking about it, especially to a…non-witch." Molly knew she'd been about to say "mundane," but stopped herself as if the word were offensive.

Molly was a mundane. She'd come to terms with that fact years ago. It didn't hurt anymore. She almost told Bobbi the whole story then, the story of Koro and the four stupid girls who'd fallen under his sway thirty years ago.

What stopped her? Fear, maybe and a good dose of self-targeted blame.

As she tucked the basket back on its shelf, she caught a glimpse of a familiar face outside.

"Looks like your new beau is right on time for your date," she said.

Bobbi's face melted from anger to happiness. The bell chimed again and William Fain walked in.

"Hey, babe." William opened his arms as Bobbi fell against him. She tilted her head back for a kiss.

Molly pinched back a comment. Bobbi had never been demonstrative with her boyfriends before, not even with Quinn. Molly had been disappointed when that relationship ended. They'd been a good match.

She didn't know what to think about this new one. William wasn't exactly ugly, just plain. A bit pudgy and round-faced. Dopey looking. Not the sort of man who turned a girl's head. But Bobbi seemed smitten.

"I'm ready to leave," Bobbi said. The daily receipts littered the counter, but she left them. This wouldn't be the first time Bobbi shirked her duties to spend time with William.

"I've got a few errands to run in town. Let's meet at your place later." William smiled, an expression more like painful gas on his ruddy face. "I've got a new…uh, recipe for you to try."

Bobbi laughed. "It's okay. Molly knows all about witches. You can say spell."

"Fine, I've got a new spell. One that's best cast sky-clad." His eyebrows waggled like an old-timey vaudevillian.

"Well, I'll let you two kids get on with your evening." Molly grabbed her purse from behind the counter and headed for the door. She had nothing against young love, but William Fain gave her the creeps.

William and Bobbi barely noticed her leave.

Investigation

Heights made Quinn dizzy. The balmy wind brought him no comfort as he scaled the fence behind Bobbi's house. October should be cool with frost to welcome the spirits of Samhain. Warm winds brought unrest at this time of year.

Grabbing a low branch, he pulled himself up and settled into the crook of an old cottonwood. The tree's bare branches gave him no cover, but the night was moonless, and he settled an obfuscation spell over himself. None of the neighbors would see him.

He pulled a small pair of binoculars from his jacket and surveilled the house. They weren't night vision, but he'd enhanced the lenses with a clarity spell and from his perch, he had a clear view into the dining room with the living room beyond. Bobbi and the mysterious William Fain ate at the table with candles and…was that champagne? This guy was going for broke tonight. He obviously didn't know Bobbi was a beer and chips kind of girl. Or maybe she'd only been that way with him? Could he have been so blind?

Quinn watched for a few more minutes. Something wasn't right. He could feel it in his bones. He should have brought Abilene with him. She could read Fain's aether better. Quinn's sensate skills weren't strong enough, but he could feel Bobbi's aether, even from a distance. They'd connected—literally—when they rejoined the core to the ley-line. He'd recognize her magic anywhere.

And tonight he could tell something was wrong. Her aether felt compressed. She burned bright, her magic eager and curious as it always was, but the brightness swirled around her in a tight ball, like a protective shield.

Maybe it was nerves or hesitation that gave her aether an odd flare—nerves because Bobbi was really into this guy.

The thought of her with someone else tightened his gut. He wasn't a possessive man, but some feral part of him wanted to claw past his good nature and snarl: *Bobbi is mine.*

Despite this savage side, it wasn't jealousy that brought him out to spy. If Bobbi wanted to break up with him, he'd deal. But she hadn't said a word. When she canceled her weekly magic lesson with Abilene, he hadn't worried. They were busy at the coven, training new vestals. Bobbi was busy too. She brought her spinning wares to fall festivals all around the state. So he'd let it slide.

When she canceled this week's lesson by text, doubt nagged him, but he'd been caught up in Siranda's latest prophecy of doom. The coven's seer was completely mad, but every now and then, she babbled a kernel of truth, and it was his job to follow up on each lead. So, he'd put his worries about Bobbi aside as he chased down another dead end to finding Koro, the demon who'd attacked the coven in August.

Then Gavin came home this morning with news of his encounter with Bobbi in Ashlet.

"Did you know she was seeing someone new?" he'd asked. No, Quinn hadn't known. To be fair, he and Bobbi hadn't made any formal declarations to each other. They were taking things slow, savoring the sweet intensity of a new relationship. Or so he'd thought.

Bobbi laughed at something Fain said. She touched his face in a way that was altogether too intimate. With his free hand, Quinn gripped the rough branch under his fingers, wishing it was someone's neck.

Bobbi stood to clear the dinner dishes. Fain followed, never more than a step away. He nuzzled her neck. She kissed him. They moved into the kitchen, embraced by the sink, their silhouettes plain in the window. Quinn put down the binoculars. He didn't know what was worse: watching them kiss, or the next moment, when they left his view and headed down a hall leading to her bedroom.

He waited. His aether was weak and a wave of dizziness swept over him. Even the simple obfuscation spell taxed him. He clutched his cockroach necklace in one hand and a branch in the other. The talisman was a magic battery, a vessel for storing aether. He only used it when he had no time for exhaustion, like tonight. The roach amulet gave him a boost and the weakness faded.

He returned his attention to the windows, scrutinizing empty rooms. They were still in the front of the house, outside his view. He didn't want to think of what they could be doing.

Below, a patch of burned ground showed where Bobbi had attempted her fire spell less than three months ago. It felt like a lifetime since the night he burst through the back gate to find Bobbi spell-locked and near death, aether glowing around her like the halo of an angel. She'd looked so fragile, he thought he might break her as they ran for the car.

But she wasn't fragile. A streak of steel ran through Bobbi. More than once, she'd faced horrors with strength and grace. She killed a wraith, for gods' sake. Not even Jane could do that. Bobbi was a burning coal of untapped aether, and he'd been looking forward to learning exactly how far magic would take her.

A girlish giggle came from inside the house. Quinn cringed. How had he missed the signs? He thought they were heading for a future together. William Fain blindsided him. Had he misread Bobbi's intentions? He thought back to their last encounter.

They'd planned for dinner and a movie, but conversation had flowed through the meal, then coffee, then digestifs. They missed the movie entirely and only left when the tired waiter extinguished candles on nearby tables. The whole night, they'd touched in little ways—a finger curled around a thumb, a brush of hair away from her face. They were heading for the bedroom, but he didn't rush it. They had a lifetime to explore each other sexually, but only a few first dates to savor what was coming. Dragging out those exquisite moments had felt like the best decision he'd ever made. She'd felt the same. He was sure of it. He couldn't be that witless.

No more sound or movement came from the house. He shifted on his perch, made more uncomfortable by thoughts of that last date.

Were they in the bedroom? He didn't know what to do. He couldn't burst through the door and confront them while they made love. But he couldn't sit in this tree and imagine Bobbi with her legs wrapped around another man either.

He had to admit defeat. Bobbi had moved on. He hadn't thought she was the callous type—to drop a guy without so much as a text—but he'd been wrong before. He slid sideways, reaching down with one leg for the fence.

The patio door slid open. He froze, then pumped more aether into his obfuscation spell, ignoring another surge of dizziness.

Bobbi came out carrying a tray with candles and other accessories for an altar. Fain followed with the champagne and two glasses. He was plain with a round face that had no angles, slightly paunchy and dressed in a collared t-shirt. He was the innocuous boy next door.

Quinn sat as still as possible, barely daring to breathe. Obfuscation spells worked best on mundanes. He wasn't sure about Fain, but Bobbi had enough sensate magic to spot him if she made an effort to really look.

"Such spells are best done sky-clad." Fain spoke with a faint British accent. It sounded fake. His lips shone wetly in the dim light.

"You're kidding. It's too cold." She shivered, despite the warm wind.

"You won't feel it. Trust me." Fain pulled her to him and kissed her. Bobbi's arms circled his neck. Quinn held his breath until they broke apart.

"Don't you trust me?"

"I do, but I've never cast a spell in the nude. It feels awkward." Bobbi placed her tray on the low table she used for an altar.

"Are you afraid I'll ravish you?" He dipped her into an exaggerated bow, like a ballroom dancer and pretended to bite her neck. Bobbi squealed. Quinn's heart hurt.

Fain righted her. "I promise, my dear, I will ravish you one day when the time is right. And on that day our worlds will change."

This guy was smooth.

"But not tonight?" Bobbi sounded both relieved and disappointed.

"Not tonight," Fain said with a leer. "Tonight we practice magic, so you can learn to control it and not drop baskets on the heads of irate customers."

There had to be a story behind that comment, a story Bobbi would have once confided in Quinn.

Fain set up the altar, candles, bowls of salt and water, athame and incense—all very traditional except for the missing deity figures. Bobbi had statues of the Lord and Lady. Abilene had given them to her at their first lesson. Fain chose to leave them out of his casting preparations. That spoke to ominous intentions.

Bobbi stripped off her blouse and pants. She slid the bra from her shoulders and shimmied out of panties. She was stunning, long limbed, with skin somewhere between pink and gold. Her blond hair hung loose and the wind teased it against her breasts. Quinn wanted to look away but couldn't.

This is so wrong.

He was invading her privacy. For what? Because Gavin thought she was acting strange?

Bobbi hugged herself in the cool air. Fain ignored her as he placed the last touches to the altar.

Quinn shifted on his uncomfortable perch, painfully aware of his growing desire.

"What are we casting tonight?" Bobbi settled on the ground in front of the altar.

"This is a prosperity spell," Fain said. "It was originally used by farmers who wanted to multiply their sheep. I thought it was suitable."

"Cute. Go forth and multiply thy wool," Bobbi said.

"Something like that. Now center yourself. If nothing else, this spell will give you quite a boost of energy."

Bobbi closed her eyes. The hot wind tossed her hair and puckered her skin.

From his pocket, Fain took a small red statue and placed it on the altar. Quinn drew aether from his necklace and sharpened his vision enough to make out details. The round statue stood no more than three inches tall, with blackened features. Horns protruded from its forehead. That was no deity figure. Quinn's suspicions flared. He let the vision spell drop and hung onto the tree as fatigue overtook him. He clutched the cockroach again, hoping it held enough juice to keep his obfuscation spell going.

Below, Fain walked around Bobbi, lecturing like a professor. Quinn fumbled for his phone and hit record on the video app.

"Let your aether wash over you. Let it guide you to prosperity," Fain said, then switched to a chant in a language Quinn didn't recognize. The words were guttural and stark. Primitive.

Quinn knew several varieties of prosperity spells. They spun positive thinking into a weapon that could strike at your enemies in subtle ways. In truth, most were nothing more than ego boosters that left the caster with immense self-confidence to win a new job, wow a new client or play the stock market.

Fain's spell was different, and Quinn's unease deepened.

"Open your eyes. Look into me. Trust me," Fain said. Her gaze locked on his. He continued to chant. Quinn felt the telltale burst of soother magic. Anchoring aether to a word like "trust" was a classic soother trick, one he'd used himself in many negotiations.

He's soothing her!

Bobbi's aether spread from her in a brilliant blue swath, but Fain's chanting didn't direct it. He contained it. Bobbi's stern concentration melted to a dopey grin. Fain wrapped her in his magic, cocooning her with the chant. Did she even hear the dark, eerie incantation slipping from his tongue?

Bobbi's eyes glassed over.

"There, now. Don't you feel better? Powerful?" Fain tucked the red statue back into his pocket.

"Yes. Powerful." Bobbi swayed. Fain gripped her bare shoulders.

"Next time, we'll try something truly spectacular." He patted her arm. "Won't that be nice?"

"Nice."

Fain helped her to her feet and led her back inside. They left the candles burning.

Quinn's aether howled like an injured wolf.

ALTERCATION

Quinn's headlights cut the night. Taunton Road wound through the hills north of Ashlet. He drove it often and knew every bend and bump even in the dark. He stopped fifty feet past a steep curve, made a three-point turn and parked his car across the road, blocking the oncoming lane.

It was a risk. Someone other than William Fain could come by and they might not have time to stop.

Quinn didn't care. Rage boiled in him like lava ready to overflow.

Sitting in his car, he watched the video of Fain soothing Bobbi twice before headlights lit the night. He got out and stood in the road. The approaching car slowed as it rounded the bend. An old, flame-red Dodge Charger, stopped in front of him. Big surprise. Fain was a Dukes of Hazzard geek.

He leaned out the window.

"Something wrong? Hit a deer?"

"Get out."

"What? Who are you?"

"Get out of the car." Quinn's patience ran dry. He would gladly reach through the window and haul Fain out by the throat.

Fain opened the door and got out. He stood as tall as Quinn, but with a chunky soft build, like someone who spent too much time behind a computer. He smiled faintly, as if the world amused him.

"What did you do to her?"

"Look, I think there's some mistake."

"Bobbi. What did you do to her?"

Fain's eyes narrowed. The smile twisted to a sneer.

"You're him aren't you. Quinn something-or-other. Bobbi told me about you. Did she tell you about me?"

Quinn let silence answer.

"No, I can see she didn't."

"You soothed her. Is that how you plan to get her into bed?"

"Oh, I have big plans for Bobbi. Fucking her is only the start."

Quinn stepped into Fain's space.

"Is that how you get women? Pathetic."

Fain's smile slipped. Quinn could soothe too. He willed his aether to poison Fain's temper.

"Bobbi wouldn't touch you otherwise. Look at you. Fat, plain and dull."

Fain's face crumpled in rage.

Come on. Do it. Throw the first punch.

He leaned in. Their eyes locked.

"The only chance you have with her is drugged or spelled."

Fain shoved him.

Quinn grinned. "Was that supposed to hurt?"

Fain swung a punch. It glanced off Quinn's shoulder.

Quinn's fist landed squarely on Fain's mouth, splitting his lip with a spray of blood. Fain slammed against his car, but he wasn't down for long. Blinded by blood and mad with fear, he came up swinging.

The kid was tougher than he'd given him credit for. Or at least persistent. Quinn leaned sideways to avoid a clumsy hit, then grabbed Fain by the throat, pressing him against his car door. Quinn struck him in the mouth again, then held him there, ducking quickly to press a thin disk to the underside of the car, while Fain choked on his own blood.

Fain babbled like a hysterical child, tilting his head back to deflect another strike, but Quinn was done with the fight. He'd made his statement. He grabbed Fain's chin, wrapping a hand around the blood-smeared jaw, and dragged Fain's gaze down to meet his.

"Bobbi is not yours to play with. You hurt her and I will kill you. Does that sound like an empty threat?"

Fain tried to shake his head but Quinn held him in a vice grip.

"Good." He let go and shoved Fain one more time because it felt good.

Fain fell into his car. The wheels spun as he veered around Quinn and sped off down the country road.

Quinn watched until the tail lights disappeared, then sat in his dark car for a long time.

Soothing was dangerous magic. A soother could affect another person's emotions for good or bad. But magic wasn't a precise weapon and the soother could be as easily affected as the target.

He slammed his fists against the steering wheel.

How much of his rage was from magic and how much was from seeing Bobbi manipulated by that creep? Did it matter?

He breathed deep until the anger faded.

He'd learned a lot tonight. Bobbi's new romance wasn't real, and William Fain had a hold over her. Quinn cursed himself for not teaching Bobbi to recognize soother magic sooner. But with the upset at the coven, he'd barely had time to teach her anything. Then, two weeks ago, Siranda had rambled on about Koro, something about being in a club in Miami, and Quinn flew out to check. It was a dead end and a waste of time—time Fain used to hook Bobbi with his magic.

Fain's aether was weak though. Any well-trained witch would have sensed Quinn's soother attack and taken measures to block it. Fain hadn't even tried.

So where did he find the power to ensorcell Bobbi? He thought back to the ritual, the dark chant and the odd deity figure. Someone was pulling Fain's strings. And he had a good idea who.

Before starting the car, he checked his phone. The signal for the tracker he'd planted on Fain's car flashed reassuringly. His Dukes-of-Hazzard-mobile moved fast, and not toward Bobbi's house.

His hands shook from the sudden release of adrenaline. Blood dried on his knuckles. He wiped it with a handkerchief and winced. His joints were bruised, but the blood was Fain's. Studying the dark stain, he wished his sensate abilities were stronger. Power stirred in that blood, but he couldn't tell what kind. Carefully, he folded the handkerchief and sealed it in a plastic bag.

Abilene could tell a lot from a drop of blood. If Koro controlled Fain, she would know it.

CONFRONTATION

I had never been so furious.

Quinn thought he could butt into my business through some sense of what? Misplaced chivalry? Did he think I was so naive, so weak I couldn't take care of myself?

"How dare he?" I pounded the keys on the cash register and it spit out an end-of-day receipt.

William had just left, after telling the horrific tale of his encounter with Quinn last night.

"Are you certain he's telling the truth?" Molly's tone was infuriatingly reasonable.

"Why would he lie?" Poor William. His lip had been swollen in a pout. It would have been adorable if the reason behind it wasn't so dark. What the hell was Quinn thinking?

"Maybe you should speak to Quinn, get his side of the story before you jump to conclusions," Molly said.

"Oh, I jumped already. Believe me. I'm at the sentencing stage."

Molly shook her head and turned away.

I pulled out my phone and texted: *We need to talk. NOW.*

Quinn only went outside the ward a couple of times a day to check his messages. I'd have to wait for his call.

I closed the cash register as the ladies knitting club arrived for an evening class. Molly ran these twice a week. Usually, I tried to duck out before they arrived.

"There she is!" Mrs. Davereau hustled through the door with her oversized knitting bag. The rest of the knitting brigade filed in behind her. "I hear you have a new special someone." Mrs. Davereau gripped my hand across the counter.

"Yes, I do." If she pinched my cheek I was bolting.

"And what's his name?" She wasn't leaving until she got the details.

"William. He's…" I couldn't think of a word to describe William. "Nice."

He was nice. Ordinary almost. And considering my usual bad-boy fixation, that seemed like a step toward maturity. Thinking about William's touch bewildered my brain with waves of happiness.

"I'm sure he is, dear." Mrs. Davereau patted my hand. "And this must be him now."

The door chimed. I looked up and froze.

"No. Definitely not my boyfriend."

Quinn stood in the doorway. He looked gaunt, as if he'd missed a few nights of sleep. Fatigue etched the lines of his face into something raw and imposing. His hair was longer and curled helter-skelter across his brow. Blue-black eyes challenged me. I pulled away from Mrs. Davereau's grasp. My legs jellied. This was silly. Quinn and I were long gone. I'd moved on. Just because the sight of him triggered some vestigial desire that didn't mean I had any real feelings for him.

"You bellowed?" He held up his phone.

"Uh, yeah. You have some explaining to do." And he could have done it by phone. He must have already been in town to have shown up so quickly. "But not here," I said through gritted teeth. The knitting bees had settled into the lounge area of the store, but they were noticeably quiet. All ears perked our way.

Molly greeted Quinn with a smile.

"It's good to see you, Quinn. Some of us have missed you around here." She looked pointedly at me and I rolled my eyes. During our brief relationship, Molly had fussed over Quinn like a mother hen. It turned out Jane had also been a friend of my mother's in high school. Some falling out between Molly and Jane had caused a decades-long rift, but Molly didn't hold the grudge against Quinn. She thought he was delightful and took pains to mention it to me often. And at the most awkward moments.

"Isn't he the handsome one, Bobbi?" I turned away, pretending to sort receipts I had already sorted. "Look at those shoulders." Molly wasn't letting go any time soon. "I bet you still throw a mean baseball. I remember you had quite an arm as a boy."

"Mrs. McFadden." Quinn's smile was genuine as he leaned in to kiss her cheek. "I don't have much time for baseball these days. You're looking lovely as ever."

"Flatterer." Molly fluffed her hair. Today, she wore it loose with bright feathers woven among the grey curls.

I shoved my papers into a drawer and faced Quinn, glad to have the solid barrier of the counter between us.

Quinn quirked an eyebrow. "Care for a walk?"

"Fine."

I needed to leave the prying eyes of Ashlet's gossipmongers behind.

Half a dozen cheery voices called out in goodbye as we left. I heard a few titters and could imagine the old ladies nudging each other and whispering about the young couple out for a romantic walk.

Let them think what they wanted. This encounter was all business. My heart battered my chest in response to the coming confrontation, not because Quinn affected me in any way.

I turned my thoughts to William and his sweet smile. My heart rate slowed and I took a deep breath.

A gust of warm wind blew leaves up the sidewalk as we left the store. I shrugged my sweater tightly around my shoulders but I didn't really need it. The night was unseasonably warm.

We headed across the bridge. The roar of the Anneke River flowing over the dam made conversation impossible.

Now that I'd trussed up my nerves, anger returned. Sweet righteous anger. Quinn had his chance. Things didn't work out. That didn't mean he could sabotage the first good relationship I'd ever had. I glanced sideways. He watched me.

On the other side of the bridge we turned into the park. We were alone. The kids' playground lay in shadow, wind rocking the empty swings.

I stopped and turned on him.

"You had no right to interfere."

"I had every right."

"Why? Because we dated a couple of times? Because we kissed? All of a sudden you're my keeper? You punched my boyfriend in the face! Who does that? I really want to know. Tell me, by what right do you decide who I go out with?"

He studied me with no anger in his expression. He looked sad.

"Fain is Koro's agent."

"Still no reason...what?" I wasn't prepared for that. "Don't be ridiculous. William is just William."

"It's true. He's soothing you. I saw it. Last night at your place. He had some kind of talisman."

"You spied on me? Oh, this is great." I turned away. My stomach churned with emotions I couldn't identify.

"Listen to me, Bobbi. I felt his magic. He's controlling you." He grabbed my arm. I yanked it away and picked irritation out of the seething mass of emotions in my gut. I wrapped it around me like a security blanket. How had I ever thought this man was attractive? I saw him now for what he was. An arrogant manipulator. My way or the highway kind of guy.

"You're pathetic." I put all of my loathing into those words.

"I can prove it," he said quietly. He pulled a handkerchief from his pocket and unfolded it carefully. "Abilene tested his blood and found Koro's aether in it."

Dark stains spotted the cloth. William's blood. I closed my eyes. He'd hurt William to get his blood.

"You are unbelievable." I opened my eyes and pinned him with my glare. "Here's what's going to happen. You are going to leave me alone. You, your sister, your mother, your whole bloody coven. Leave. Me. Alone."

I turned and ran back over the bridge. The rushing of the river didn't quite mask the sound of Quinn calling my name.

Intoxication

Dracula stalked the sleeping woman. I sipped my wine, watching the melodrama on TV with faint interest. William always chose the best vintages, and I could put up with his classic movie fetish.

"You wouldn't believe how arrogant he was!" I said for the third time. Bela Lugosi's mesmerizing eyes filled the screen.

"I can believe the arrogance. But I don't like the idea of you and him alone." William leaned back on the couch.

"Jealous?" I wrapped my arms around his neck. The cut on his lip had scabbed over. I wanted to kiss it.

William frowned and untangled himself.

"He's dangerous, Bobbi. Promise me you won't see him again." The TV defined his face with flickering shadows. He held me at arm's length. I hated it when he did that. I wanted to be close, to feel his aether around me like a shield. It was a visceral feeling. A *need*.

"I promise."

He smiled and I tucked my feet under me, scooting closer to the warmth of his body. My head lay on his shoulder.

"Look at this part." William gestured at the TV, bouncing my head from its perch. "Look at the dramatic use of lighting on Dracula's face. It was revolutionary!"

He was so excited. His aether circled me, a safe haven of energy and love. Lugosi snuck up on his next sleeping victim. She looked so peaceful, as if the vampire bite was a happy dream.

"What else did he have to say?" William's tone was calm, but I felt the edgy undercurrent. I shouldn't have brought up my encounter with Quinn. It would ruin a perfectly good Friday evening. I wanted to forget about Quinn and relax in the glow of warmth around us, but the words erupted from my lips.

"He said you were working with Koro."

"Who's that?" His thumb stroked the underside of my palm. Up and down, in a mesmerizing junction of senses.

"Some guy. I don't know. They don't like him much." Shadows of memories lurked behind those words, but they weren't important. What did I really know about Koro? He was Jane's enemy. But Jane was a hard woman. She probably had dozens of enemies. The connection fuddled in my brain.

"He's got something against the coven, I guess." On the screen Van Helsing confronted Dracula with a mirror and the monster cringed.

"He also said you were using magic on me. Soother magic."

The thumb stopped its caress. William pushed me off his lap. The room felt ten degrees colder.

"That's ridiculous."

His words fell like icy rain.

I blinked and my eyes cleared.

"Who are you?" I stared at the stranger on my couch. "What are you doing here?"

"Don't be silly…" The round face morphed into a grin, badly lit in the dark room. I knew that face, and yet…it was completely strange too. I pushed away, my hands sinking into the couch. He grabbed me.

"Bobbi stop!"

No! I had to get away. This was wrong. All wrong. It should be Quinn beside me not this round-faced man I didn't even know! I tried to stand but my limbs were heavy. Panic constricted my chest.

I shoved. A hand dug into my shoulders. Hard fingers wrapped my chin, forced my eyes upward.

"Bobbi, look at me. Do you know who I am?"

My eyes betrayed me. They looked at the face, that hated face. Pale blue eyes bore into mine.

William.

"Yes."

He held my eyes with his deep, sincere gaze.

"I would never do anything to hurt you. Trust me."

I breathed a sigh and felt everything loosen. Quinn and his maniacal accusations faded to a dim memory.

I cupped William's face with my hand. Such a sweet face, ruddy and bright-eyed. His lips were always a bit puckered, inviting a kiss. He made me feel full. Overflowing. Never in my life had I felt so connected to another human being.

"I trust you."

He smiled and the world came into focus again. Everything would be all right.

"Did you practice the prosperity spell again?" he asked.

"I tried, but I couldn't get it right. I guess I'm tired."

He pulled me onto his lap. His arms wrapped around me, his aether bundling us in protective energy.

"You should rest," he said. "You've been working so hard. And all this confrontation must be exhausting."

It was exhausting. It felt good to have someone understand me so completely. I laid my head against his chest. Fingers ran through my hair. So good. He tipped my chin up and his lips covered mine. I leaned in to him, needing to feel closer, to press every bit of my body against his. I pushed his hands down my shoulder, hinting they were free to explore further. But he held himself in check.

Again.

"We could take this into the bedroom." I wanted him so badly, I thought my wellspring would burst from need.

"Soon." His eyes darkened with intensity. "When I make love to you, it will change the world."

I lay back and closed my eyes. His aether wrapped me in calming vibes. I could wait. What girl didn't love to be pampered and cherished?

"I brought you something," he said. I opened my eyes. A small statue sat in the palm of his hand. Red, with black grotesque features, like a squatting gargoyle. I instantly wanted it.

"So cute!" My hand tingled when I held it.

"It's a protection talisman. It'll keep you safe when I'm not around. And I want you to promise me something."

I didn't answer. The talisman spread warmth up my arm and into my chest. He nudged me.

"Hmm?"

"Promise me that if Quinn comes around again, you stop him. Do whatever it takes to make him go away. Same goes for anyone else who tries to fill your head with nonsense."

"You take such good care of me." My words slurred from wine or sleepiness. I clutched the statue to my chest and leaned on him.

On the TV the mad Renfield cried, "Master! Master! I am here!"

PREDICTION

The wind was too warm. Gavin couldn't help feeling that the odd weather was an ill-omen as he sat on the curb outside The Woolery, waiting for Bobbi. Inside, Molly escorted two young women through the selection of wool roving. He'd listened long enough to become numbed by the array of colors and textures. When Molly started on the differences in felting needles, Gavin had decided to wait outside.

Ten minutes later, Bobbi appeared, balancing coffee and two takeout bags. Gavin stretched, rose and took the coffee.

"Is this a late lunch or an early dinner?" he asked.

Bobbi ignored the question. "Are you here to try and convince me that my boyfriend is evil too?"

"Such ego. Not everything is about you."

Inside, Bobbi dumped the bags on the counter. Gavin sipped her coffee and made a face.

"Have some coffee with your sugar," he said.

"I like it sweet." She grabbed the cup. "So what do you want."

Bobbi leaned on the counter and ate a fry from the bag. She offered him one and he shook his head.

He didn't know her well. The first time they'd met, he'd been angry because Siranda, the coven seer, was upset by the stranger in their midst. Gavin's job was tough enough. He didn't need newbie witches making things worse. He might have expressed this opinion. Loudly. And within Bobbi's hearing.

The next time they'd met, she berated him in front of his vestals for letting a witch die while on duty at the core.

She had balls, he had to give her that. He could see why Quinn was raging around like a constipated bull. Quinn liked to take things slow. He had that whole suave and debonair thing going on, or so he thought. Gavin knew better.

Quinn took forever to get it on with a woman because relationships scared him.

"I came to take you up on your offer." Bobbi stared at him blankly. "To visit my mother," he prompted.

"Oh, right. You're going today?"

"Yeah, it's my sister's birthday."

"Nice. Will she be joining us?"

Gavin let silence drop like a curtain between them. He never liked this part. "She's dead."

Bobbi looked up with the silent "Oh!" on her lips that inevitably appeared when people faced the social awkwardness of death.

"This day is always hard on Mom, if she remembers. I could use some back up."

"Of course. I'll let Molly know and we can go."

Riverview Psychiatric Hospital was a large manor house, once owned by the founding family of Ashlet. Since the thirties, it had gone through many incarnations, from boarding house to squatters' den. Twenty years ago, the state bought the land and turned the house into a hospital.

To Gavin, it felt more like a retirement facility. The patients were all elderly. Even those who weren't seniors grew old quickly in a place like this. The industrial grey walls turned every complexion to ash. The stillness inside was oppressive, as if the inhabitants waited for someone who would never come. Nothing ever changed in Riverview. No one left, except on a stretcher with a sheet over their face. Even the few outbursts of patients only ruffled feathers before the birds settled down to wait some more.

Gavin hated it.

Asking Bobbi to join him wasn't just for Quinn's benefit. Yes, he'd agreed to spy on her, but he genuinely welcomed the company.

They signed in at the front desk. The receptionist barely looked up from her magazine. Gavin was a regular visitor. They passed several residents in the front sitting room. Two people played cards before a muted TV. Bobbi's eyes were wide as she took in the dark interior and the bath-robed patients.

A man stood in the corner with his forehead pressed against the wall.

"Hey, Joel." Gavin waved. The wall-gazer didn't answer and they went upstairs.

His mother's nurse, Tanya, met them on the landing. She carried a bundle of dirty sheets.

"She had a quiet morning," the nurse said. "I was about to bring her tea. Want some?"

"Thanks. This is my friend Bobbi," Gavin said.

"We've met." Tanya smiled. Bobbi's eyes squinted at her cheery face. She was short with broad shoulders and thick curly hair. She had an air of strength about her, both physical and emotional. "You don't remember me."

"At the library," Bobbi said.

Tanya nodded and turned to Gavin. "Bobbi came to a few of our coven meetings. I haven't seen you around in a while. Did you decide that witchcraft is not for you?"

"I've been busy," Bobbi said.

Tanya shrugged. "It happens. We aren't all in tune with the Mother."

Gavin stifled a snort. Tanya pinched her lips.

"Gavin doesn't believe in witchcraft," she said.

Bobbi smiled faintly. "I guess it's a hard thing for most people to believe." She shot him a dark look.

"Don't worry. It doesn't matter if you believe. The Great Mother believes in you," Tanya said.

Gavin was glad her arms were full of dirty sheets. She had a hugging look in her eye.

"Well, we still meet every second Tuesday at the library, if you're interested," she said. Bobbi made a noncommittal noise. Tanya descended the stairs, tossing back a smile and a "Blessed be."

Bobbi waited until they were alone and whispered, "I looked them up last year, hoping they could help me master magic. They had bake sales and sit-ins. Not a real witch among them."

Gavin grinned. "I guess our coven was a bit of a shock after that."

"I'd given up trying to find others to help me." Bobbi frowned.

"You could come visit, you know. I think Quinn is over all that blindfolding, cloak and dagger stuff."

"Don't even mention that name. You promised."

"I'm just saying Quinn isn't the only witch in the sea. All's fair in love and magic."

Bobbi laughed. "You are the master of mixed metaphor." Her tone turned serious. "But I can't go back. Not now. Not after those horrible lies Quinn told."

Lies, right. He saw no point in having this conversation now. Bobbi was firmly under Fain's sway. Besides, Quinn hadn't asked him to convert her to reality. Just to keep an eye on her.

He reached for the door to his mother's room and stopped.

"I told you today is my sister's birthday. There is something else you should know." The words had trouble forming on his tongue. He'd never spoken them out loud.

"My mother was an addict back then. Ivy, my sister, died of neglect. They found her in her crib. She starved to death." That was all he could get out before anxiety battered him.

A cold, dark room, full of trash and sharp things that hurt his tiny fingers… his only dim memory of life with his mother before social services took him away.

Bobbi gripped his arm and he instinctively jerked away from the touch.

"I'm so sorry." Her face was pinched in anger but that was better than pity. He didn't want platitudes. He smiled, took a deep breath and opened the door.

Stacy Beal sat by a large, arched window. Her hair, once thick and black, hung in thin white wisps. At least it was clean. Tanya took good care of her.

"Ma? I brought you a visitor." Stacy didn't turn. A blanket covered her lap and an open book lay on that, but she didn't read. She stared out the window. She always stared. Her shoulders shuddered.

"Are you cold?" Gavin took a shawl from the end of the bed and draped it over her shoulders. Stacy shrugged and let it fall to the floor.

"He was here, you know." Her thin voice was like ice scraping off a window. "He comes when no one sees. But I see. *I see.*"

Once again Gavin was struck by Stacy's resemblance to Siranda, the coven's mad seer with her pale face, stringy hair and rambling nonsense. He looked at Bobbi, transmitting an apology with his eyes. She stood quietly by the door as if any movement might startle Stacy.

"Ma, this is my friend, Bobbi. I thought we could take a walk outside."

Stacy turned her head to look at her son, but she didn't really see him.

"He can't take me back there. He knows that. It's not allowed. But he comes for me anyway." Her cracked lips widened in a smile. Her right front canine was black and dead. "He still wants me."

"Maybe today isn't a good day for a visit," Bobbi said.

Stacy turned sharply.

"Hannah?" Her eyes narrowed, then widened. "You can't be here! You can't be here when he comes!"

Gavin hadn't seen his mother stand in over two years, but from some deep reserve, Stacy found strength. She rose, letting the book and blanket fall, and lunged at Bobbi.

"You have to leave! Hannah! He's so angry at you. Go! Before he finds you here. Go!" Her thin face creased with fear. Gavin froze. He didn't want to touch Stacy, had never touched her, but panic gave her strength and she moved fast. She looked like a hollowed-out scarecrow with bony fingers clawing at Bobbi, who tried to fend her off. A swipe of her nails cut a red line across Bobbi's chin.

The bedroom door opened and Tanya came in, carrying a tea tray.

"What is going on in here? Miss Stacy, you shouldn't be up!" She dropped the tray on the bedside table and grabbed Stacy's hands, prying Bobbi's shirt from their grip. "Come on, now. Let's get you back to bed." Over her shoulder, she shot Gavin a dark look. "You should leave."

Bobbi grabbed him by the arm and shoved him through the door. For once, Gavin didn't resist the touch. In the hallway, he leaned against the bedroom door. Stacy's cries faded to a muffled whine, interrupted by Tanya's placating words.

"Who's Hannah?" he asked.

Bobbi's face was pale. "My mother."

RECOLLECTION

Molly could tell something was wrong. From her vantage at the store's big front window, she watched Bobbi and Gavin approach the Woolery. They crossed the bridge, not stopping to take in the view of the Anneke River. The unseasonal wind grabbed at their clothes and hair. Bobbi looked like she'd witnessed a fatal car crash. And Gavin…well, that boy was hard to read, but even his spritely facade had cracks.

She'd known it was a bad idea for Bobbi to visit Stacy, but she'd held her tongue. It was time. Time for secrets to be revealed. Time for the great wall of silence Jane had erected around them all to crumble. So she'd let the encounter happen and now she would pick up the pieces.

She hurried to the back to make tea.

The bell above the door jangled and she heard Bobbi and Gavin settle in the shop's lounge area. The knitting bees were gone and Danielle had the day off. Molly locked the door and turned the sign that said "Be back in 15!" with a bright smiley face.

"Do I look like my mother?" Bobbi asked. Molly took the time to sit and pour tea before answering.

"Yes."

No need to tell Bobbi she was almost an exact replica of Hannah—same blue eyes, same curl to the blond hair. She even walked like Hannah. Sometimes, when Molly saw Bobbi from the corner of her eye, she could imagine her childhood friend hadn't been dead these past twenty years.

Bobbi stirred her tea. She'd been off lately. Not quite her normal, positive self. After an enlightening visit from Quinn last night, she understood that Bobbi's behavior had much to do with William Fain's sudden appearance in her life. Molly knew that punk was bad news the first time he awkwardly flirted with Bobbi in the shop. Buying wool for his aged aunt. Bah! No one believed that. William Fain had deceiver written all over him.

But Molly had to tread carefully. Fain was not the issue. His presence in Bobbi's life only complicated a story long overdue in telling.

"Why would Gavin's mother know my mother?" asked Bobbi.

"We were all friends," Molly said. "Jane, Hannah, Stacy and me." She turned to Gavin. "Jane might have already told you that." He nodded. "But she didn't tell you everything."

"Well, you'd better tell us now." Bobbi's voice hardened. "I don't like having things kept from me."

"The way you kept your magic from me?" snapped Molly. "Oh, don't look like a sheep. For years, I wondered when you would recognize the power inside yourself. I'm sure Jane wondered too."

"Jane?" Bobbi looked confused. "She knew about me before this summer?" Molly nodded.

"The High Priestess of the Hidden Coven knows about all witch activity in this area, even those witch wannabes who meet at the library and pretend to commune with the Great Mother. But you, Bobbi, you are special. As is Gavin."

"Gavin?" Bobbi glanced at him as if she'd never considered him before.

"Yes." Molly sighed. Jane wouldn't thank her for this, but Molly didn't give a rat's fat ass what Jane wanted. Not anymore. Not in a long time. "Gavin is your half-brother." She let that sink in. They stared at each other.

Gavin spoke first. "But how?"

That was a loaded question. Where to begin with the answer? Molly put her thoughts in order. Best to begin at the beginning.

"We were young and foolish, fresh out of high school. Girls at that age can be reckless. We had a whole summer ahead of us before college. One last hurrah of youth. We spent our days working at minimum wage jobs and our nights fantasizing about the men we'd meet in college." Molly could see them in her mind's eye, four brave and beautiful women, oblivious to the world barreling down on them.

"Hannah found the grimoire. We thought it was a joke, had a few laughs pretending to cast spells. I didn't believe in magic." Molly laughed roughly. "Who would, really? But Jane and Hannah insisted they felt something when we read the spells. Jane convinced us to call Kororaeth."

"Koro? You called him?" Gavin's expression reflected the disgust Molly felt at the memory.

"Yes. I'd like to say we were innocent, but really we were stupid and arrogant, thinking we knew all there was to know in the universe."

Molly closed her eyes and remembered their faces. Her friends, so young and happy. Stacy stole a bottle of sherry from her father's liquor cabinet. They passed it around, along with a cigarette and watched Jane dip her brother's hunting knife through the flame of a black candle three times, invoking Koro's true name with each pass.

The noise began like an itch in Molly's ears. Jane and Hannah intoned the words from the spell, written in some language none of them understood. Who knew if they even pronounced them right? The candle went out and Stacy screamed. Molly thought Jane was tricking them until the noise grew like a tornado in her head.

And the ground fell away. Their world disappeared and they plunged through darkness that had texture. Hot, then cold. Viscous like oil, then sharp as cut glass. Molly landed with a bone crushing jolt on wet stone. Someone whimpered nearby. Her body hurt, stomach churned and she leaned over to vomit.

"He kept us prisoner for months. At first, he left us alone in the dark. We were hungry, scared and hurt. Later, after he had his fun with us, we grew to relish alone time. But in the beginning it felt like hell." They had been so naive. Hell was relative.

"I don't know how long we were there. Time has no meaning in his world."

"His world?" Bobbi asked.

"Yes, I believe we were in another dimension," Molly said. "I can't prove it. But I feel it, here." She pressed her hand against her heart. "He tortured us for months, but when we finally returned, only hours had passed. No one even knew we were gone. Two months later, we all discovered we were pregnant."

Gavin's face turned to ash. Bobbi's was unreadable.

"I miscarried in the fifth month. Jane's baby was stillborn." Or so she said. Molly didn't want to get into that age-old argument right now. "But Hannah and Stacy carried you both to term."

"Us?" Bobbi's voice cracked. "You're saying we're the children of a demon?"

Molly nodded. Nothing she could say would convince or comfort. Better to let them digest the news in their own time.

"Stacy said 'he' came to see her," Bobbi said. "She wanted us to leave before 'he' got there. Did she mean Koro? Is he here in Ashlet?"

Gavin shook his head. "My mother is sick, Bobbi. She sees things that aren't there."

"Koro can't manifest on our plane," Molly said. "He can only take foolish witches who open the door to his dimension or manipulate someone into being his agent in our world."

Silence hung in the room like oppressive weather.

Slowly, Bobbi's face turned livid red. "That's what this is about. You're all thinking it. You, Quinn, Jane and Abilene. You all think William is working for Koro and I'm just some dupe he's manipulating."

"The truth is, we don't know where Koro is or who's working for him," Molly said. "But I do know that he would do anything to cross worlds. And you two may be the key he's been waiting for. Jane says…"

"Get out," Bobbi said. "Both of you. Just get out."

"You must listen to me…" Molly reached for Bobbi's arm, but she pulled away.

"You know what? Never mind. I'll leave. You two can go on talking your nonsense. And when you talk to the High Mistress, you can tell her to butt out of my business too." She stood and rushed out, leaving the front door wide and swaying in the wind.

In the silence that followed, Molly gathered the tea tray.

"I'll call Danielle to cover the rest of her shift," she said. Bobbi hadn't even considered the store's schedule before running out. It only highlighted the muddle in her mind.

"Tell me about him. My father." Gavin's words stopped her and she sat back heavily in the chair.

"He's a demon, I know," Gavin said. "Tell me what he wants with me and Bobbi."

"Demon is a loose term. Any being from a lower dimension can be called that. Some of those creatures are nothing more than vermin. Others are peace seekers who want to be left alone. Koro is a monster."

"Is he the reason you and Jane are no longer friends?"

Molly considered her words carefully. She had no love for Jane, but once they had been as close as sisters. Jane saved Gavin from a brutal life. She might have had ulterior motives, but the fact remained; Jane took Gavin in when no one else would. And if her brand of love was a little twisted, how could Molly truly fault her for that?

But she wouldn't lie to Gavin.

"How much about our time with Koro has Jane told you?"

"Nothing. I only know that she faced him once. She won't talk about it."

Gavin's gaze reflected his eagerness. He was hungry for knowledge.

"Do you want to know the truth? It's not pretty."

Gavin nodded once, short but with no hesitation.

Molly sighed, closed her eyes and mentally prepared to put herself in hell again.

"Koro takes pleasure in pain." She didn't see any reason to sugarcoat things. "He raped each of us, taking turns like it was a game. If we fought back, he beat us. If we cried or looked away, he beat us." She opened her eyes. Gavin watched her, his face gone white.

"Once, he beat Stacy badly, broke her nose and arm. Right in front of us." She never knew which was worse, having it happen to her, or watching him rape her friends, knowing she couldn't stop him. "Stacy's eyes were swollen shut and blood poured down her face. He drank it. Licked it right off her cheek and…he smiled."

Panic washed up her spine in a wave of trembling. Even after all these years, that bastard had power over her. The power of fear.

"Stacy was never the same after that. When Koro came for her again, she wasn't even healed from his last visit. Jane intervened."

"She what?" Molly ignored Gavin's outburst. She had to finish the story quickly now.

"While Hannah and I cowered in the shadows, trying to make ourselves small and insignificant, Jane stood up to a demon. She told him to leave Stacy alone or she'd kill him. I think she meant it." Molly could still hear Koro's booming laughter filling their small prison cell as if amplified.

"Koro nearly killed Jane, but I don't think she ever forgot her vow. She will kill him one day."

"You think he'll come after me?"

"I think he'll try to seduce you with promises of power. He'll shower you with affection, then sacrifice you for a drop of your blood."

"It's always about blood."

Molly nodded. "Blood is life. Life is power. I can't say how he will use you. But he had a plan when he impregnated us, one he has waited a long time to finish."

Outside, the sun was setting, but Molly couldn't shake the feeling that speaking the demon's name had the power to make the world go dim.

ZOMBIFICATION

Shadows spilled like ink beneath the cottonwood tree. Quinn crouched inside the fence surrounding Bobbi's property. The sun had barely set and he waited impatiently for full dark. The weather was still warm, more like July than October. Now the portentous warm wind blew in fitful gusts. It made a racket of crackling leaves, dust tossed against the fence, and clattering branches. Quinn worried he wouldn't hear an approaching car above the noise.

His phone vibrated and a text from Gavin appeared on the screen.

B on her way. She's upset. Talk later.

Upset about what? He texted back, but Gavin didn't answer. *Damn him.* Gavin couldn't be trusted with one simple assignment. Spend time with Bobbi. That's all he'd asked. What the hell had he said to her?

He couldn't wait for the cover of darkness any longer. He ran across the empty yard to the patio door. His legs shook with fatigue. When was the last time he'd slept? He couldn't remember. He'd been watching Fain's movements with the GPS tracker for two nights, in between hours of intense research on how to break a soothing spell and anything he could find about Koro and demons in general.

He was exhausted, and a touch of the cockroach on the cord around his neck didn't help. The bug talisman was dry.

Damn. He should have taken time to replenish it. He waited for a bout of shaking hands to pass before trying the sliding glass door.

It was locked. He knew several spells to get inside, but with Bobbi's keen sensate abilities he didn't want to expend too much aether, not that he had any to spare.

Thankfully, like most home owners, Bobbi had no idea how easily those patio doors could be picked. He pressed his hands on the glass and jerked up sharply. The lock popped as the flimsy mechanism fell free. He slid the door open, and wiped his fingerprints off the glass.

He'd really have to school her on home security when this was over.

Inside, the house was dark and he didn't dare use a flashlight or a vision spell. So, he headed through the kitchen, moving slowly until his eyes adjusted.

Down the hall, he found her bedroom lit from outside by the light over the garage. The bed was neatly made. A robe hung over the rocking chair by the window. A jewelry box sat on her bureau along with a small lamp. Nothing else.

He was looking for the red statue. If Fain expected to keep Bobbi under his sway, he needed some kind of talisman to continue soothing when he wasn't around. Quinn suspected that odd demon statue was it. Breaking it might rupture Fain's hold on her. Maybe. Or maybe the statue was only a catalyst for the spell and now that Fain's claws were deeply embedded in her psyche, he no longer needed it. It was still worth a try.

He opened drawers, checked under her pillow. Nothing.

Inside the master bathroom, he opened the medicine cabinet. He didn't expect to find the statue in here, but would he find a second toothbrush? A man's razor?

No. The bathroom was clean and seemed to be stocked only with Bobbi's things. A tightness eased around his heart. She hadn't welcomed Fain into her life that completely. Not yet.

He should feel guilty for spying on her. He didn't. She had no one to look out for her. No one who understood the real danger she faced. Jane wanted proof before they moved against William Fain.

"He's soothing her!" Quinn had said, ready to pull out his hair.

He'd shown Jane the video, but she dismissed it with the wave of a hand.

"Tell me you never used your power to get a pretty girl into bed," she said, with her usual infuriating calm. "That doesn't mean he's working for Koro, only that he's horny."

Even the handkerchief with Fain's blood hadn't moved her.

"I want you to stay away from that woman," was all she said.

This was why Quinn had left the coven ten years ago. Jane was dead inside. He'd felt it all his life. Bitterness bled into all her relationships, keeping even her closest family at a distance.

When his father died, Jane's aloofness reached a new plateau. He'd left the coven, traveling down south as head of security for a company that catered to visiting dignitaries. He came back for good three years ago, when Abilene was fourteen and Jane began grooming her to take over as High Priestess. Abilene was brilliant and a powerful witch, but young. She needed other influences in her life to balance Jane's cold, authoritarian views.

So he'd come home. And Jane hadn't changed. She saw no reason to interfere in Bobbi's affair as long as it didn't touch the coven. That Bobbi was being mind-fucked by that bastard was of no concern.

He bared his teeth at his reflection in the bathroom mirror. He'd get the proof. Then he'd see William Fain on the wrong side of hell's door.

In the living room, he checked the bookshelf and the stack of DVD's under the TV. He closed his eyes and tried to sense any odd magic in the room.

There.

Behind a sofa cushion, he found the statue. The terra cotta face had been oiled to a deep red. Nubs of blackened horn protruded from its head. Quinn's fingers tingled when he touched it. He tried to sense its purpose, but could only read its vague malevolent aether.

Wind blasted the front window, and he nearly dropped the statue. Behind the wind came the distant rumble of a car.

Bobbi was home.

He glanced at the room, hoping he'd put everything back the way he'd found it. He adjusted a throw pillow, then slipped out the patio door, hiding in the shadows behind the barbecue.

A door slammed and voices came from inside. She wasn't alone. He had no time to make it to his spy nook in the tree, and the way his legs shook, he wasn't sure he could climb it.

The voices rose. Gavin was right. Bobbi was upset.

He could see them in the kitchen. Bobbi tipped her face up to Fain's, then pressed it against his shoulder.

Was she crying?

Quinn had been watching her for days. She walked and talked and smiled like a normal person, but that was Fain's aether masking the real Bobbi. Maybe he should thank Gavin for provoking some kind of emotion from her. Something had reached her through the fog of magic. Something powerful. He wanted to call Gavin and find out what happened, but without an obfuscation spell, he didn't dare move.

Fain led Bobbi into the living room, stopping to open the patio door, and slide the screen into place.

Quinn crept closer.

"You can tell me anything." Fain wore a tight golf shirt that did nothing to hide his paunch. His eyes darted from side to side as if he expected an attack. Bobbi's gaze fixed on his face. She didn't look upset, though her eyes were red-rimmed as if she hadn't slept. Her face had a dreamy look. Fain had already been working on her.

"I have a brother," she said in a flat tone. "His name is Gavin."

Quinn's world shifted. *Gavin?*

"And Koro is real. He's a devil or a demon. I'm not really sure." Her forehead wrinkled with confusion.

"Koro?" Fain frowned.

"Yes. I don't really understand all of it. But he…he took my mother and some other women. He took them away." A long moment passed. Bobbi licked her lips and went on in a dead voice. "He let them go. They were pregnant. All of them. I am his daughter."

Holy fuck. Jane what have you done? His mother was involved in this horror. Quinn had no doubt. Always, she'd hidden something about Koro from the rest of them. Now he knew. For one terrifying second, he wondered if he was also a spawn of that demon. But no, Gavin was two years older. If Jane was involved, it had been before she met his father.

Dustin. The grave in Ashlet cemetery. He'd had a brother. Jane visited his grave once a year on the anniversary of his birth and death. Was Dustin also a child of Koro?

"Who told you this nonsense?" Fain laughed and pulled away from Bobbi. He fidgeted, shoved his hands in the pockets of his jeans, yanked them out and tugged at his shirt. The man wasn't comfortable in his own skin.

"Molly."

Molly McFadden? What did she have to do with all this? Quinn inched backward, ready to sneak away and get some answers from his mother.

"Would it be such a bad thing?" asked Fain. "Being the daughter of the Great One?"

Great One? Quinn stopped and turned back to the scene in the living room. Fain gripped Bobbi by both shoulders, forcing her to look up. He seemed to come to a resolution.

"What do you mean?" Bobbi's voice stuttered. The light caught her giant eyes.

"I mean that if I was the descendant of Koro, I could do great things. I could be great. Maybe you should think about that." He held her gaze and

Quinn felt aether pouring from him.

He had power but it was wild, untethered by practice or discipline, and soother magic wore off over time. He needed to keep Bobbi dosed, until his plans were complete, whatever those were.

Quinn remembered the night in Jane's garden when he'd inadvertently soothed Bobbi, and how violated she'd felt. With good reason. She would be horrified to know someone had such a hold over her emotions. And part of her did know. Somewhere, inside her mind, Bobbi was screaming to be let loose.

He would break Fain's hold on her and he would break Fain, but he wasn't sure Bobbi would ever be the same.

"Relax," Fain said. "You are the seed of the Great One. The blood of the seed will call the father and he will provide for you."

"Yes." Bobbi's mouth hung slack.

"He's been watching over you for a very long time. He's getting ready to meet you. That's why he sent me."

"When?"

"Tomorrow."

Samhain. Tomorrow was Samhain, the one night of the year when dimensions were more easily opened.

"Tomorrow." Bobbi's voice fell flat. Her face lost all vigor. Fain had her completely under his control. He kissed her forehead and patted her cheek as if she were a small child.

A moment later, Quinn heard a car pull out of the driveway. Fain had gone.

Bobbi puttered in the kitchen, her face barely visible in the window above the sink. She wandered around the house, a glass of wine forgotten in one hand, touching knickknacks as if trying to remember who put them there.

Quinn backed out of his hiding spot behind the barbecue, still gripping the red statue. He had to get back to the coven. It was long past the time for Jane to come clean about Koro. He took two steps toward the back fence and the patio screen squawked.

Bobbi stepped barefoot onto the deck. Quinn froze.

"You!" Her voice rose in surprise but her eyes were dead.

Quinn hadn't meant to face her tonight, not while his aether was so dangerously low. Not while Fain's hold on her was impenetrable. But now he had no choice. He would make one last attempt to reach her.

"Bobbi, listen to me. Fain is soothing you. Look, I can prove it." He held up the statue.

She whipped a hand forward. Her wine glass smashed the statue, shattering both in an explosion of glass, wine and terra cotta shards.

The sound shocked Bobbi to stillness. He waited, looking for a sign that Fain's spell broke with the statue.

Her face twisted with rage.

"He told me about you." She wielded the broken stem of glass like a knife. "He told me you would try to come between us. He told me to stop you no matter what." Blood dripped down her arm from a cut on her thumb.

Quinn held his palms out as if trying to placate a wild animal.

"Bobbi, please. You know I would never hurt you. Think about it." He inched forward. Her lips twisted in an ugly snarl. Tangled hair fell across her eyes, sunken in deep shadows.

Bobbi swiped the air in front of his nose. He grabbed her hand, twisting, trying to force her to let go of the glass blade.

She made a sound like a rabid snarl. Quinn spun her and pinned her arms. He hated this. He didn't want to be the aggressor, but she had to listen to him. He was glad his aether was dry because he wasn't sure he could resist soothing her to open her mind. And that was the last thing Bobbi needed right now.

No, he'd have to use plain old persuasion to get through to her.

"You know me, Bobbi. Remember us. Remember the time we spent together. That hasn't ended. You've only forgotten." She squirmed against him and his senses filled with the scent of her hair and the feel of her body against his.

Then she tensed. A keening noise came from her throat. The wind picked up and screamed through the yard. The patio table jerked upward and slammed into his side. He grunted as pain lanced his leg, but he held on to her. The barbecue crashed into the wall. The sliding door smashed closed, then open again. Chairs spun around them.

Bobbi shrieked as kinetic aether burst from her in a chaotic frenzy, then she went limp. The chairs dropped with a crash and the night calmed. Quinn released his hold and she crumpled to the ground, staring up with wide, unseeing eyes.

A lone tear dripped down her cheek. Her fingers relaxed and the wineglass stem broke on the patio stones.

Quinn lifted her into his arms and carried her inside to the couch. She lay like a rigid corpse, as if her muscles were fighting themselves. Fain's magic controlled her, but something inside rebelled. He took comfort in that. He could do little else.

By the time he'd cleaned and bandaged the cut on her thumb, her eyes had closed and her breathing calmed. He wanted to stay by her side, but that was not an option. She was too deep in the magic. If she woke and found him, she'd only attack again. He tucked a blanket around her and left.

He had questions for his mother.

DIRECTION

Ashlet cemetery lay in darkness. Quinn waited with Molly as Jane and Abilene parked in the near empty lot and joined them.

"What's she doing here?" Jane glared at Molly. Her feet crunched dried leaves as she swept past gravestones toward them.

The two women faced each other. Abilene hung back warily. Jane was impeccably dressed as always, her silver hair catching the moonlight. Of the four of them, only Molly had no magic, yet she looked the most like a hedge-witch with black hair streaked grey, sticking out in kinky waves, and layers of bright clothes and scarves despite the warm weather.

Quinn hadn't mentioned Molly's attendance to this late night meeting when he called his mother to join him. The two women had been friends in high school but a falling out shortly after left them bitter enemies.

Too bad. He needed answers from both tonight.

He'd spoken to Gavin and understood the basics of what happened all those years ago, how four young women fell victim to Koro, but he wanted to hear it from Jane and Molly. Then he would make his mother understand that the time for collecting proof was over.

"And why are we meeting in this gods-forsaken place?" Jane asked.

"The place you buried my brother?" Quinn said. "Let's hope the gods have not forsaken it."

Jane pursed her lips but didn't answer. She made one obligatory visit a year to Dustin's grave. Did she ever think about her lost child, the one who only lived for a few moments? Quinn knew about baby Dustin because his father, Henry, had thought it was important to acknowledge his brother's existence. Dustin wasn't even Henry's child.

A car door slammed. Moments later, Gavin joined them.

"We're meeting here because it's neutral ground." He glared at Jane and

Molly. "And because I've been tracking William Fain by GPS. In the past four days, he's come here twice, in the middle of the night." Unfortunately, Fain had been gone both times when he arrived, so Quinn didn't know the reason for those midnight visits with the dead. "If what I suspect is true, tomorrow night this will become our battleground."

They stood around a small grave-marker, a simple flat stone embedded in the ground. Grass encroached on the edges of the stone, nearly obscuring the name: Dustin Redner.

Abilene knelt by the grave, closed her eyes and recited a quick prayer for their brother. Jane turned away.

Jane Smith had been born Arabella Redner, then became Arabella Mason when she married. She gave up both names when she was anointed as High Priestess. Tradition granted her the right to choose her witch name. Most chose dignified or grandiose names that paid homage to the Lord and Lady. Arabella said she represented every witch and would take a generic name to suit: Jane Smith.

Quinn wondered who Arabella Redner had been.

"You won't even look at the gravestone of the child you murdered," Molly said.

"I didn't murder him." Jane didn't lose her equilibrium, though Molly looked like a spitting cat ready for a fight.

"Please," Quinn said, "I didn't bring you here to rehash old hurts. Bobbi needs us. She's completely under Fain's influence."

Jane made a noise to interrupt, but Quinn held up a hand. "Mother, you asked for proof. I'm getting to that. But first I want you to hear what happened this afternoon. Gavin?"

Gavin nodded. "I took Bobbi to see Mom. If I'd had all the facts, maybe I wouldn't have." Gavin glared at Jane, then Quinn in turn. "Mom freaked out when she saw Bobbi. She thought Hannah had come back from the dead. I guess they look alike." He took a deep breath and Quinn resisted the urge to shake the story out of him.

"Then Mom started babbling about 'him,' saying we should leave before 'he' got there."

"Koro," Abilene said.

"We don't know that," snapped Jane.

"Molly, what did you say to Bobbi about it? She was clearly upset tonight," Quinn said.

"I told her the truth, since none of you felt she needed to know it. I swear, all these years, I've kept your damned secrets but not anymore. Bobbi is a powerful witch, even I can see that." She turned on Jane like wildfire. "You promised if she ever came into her powers, you would tell her the truth."

"Molly, please." Quinn prayed for calm. "Just say it."

Molly crossed her arms. "I told her that she and Gavin are the offspring of Koro."

Abilene sucked in a breath and turned to Gavin. "What?"

Gavin shrugged. Moonlight filled his eyes with shadows.

"It's the truth," Molly said.

Quinn faced Jane. She nodded. "Dustin, too?" he asked. She nodded again.

"Is that why we're here?" Abilene said.

"Fain said something earlier." Quinn remembered the fanatical look in Fain's eye. "Something about the blood of the seed calling the father. Well, this ground is saturated with blood of the seed. And Fain is planning something big. I think it's going to happen here."

"Like a rite?" Gavin asked.

"Like a sacrifice." Quinn let that sink in. "He's been soothing Bobbi for days. She's as pliable as pudding now. I think he's going to bring her here for a blood sacrifice."

"To what end?" Molly asked.

"Samhain," Abilene whispered. "By the Lady! Tomorrow is Samhain."

Quinn nodded. On Samhain, the veil between worlds thinned. With the proper rites, witches could speak to dead loved ones. Some could even call the dead back to life. And demons could break through from whatever hell detained them—if they had the proper acolytes in this world to perform the sacrifice.

"He's going to call Koro to manifest on this plane," Quinn said. "He'll no longer have to work through human agents. Koro will stand in our world with all the power of hell at his fingertips."

And his first target would be the coven that had defied him for so long. Koro almost destroyed the Hidden Coven when Aidan, acting as his agent, brought in the wraiths. Now Koro would need no such help. His touch would burn through their ward like hot coals through paper. Then he'd drink every witch in the village dry. Quinn's friends and family would die or become wraiths in Koro's dark army as he sought out other covens in his relentless pursuit of aether.

"And that's why you killed your baby and mine." Molly wasn't letting it go. Quinn reigned in his impatience. Bobbi was most important, but they needed to work as a team. Better to have old grudges aired now.

"You knew. We all knew. He told us time and again. He would claw his way into this world through our wombs." Molly was shaking now.

"I didn't kill my child." Jane's expression was flat, but Quinn knew his mother well enough to see anger building around her eyes. Jane was hard to read, but she had tells—a slight lowering of lashes, a tightness in the nostrils. As a child, he'd learned to read those signs and make himself scarce.

"You miscarried. I had nothing to do with it," Jane said.

Molly looked like she wanted to punch her. She stood with eyes blazing fire, fists clenched and mouth working on a curse. Then she took a deep breath and walked off into the shadows of a stand of cedar trees. Quinn let her go.

"You have no proof Fain is working for Koro," Jane said.

"I heard him!" Quinn said. "He didn't even try to deny it. Bobbi is so far under his spell, he thinks he can do as he wishes. She'll come like the lamb to slaughter."

"So we'll be here ready to stop it," Gavin said.

"We'll have to break his hold on Bobbi first." Abilene made choking motions with her hands. "Or we could find ourselves fighting both of them."

"Agreed." Quinn had been thinking the same thing.

"What if we consecrate a circle around Dustin's grave?" Gavin asked. "Are we sure he's going to perform the rite here?"

"Not sure, but it's a good bet," Quinn said.

"He might sense the aether we lay down." Abilene was right. They had no idea of Fain's capabilities. But it was a chance they'd have to take. Molly wandered back to their circle, her expression composed but determined.

Jane crossed her arms. "Even if Fain is Koro's agent. We don't know what he's planning. The grimoire we used to call him was very vague on the subject."

"Where is this grimoire now?" Abilene asked. "Maybe it could give us some idea what kind of rite Fain is going to do."

"Lost," Molly said. "Hannah had it last, but it was never found after the fire."

"Doesn't matter," Quinn said. "I'm going to kill him before he lays a hand on Bobbi." One way or another, Fain would never complete his rite, never bring Koro into this world. Never hurt Bobbi. Except he already had. He'd enslaved her, broken her and turned her will into his own. Would she ever heal from that? He had to put those thoughts out of his mind, had to focus on freeing her, then together they could heal the rest.

"Do you think you'll be able to break Fain's soothing spell?" Quinn asked. Abilene bit her lip and nodded. "Then, you three go home and get supplies. We'll meet back here in the morning. We've got work to do."

"Where are you going?" Gavin asked.

"I'll stay in town tonight. Maybe get a room." Quinn didn't want to be isolated on Coven Island, in case Bobbi somehow managed to break Fain's hold. She might reach out to him and he wanted to be ready.

As they walked to their cars, Molly slipped a hand around his elbow.

"You'll be staying with Emmett and me tonight," she said. "No need to waste money on a room."

Quinn smiled and thanked her. With friends like Molly, Bobbi might have a chance.

Affliction

The dirt road twisted like an evangelist's sales pitch. No city lights penetrated this deep into rural country. The moon had long since set. Molly drove with a lead foot. Her taillights winked at the far limit of Quinn's headlights. If he slowed to round a bend, he'd lose her. Finally, they turned onto an even more dubious lane, drove through a tunnel of overhanging trees and stopped in front of an old farmhouse.

Quinn got out and shut the car door, an unnaturally loud sound in the dark. He'd never been to Emmett's farm at night. It seemed even more isolated than it did in daylight. The house was hidden from the road by ungroomed forest on either side of the drive. This gave way to pastures and barns behind the house.

"Emmett's probably asleep," Molly said. "Let's try and keep it that way. I haven't told him about Bobbi." She paused. "Emmett can be irrationally overprotective when it comes to his children."

Quinn nodded, though he didn't think Emmett's concern would be irrational in this case. His daughter was about to be sacrificed to a godsdamned demon. But they didn't need another civilian involved.

Inside, Molly turned on the light above the stove, leaving most of the kitchen in shadow. She put on a kettle without asking if he wanted tea. Neither of them would be able to sleep right away. Quinn wasn't sure if he'd sleep at all.

He checked his phone for the tell-tale blip of Fain's tracker. It was moving fast on Interstate 76, a hundred and fifty miles away from Ashlet. He slammed the phone down on the table.

"Something wrong?" Molly asked.

"It's Fain. He's halfway to Pittsburgh."

"So?"

"So, either he's leaving town the night before his big reveal or he found the tracking device and put it on another car."

"Well, we might not know where he is now, but we know where he'll be tomorrow night."

Quinn nodded. It would have to be good enough. Still, he didn't like running blind.

"I have to confess, I had an ulterior motive for inviting you here tonight," Molly said. Quinn quirked an eyebrow and grinned.

"Now don't you flirt with an old lady. I'm already living in sin. I don't need more excitement."

Molly and Emmett had been living together for over a year. Quinn didn't know either of them well, but from what Bobbi told him, Emmett had been devastated when Ellen died. She was happy when he let Molly into his life.

"There are things you need to know, things your mother won't tell you."

"You mean there's worse news than Bobbi is the daughter of the demon who's trying to wipe out my coven?" He sounded like a smart-ass, and Molly frowned.

"I've kept silent for too long. And I'm ashamed to say Jane bullied me into that silence."

Quinn understood. Jane bullied everyone.

"Is this about your baby?"

Molly sighed and seemed to deflate. The kettle whistled. She rose and filled the teapot, then fussed with milk, sugar and mugs—a delay tactic. Finally, she sat, poured the tea and looked him straight in the eye.

"This is about Bobbi."

"What about her?"

"Do you know how her parents died?"

"In a house fire." Bobbi had told him, but not the details. "She was very young."

"Six. Her sister was only three. But they were already dead when the fire started. It was a cover up."

"For murder?"

"For kidnapping. A man named Edward Wallis took Bobbi. He was Koro's agent at that time. But Hannah and Ben Cole were waiting for him. They died trying to stop him from taking their daughter."

"They knew what he was? What Bobbi is?"

Molly nodded. "Ben was Paragon."

Quinn nearly dropped his mug. Paragon was the group of scholars and warriors who patrolled the underworld of the supernaturals, keeping regular humans safe from forces they wouldn't even believe. Paragon was legendary. They were the superheroes every witch child aspired to be. They took only elite witches whose powers were off the scales. And aether wasn't their only measuring stick. A paragon warrior went through boot camp that would put the Navy Seals to shame. Their scholars had access to archives going back thousands of years.

Paragon had set a dedicated agent to protect Bobbi, an act that spoke volumes about their concern for Koro. He posed a serious threat to all mankind, both witches and mundanes. Or maybe they thought Bobbi would one day be the threat. Did Paragon have agents watching Gavin too? Jane had close ties to the group. That's probably why she adopted Gavin. What would she have done if Gavin had embraced his demon heritage? Would Jane have turned in the boy she considered a son? Quinn didn't want to look too closely at that question.

"Ben was tasked with protecting Hannah and her child," Molly said. "They fell in love and married. Paragon thought it was a good resolution for a long-term problem. Koro would never stop hunting his children."

"Why?" Quinn felt warm. He loosened his collar.

"I'm not sure. I remember something in the grimoire, the one we used to call him that first time. His children—or the blood of his children—can help him to manifest on earth. The exact wording was vague."

But the grimoire was lost to them now. No help there. He rubbed his face. Gods, he was tired.

Molly had confirmed his suspicions. Koro needed his child in order to manifest. But why Bobbi and not Gavin? Because Bobbi was an easier target, living alone without the protection of a coven?

Koro couldn't directly affect their world as long as he was trapped in his. He could only use naive witches to do his bidding. That was how he'd trapped Molly and her friends. William Fain was another of his victims, though Quinn had a hard time feeling sorry for him. Koro might work through him, but Fain enjoyed the work. Quinn had seen the lust in his eyes. Koro had probably promised him power and riches for his service.

Fool. If Koro manifested, there would be no haven for any witch. Koro drank aether. The wraiths that had attacked the coven this past summer were the remnants of witches he'd drained. All he needed was one foolish enough to call him and the demon could kill an entire coven. And each death made him stronger. It might already be too late to stop him.

Gods, it's hot in here. His hand trembled as he raised his mug.

"Does Bobbi know?"

Molly shook her head. "Wallis ran. He had Bobbi for three weeks before Paragon agents found them. She doesn't remember any of it. We don't know where they went or what he did to her."

"We?" Molly spoke as if she was intimate with Paragon's inner circle.

Molly's mouth moved in answer, but a roar like a train rushing through his head drowned her words. His vision blurred, darkened at the edges. Pain shot through his limbs into his chest, a red hot poker right to the heart.

No! Not now. Not here.

He was having an attack. He'd felt the signs all night, but hoped…

Aether flushed from him in a massive surge. The lights flickered. He swayed in the chair.

Molly reached for him, her face concerned.

He clutched the petrified cockroach, but the amulet was dry. He'd expended too much aether this week with no time to replenish it.

Molly shook him. He wanted to tell her he'd be fine, but his arms trembled, fingers tingled and pain lanced his spine in waves.

The floor crashed into him and the world went silent.

CPRESCRIPTION

olly fell to her knees and shouted for Emmett. Quinn spasmed, legs
and arms locked straight and rigid. His eyelids fluttered, showing only
whites underneath. Should she hold him down? Would that hurt him
more? His complexion went from white, to purple, then to a sickly grey-green.
Sweat popped up in beads on his forehead.

"What the hell happened?" Emmett rushed into the kitchen in his
pajamas, hair spiked on one side.

"I don't know. He's having a seizure."

Quinn's flailing leg kicked the table. A mug smashed on the floor, spilling tea.

Emmett laid his hands on Quinn's chest and closed his eyes. Molly couldn't
sense magic, but she knew Emmett was pouring his aether into Quinn in an
effort to heal. The flailing slowed. Quinn's head thumped against the floor,
then he lay still.

"That's no ordinary seizure," Emmett said. He left the room and returned
with his kit. Emmett was a med-mage, though he rarely practiced anymore.
In the year-and-a-half she'd been living at the farm, Molly had never seen him
take this kit from the shelf in his closet.

He opened the black leather bag and took out a small glass cup rimmed
in gold. He filled it with a clear liquid from a bottle, then opened a leather
case and chose a blade from the array of gleaming scalpels. He hadn't used this
equipment in years, but it was spotless.

He nicked Quinn's finger and let blood drip into the cup.

The blood swirled, turning the water faint pink.

"He's dry." Emmett stirred the mixture with a glass stick.

"What do you mean?"

"His aether. He's running on empty."

"But he hasn't done any magic. I've been with him most of the evening.

He just fell over." Molly chewed on that for a moment. He'd been fine, then his color drained and he hit the floor.

"Is it a curse?" she asked. Maybe William Fain was on to them and he was already wiping out the competition.

"Not a curse." Quinn's voice rasped like chalk on sandpaper. He tried to sit up, but Emmett held him down.

"Take it easy," he said. Quinn lay back on the linoleum and closed his eyes. Emmett prepared a syringe, talking as he worked.

"It started off as a curse though didn't it?"

Quinn nodded and grimaced as Emmett stuck him with the needle. "But the curse was only the carrier for the disease. You've been infected with mawr."

By the gods. Molly sat back on the floor. She might only be a mundane, but she'd lived with witches for long enough to know that mawr was deadly. A mystical illness, mawr was likened to leukemia for supernaturals. An entity of unknown origin lived in the host, feeding off aether. Fifty years ago, it was considered a myth. There wasn't enough magic in the world to sustain a mawr infection indefinitely. But the world had changed, was still changing. Magic bled from the ley-lines, boosting the powers of witches and other supernaturals and carving a new habitat for mystical viruses.

Mawr was painful, frightening, and incurable.

Quinn opened his eyes and pinned Emmett then Molly. "Don't tell Jane."

Molly shook her head. "How can you keep it secret?" The symptoms of mawr ranged from seizures to hallucinations. And pain. Horrible pain.

"Amulet." Quinn touched the strange bug on his necklace "A friend..." He cleared his throat and tried again. "A friend gave it to me. A voodoo master. It's a receptacle for storing aether. I use it to give myself a boost when I feel an attack coming on."

"Didn't help much this time," Emmett said.

"It's empty. This is my second attack this week. With everything going on..." His voice trailed off. Molly tensed. He almost spilled the beans about Bobbi. Thankfully, Emmett was too busy fussing with the bottles in his case. After a moment he selected one and put it on the table. He helped Quinn back into his chair. Molly poured more tea and he topped off the cup with the tincture.

"Drink."

"You're Paragon too." Quinn sipped the brew and made a face.

"Drink it all," Emmett ordered, then his tone softened. "I was Paragon. Med-mage of the First Order. I'm retired now."

"You're the one who saved Bobbi after the fire all those years ago."

Emmett gave Molly a sharp look. He didn't tell other people his secrets without good cause. Molly nodded. Quinn needed to know.

"And I've been watching over her ever since," Emmett said. "Just like your mother watches over Gavin."

"I always knew she had some other reason for taking him in." He leaned back in the chair. His color was returning, but he looked like he'd been ravaged by weeks of illness.

"Don't be too quick to judge her," Molly said. "The gods know, I'm not Jane's biggest fan, but she can be as harsh on herself as she is to others."

Quinn didn't look convinced. What must it have been like to grow up under Jane's stern gaze? Molly hoped he'd get the chance to know the affection he deserved. That might never happen if they didn't stop Koro.

At least Molly could make him understand his mother better. She'd told Gavin the truth. Time for Quinn to hear it too. She looked at Emmett, the old dear. The story wouldn't surprise him. They had no secrets, but he didn't like talking about Koro. He was a lot like Quinn, and he'd never forgiven himself for letting Ben Cole's killer get away.

Men. Sometimes she thought they carried around their guilt like trophies.

"Koro hurt Jane the worst…" she started. A loud thump came from above. Quinn held up his hand. All eyes looked up. Above them the hallway lead to the bedrooms and above that only attic.

They waited in the heavy silence, straining to hear. Quinn put a finger to his lips and stood, careful not to let his chair scrape against the floor. Another dense silence.

"Could be a broken branch hitting the roof," Emmett said. They all looked to the window and the wind-blown trees outside.

Every light bulb in the kitchen exploded.

DISRUPTION

The kitchen fell into darkness. Quinn's ears rang with that peculiar tingling silence after a dramatic explosion.

"Not a branch," he said. He'd done enough security details to know the thud came from inside the house. Someone dropped a heavy tool, flashlight or screwdriver, then panicked. Someone with kinetic or electrical magic strong enough to blow every bulb in the place.

Someone who was still inside the house.

Quinn stepped around the table, feet crunching on broken glass. "Stay here," he said quietly. Molly followed him as far as the doorway, pulled a knife from the butcher's block and handed it to him. Quinn mouthed a thanks and slipped into the dining room. Beyond, the front foyer lurked in shadow. A bit of stray light gleamed off the stair railing. He could chance the stairs, but if someone waited at the top, they'd have a clear advantage.

Emmett's tincture boosted his aether enough to get him standing, but he didn't like his chances if it came to hand-to-hand combat. He listened to the dead silence from above, deciding if he should make a move.

A black figure leaped down the stairs and tore open the front door.

Quinn flung the knife, but the intruder was already gone and the blade ricocheted off the open door. Kitchen knives were lousy for throwing.

Outside, the strange hot wind screamed through the trees. Quinn's gaze scanned left and right, catching flying leaves and tossing branches, but nothing else. He stepped off the porch. The wind died. Nothing moved.

The tunnel of trees loomed in the driveway, enticing like a road to hell. Somewhere in those shadows, the intruder hid, assessing his pursuer.

Quinn had no weapons—no gun or knife. And his aether was dry. No magic to launch an attack either. He couldn't even soothe the guy, maybe drench him in fear until he collapsed in a quivering heap. It had worked for him before, but mawr left him vulnerable. Of course, the intruder didn't know that.

Stepping onto the drive, Quinn winced as his shoe scraped gravel. He was an open target now. He crouched and waited. The world spun. He had enough for one burst of energy before his body gave out on him. He'd have to use it wisely.

He listened. Leaves whispered as they settled. The skin on the back of his neck prickled. From his right, something rustled. A branch cracked.

A figure shot from the bushes and sprinted down the drive. Quinn gave chase.

His limbs were rubber. He had nothing to give to this pursuit. The figure ahead, dressed all in black, weaved between the trees lining the drive, gaining ground even with this twisted path. Quinn stumbled down the long drive, hoping now for at least a glimpse of the intruder, though he had little doubt to his identity.

A rock hit him in the forehead. Blood dripped into his eye as branches were flung across his path and more debris pelted him. With his magic, the intruder lobbed anything he could find, trying to slow the chase.

Quinn ducked into the bushes. A thick dead branch flew up from the ground and jabbed him in the stomach. He stumbled. Rocks bombarded his chest, knocking him backwards. He tripped and fell flat. Branches pinned his arms and legs. He struggled, pulling against these unnatural bonds. The branches held him down with a force stronger than gravity. A rock landed on his stomach, pushing all the breath from his lungs.

"Who's the bully now?" Fain leaned over him, his expression smug.

Quinn's chest ached for air. He sucked in a painful breath.

"What are you planning to do to Bobbi?" The words grated in his throat. Fain laughed.

"You don't get it. This isn't the kind of story where the villain wastes his time telling the hero all his plans." With a flick of his hand, he raised another stone. "I'd rather kill you and get on with it."

"You're wrong. You've already given away everything." Quinn could feel another attack of mawr coming on with the tell-tale tingling in his fingers.

"What do you mean?" Fain squinted at him. A fist-sized rock hovered above Quinn's head.

Quinn gritted his teeth, hoping it looked like a grin.

"This isn't the kind of story where the hero tells his secrets."

Fain's lips twisted in a sneer, then the tree beside his head exploded with a crack of gunfire.

"Get off my property!" Emmett yelled from the shadows. More gunfire. Quinn twisted as the rock fell. The branches loosened and he turned enough so the rock hit his shoulder. He rolled, clearing the debris, and came up in time to see the distinctive round lights of a vintage Charger through the trees. The car revved and spit gravel as Fain fled.

Molly and Emmett met him halfway back to the house. She rushed to grab Quinn's arm as he limped up the drive. Blood dripped from his forehead.

"Is someone going to tell me what the hell is going on?" Emmett growled. He'd run outside barefoot, still in his pajamas, but the old med-mage couldn't look ridiculous, not with the fierce glare in his eye.

"That was Bobbi's new boyfriend," Quinn said. "He didn't want to stick around for tea."

Ten minutes later, with the glass swept up, they sat around the kitchen table. Emmett cleaned the wound on Quinn's forehead and taped it with butterfly strips. The bruises on his shoulder and stomach dulled to angry aches.

They'd brought Emmett up to speed. He wasn't happy they'd kept it from him. Quinn suspected Molly would have some appeasing to do later.

"So after all these years, Koro is finally making his move," Emmett said. "I'd begun to hope he'd given up."

"Time is meaningless for Koro," Molly said. "Twenty years or a thousand. It's all the same to him. He'll never give up."

Emmett grunted. "I guess we'd better set up some wards. With all the comings and goings for Ellen's animal rescue, I let them expire years ago. It was easier than keying so many strangers to the ward. And Bobbi doesn't even live here anymore. Seemed pointless."

Emmett was beating himself up with self-recriminations. Quinn could relate.

"I doubt Fain will be back tonight," he said. "And I've got nothing to give to a ward. Let's just clean up this mess."

After checking the house, they'd found the door to the attic stairs open. Fain had been trying to get up there. They also determined that Fain had not blasted the entire electrical circuit in the house. He had telekinetic magic. And damned precise magic at that. Up until now, Quinn had thought Fain some bumbling incompetent. He soothed with the finesse of a sledgehammer. But what if soother magic wasn't his primary talent, the way Quinn could read an aether signature, but not on the level of Abilene's sensate abilities?

That knowledge could help them in the fight to come. Quinn hoped it would be enough. Fain obviously knew they were onto him, had probably followed them from the cemetery.

Molly poured tea but before Quinn could take his, Emmett dropped a dollop of thick black liquid into it.

"What's that? Molasses?" Quinn sniffed it and made a face.

"A molasses base, but it's chock full of aether boosting herbs," Emmett said. "Drink it."

Quinn obliged him. The drink was hot and spicy and prickled on the way down.

"Do you think he'll switch locations for the rite tomorrow?" Molly asked.

"No, he's too arrogant," Quinn said. "But he'll know we're coming now. We can't take anything for granted."

Emmett packed up his med kit. "I agree. Koro brought Molly and her friends to him for a reason. To make children. To have his blood born into our world. Dustin's blood has been feeding that cemetery for years. It's Koro's hallowed ground. If only we had Hannah's grimoire, we might know what he's planning."

Molly frowned. "I wish I'd read it more carefully. I thought the grimoire was a joke back then."

Emmett patted her hand. "It's no one's fault. You couldn't have known."

"The grimoire." Quinn's thoughts were sluggish. He was tired beyond exhaustion, but an idea nagged at him. "Was it really lost in the fire?"

"Who knows," Emmett said. "It wasn't among Hannah's things, but much of the house was a charred ruin."

"So it's possible the grimoire still exists," Quinn said. "Or at least that Fain believes it exists. Maybe that's what he was snooping for." He felt a kernel of hope. "Maybe something in the grimoire is important enough for Fain to risk sneaking into an occupied house."

Emmett smiled. "Something like a way to defeat Koro."

Quinn returned the grin, but his eyes were hard. Yes, Fain's little blunder had definitely been enlightening.

ⲔPREPARATION

Cemeteries made Gavin uncomfortable. Not for the usual reasons. He had no problem with the dead. He'd seen necromancy in action, even tried a few dark spells during his reckless youth. The dead usually stayed dead. They mostly poked at the veil separating their world from the living. And ghosts rarely had anything important to say.

It was grief that bothered him, such a raw emotion. Funerals were the worst. Mourners wept, spilling aether along with tears, saturating the ground with sadness and anger. Walking through the cemetery, he could feel it in every blade of grass and every swaying branch.

Gavin knelt by a grave and touched the brown grass growing over the stone marker. Dead blades turned vivid green, then writhed and curled backward, revealing the name: Dustin Redner.

He should feel something. Jane's baby lay cold and decayed beneath his feet. His brother. Was that why she'd taken him in? He'd never questioned her motives. She was Stacy's friend. That's what you did for friends in need. But was Gavin meant to replace the son she'd lost?

His sister was buried in a grave like this too. He didn't know where. He'd never asked. Maybe when this was over he'd find out.

Samhain fell on another warm Sunday. Gavin watched churchgoers stroll the grounds. A few knelt in honest bereavement. Did they know that on this day, their lost loved ones might actually hear their prayers?

He strolled to the columbarium at the top of the hill, where Quinn waited with Abilene. She carried a backpack of supplies. Gavin had a similar bag for him and Jane. Once the sun went down, Abilene would begin the spell to break Fain's hold on Bobbi. Jane and Gavin would consecrate the ground around Dustin's grave, creating a circle of the Lord and Lady's protection to counteract any dark magic Fain might conjure.

"We've got an audience," he said.

Quinn glanced at the mourners then at the sky. The sun already tipped to the west.

"Not for long," Quinn said. "We'll start the setup in the columbarium. Hopefully, no one will bother us there."

The columbarium was a reliquary for cremated remains, a stone building no bigger than ten by ten, walls lined in locked compartments filled with urns. With only one door and no windows, it would shield the candle light as Abilene tried to break Fain's hold on Bobbi.

"Do you think it'll work?" asked Gavin.

Abilene dumped her pack and shrugged. "I'm going to try. I only hope he's not a sensate as well as a soother. This place is too close."

The building loomed over the cemetery, a stone sentinel on the highest ground. Strategically, it gave them a good view of the target grave. But Fain would also be able to see them. Worse, if he had any sort of sensate magic, he'd be able to feel Abilene's spell brewing long before it took effect.

"I don't like it either," Quinn said, "but it's all we've got."

Abilene shrugged and went inside to begin her preparations.

Quinn huffed out a breath and leaned against the marble wall. He looked like crap, eyes sunken and ringed in shadows, skin an unhealthy grey. Tape covered a cut on his forehead, and his chin and right cheek flaunted more bruises.

"Did Molly put too much Irish Cream in your tea last night?" Gavin asked. "You look like you've been in a bar brawl."

"Had a little visit from Fain. Seems he has some kinetic magic too."

"And you couldn't fend him off?" That was unusual. Quinn was one of the strongest witches he knew and a decent fighter. He studied the wan face beneath the bruises.

"You had another attack, didn't you?"

"I'm fine."

He wasn't. Gavin had been with Quinn in Port-au-Prince when the voodoo priest cursed him. He'd nursed him through his first attacks of mawr. Then they scoured the city looking for the priest and found him dead in an alley, a bullet through his brain and rats already eating his soft parts. They never discovered who paid the priest to curse him.

"You should tell Jane. She's going to know," Gavin said.

"She'll be focused on Fain. It'll be fine."

"Maybe for tonight. But she will find out eventually and when she does, she'll be pissed that you hid it from her."

Quinn gave him a look. "Do you think I care? Right now, when Bobbi is locked in some soother spell, about to be sacrificed to a demon, do you think I care about hurting Jane's feelings?"

Gavin shrugged. There was no reasoning with him. Not now, not yesterday and not tomorrow.

They watched in silence as the sun retreated into the trees. The mourners left them alone with the dead. At sunset, a strong, hot wind blew in, sending dead leaves billowing up the gravel paths.

Jane arrived and Gavin hurried to help her lug a large box. He hefted it onto his shoulder with a groan.

"What are you carrying? Rocks?"

"Black salt," Jane said grimly. "It was ridiculously expensive and I drove half way to Philadelphia to get it."

They decided on the layout of the circle, about a twenty foot diameter, and hoped Fain would set up his rite inside it. Then, when he least expected it, they'd spring their trap.

"Spread the salt sparingly. It's all I could get," Jane said.

As Gavin sprinkled it around the perimeter, Jane's black salt made sense. It sank into the grass unseen. White salt would have shone in the waning moon and given away the trap.

Even so, they didn't know Fain's full capabilities. If he had sensate magic, he'd feel the aura of the circle. Gavin's flora magic didn't have many practical applications, but masking a sacred circle was one of them. He finished spreading the salt, then walked the perimeter, pulling at the aether of the grass beneath his feet. He didn't make the grass grow, but expanded its magic like a shadow to cover the power of the circle. It wasn't foolproof, but it would have to do.

Jane set four candles at the cardinal points. She lit each one, calling the spirits of the four winds. At each point, she dipped her athame through the flame, then stabbed the blade in the ground, driving her aether deep into the earth to anchor the circle's protection.

Gavin watched her work. She was focused, her mind turned inward. To anyone else, she would have seemed cold, as if she didn't care that the grave beneath their feet held the bones of her child. Or that they were trying to stop the demon who'd tortured her.

Molly believed Jane had killed Dustin to stop Koro. Gavin knew better. He saw past her unforgiving exterior to the kind heart beneath, the one who'd given a home to a neglected boy.

"I know you didn't kill him," Gavin said. Jane looked up and he pointed to the small grave marker. "Dustin."

"Thank you."

"After all, if you believed that his death would stop Koro, you'd have killed me too, right?" He'd been only three years old when Jane took him in, a helpless toddler. "And Bobbi."

Jane put down the candles.

"It has nothing to do with what I believe. I didn't kill Dustin. Molly blames me for her miscarriage. She thinks I poisoned her. But she's had three more miscarriages since. In her heart, she knows the truth, but it's easier to blame me than accept the fact that she is incapable of bearing a child."

Gavin searched her face. Her eyes were hard. They were always hard. But could he blame her for that? The things she'd endured in her life—rape and torture, death of her son and husband, the loss of her three best friends, one from death, one from madness and the other from imagined betrayal. It was a wonder Jane could feel any emotions. And he knew she did.

Not the most demonstrative mother, Jane had shown her love in other ways. She'd taken him in, the dirty, battered kid of an addict. He hadn't even been potty trained. Nor could he speak. She spent hours every day, teaching him, coaxing him out of his shell. She spent money on doctors and therapists. She gave him the confidence to overcome his abnormal beginnings.

And now he knew the truth. He was the son of a demon who'd raped and tortured her, and his blood could help that demon manifest in their world. And yet, she had given him the most difficult gift of all: his life.

If she was hard as granite, it was because she needed to be—for all of them.

"If he succeeds," Gavin said, "if Fain manages to bring Koro through the veil, can we stop him?"

Jane frowned. "I don't know. Let's hope it doesn't come to that."

Gavin turned away, but Jane caught his arm. That was odd enough to make his heart pound. Everyone knew he disliked being touched, and Jane respected his quirk.

"If things go badly, we may have to end this anyway we can." Her blue eyes willed him to understand, and he did. If they couldn't stop Fain, if they couldn't break his hold on Bobbi, they would have to kill her. Keeping Koro out of their world was too important.

"I need to know you'll back me," Jane said.

Gavin nodded once, then squeezed her shoulders to show he meant it.

Anticipation

Quinn watched Gavin hug Jane. The rare moment of affection was over quickly and they went back to work consecrating the ground.

He should be jealous of Gavin's relationship with her, but he wasn't. Jane was a hard woman to love. Gavin saw through her cold facade, but Quinn had long ago given up that struggle. He wasn't sure anything under the facade was worth it.

He wasn't the problem. He wasn't unloved or unable to love. Abilene had held his heart in her hands since the day she was born. And he'd loved his father with the pride and admiration only a son can have.

And now he'd found Bobbi. He hadn't wanted to love her. She was brash and uncouth. She blundered into things she didn't understand. She was stubborn. And she didn't let him get away with any crap.

In the last month, they'd spent time together in magic training and a few afternoons in pure fun. She didn't let him sit at home endlessly reviewing training manifests. She made him go out into the world and discover new places. They'd gone to an apple festival, of all things. They'd eaten fritters and drank hot cider while listening to Celtic drummers. And he'd loved it.

She brought him to Emmett's farm and showed him how to brush the horses. Quinn had never been on a horse in his life until she bullied him into the saddle on an old nag. His backside ached for days after, but the sight of Bobbi on horseback with the wind pulling her hair had been payment enough for the discomfort.

Those dates were only a few weeks ago but they seemed a lifetime away. And Bobbi was a world away. She had one foot in Koro's dimension, and the demon would use that foothold to manifest here. But what if Koro's intention was to yank Bobbi into his world just as he had with her mother? Neither scenario was acceptable. He had to stop Fain before he began whatever dark rite he had planned.

Hours later, Quinn still waited in front of the columbarium, keeping an eye on the road.

Where were they? It was nearly midnight. If Fain was going to show, it would be soon. Had he chosen a different site after all? Had their run-in last night spooked him? Ashlet had only one other cemetery, and it didn't hold the bones of Koro's offspring. No, they had to be coming here. But where were they?

He paced.

Wind howled. The spirits were restless on Samhain. Quinn could feel their presence, like the weight of a brewing storm. Once or twice, he saw wispy forms flitting between the headstones.

Molly and Emmett hid among the trees, their first line of defense. If Fain brought backup, they were ready to take them out.

Inside the small building, Jane and Gavin tried to stay out of Abilene's way as she fussed with the preparations for her spell. She'd melted a taper to the bottom of a silver bowl. Silver conducted aether better than other metals. Water filled the bowl until only the tip of the unlit candle showed above it. When the candle burned down to the water, the spell would take effect. Fain's hold on Bobbi would be broken.

Abilene poked her head out the door for the fourth time. "I think I should start now."

"It's too soon. We have to be sure he's coming," Quinn said.

"But I need time to prepare. If we wait until they get here, it might be too late."

"Fine." She needed to be doing something. He got that. The waiting was killing him too.

Jane came out to stand with Quinn. She wore her white ceremonial robe and carried her staff. She meant business.

"You glow like a beacon in that robe," he said.

"I'll stay hidden until I'm needed."

He hoped it wouldn't come to that. Jane was the strongest witch he knew. If she needed to intervene, it would be because all other tactics failed.

"Thank you for being here, for helping." Quinn said. "I know this must be hard for you."

He watched her inscrutable face, looking for any hint of softening.

"I'll do what must be done. I always do," Jane said and returned inside.

Quinn paced to the edge of the building and back. Emmett finished his tour of the cemetery and trudged up the hill from the back end. He leaned against the marble wall and shoved his hands deep into the pockets of his jacket.

"Damn, but I would love a cigarette, right now."

"Sorry, I don't have any," Quinn said.

Emmett shrugged. "Gave 'em up fifteen years ago. Ellen thought I'd die before her. Funny how things go." Ellen had died many years ago, too long for Quinn to offer condolences. They watched an eddy of leaves in silence.

"You should prepare yourself," Quinn finally said. "For when you see Bobbi."

"What? You think I can't handle a little magic? I've been fighting sorcerers since before you were born."

"I know you can handle yourself."

Quinn could sense his aether. It was tough as old boot leather.

"But Fain has really done a number on her. She's changed. Your first instinct will be to run over and pull her away from him. You can't."

"I know. Molly already warned me. You've got to break his hold on her first." He nodded towards Abilene's altar. "I get it. I won't go all cowboy."

"By the time this night is over, we might need a cowboy."

The wind blew hot and stale, more like the air through a bus terminal than a fall evening in the country. It howled through the trees. Dead leaves rose up and swirled like specters before dropping to the ground again.

Then the real specters came out. He'd seen them in his peripheral vision since sundown, single spirits seemingly lost or hovering above random headstones. Now they marshaled as a unit, over a dozen of them, shimmering bodies lined up at the base of the hill. They didn't approach further, but they didn't recede either.

"Well, that's not good," Emmett said.

"What does it mean?" Quinn asked.

"I don't know, but we'll have to go through them to get to Fain, if he ever shows."

"Can they hurt us?"

"Depends on who's pulling their strings. A ghost can't do much damage, unless Koro has gifted them some kind of power. Regular bullets won't do much good, but I've got a few surprises left." Emmett patted the rifle slung over his shoulder.

Quinn watched the ghosts milling around the base of the hill like a pool of glowing spirit. They waited. They were all waiting. Abilene with her spell-breaker that might or might not work. Jane with her staff at the ready, Gavin, Molly and Emmett. His little army seemed pathetic in the light of what they faced. Before this night was through, they might have to battle a demon. He'd never heard of anyone winning that fight.

Wind slammed against the marble wall. Clouds flitted across the sickle moon. Headlights broke the darkness as a car wound up the road to the cemetery.

Quinn pushed away from the wall. "Show time."

ɪMPREGNATION

The night went deathly still. Gavin watched Abilene's candle burn. She sat like a statue inside the circle she'd drawn on the marble floor. Eyes closed, legs crossed, he knew she was reaching for Fain's aether that held Bobbi captive. Abilene was the best sensate they had, but it was tricky, delicate work. Life was magic and so were spirits. She had to pick through all the aether swirling around the cemetery on this holy night to find the right one.

Gavin and Jane stood silently in the dark, cramped space. Abilene mouthed an urgent chant.

Quinn's whisper reached them from the door. "It's time."

Sweat broke out on Abilene's forehead as she focused all her energy on the flickering candle.

Quinn's heart screamed for action as Bobbi walked up the path with mechanical steps, her head bowed, hair loosely covering her face. She stumbled. Fain didn't steady her. He prodded her on like a cow to slaughter.

His flashlight beam cut the night.

Good. He wouldn't see much outside its range. Every good security guard knew flashlights killed your night eyes. The beam flicked back and forth as Fain read the names of the grave markers.

He stopped at Dustin's grave. Bobbi stopped too, head drooping, arms hanging like dead vines.

Emmett slipped back into the shadows to take up his position, but it looked like Fain had come without backup.

He's as arrogant as I thought. Quinn hoped that arrogance didn't mean he had other tricks up his sleeve. He slipped a knife from the sheath at his belt.

His aether was low, and he'd need every weapon in his arsenal.

Fain crouched, brushed a hand across the grave and looked up. Quinn was confident he couldn't be seen against the dark marble wall, but would he see the ghosts? Not every witch had an affinity for the dead. To Quinn's eye, the wall of spirits shifted and flowed restlessly. Fain might not see them at all, but Quinn was done underestimating this witch. Ghosts were solitary creatures. They didn't gather unless someone controlled them.

Fain stood and brushed his light across the ground, his pudgy face folding into a frown. The flashlight beam moved in an arc, then he bent to inspect the grass.

Shit. He could feel the circle. Their trap was discovered. Fain yanked Bobbi backward. She stumbled again and fell. This time he let her lie where she'd fallen, right on the edge of the sacred circle that Jane and Gavin had consecrated.

So Fain could sense the magic, but not its exact dimensions. They might have a chance to pull this off.

Quinn's fingers tightened on the blade in his hand. They itched to slit the bastard's throat.

The ghosts attacked.

"Any time now, little sister," Gavin said.

"I'm trying." Abilene gritted her teeth. "Got it."

Even Gavin's weak sensate ability felt the tug of power as she drew Fain's aether toward the candle. To break the spell, she needed to plunge the aether into the sanctified water, where it would be trapped. And when the candle burned down, the spell would shatter.

Abilene swayed. Gavin dared not steady her. If he broke the circle of salt she sat in, all her efforts would be ruined.

Another fraction of an inch to burn.

"Incoming!" Quinn shouted.

A blue light whisked through the door and right through the back wall, followed by a gust of wind. The candle flame fluttered erratically. Hot wax hissed as it hit water.

No! The flame must burn out in the water. If the wind put it out, they were done.

The flame steadied. Abilene gulped air.

"What the hell was that?" Jane snapped.

Gavin stood in front of the candle, trying to block the wind with his body. He peered into the night. A wall of shimmering ghosts stalked up the hill toward them.

"The spirits. They're attacking."

"Block them!" Jane said. Aether gathered in the tip of her staff.

Another ghost blew in and flew around the small room, funneling the wind. The candle sputtered. Jane's staff blazed and the spirit hit Gavin.

It hit him!

They couldn't fight insubstantial spirits, so Jane had made them corporeal. Gavin shot out a hand and grabbed the ghost by the throat. In life, it had been a young man with long hair and a sharply cut face. He stared at Gavin in surprise, translucent blue hands grasping at the fingers on his throat. Gavin unsheathed his knife, doubly blessed this morning by the Lord and the Lady, and plunged it into the ghost. Surprise jolted the spirit's face and he dissipated into wisps of aether that slipped through Gavin's fingers.

Outside the remaining spirits howled and charged. Gavin loosed his magic. It dug into the ground and pulled at roots from far away, calling them to do his bidding. Branches shot up in front of the columbarium, blocking the door.

The ghosts pounded at the barrier of branches and vines, wailing in fury at their now unreachable quarry.

Quinn ignored the ghosts running for the columbarium. Gavin and Jane would have to deal with those.

Only Bobbi mattered now. Quinn's heart lurched as Fain picked her up. She hung limp in his arms. How much soother magic did it take to turn a woman into a rag doll?

He ran down the slope, two ghosts trailing behind. They were nothing more than a nuisance until one of them tripped him. He stumbled. No time to wonder how they had become corporeal. He punched the first ghost in the jaw.

Shots fired from the shadows and the spirits disappeared in puffs of aether. The med-mage was making good on his promise. Of course a Paragon would know how to defeat ghosts. He left Emmett to his target practice and ran on.

Two hundred yards to go. He didn't bother hiding. They had lost their surprise advantage.

Fain raised Bobbi's arms above her head and pulled off her shirt.

Quinn put all his energy into running. Fain looked up and flicked a wrist. A headstone jolted from the ground and hurled at Quinn. He dodged, but the stone clipped his ankle and he fell. Another sailed over his head and shattered against the monument behind him. He had no aether left to make a shield, but he pushed himself up and staggered forward, one slow step at a time.

Below, Fain spun Bobbi, unclasped her bra and flung it aside. Her jeans caused him more trouble and he slit them with a knife. Bobbi crumpled to the ground again. He left her like that while he lit candles in protective glass votives and set them in a circle, then ringed them with salt. Fain's smug face showed him completely at ease, as if Quinn's presence was of no consequence.

That worried Quinn. Had he booby-trapped the cemetery? Had they missed something in their preparations?

Quinn's ankle gave out and he fell to one knee. Fain grinned and waved to him. A screen of gravel hit Quinn in the face, blinding him. He swore and hobbled down the hill, clutching his knife like a life-line, weaving through the graves to make himself an unpredictable target.

Fain advanced on Bobbi, knife gleaming in the candle light.

Come on…wake up!

Bobbi lay like a corpse. Fain swiped the blade across her chest.

"Now Abilene!" Quinn shouted and lunged.

Ghosts pounded on the screen of brambles.

"Abilene! We need that spell broken now!" Jane hissed.

"It's almost there," Gavin said. Abilene couldn't speak. She held herself rigid, her will clamped on Fain's aether. The candle burned at water level. Only a thin rim of wax held back the water.

A hissing scream came from outside and one of the ghosts disappeared in a puff of aether. Behind it, Emmet's eyes peered through the branches.

"All clear," he said, "but you'd better hurry."

Outside, Quinn screamed.

Inside, all eyes watched hot wax leak into the water.

Quinn jumped over a headstone and skidded on gravel. He gasped from pain and exhaustion, but Bobbi lay only a few feet ahead, her expressionless face smeared with blood. From deep in his soul, he found the strength to lunge for her.

Fain looked up from his wet work and spoke one word. Fire exploded in a circle around him. Flames leaped, blazing white hot.

Quinn didn't stop. He ran into the ring of fire.

And smacked into a ward.

He fell, hitting his head against the ground and lay stunned. The bastard had salted his circle with black powder to ignite a shield.

He wouldn't be able to get through it. Not with his aether so dangerously low. He sat, considering his options while Fain leered at him through the flames.

"Did you think I wouldn't be prepared for you?" he said.

Bobbi lay naked and vulnerable, arms bent at painful angles. The cut on her chest leaked blood between her breasts. Her eyes stared at the black sky. Fain shoved her with a toe.

A candle fell over in the wind and extinguished in the grass. Quinn jumped up, hoping the break in the circle would mean a flaw in the ward. He pounded on the barricade of flame. His fists sizzled and the air filled with the stink of burned hair, but the ward held.

Fain smiled, righted the candle and relit the wick.

Quinn was fueled by rage now. Bobbi might be a zombie, but somewhere inside she was aware. She felt the wind across her bare skin. She hurt from the unnatural bend of her limbs. Some part of her screamed in fear.

Fain hovered over Bobbi, assessing. He looked at her naked body, not the way a man looked at a woman, but the way a butcher looked at a carcass of beef.

Then he sliced across her chest again.

Quinn roared.

The candle hissed. The flame went out. Abilene fell over in the darkness.

"Get that hedge down now!" Jane said.

Gavin pulled at his magic, reeling in the energy he'd so recently poured into his barrier. The vines wilted and shrank. Jane blasted the brittle branches with a flare from her staff and was gone.

"You cut her again, and I'll kill you."

Fain grinned, dipped a finger in the blood trailing down Bobbi's chest and licked it.

His face contorted, eyes bulged. A second face superimposed on his own. Black eyes, bulbous brow, with the hint of protruding horns. Fain wore this new face like a badly fitting mask.

"I am not finished with the blooding, witch." A commanding voice boomed from his throat. "When I am done here, I will come for you." He pointed a hand that had turned skeletal.

Koro. The blood, the magic, the thinning veil of Samhain. It was enough to bring him forth and now he rode Fain, a master in complete control of his puppet.

He bent and sliced another line on Bobbi's chest, making a cross of blood.

The unnaturally loud voice boomed again, incanting the rite that would release Koro from his dark prison and bring him fully into their world.

He's going to kill her!

Quinn pounded uselessly on the ward, not caring that every strike lashed his fists with hot pain.

The Fain-Koro creature dropped the knife and unzipped his pants. He gave Quinn one last leer before turning back to his prey.

Holy gods, he wasn't going to kill her. He wanted something much worse.

From behind Koro, Bobbi screamed.

It was the most beautiful sound Quinn ever heard.

RESUSCITATION

Something wet dripped down my breast. I sat up. The world spun. I wiped my chest and stared at my fingers.

Blood.

My eyes slid sideways.

Fire. Black sky. A face through the flames. Frowning. I knew that face.

"Quinn?" The name stuck in my throat. Thirsty. I was so thirsty.

"Lie down!" Hands shoved me flat. William filled my vision, his lips twisted in anger. Something was wrong with him. His appearance flowed and morphed. A huge nose seemed to lay over his. Stubs of black bone protruded from his forehead, then were gone. His eyes shifted from William's pale blue to black and back again as if I watched a flickering screen.

Then the features solidified into a brutish brow with stubby horns, bulbous nose and thick, wet lips. William, but not William.

Oh gods. I let him touch me? Kiss me? I had loved him!

Everything I felt for him dropped away like stones, leaving only terror.

William yanked his pants, freeing his fully hard cock.

"Take me."

I jerked away. Searing heat stopped me. A wall of flame rose at my back. Someone yelled in the darkness.

"You think you're so high and mighty." Flames lit the round face as it morphed back to William. "You wouldn't give me the time of day. But I made you want me. Stupid bitch. I told you we would change the world."

The face morphed again and I stared at the aspect of a demon.

Koro lunged.

"Jane! I need you!" Quinn screamed. He battered the ward, ignoring burned flesh. Inside, Fain jumped on Bobbi.

"Mother, now!"

Jane seemed to float over the ground in her glowing white robe. The rest of the crew tumbled through the darkness behind her. Jane reached the ward and pushed Quinn away. She took a deep breath, and spoke in the language of power, calling to the Mother to join aether with hers.

Quinn had heard this language a dozen times in his life. While she spoke, he understood her perfectly, but afterwards, he would never be able to recall the words. More spirits gathered, drawn by the aether. They milled around like a medieval crowd eager to see an execution.

The wind puffed Jane's robe and swelled her hair. In the glow of aether, her face was stark, her eyes without mercy. She raised her staff to the sky, gave a primal scream and slammed it into Fain's ward. It boomed like thunder.

The ward held.

Bobbi screamed as Fain tried to consummate the rite. Quinn could do nothing but watch.

I jerked up my knee, caught him in the thigh. His full weight crushed me as he fumbled, trying to penetrate. His cock jabbed my thigh, my stomach. A zipper scraped my flesh. I struck out. My fist connected with bone.

He smacked his forehead against my cheek. Pain shot through my eye.

A deep voice rumbled, hot and wet in my ear.

"You will take me into you, daughter. You are my vessel. I made you strong to bear me into this world. Take me or I will break you."

I couldn't breathe. The world dimmed and closed to nothing but the stench of the man-demon smothering me and the pain of his blows. My teeth clamped onto his ear and I tore off a chunk of flesh. Blood filled my mouth. I gagged and spat, crying, choking. The beast-man screamed and hit me again.

Thunder boomed.

Jane's staff crashed into the ward, her face set in concrete, eyes blazing with inner fire.

Boom!
The tip of the staff shone.
Boom!
Quinn's ears hurt from the sound.
Spirits shrieked and scattered, terrified by the awesome display of power.
Boom! She struck again. Red cracks zigzagged across the ward.
One more strike and with a sound like the shattering of the sky, the ward fell. The mage fire vanished. Jane crumpled in a heap of billowing robe.
Quinn dove for Fain.

The pressure vanished. I rolled, coming up hard against a stone block. A headstone?
I wiped my eyes with a bloody, shaking hand. My mouth tasted of blood. I spat.
A cry of pure pain. I spun. Two figures wrestled at the edge of the candle light. William's high voice whined. Quinn pinned him and punched. Blood splattered both of them. William shrieked. He bucked and clawed the ground, snatching a candle and smashing the glass votive across Quinn's face. Quinn jerked sideways, his face exploding with cuts, eyes full of glass. William squirmed, reached and came up with a knife. He lunged at Quinn, the blade arced high to strike Quinn's back.
He never reached it.
A spectral figure in white rose behind him. Jane, eyes firing fury, raised her arm to strike. She called to the Lady and sank her sacred athame into William's back.
"Never again!" she screamed.
Fain's eyes rolled, mouth gaped. His features shuddered and shifted back to human. Jane pulled back and struck again. The knife slid into his neck. Blood spurted. His knees buckled.
Jane plunged the blade again. And again. And again.
"Never! Never! Never!"
Abilene circled arms around her mother and pulled her back.
Jane dropped the knife. Her regal features crumpled and she wept into Abilene's embrace.
Through a haze of tears, I saw William breathe his last breath. A bubble of

blood popped on his lips and his aether blew away on the wind.

Quinn sat up. His face was a mess of blood. He reached for me and I fell into his arms, smearing my blood across his shirt.

And I broke just as Koro wanted. Sobs tore through me, loosing the rage that William had pinned behind a wall for days. Snot and tears streamed down my face. I pounded on Quinn, my blows striking his chest, shoulder and arms. He didn't stop me. I shook and raged until my muscles gave out and I sagged against him.

"I got you," he whispered and kissed the top of my blood-matted head.

Contrition

Horses sprinted through the frost-painted pasture. As a kid, the sight of horses galloping never failed to thrill me. Every day, I woke eager to do my barn chores and feed the animals. Now, even the sleek, glossy horses shining in the morning light did nothing to comfort me. I pressed my bruised face against the cool glass and watched it fog.

Like my brain for the last week.

Two days had passed since the events in the cemetery. I'd spent one of those sedated at the hospital and the next in my old room at the farm, unable to sleep, staring out my window, waiting for the next monster to attack.

I rose and threw on a housecoat. The motion tugged at the stitches across my chest. My bare feet cringed against the cold floor. The weather had finally caught up with the calendar and the day was chilly. Emmett had started the old furnace. The house groaned and creaked as I headed for the bathroom. Downstairs, Emmett and Molly tiptoed around, afraid to disturb me, afraid I'd break if they spoke too loud.

It was a possibility.

The mirror in the bathroom, yellowed around the edges and shot through with fine cracks, did nothing to enhance my appearance. The bruise on my cheek was deep purple and swollen. I could look forward to the gradual fading to green, then yellow. A hairline fracture, the doctor said. I'd been lucky that William hadn't struck me a few inches higher or he might have damaged the eye socket.

Yeah, lucky.

My bottom lip had scabbed. I felt like bits of William's ear were stuck between my teeth and no amount of flossing could change that. He'd turned me into a rabid beast.

I looked into my eyes and didn't know the person who stared back.

I had loved him. He made me do things—kiss him, touch him—but worse, he twisted my love into a tool. My emotions were no longer my own.

At least I'd been saved from one hellish fate; William hadn't raped me—and even if I'd wanted it, begged him for it, it would have been rape. But he'd been saving that special pleasure for Samhain and his midnight picnic in the cemetery.

I splashed water on my face and went downstairs to find some answers.

"Where's Emmett?" I asked Molly, who sat with her ubiquitous cup of tea in the kitchen.

"In the big barn. Do you want breakfast?"

I ignored the question and slipped my feet into muck boots. Outside, the wind whipped my housecoat, exposing bare legs. I ran across the yard to the bigger of the two barns, and hauled open the door.

"I want to know things."

Emmett looked up from stacking bales of hay. His brown eyes were haunted, but he nodded.

"Let's go inside," he said.

I planted my feet. "No. Here. Now. Tell me why William waited to…fuck me until Samhain." The curse word fell like a hand-grenade. I'd dropped all my anger into it—anger at William, anger at myself for being a victim. Anger at Emmett for hiding the fact that he was a Paragon med-mage. There was more anger to go around, but I'd get to it.

Emmett sat on a hay bale.

"He wasn't trying to kill me. He was trying to rape me. Why?"

"Samhain is unique. It's the night when the veil between worlds thins and Koro could more easily possess him."

"And you know this because you were a demon hunter for Paragon." I had learned a few truths in the last couple of days, and they didn't all sit well.

He spread his hands across his knees. "I never actually did any of the hunting. I was more in the research and development side of things."

"A med-mage," I said. He nodded. "But my father…" I closed my eyes. He wasn't really my father. "I mean Benjamin Cole, he was a hunter, a knight of Paragon."

"He was also your father in every way that's important. He loved you."

I waved my hand as if this was of no importance, but a lump lodged in my throat. Ben Cole had always been my father, a giant of a man with a deep laugh. I had few memories of him, but even those were tainted now. Another precious thing William Fain took from me.

"So Koro was riding in the passenger seat on Samhain," I said. "But why? He wasn't trying to sacrifice me." With dark magic it was always about blood. And William's rite had started that way. My hand came up to touch the bandage covered stitches on my chest. He blooded me, but that had only been an opening gambit, a way to let Koro possess him.

A horrifying thought cut into my mind.

"He was trying to impregnate me, wasn't he?"

Emmett nodded slowly. "I think so."

William had planned to plant his seed—my father's seed—in me and grow what? Another demon? Did they think I'd willingly carry such a beast to term? That Jane wouldn't murder me as soon as the ward fell?

"Why?"

"There is precedent. A demon can manifest by implanting his seed in a human host." Emmett's shaggy eyebrows lowered in that way they did when he was holding back real emotion. "And it happens fast, within minutes. Most human women are too weak to carry a full-blood demon to term." He didn't explain what that rapid gestation would do to a woman. I could imagine— stomach bulging, organs tearing as a fully formed demon burst from my womb.

By the gods. I thought I would vomit.

"In essence, he births himself, but he needed a strong woman to be his vessel."

"One with demon blood," I whispered. That was why Koro had stolen four human women twenty-nine years ago. He couldn't find a host, so he made one.

"He's been looking for me all this time?"

Emmett nodded. "He can't interact on this plane. He can only work through possession. And contrary to Hollywood myth, it's not easy for a demon to possess someone. He needs to find a willing host. And when he does, that host must stay off Paragon's radar. We've stopped more than a few possessions before they became deadly."

"That's why you took me in. To watch over me."

"At first, yes. Your parents weren't really friends of ours, though we knew them through Paragon, of course."

"I was a job."

"No!" Emmett rushed over and squeezed my shoulders with his big hands.

"Never that! You were a child in need. We took you in and you became our daughter." He shook me a little. "Never doubt that. I love you as much as I love Grace and Jennifer," he said, naming his flesh-and-blood daughters who I'd always thought of as sisters, "and probably a little more than I love Ryan." He grinned and I half-sobbed, half-laughed. I couldn't help it. I loved Ryan like a brother, but he didn't make it easy.

I wiped my eyes. "One last question: did Koro kill my parents?"

"Yes."

He'd been hunting me for nearly three decades. And he wouldn't stop. William was dead, but he'd find another host and come for me. And I, the untrained witch with enormous powers, wouldn't be able to stop him.

"I could go for that tea now," I said.

I sat on the front porch watching horses zip around the pasture, a forgotten cup of tea in my hand. The cold weather made the animals frisky. The shadows were long and blue along the fence when a car pulled into the driveway.

Quinn.

I hadn't exactly been avoiding him…yes, I was. I didn't want to deal with my jumbled feelings right now. We'd started something good, possibly something amazing. It had all turned to shit. The cost of William's betrayal grew ever higher.

Molly had filled in some of my missing days. Quinn had spied on me and learned the truth before anyone else. And he'd fought for me. But he'd also soothed me once, by accident. He'd confessed immediately and promised never to do it again. But the thought of that awful magic taking hold of me made the breath hurt in my chest.

Quinn's feet kicked up dust in the driveway. He limped slightly. One eye was covered with a white patch. I remembered the glass votive shattering over his head and winced.

He walked to the edge of the porch. His one blue eye, as dark as the falling shadows, ranged up and down my body, taking in my bruised face, disheveled clothes and the bandage sticking up through the collar of my shirt.

"I went by your house," he said. "You weren't there."

Ah, we'd reverted to the awkward conversation phase.

"No. I didn't want to be alone."

He nodded as if that made sense. We stood watching each other like strangers for a long minute.

"How's your eye?"

"Doc says it's just a scratch."

I doubted that, but I didn't press.

Horses trotted past the drive, glowing in the last light of day.

"I'm sorry I didn't stop him," Quinn said. "Sooner, I mean."

"No!" I suddenly felt foolish, ungrateful and a whole host of other unpleasant emotions. "I should thank you. You saved me when no one else could, when I didn't even know I needed saving."

My verbal explosion seemed to release something in him. He sagged and sat heavily on the porch by my feet.

"I shouldn't have let it get so far. I should have taken you away as soon as I realized what he was doing."

I laid a hand on his shoulder.

"It wouldn't have made a difference. Koro would have found me anyway. He will always find me." That truth was a cold hard stone in the middle of my wellspring. My aether could pool around it, cover it, mask it, but the truth would remain. Koro would come for me.

"We found out about William Fain," Quinn said. He turned to see my expression. "I could tell you about him, if you want."

I nodded. Nothing he could say would hurt me further. William was dead.

"He was from the Crestlayan Coven, near Charlotte. They're an old coven with a few hereditary families. Fain was the last of his line. His High Priestess said he always felt like he had something to prove. He was reckless. She wasn't surprised that he would open himself to possession. They're coming to claim the body."

I let those words work through me, sought an ending within them, but found none. I hoped they burned his bones and scattered the ashes.

The sun dipped below the tree line, sucking color from the world as it went.

"He made me love him," I croaked.

Quinn shook his head. "I should have taught you to detect soother magic. I never thought…We'll make it a priority in your training. I promise."

His one good eye pleaded with me, but I couldn't give him what he wanted.

"I think Abilene should take over my training. For the next little while at least."

"You don't think I would ever soothe you?"

"Not on purpose." How could I make him understand? "I just need a little time…to find my real emotions again."

He nodded and rose. We stared at each other, the few feet between us were an unscalable gorge.

"I'll tell Abilene to expect your call as soon as you're feeling up to it." He turned to go.

I couldn't leave it like that.

"Quinn!"

He turned. The last light caught the gleam of his dark hair and deepened the shadows on his face. He looked so tired. I had done that to him.

"We're okay," I said. "I mean, we will be."

Quinn smiled and I felt a bit of life return to my dead heart.

Book 3

TRIGGER MAGIC

Invasion

The sky broke. Fat heavy raindrops pelted the roof of my car. Tired of spring, Mother Nature just wanted the job done. I turned off the engine and sat in my driveway.

To get soaked or not to get soaked?

Lightning reflected off the dark windows of my single-story house. The rain increased, and was that hail? Yep. Ice pellets pinged off my car as if daring me to break for the house. I closed my eyes and leaned against the headrest.

I'd been awake since before dawn helping my father at his Open Gate Farm Tour fundraiser. Now close to midnight, I needed sleep. Emmett wanted me to stay at the farm, but I had to work tomorrow. I wanted my bed for tonight and my bathroom and closet in the morning.

The hail stopped, giving me a small reprieve. I readied myself to dash for the door, wishing I knew a spell against weather.

Wind nearly ripped the door from my grip as I jumped from the car. Hailstones crunched under my feet. Cold water dripped into my eyes and plastered my clothes to me by the time I reached the door.

Lightning crackled again. I froze. Something was wrong. I wasn't proficient enough with wards to protect my entire house, but I'd set up a few magical trip wires around the perimeter. I should have felt a tingle of aether as I passed over them, but I didn't.

The wards were gone.

I unlocked the door and flicked on the light switch. Nothing.

Just perfect. The storm knocked out the power. Or had it? I peered back into the rain. Several porch lights glowed up and down both sides of the street.

As a sensate, I could detect the presence of aether, a less useful talent than it sounded. All living beings gave off aether or life-magic and continually scanning for it was overwhelming. But in the aftermath of events from last fall, I'd practiced discerning useful information from all that noise.

My house felt off. Mentally, I picked through the familiar aether signatures. I'd started to think of these in connection to my other senses. The houseplants gave off their peculiar earth-scented aether. A faint orange tinge remained on the couch where the neighborhood cat slept on cold nights. And something else. A jittery aether, like the sound of cicadas buzzing in the summer heat. This aether was too fresh. The intruder still hid in the house.

A blast of cold air told me a window was open somewhere. With quiet steps, I headed into the kitchen. The storm raged overhead as lightning and thunder collided. Each flash ignited the room, then left me blind.

"Hello? Who's here?" My voice rang too loud in the dark. I passed through the kitchen into the dining room. Rain blew in through the broken patio door, and shards of glass littered the floor. Lightning briefly illuminated my backyard, empty except for the patio furniture neatly piled under a tarp for the winter.

Turning back to the quiet house, I called up my aether ward, struggling to make the protective spell big enough to surround me. It wouldn't deflect bullets, but like Kevlar, it would slow them down enough to keep me alive. And it would protect me from all but the strongest magic attacks.

I grabbed the phone a dialed 911.

"What's your emergency?"

"Someone's in my house," I whispered.

"What's your name, ma'am."

"Bobbi Cole. Please send someone…"

Thunder clapped and lightning burst through the windows. I dropped the phone and heard the operator's tinny voice from where it lay on the counter.

"Ma'am? Please get out of the house, if you can. Ma'am, are you still there? Bobbi?"

A crash came from my bedroom.

I slipped a knife from the rack, and wrapping my ward around me like a cloak, stepped toward the back of the house. Something loomed at the end of the hall. Lightning flashed, and I recognized the hanging stairs that led to my attic.

"The police are on the way!" I called into the gloom.

A ball of light struck me in the chest and exploded. Crackling energy raced across my skin, pain and heat in its wake. The ward took most of the hit, but the blast knocked me backward. I fell, dropping the knife and ward. My eyes burned with hot tears as the intruder rushed past me. I kicked out, trying to trip him. My foot glanced off his ankle. Another bolt of white-hot light ripped into the wall beside my head. I flattened myself to the floor.

He flung open the front door, and it slammed against the inside wall. Rain blew into the foyer. Lightning cracked, and behind the pealing thunder, I heard the wail of sirens.

When the police arrived, I sat slumped in a daze beside the scorched drywall, the paint around it black and peeling. I touched my sore chest where the other bolt hit me. What damage would it have done if I hadn't been shielded?

Five months ago, my demon father possessed a creep named William Fain and pushed him to use me in a dark rite that I didn't completely understand. If he'd succeeded, Koro would have birthed himself into our world, tearing me apart in the process. And no one—witch or mundane—would have been safe from his lust for aether.

William taught me a healthy fear of soother magic. To this day, while I lay in that paralyzing moment between wakefulness and sleep each night, I could feel his slithering magic enfolding me, taking away my will, and I'd shoot upright with a scream lodged in my throat.

Until tonight, soothing was my least favorite kind of magic, but being attacked by a galvanic mage sucked too. The bastard shot me with a bolt of electricity. My muscles still hummed and twitched, and I didn't even want to look at my hair.

As the police searched my house, I brooded at my kitchen table. Why me? Why did I always end up in the crosshairs of some maniac magic user? Of course, the answer to that was easy. It was in my DNA. Koro would never stop coming for me.

The officer who took my statement suggested I interrupted the burglar before he could steal anything. He told me to get a copy of his report from the precinct and to go through all my belongings carefully for the insurance. I once again refused his offer to call the paramedics. As far as the police were concerned, I'd only been knocked down. No way to explain the burn mark on my wall, or the bruise blossoming on my chest, so I ignored those.

"Is there anyone you can call?" the officer asked, after they helped me board up the broken window. "We'll have a car in the area tonight, but you shouldn't be alone."

I nodded. As soon as they left, I dialed Henry's number. It went straight to voicemail. Damn. I forgot he went on some secret Paragon mission.

Since Koro's attack last fall, Henry Garza had been teaching me defense, both physical and magical, with varying degrees of success. A kick-boxing instructor for mundanes by day, Henry was also a Knight of Paragon, the group of warriors, healers and scholars who protected the mundane world from all things supernatural. My adopted father, Emmett, put me in touch with him when my nightmares of Koro and William Fain became a risk to my health.

It turned out that kicking the crap out of things helped. Blowing stuff up with balls of magic fire was also cathartic, even if my spells tended to get away from me. But I improved with every lesson. I'd only set the dojo on fire once last week.

Henry taught me to ward my house and my body. When he learned of this attack, he'd offer praise and disapproval. Praise for calling up the ward under duress, and disapproval for letting it drop after the first attack. I'd take the criticism if it meant I didn't have to spend the rest of this night alone. But Henry was away, and I had no one else to call.

That wasn't entirely true. Every day for the past five months, I wanted to call Quinn. Even now, my finger hovered over my phone. He would come. I knew he would, but I hadn't called him when things were good, and it seemed unfair to reach out now. Quinn wasn't my protector. I had no right to ask him to save me. I sighed and put the phone down.

Unable to sleep, I spent the dark hours of pre-dawn sorting through my jewelry and other precious effects, even though I knew all would be in order. Whatever the intruder sought, it wasn't mundane valuables. Other than a broken lamp in my bedroom, I couldn't find anything missing or damaged. The police had poked their heads into my attic, but found only boxes of books still unpacked from my last move.

Nothing out of place. Nothing missing.

I went to bed and managed only two hours of sleep before my traitorous alarm woke me.

In the harsh morning light, the burn mark in my foyer looked even worse, and my chest ached. I left another message for Henry before heading to work.

I owned a small fiber shop on Main Street in Ashlet. Mondays at the Woolery were quiet, and I hoped to use the time to practice that warding spell. I needed to learn to keep it intact even while under fire from an enemy. If the intruder had better aim, he would have killed me.

So preoccupied with my thoughts, I didn't notice the buzzing sound in my ears until I unlocked the store.

I stood in the open doorway with shock locking my legs in place.

The store was a mess. Baskets of wool were pulled from the shelves and left in heaps on the floor. The book and magazine section was torn apart. Chairs were toppled in the lounge and my cash register lay open and empty on the floor beside the counter.

I stared at the ransacked chaos and suddenly recognized the buzzing noise I'd been hearing all along. It was an aether signature—the same one I'd detected in my house last night.

I picked up my phone to call the police again, but I needed more than mundane help this time.

REUNION

Quinn paused with a fork halfway to his mouth. Something twanged his aether like a chill down his spine followed by an echoing shock wave. Squirtsburger opened one eye, decided the sound was none of his concern and curled his tail around his nose. Cats were attuned to the aether world; they just didn't worry about it. That was Quinn's job. Any possible threat to the coven should be taken seriously, especially this week, with the village full of VIP guests.

Several Paragon agents, along with the heads of influential covens came to discuss the demon Koro, his previous attacks and inevitable future attacks. They chose the Hidden Coven to host these talks because of its combat-rated ward. It was an honor for the coven, but it meant that Quinn hadn't slept for more that a couple of hours at a time in days. Now, after all the formal dinners, presentations and debates, Quinn finally had a moment of solitude.

Again the shock wave sounded as if someone knocked on a giant door. Lightning flashed, followed by a rumble of distant thunder, then another bang.

Despite fatigue and hunger, he put down the fork. Supper would have to wait.

A cold wind blew around the empty village square as he left his cottage. One or two faces peered through half-cracked doors, those witches with sensate abilities. Quinn motioned for them to stay inside.

Bang! It seemed to echo from all around. He stood in the village square, turning in slow circles. Bang! It came again, and again, more insistent now, and suddenly, he recognized the noise. Jane's staff made the same sound last fall when it slammed into William Fain's ward.

Someone was trying to break into the coven.

Abilene ran into the square with Jane on her heels. Both his sister and mother had off-the-chart sensate abilities so it didn't surprise him that they were attuned to the sound.

"Can you hear it too?" Abilene asked.

Quinn nodded.

"What is it?"

"Ward," Jane said, her face grim. "Someone's trying to crack it."

Quinn pointed to the guest cottages. "Abi, rouse the Paragon agents and meet us at the ward." A dozen Paragon knights remained on the island. If Koro was banging on their door, he hoped it would be enough. Memories of the demon's first attack tore at him—a hellish night of fires burning through the thatched cottages and wraiths loose inside the ward, killing indiscriminately. He couldn't let that happen again.

Abi ran for the guest cottages, where the knights were already mustering.

Quinn glanced at Jane, who simply said, "Go. I'll catch up." He didn't need to lead her to the spot on the coven perimeter where the sound originated. Every bang made Jane wince. She could pinpoint it more easily than him. He ran up the path leading to the vestal house. The young guards set to protect Siranda and the core snapped to attention.

"We may be under attack." Quinn pointed to one guard then the other. "You, wake Gavin and the vestals. You, come with me."

His foster brother, Gavin, didn't have a strong sensate ability, but he was a good man to have at his back in a fight.

Ignoring the path, Quinn dodged trees and took a straight route to the ward's edge. He clutched his cockroach necklace to boost his aether and ran faster. The young guard did his best to follow.

The sun set later these days and the last tinges of daylight faded into the forest. Branches slapped his face and clutched at his clothes, but he didn't slow. The sound of rushing water grew in harmony to the constant battering at the ward. He slid the last few feet down an embankment to the edge of a stone jetty.

And found Bobbi.

She stood in the river up to her knees with a backpack slung over one shoulder. Her blond ponytail hung in a long wet hank and dirt was smeared across her cheek. She was beautiful.

Quinn leaned against a tree and crossed his arms, trying for nonchalance though his heart hammered in his chest.

Bobbi raised her fist glowing within a protective glove of aether and pounded on the door to the Hidden Coven.

"What do you want?" he asked.

"Just let me in."

"Not by the hair on my chinny chin chin." He grinned.

She glared and pounded again.

"Open the ward, Quinn."

The guard finally caught up, making enough noise to scare away a bear.

"Stay here," Quinn said to the boy. He strolled up the jetty, taking time to assess the situation. Bobbi's teeth clenched. Was she angry or cold? Both, he decided.

The last time she'd left the coven, Quinn insisted she go blindfolded. She'd bristled at the blatant mistrust on his part, but his security instincts were right. What if she'd led Fain back here? As much as it pained him to treat her like an outsider, that's what she was.

"How did you find us?"

"Easy." Bobbi shrugged. "I'm a super sensate, remember?"

He gave her his best I'm-not-buying-it look.

"Fine. I drove fifty miles into the middle of nowhere, then hiked another two through the woods and swam the last stretch through ice water because that was the only way I could find this jetty."

He thought of the last time they'd stood here, when he'd hugged Bobbi close so they could pass through the ward together, and saw the same thought reflected on her face.

"And you thought you'd just break down our ward? Do you have any idea what that would have done to the vestals linked to the core?"

Bobbi stood straighter. "You still think I'm a bumbling idiot when it comes to magic, but I've learned a lot in five months."

"So I heard."

He kept tabs on her through Emmett when he went to the old med-mage for his weekly inoculation. Emmett set Bobbi up with a Paragon mentor. She needed proper magical education, and he understood why she turned to someone else, but it still hurt.

"I wasn't trying to break through it. I needed to get your attention. It's cold out here." She crossed arms over her wet chest.

Lord and Lady, she looked good. Even sporting the drowned rat look, the sight of her made him want to open a door he resolutely shut some months ago.

"You could have called instead."

"I did, which you would know if you checked your messages."

Quinn walked through the ward, no barrier to him since he was keyed to it, and checked his phone.

"You're right. Look at that. Three messages. All from you. I guess I've lost the habit of checking them. Seems sort of pointless when everyone who would be calling me lives inside the coven." That sounded petty even to his ears.

Bobbi didn't take the bait. Her mouth set in a grim line. She looked exhausted and scared. The alpha protector in him wanted to gather her in his arms, hold back the night and whatever terrors she brought with her, but her fierce gaze said all he needed to know. She wouldn't thank him.

William Fain broke Bobbi, violated her in body and soul, and she hadn't yet found all the pieces of herself. Quinn should have acted sooner to stop Fain. At least he could respect her boundaries now.

"So are you going to let me in?" Bobbi squeezed water from her ponytail and glared at him.

"Are you going to tell me why you're here?"

Her defiance crumpled. "I need your help."

ⅭDISCUSSION

Paragon dedicated an entire team to the koro problem. I should have been happy that such a powerful organization cared for my well-being. I wasn't. I didn't like being a burden or the cause of so much potential destruction. At the very least, they could've had a better code name, something snappy like Team Demon Slayer.

While I changed into dry clothes, Abilene brought me up to date on the recent gathering of witches at the coven, all there to discuss the threat of my father.

"Considering his blood runs in my veins, you'd think I would've been invited to the table," I said, drying my hair with a fluffy towel.

"You're here now." Abilene shrugged and looked away. Of course, they didn't want me in the discussions. I was part of the problem, and my death might be part of the solution.

She led me to the living room. I sat and accepted a mug of coffee from Gavin. At least he looked friendly. The rest of the crowd did not. It felt like I faced a parole board.

Across the room, next to Jane's austere altar, sat Colonel Bert Donner, head of the local Paragon chapter. A tall, broad-shouldered man, Donner wore power like a cloak and made me want to sit up straighter. He watched me with flat eyes as I told the assembled group about the two break-ins.

Beside him sat Myra Aoki and Grant Siskin, two of the thirteen witches who founded the Hidden Coven and built the core, the giant pulsing construct that fueled the ward. Myra, a small dark woman, listened to my story intently, but Grant's ancient wrinkled head bobbed as he fought sleep.

Henry Garza came next. He shot me a reassuring smile. At least I knew where Henry had disappeared to. Dark-haired and olive-skinned, Henry was always ready with a smile or a pat on the back. In the months we'd been training together, Henry pushed me to work harder and smarter, and I'd come a long way in that time.

I still had a lot of catching up to do, as Colonel Donner so helpfully pointed out.

"You're a sensate. You must have detected the intruder's aether signature. Why didn't you put a tracking spell on him as soon as he ran?"

I thought of those hectic moments after the attack with the wall smoldering behind me and lightning only intensifying the dark. What could I tell him? I was too scared? Too weak? Too stupid? He could have his pick.

Henry cleared his throat. "Bobbi and I have been focusing mostly on defensive magic, given the circumstances. She can call up a decent ward, but we haven't covered other basic offensive spells yet."

That was Henry's superpower: pure calm reason.

"And what if Koro finds another agent with soother magic?" Jane asked. "Will she fall prey to that again?"

Thank you, Jane, for reminding me what a victim I was.

"I admit I have been unsuccessful in teaching Bobbi about soothing magic, but the fault is mine." He spread his hands wide. "I have no soother magic and so have no way to show it to her." Henry's eyes rested on Quinn. "Perhaps she would benefit from time here at the coven. Mistress Abilene can teach her to use her sensate magic for tracking and Quinn can…"

"I'm not sure staying at the coven is a good idea." I cut Henry off before he could finish. My vulnerability to soother magic was a raw wound. "I'm Koro's prime target. The coven has solid wards, but we already saw how one angry teenager could easily dismantle those."

When I first visited the coven, Aiden, a boy with a chip on his shoulder, let wraiths inside the ward. The monsters killed over a dozen witches. Only my desperate and foolish act kept the core secure and the ward active.

"Even so, this is the safest place for you to be right now," Donner said. "With Mistress Jane's permission, we'll leave knights here to guard the core while you train. I don't need to impress upon you all how vulnerable Bobbi and the coven are right now." All eyes turned to Jane who pursed her lips and nodded once.

I felt like such a welcomed guest.

"I didn't come here to stay. I only wanted advice and maybe some help warding my house and business, until I find out who's stalking me."

"We all knew you'd end up back here sooner or later," Jane said. "I hoped we had more time before Koro could successfully trap a new agent into working for him."

None of us spoke of the worry behind those words. Koro was ramping up his efforts. That meant no one was safe.

The discussion rambled on. The long walk, the swim in the icy water and a near sleepless night left me exhausted. I could barely sit up straight by the time the party broke up. Then I had to face the sleeping arrangements. Colonel Donner occupied the spare room in Jane's house. The other Paragon knights filled the guest cottages.

"I guess you're staying with me tonight," Quinn said as everyone left. His sneaky eyebrow arched, even as he tried to hide a smile.

Just great. We hadn't spoken for five months. Now, we were having a slumber party.

I followed him home, feeling like a lost puppy. He made up the spare bed, a pull-out couch in the middle of his one-room cottage, his bed only a few feet away.

The room was dim and warm. The rest of the world seemed far away. I was alone with Quinn. He'd changed into sweats and a cotton t-shirt that hugged his shoulders. I wondered if it was soft. It looked soft. I could run my fingers along…

"Do you want an extra pillow?"

I looked up. His eyes, always dark, were hidden in shadow. A sudden memory overtook me: Quinn leaning over me in Jane's garden for our first kiss. I shook my head. There would be no kissing tonight.

He watched me, and I couldn't seem to break free from his gaze. I had so much to say, but the words stuck like a hard lump in my chest. I wanted him to know how, as each day passed without me picking up the phone, it became harder and harder to break that silence. How many words would it now take to fill the gulf between us?

"Do you snore?"

His answering smile was slow and came from somewhere deep.

"I don't know. It's been a long time since anyone could tell me. But if I do, feel free to throw a pillow." He turned for his bed.

Tomorrow. I would make everything better tomorrow.

♌DIMENSION

I walked to center field and stretched. The practice yard cut into the woods about a mile from the village square. A sacred circle, reinforced many times over the years, bordered it. The hum of old aether strummed across my senses. Within this protection, the Hidden Coven taught its youngest witches magic.

The coming battle practice would be tough and already, my energy lagged. I'd spent a long night staring at Quinn's ceiling and listening to him sleep. He did snore a bit, but the sound anchored my whirling thoughts.

Standing at the ward's edge yesterday, I'd been excited and terrified to see him again. That feeling hadn't left me.

We ate a polite breakfast together. *Please pass the butter,* and *Thank you, did you want any jam?* It was like having tea with the Queen. I remembered our first date. We talked so much, we closed down the restaurant, but the five-month silence turned us into strangers again.

Quinn watched me from the sideline. Once, I could read every thought flitting across his mind. Now, his hooded gaze hid him well. He could be angry, anxious or excited. I couldn't tell.

Laughter rang through the trees. Abilene and Henry stepped into the clearing. Her hand touched his arm as she laughed at something he said. Abilene turned eighteen over the winter, and she shone with youth and vigor. She also seemed to have a crush on my mentor.

"You'll have to tell me more of your Paragon adventures later." Her cheeks were tinged pink.

Henry leaned in and spoke in a theatrical whisper, "I could, but then I'd have to kill you."

Abilene giggled. Yep, she had it bad.

I couldn't blame the kid. Henry was older but not too old, and he had that whole dark, smoldering thing going on. He walked with a dancer's loose-hipped gait and seemed to radiate readiness for sex or battle, whichever came first.

More than once, when he had me in a choke hold, I'd wondered what his hands would feel like in a more intimate touch. The first time that happened, it led to a panic attack and some very unsexy hyperventilating on my part. Henry helped me through those episodes by teaching me to fight back. It felt good not to be helpless anymore.

"Are we ready to do this?" Henry asked. "Bobbi, call up your ward. You two attack with everything you've got and we'll see how long super-girl can hold up."

Abilene smiled. Quinn showed me his teeth.

I sheathed myself in aether and found my fighting stance. "Bring it on."

An hour later, I guzzled my third bottle of gods' water. A ley-line ran under the coven and boosted aether in the local spring water. This magic fuel kept me going as the morning wore on to noon. I fought to hold my ward steady while Quinn and Abilene pelted me with aether bombs.

"Don't forget about your feet!" Henry called. "An arrow to the foot can take you out as easily as one to the heart!" I gritted my teeth and poured more aether into the lower section of my ward. "That's right. You've got this!"

Too bad he forgot his pompoms.

A personal ward was a tricky thing. It had to extend far enough to cover my movements, but not so far that it wasted aether. I'd never held one for so long.

Quinn channeled his firebug magic and lobbed another orb of flames. I let it glance off my shoulder, feeling only a mild burn. He alternated the magic assault by throwing rocks, so I could feel the difference between an aether attack and a physical weapon strike. I wasn't the only one tiring. An hour ago, his missiles had been the size of bowling balls, now they'd shrunk by half. They still hurt when they crashed into my ward.

"You're doing great," Abilene said. Her cheerfulness seemed to know no bounds. If I didn't have to concentrate so hard, I would have thrown something at her. Abilene's attacks were more insidious than her brother's. Instead of an outright assault, I could feel her aether poised like a corkscrew behind me, down at my ankle. With gentle pressure, she ground away at my protection. The strategic assault was annoying and kept my attention averted, even as I blocked another of Quinn's fireballs.

"Let's break for lunch." Every one of my muscles ached and a cramp nagged at my foot.

Quinn grinned. "Getting tired?" He tossed three more fireballs in quick succession. I blocked them, but they cost me. I lost focus and Abilene's aether drill dug into my ward.

I had to do something. With little energy left, my choices were limited.

"You're stuck in your head," Henry said, seeing my desperate attempt to hold up the ward. "There is aether all around you. Use it."

Once, I pulled aether from the ley-line and connected it to the core. It hadn't been easy. As a complete neophyte, I had only my strange attraction to the core to guide me. Could I do it again, tap into the ley-line to fuel my flagging ward? It would be like using a nuclear bomb to power a transistor radio. I'd have to finesse it, but Henry was right. In a real battle, I would need to grab aether where I could find it.

Ducking under another of Quinn's assaults, I used the movement to press my hands to the ground. Pulling back the aether fueling my ward—except for the protection from Abilene's grinding attack—I plunged it into the earth in one wild, desperate plea to the Lord and Lady.

My sensate practice paid off. Immediately, my aether connected with a stronger power that flooded all my faculties. It was a train rushing through my head, a hot drenching rain, a spicy tang on the back of my tongue, and the stench of burned hair all rolled into one massive flare of aether.

I reeled. This wasn't the aether signature of a ley-line. I tried to withdraw, but my magic latched on to the strange, dark power.

"No!" Henry's yell chimed faintly as the alien aether filled me with giddy strength.

Magic burned through my senses until it sizzled from my pores. My hands glowed with energy that zinged between my fingertips, sparking an aether explosion in mid-air.

Abilene screamed. I felt rather than saw her fall to the ground.

The eruption stretched like a sphincter and opened into a gaping maw. Magic streamed into it, a screaming river of power, horrifying and beautiful. I raised a hand to touch the shimmering ring hanging in the air before me.

Not a ring. A hole.

Through its rippling surface I spied another world full of red shadows, bright sunlight and rolling dunes.

Quinn's desperate face blocked the view. His hands gripped my shoulders, and he spat words I couldn't hear inside my bubble of aether. Then it popped.

Sound, light and pain blasted me.

Oh, Lady, *it hurt*.

I used too much aether, and the hole drew more, pulling it from my veins like lifeblood.

"You have to close it!" Quinn yelled.

"I…I can't." My stomach folded on itself, and I crumpled, arms pressed into the lashing pain.

Quinn shouted a spell. He grabbed the hole's gaping edge. It wobbled like a soap bubble. His hands glowed as he pulled downward. I knew Quinn's aether as well as my own, and I could feel his power burning away. Sweat streaked his face as he struggled to pull the lips of the gap together.

I could do nothing but watch in fear and dread. He was using too much aether! I reached a hand to help, but had nothing left to give.

Quinn strained. The power of one man fought against a tear in the universe. It was impossible. It was suicide. His jaw bulged, and the tips of his fingers turned black, but he didn't let go.

He dragged the edges together. One inch…two. A primal yell burst from his chest. His eyes rolled back and he fell. His arms and legs jerked in a seizure, and he lay motionless.

The hole still gaped open, but Quinn's intervention severed my connection to it.

I fell to the ground, forced my shaking arms to bear my weight and leaned over Quinn. He was breathing. I rested my head on his chest and listened to the erratic beating of his heart.

"What in the hell happened here?" said a sharp voice. I looked up. Gavin's angry glare fell on me and Quinn, then on Abilene and Henry, both unconscious in the grass. A yawning tear in the fabric of space hung like a disembodied eye above us.

"We had an accident."

Affliction

The tang of burned magic clung to my clothes. Late on Tuesday, I fell asleep fully dressed and woke the next day near noon, groggy, sweaty and tense. I sniffed myself and wanted to head straight for the shower, but I needed to check on Quinn first. That would mean going through Jane.

The High Priestess of Hidden Coven wasn't happy with me. My little magic battle practice caused a rip to open between dimensions. Yes, an actual rip. In dimensions.

Jane had posted two Paragon knights to guard the opening. I didn't like to think of what might come through. There were infinite worlds it could have opened to. It could be a realm where purple butterflies ruled. Or a realm with sentient trees made of spun sugar. Or a demon realm filled with bloodthirsty monsters.

Lady, let it be butterflies.

I threw on clothes and headed out.

The explosion of magic had knocked Abilene, Henry and Quinn out, and when I finally gave in to my exhaustion, Quinn still hadn't recovered. He slept in Abilene's room, where his sister and mother could keep an eye on him.

The walk from his cottage took me straight through the village square. Witches stopped their chores to watch me pass. No one spoke, not even Olga, who stood at the cart laden with her famous hot cross buns. She nodded but offered nothing more.

Last summer, I lived with these people for a week. At Jane's insistence, I shadowed many of them, learning their arts and enjoying their simple way of life. I saved them from Koro. But none of that mattered. I was a pariah now. Once again, my ignorance endangered everyone I cared about. I opened a hole in the universe. By the Lady's grace, who did that?

I ducked my head, ignoring whispers and stares as I hurried toward Jane's house.

Henry and Gavin drank coffee at the kitchen table. Henry's swarthiness tinged toward green rather than golden this morning. Dark shadows ringed his eyes. He smiled and raised his cup in salute. Gavin looked grim.

"They're upstairs," he said.

I headed for Abilene's room. The two women sat beside Quinn's bed. One silver-haired and one raven-haired, both silent and straight-backed. Abilene held Quinn's hand. Her haggard face showed the effects of a sleepless night.

I hung back in the hallway, an intruder in a family moment.

"Tell me again what happened," Jane said.

"I'm not sure." Abilene's voice hitched. "I think she tried to draw aether from the environment, or maybe from the ley-line. Then…nothing. I blacked out."

Jane said something very unmistress-like followed by, "That bloody fool. Doesn't she know how dangerous environmental magic can be?"

"No, she doesn't." Gavin pushed through the door, dragging me along. I hadn't heard him come up the stairs. "How would she know, when you've done nothing to teach her?"

I fought not to squirm under Jane's glittering gaze.

"I was under the impression that the Paragon knight was teaching her."

"Henry is a battle mage. He can't show her everything, and you know it. Every child in this coven has a dozen teachers. Why should it be different for Bobbi?"

Mother and son continued to toss arguments back and forth. Abilene fought for both sides, but I tuned them out when I got my first good look at Quinn lying in the bed.

He looked dead. His bare shoulders were shrunken against the pillow, his face grey and slack. By the gods, had I done that to him? Had my ignorance and incompetence sapped him so completely? Dark hair fell across his forehead. My hand shook as I reached to brush it aside, revealing the jagged scar snaking into his eyebrow, a trophy from his battle with Koro at the cemetery.

At least his skin was cool and dry. No fever, no sweat.

"What's wrong with him? Why won't he wake up?" My voice cut across the argument and everyone fell silent. I looked from one face to another. Abilene stared at her pale hands. Jane glared at me. Gavin shoved his hands in his pockets, shrugging his shoulders.

"Quinn's recovery will take longer," he said.

"The blast didn't knock him out." I tried to piece together the events, but they blurred in my mind.

"Tell me what happened," Jane demanded.

I took a shuddering breath. "I remember plunging my aether into the ley-line. At least I thought it was the ley-line."

I didn't think Jane could pinch her lips together any tighter but she did.

"And then…an explosion. Abilene fell immediately. I didn't see Henry, but Quinn stood farther away. He was fine. Until…" What had he done? "He tried to close the tear. And he just fell."

"My son has mawr," Jane said. "Did you know?"

"Mawr? I don't even know what that is."

Jane pinned me with her gaze as if trying to pull the truth from me by sheer will.

"That wasn't a ley-line you tapped into. Somehow, you found the aether of another dimension. It must be your unique heritage that drew you to it." Kudos to Jane for finding the politically correct term for demon blood.

"I'm sorry. I didn't know."

"Yes, well that's a problem for another day. For now, I'm going to try and clean up the mess you made. With any luck, I can close that hole before anything really nasty comes through." She turned and left.

"What's mawr?" I asked. Gavin slumped in a chair.

"It's a mystical disease, contracted through a curse."

"A curse? Did I do that, with the explosion?"

Gavin shook his head. "Quinn's been suffering from it for years. He got it when we were working in Haiti. Someone hired a voodoo priest to curse him."

"I don't understand. Why hasn't he found a way to break the curse before now?"

"The curse is only a vessel for the contagion," Abilene said. "It delivers the disease then goes dormant. The disease is hurting him now. It drains his aether too quickly. That's what the necklace is for." She pointed to the petrified cockroach laying on his bare chest. "It's an aether vessel for when his reserves run dry."

By the gods, he lobbed aether missiles at me all morning. Why didn't he stop?

"When he tried to close the rift, he overdid it, is that what you're saying?"

"Yes," Gavin said.

"So replenish him. Feed him your gods' water or whatever!"

"It's not that simple." Abilene smiled sadly. "He pushed way past his limits. There may be internal damage—brain damage."

I shut my eyes. This couldn't be happening.

"We won't know until he wakes up," she said. We all understood the last unspoken part of that sentence.

If he wakes up.

Gavin and Abilene left to find breakfast. I wasn't hungry. My stomach churned with suppressed emotions. I sat by Quinn's bed wondering why I wasted so much time finding my way back to him. I held one of his hands, my thumb rubbing the edge of his palm with nervous energy as if I could rub the life back into him.

His chest rose and fell in slow waves. Too slow. Other than that, he lay utterly still. My gaze snagged on the odd bug talisman. Quinn once told me it was a protection charm. All this time, he'd been suffering in silence. I touched the bug with the tip of one finger. It was startlingly realistic and pretty, if creepy. An inch long, the roach's chitin body shone purple and green in the sunlight streaming through the window. How often had I seen Quinn grip it, seeking nourishment for his waning aether?

"You didn't eat," Abilene said from the doorway. She carried a tea tray. "At least drink something. If you're not careful, you'll run your aether dry too."

I nodded and accepted the cup of steaming tea.

"There must be a physician somewhere who could help him," I said. "Maybe we can call one of the other covens."

Abilene shook her head. "There's no cure. It's amazing he's kept himself alive this long." Her eyes glistened with unshed tears.

I moved aside. "I'm so sorry. Here I am hogging his bedside. Do you want to sit here?" Quinn adored his baby sister. Maybe her presence would win through the veil of consciousness and wake him.

"You shouldn't have come back." Abilene's normally animated expression turned grim and flat. I caught a glimpse of the hard woman she might become, the woman Jane was grooming her to be. "I'm sorry." She shook her head, and the old Abilene returned. "It's just that he seemed to finally be getting over you. But I think he needs you now, more than me. He might not admit it, but he missed you."

I nodded, letting my guilt be the instrument of my self-flagellation.

Shouting from downstairs brought us to our feet.

Jane came out of her study and met us in our mad dash to the kitchen where a young witch bounced from foot to foot.

"Something came through the rift!"

BATTALION

I heard the beast before i saw it. A high-pitched roar, like a lion trying to speak whale, echoed up from the forest. Witches ran in every direction. Some had weapons—pitchforks, fireplace irons, knives—others only bare hands and magic.

Henry and the remaining Paragon knights joined us as we ran through the village square. At the trailhead leading to the practice yard, a creature jumped from the trees. Henry cut it down with his sword before I even got a good look at it. A sword would have been a great idea. I had only a knife and my scattered wits to defend me.

Creatures jumped from tree to tree. A few were ape-like with purple leathery skin and long arms. Others scuttled through the underbrush. They were furred, scaled or winged. A fat black beast resembling a razorback boar lunged at us. Henry's training came back to me in a flash, and I kicked it in the head, putting everything I had into that strike. A shock of pain burst up my leg. The beast barely paused long enough for Henry to stick a blade in its eye.

Henry winked. "That's two for me."

I hefted my knife and smiled grimly. "I'm just getting started."

The beasts seemed more intent on fleeing than attacking. We ran on, stopping only to cut down the creatures stumbling into our path. Someone had lit the torches surrounding the practice field, not for light but protection. The flames activated the sacred circle and the air was heavy with charged aether.

A colossal brute stood beside the rift, flexing his massive arms in preparation for a fight. On the other side of the iridescent doorway, a sandstorm blew across the alien desert. More small creatures slipped through the rift and ran for the trees. The brute roared.

"What is that thing?" I asked.

"A minor demon," Abilene said. Minor? The beast stood a full three feet taller than any human. Curved horns crested his head. Bony plating layered his neck, and his arms were molded with sinew. A face with bulging eyes, protruding brow and thick skin hanging in folds turned toward us. He opened his muzzle and bellowed again. Finger-length fangs dripped with spit over thick black lips.

Above the uproar, a shrill noise like a drove of pigs all squealing at once shred my nerves. Someone threw a pitchfork, but it only clattered off the beast's bony armor. He turned to assess the threat, revealing his back. The plating ended at his shoulders, and two rows of heads protruded from beside his spine. No more than hollow-eyed skulls, the gaping mouths were the source of the piercing squeals.

Jane stumbled into the clearing. The long run left her breathless.

"That's a berserker," she said. "See those heads embedded in its back? They're running the show. Like parasites. They've taken over the demon and driven him mad."

Perfect. An insane minor demon.

Abilene rushed over to support her mother with Gavin not far behind.

"How do we kill it?" he asked.

"We don't," Jane said. "As long as one of those skulls is alive, it will force the beast to keep moving. We have to push it back through the rift and close it. Until then it can't leave this field."

Colonel Donner appeared and started barking orders. Two firebug knights lobbed bombs at the demon. A circle of witches protected them with a reinforced ward. Another young witch, just a boy, lunged at the demon and jabbed his foot with a spear. The demon turned and backhanded him across the field. The knights took the advantage. Fire exploded on one of the skulls and the keening shrieks ramped up. Abilene joined the firebugs, lobbing her flaming missiles.

"Can I help you close the rift?" I asked Jane. She hadn't seemed confident about closing it this morning.

"Just get that thing into the hole." She walked off with a storm in her eyes.

I grabbed two women lingering on the edge of the melee.

"Can you produce a personal ward?" One woman nodded, eyes huge with fear. "Good. Follow your mistress and make sure nothing happens to her." The witches ran after Jane.

I turned to the fight. Witches and knights attacked the beast from all sides, but it shrugged off their strikes. A man with a glowing blue sword had the best success, breaking the tough hide with one strike. I recognized him. Kirk was the blacksmith I'd spent time with during my first stay at the coven. His broad shoulders bulged as he swung the massive sword. He took a hit from the demon but shook it off. Sweat flew from his red curls. Black blood oozed from several wounds on the beast's arms and legs. Kirk was trying to bleed him out. The demon tired of dodging the sword and grabbed the blade in his giant hand. Smoke curled up from within his grip. Kirk hung on and the demon flung him backward. He landed twenty-feet away and didn't get up.

Others took up the attack. Gavin fought with his flora magic, calling vines from deep within the earth to bind him, but the demon simply ripped the ropes from the ground and tossed them off. Gavin was undeterred. He kept at it, coiling foliage around the beast's legs.

Henry teleported behind him, slashed at the screaming skulls, and ported a few yards away to hack at his other flank. This attack-and-dash strategy kept the demon guessing and drew his attention away from Gavin.

Kinetic witches lobbed stones that did little damage. The knights, led by Colonel Donner, struck at him with their swords. The firebugs ramped up their assault, but the demon learned to keep his back turned away from the flames. The skulls let out a new scream—a sound so high and fierce it raked along my nerve endings. And it had power. The sound seized me, and for an instant, I couldn't move. Others around me were also affected, and stood immobilized. The demon lashed out, swatting witches and knights like flies.

A firebomb hit the skulls and their sickening power released me. I fell and rolled as the demon swung his fist my way. Blood coated my throat, but I couldn't stop to find its source. All my training seemed useless against this monster. I could kick a man in the face, but what good was that against an armored giant? I had no doubt it would hurt me more than him. But Henry also taught me to fight smart.

I dove under the demon's leg and jabbed upward with my knife, trying to penetrate the softer muscle behind his knee. He roared and swiped at me. The tip of his bony fingers clipped my shoulder, and I spun, dropping my blade. My arm went numb. Another flying body hit my knees and I tumbled over it, landing with my hands on soft flesh. I recoiled at the slack face staring skyward. Another dead witch, eyes sightless, head twisted too far to the right.

Above me, bombs flared as the firebugs continued their onslaught. The battle raged on. The air stank of burned aether. No more vines hindered the beast and Gavin hung limply in Henry's arms. A small band of witches protected Abilene, but one of the firebug knights lay unconscious at her feet. Either his aether was spent, or the demon had broached the ward.

I couldn't see Jane in the chaos. I hoped she made it to the rift and was completing the ritual to close it.

Desperation fueled my limbs. I grabbed a discarded fireplace iron and lunged at the demon. His great fist rushed at my head. I ducked and came up facing the enormous back covered in skulls. Mouths gaped and fire burned in those hollow eyes. The screaming magic slammed into me, stopping my breath for a moment. I swung the iron and it glanced off the demon's scales. The backlash rang up my arm, and I dropped my weapon. I needed to hit the beast with something stronger.

Henry taught me some fire magic. It was a tricky art. Aether burned with a wick right to the soul, and I could easily go up like a torch if I lost control. In practice, I could call up flames, but I had yet to hold onto a stable fireball. If I was going to do this, I had one shot. Witches kept the demon busy with assaults from all sides. I called fire to my fingers. They tingled with the gathering aether and I let it pool in my hands, willing it to coalesce into flame. The ball wouldn't form. I struggled to hold onto the aether, but it started to slip away. In desperation, I grabbed the fire iron, plunged all that gathered power into it, and swung for the bleachers.

White hot magic sizzled up the iron like molten steel. It slammed into the demon's back. One of the skulls exploded in a flash. The iron's curved tip bit into flesh, driving the burning aether deep. The demon screamed. He flung himself sideways, craning to reach the burning pain in his back. I hung on, twisting the iron to dig deeper. Flesh smoldered.

A calloused hand grabbed my throat and slammed me to the ground. Air burst from my lungs. Black spots clouded my eyes and I sucked in pain. Crippling, searing pain. The demon loomed over me, pressing his weight on my chest. His eyes burned red. Saliva hung on the tusk-sized teeth. A drop of spit stretched and fell—oh, so slowly—to splatter on my cheek. It burned. He roared, blasting me with the stench of his gullet.

This was it. The massive teeth would close on my throat and rip out my life. My hands rose to protect my face as if those thin sticks could block a demon's wrath. My fingers latched onto his neck, flimsy digits useless against his armored skin, except a shock of power jolted up my arm. The demon flinched.

Oh, Lord and Lady...

Once, I drank the life from a wraith with my touch. Did I dare attempt it with a demon?

I did.

With both hands, I grabbed a spiny protrusion jutting from his collar bone and pulled with my will.

Foul aether poured into me, tar black and tasting of charcoal. Power filled me, exhilarating and horrifying all at once. Somewhere far off, the demon roared. His pain became my pleasure. I reveled in it, sucking his life away. I lost touch with my body and all its aches and frailties.

The magic continued to swell. It was too much! Too much aether. Too much darkness. And it kept coming. I couldn't shut it off, couldn't let go.

The demon screamed as a fireball hit the parasites on his back. I screamed for his pain and became one with the demon, bound by our shared agony and wrapped in the aether I sucked from him.

"Bobbi, let go!"

Henry yanked me away. My grip slipped. The demon fell to his knees. Fire lashed his back. The screaming skulls died one by one, burned up from the inside. As their cries faded, the demon toppled face-first into the dirt. A dozen witches ran forward to hack at his body.

"Are you okay?" Henry's concerned eyes drew me in. I could see right into his head through those brown orbs. If I reached through them, I could easily snuff out his life. So easy. I had the power. It suffused me. I had only to touch him…

"NO!" My voice thundered like a god's.

I didn't want the power. It wasn't mine and if I kept it, it would twist me into a shadow of the demon.

I thrust my hands into the earth as if it were soft sand and released the aether. Magic streamed from me. The ground buckled and tore open. A chasm yawned at my feet and the demon's corpse fell into it. As the last wisps of aether drained from me, I crumpled.

I had nothing left.

"Well, you made a fine mess." Jane peered down at me. "We have to salt and burn the corpse."

I rolled to look in the hole. The demon smoldered in ruin, at least twenty feet down. I fell onto my back and stared at the impossibly blue sky.

REPERCUSSIONS

It was all my fault. Bodies lay broken around the rift and the new crater. A dozen of them didn't move. Others moaned, shook or cried. I sat in the middle of this carnage, too weary to move, too horrified to look away. So much death. Useless death. People who had been alive this morning—eating breakfast, maybe complaining about strong coffee or sneaking an extra spoonful of jam—were now dead because of me.

Colonel Donner's commands switched from battle tactics to triage. Jane stepped over a body and turned to the rift. The head of her staff blazed blue as she began to chant. A sudden wind blasted through the field, and then the air hung heavy like pressure before a storm.

"Lord and Lady, hear my call!" Jane plunged her staff into the rift. The hole shattered, then crumpled around it, closing with a loud pop. Jane studied the space where the rift had been.

"Is it closed?" Abilene asked. She swayed on her feet but looked otherwise unharmed.

"It's patched," Jane said. "I don't know how long it will hold. Long enough for us to find a permanent fix, I hope." She turned to me. "What did you do?"

"What do you mean?"

"At the end with that iron? You hurt him somehow."

"I'm not sure," I said shakily. "I stabbed him with it."

"You did more than that," Abilene said. "You flared fire magic at the same time. I sensed it. You pushed aether up the iron. It was amazing!"

I shook my head, not wanting praise when people lay dead because of my mistake. Hurting the demon didn't make up for that.

"And the crater?" Jane arched her eyebrow.

I shrugged. "I had pent up aether. Needed to release it." I didn't want them to know I drank demon aether. I had enough suspicious looks in the village as it was.

Jane stared at me as if her glare could make me confess my sins. Another couple of seconds and it might have. Then a knight limped by with a dazed woman leaning heavily on his arm. He asked about housing for the wounded and Abilene left with them to set up accommodations.

Jane watched me with her thin lips and near-black eyes. Colonel Donner chose that moment to inspect the rift site. He ran his hands over the space where the hole had been and nodded.

"Nice work, Mistress."

"It's not permanent. We'll need to ward this area until I can find a way to close it for good."

"What about the other creatures that came through?" I asked.

"We'll hunt them down," Donner said. "I've already called in more knights."

"But they're stuck on this side of the ward, right?" That would make rounding them up easier.

"Not necessarily." Jane frowned. "The ward lets animals through. And we've never dealt with creatures from another realm. No telling how the ward will react."

I sighed. My body ached from a dozen wounds. It would be dark soon. "I guess we'd better start hunting then."

"Leave it to the knights," Jane snapped. "You're coming with me."

The core pulsed with energy. Dark tendrils of its magic sought me out as we came into the clearing with two tall cairns. The core's eager magic could easily overpower me, and I was already weak from battle. I acknowledged the probe but didn't invite it to connect with me and the tendrils withdrew.

The sun hid behind a cloud, plunging us into shadow and I shivered.

Thankfully, we weren't visiting the core today. Jane thought it would be a good idea if I met with Siranda, the coven's seer. I wasn't convinced of the rationality of this plan. The last time I met Siranda, she foresaw—with much screaming and clawing—that I would kill her.

I'm not a murderer. I don't even kill spiders when I find them in my house. But my ineptitude with magic, coupled with a deep reserve of aether that I was only beginning to grasp, left me with the real possibility that my actions might one day cause a death.

I already had. Witches lay dead in the practice yard because I'd opened a portal to some demon hell. It wasn't a big stretch to believe I would be the cause of Siranda's death. So the prospect of facing her again left me with mixed feelings. She scared the pants off me, and her self-imposed living conditions disturbed my peace of mind, but if she could shed any light on our current situation, I would face those discomforts.

Gavin met us at the door to Siranda's cairn with a frown and a bandaged head wound.

"Don't upset her." Gavin was protective of his seer.

"Sure. That's like telling the red flag not to bait the bull."

"I mean it, Bobbi."

I held up my hands in submission.

"I have no plans to antagonize her, but I can't help it if she hates me."

"Let's just get this over with," Jane said.

Inside the cairn, Siranda slumped against the sloping wall. Huge dark eyes peered through greasy hair hanging in her face. She stared at the plastered walls and ceiling that writhed with animated drawings in glowing reds and purples. She frowned as if considering something important, lifted a hand and touched the low ceiling where it curved into the wall. Another figure erupted from her fingertip to dance across the plaster. The constant movement of the drawings ebbed and flowed like a tide.

I'd seen Siranda's unique brand of magic before, but it still left me queasy. I stayed behind Gavin, hoping Siranda wouldn't see me, but Jane grabbed my arm and pulled me front and center.

The seer blinked and smiled. "You are the crooked man."

Her words provoked a memory, but it faded before I could grasp it. "What?"

"You are the crooked man!" She rose like a specter, her voice filling the small space. Gavin stepped forward and trapped her clawing hands before they struck me. He made soothing, clucking sounds and Siranda wilted against the wall.

"Can she tell us anything about the rift?" Jane asked.

Gavin tried to calm her. Siranda muttered and cursed, rubbing her hands together as if they were cold. He laid a blanket across her legs. She fussed and tossed it aside. I was struck by Siranda's similarity to his mother, Stacy. Gavin spent much of his time easing two women who would never be at ease.

"Siranda, do you know how to close the rift? Can you see it?" Gavin's tone suggested a father urging a toddler to eat her vegetables.

Siranda whimpered and pulled her lanky hair. We waited a long minute.

The drawings on the walls jittered, and my stomach turned sour.

"She can't help us," Jane finally said.

Siranda threw back her head and laughed, a good old witchy cackle that raised the hair on my arms. Her eyes latched onto Jane and the formidable witch actually took a step back.

Siranda's voice fell into a husky, masculine tone. "Forsooth, the cry of the banshee be thy touchstone."

Jane paled and fled outside.

"What was that?" I asked.

Gavin shrugged. "You'd better go see. I'll sit with Siranda for a moment."

Outside, I found a remarkable sight: Jane Smith unnerved. I didn't think it could happen. She was always so calm and unflappable. Even when she lost her shit, she did it with panache. I'd seen her kill a man, stab him in the back a dozen times, but she looked formidable doing it. The woman standing in the last bit of sunlight was diminished. And scared.

"What did Siranda say?" I asked.

"I thought we had more time." She shook her head, then turned a dark stare on me. I saw her resemblance to Quinn in those nearly black eyes.

"It was a line from a grimoire." She leaned against the stone wall. "Part of the spell we used to call Koro."

Lord and Lady, and all the gods I can muster. Why did everything come back to Koro?

"Can he use the rift to come through?" There were rules about demons manifesting in our world, complicated rituals and laws of magic that were logical only from a twisted perception.

"I don't know." Jane looked thoughtful. "The berserker isn't a full-blood demon. He's more of a mongrel. I'm not sure if a full-blood could even exist in our world. Our magic is still too weak. But if he does come through, his very existence here will shatter our natural laws."

For years, the ley-lines had been swelling, spilling magic through cracks in Earth's crust. This excess power allowed witches and other supernatural beings to flourish, but would it sustain a full-blood demon? I learned to accept that anything was possible.

"Aren't the demon realms endless?" I grasped at straws now. "Just because there's a door doesn't mean it opens in Koro's world, right?"

Jane nodded. "You've been doing your homework."

"Henry's a good teacher." Neither of us remarked on my ill-spent week trying to learn magic under Jane's tutelage.

"It's true. The demon realms are vast, even endless perhaps." Her eyes took on a far-away look as if she remembered things best left alone. "But we have no idea how demons communicate with each other. Or what kinds of magic they have protecting their realms. For all we know, your little rift could have set off a cascade of reactions."

We let that idea gather momentum for a few minutes. Then Jane did an about-face.

"Do you have any idea why Siranda called you the crooked man?"

"No, but I feel like I should." The echo of a sing-song voice rang in my mind, just beyond my reach.

"It's probably more of her ranting," Jane said. "But her message to me was clear. Siranda thinks the answer to closing the rift is in the grimoire."

"It's a mistake to take Siranda so literally," Gavin said, coming from the cairn.

"It's not a mistake." Jane's lips were planted firmly. "I've been researching ways to close the rift all day and the only lead I have is that grimoire."

"But where is it?" I asked.

"Your mother had it last," Jane said. "As far as I know it perished in the fire."

I closed my eyes and felt faint. This day just kept coming back to sucker punch me. I didn't need to ask which fire. Only one had changed my life. When I was six, my parents and younger sister died when our house burned to the ground. Only I survived.

"Do you think it's worth going back to the old house?" Gavin asked. My family lived in a stone cottage in upstate New York. Today, people would say we lived off the grid, but back then the grid was less important to everyday life.

"Paragon agents searched the entire property," I said.

"But the agents don't have your memories." Jane's regal composure returned. "Hannah knew how important the grimoire was. If she hid it on site, she would have made sure you could find it. It's your legacy, after all."

"You think I should go look for it?" I wasn't crazy about that idea.

"I'm coming with you." We all turned at the sound of Quinn's voice.

MEDICATION

The edges of Quinn's vision darkened. He leaned a hand on the cairn, trying to make it seem casual. No one needed to know what it cost him to walk from Jane's house. He felt like a truck had been sitting on him for two days. He'd come through the practice yard and seen the destruction firsthand. While the head of security slept, the coven had almost been destroyed. He'd be damned if his weakness would stand in his way again.

"Get me up to speed, and we'll leave first thing in the morning."

"You will do no such thing." Jane crossed her arms. Now that his mother knew about his illness, she wouldn't let him out of her sight. Bobbi looked like she'd been mauled by a bear, but the pity in her eyes told him he looked much worse.

Taking a deep breath, he prepared his arguments. He would take every precaution. The vestals could charge his roach amulet tonight so he'd have an aether reserve. They'd stop at Emmett's for directions to the old house and get a swig of his aether boosting tincture.

None of those safeguards would sway his mother.

"I'm going, and unless you plan to shackle me to the bed, you can't stop me."

He might have swayed a bit as he spoke.

Jane glared. Gavin looked away, but maybe—just maybe—he saw a spark of gratitude in Bobbi's eyes.

They arrived at Emmett's farm before sunrise. Molly, Emmett's new wife, took one look at their haggard expressions and insisted they stay for breakfast. She tempted them with fresh muffins and hot beverages until they gave in.

"Someone ransacked the tack room in the barn on Sunday," Emmett said as he filled his plate with fruit. "I'm still cleaning up the mess."

"That's the same day I was attacked at home." Bobbi picked at her food.

"You think there's a connection?" Quinn piled jam on his toast. He needed the sugar boost.

"I don't know. But it wasn't a mundane who broke into my house and store. And he was looking for something specific."

"William Fain broke in here last fall too," Emmett said. Bobbi flinched at the mention of her would-be rapist's name. Quinn suppressed the urge to reach for her. Bobbi hadn't recovered from her last encounter with Fain, and Quinn's failure to protect her stood like a glass wall between them. She didn't need him imposing his desires on her right now. It might make him feel better, but he could wait.

And what if she never turns to you again? The little voice in his head asked that question a lot lately.

"We thought it might be about the grimoire then," Quinn said. "But we can't be sure. All we have to go on is a vague reference from Siranda."

"You think this is a wild goose chase?" Emmett asked.

Quinn shrugged. "I've traveled farther on less of a hunch. It won't hurt to check things out. If we find the grimoire, great. If not, we'll find another way to seal the rift."

Emmett grunted. "I'm sure that between Jane and the Paragon mages, they'll figure it out."

Quinn was relieved that Colonel Donner and his knights offered to stay on at the coven until the rift could be permanently sealed. A security officer who fainted in battle wasn't much use to anyone. The knights would do a better job of beating anything coming through the rift. That brought up another nagging thought. The symptoms of his illness were affecting his performance. Maybe it was time to pass the job of security chief to someone else. Long ago, he'd vowed not to let this disease rule his life, but neither would he let his pride endanger those in his care.

Bobbi's fork clattered to the table.

"I'm so sorry." She pressed her hands to her eyes and took a long, shaky breath. "This is my fault. All of it."

Molly bustled over from the stove. "Nonsense!" She knelt by Bobbi's side and grasped her hands. "You can't blame yourself."

"I opened the rift!"

"It was an accident."

"And what about Koro? Somehow, this is all about him. He won't ever stop looking for me. I should go away…"

"None of that talk," Emmett said gruffly. "I knew about Koro when you came to us as a child. I didn't hesitate to keep you with us then, and I won't do it now."

Molly nodded in agreement.

The kitchen filled with silence broken only by the scraping of forks while they let Bobbi find her composure.

"What can you tell us about the grimoire," Quinn finally asked. Jane already gave them a description of the leather-bound tome, but he wanted to hear it from Molly too. Grimoires, especially the really old ones, could take on odd characteristics. It wasn't unheard of for one to shift its appearance for different people.

Molly's eyes closed to slits as she remembered. "It was a long time ago. Jane and Hannah handled it the most. Honestly, it gave me the creeps. But I remember the symbol burned into the leather cover." She took a small pad and pen from the pocket in her apron and drew a rough triangle with wavy lines. "Like three intertwined snakes with the head of each curled around the tail of another and an eye in the middle."

Quinn and Bobbi studied the image, and then he tucked it in his pocket.

After breakfast, Emmett wrote out directions to the old house that lay deep in the woods at the foothills of the Adirondacks.

"There's not much left," Emmett said, "just the stone foundation and chimney."

It was a long shot. They all knew it. But they had to start the search somewhere.

Bobbi turned to Molly. "You'll take care of the Woolery for me? We may be gone for several days."

"No worries." Molly smiled.

"I'm sorry I left you with a mess to clean up. I guess I panicked."

After finding her store in ruins, Bobbi had locked the door and left for the coven without a word. The old crones in the knitting circle were probably jonesing for their yarn fix.

"I've got it covered," Molly said. "Just get this done and be safe about it."

They rose to leave, but Quinn pulled Emmett aside.

"Could I have a bottle of your tincture?"

Emmett's bushy eyebrows lowered.

"You have another attack?"

Quinn nodded.

"Come with me. I've been working on something better."

Quinn followed him, leaving Molly and Bobbi to pack a cooler with food. In a back room, Emmett had set up a laboratory. The equipment was antiquated—Bunsen burners, beakers and an old microscope—but spotless.

"I decided to get back to my alchemy," Emmett said. "I've been tinkering, and I think I found a better solution than the tincture."

The old med-mage listened to Quinn's heart, took his blood pressure and peered at the whites of his eyes.

"The attack was bad, wasn't it?" he asked. Quinn shrugged. "Save your macho courage for the ladies, boy. Tell me what happened."

Quinn sighed. "I tried to close the rift after hours of battle magic practice with Bobbi."

Emmett shook his head. "Lord and Lady save me from young men who think they're invincible. Hold out your arm." He nicked Quinn's forearm and let a few drops of blood fall into a crystal cup. The liquid turned pink, then faintly purple.

"You're nearly dry again." Emmett prepared a syringe. Quinn flinched when he injected it into his shoulder, but warmth spread through him, much faster than the oral tincture.

Emmett held up a device like a self-injecting needle used for allergy emergencies. "I rigged up a few of these. They're portable and easy to use. One shot should bring you back from the brink. You get that thing charged up?" He pointed to the bug talisman.

Quinn nodded. "The vestals did it for me last night."

"That'll have to do, but I must warn you against using your magic on this trip. The disease is progressing faster than I thought. Mawr takes time to ramp up, like a steam train. But once it gets going, there's no stopping it."

He held Quinn's eyes with his piercing stare. "And your train has left the station."

EXPLORATION

It was a long and winding road.

No, I couldn't think that without hearing music.

We drove one of the coven's Jeeps deep into the Adirondacks. Spring foliage sprinkled the bare trees. The scenery didn't stir any memories in me, but the only landmarks were the odd fork in the road.

"I hope you packed an extra dilithium crystal," I said, hanging on to my seat as Quinn rounded another bend without slowing. "You drive like we have Klingons on our tail."

Quinn pressed his hand to his heart. "She's beautiful and references Star Trek. Be still my heart."

The banter felt good. The first hour of the drive passed in near silence, but as the sun rose and the coffee kicked in, we slowly regained the comfort we once enjoyed together. I could almost imagine that William Fain had never been.

Almost.

"This is it." Quinn turned onto an even bumpier lane. Grass grew between faint tire tracks. The Jeep lurched from side to side and the two large cups of coffee—which seemed a good idea at the time—sloshed in my stomach. The road ended at a hill bordered by hedges. We left the camping gear in the car and hiked up for a view of the site.

"Does any of this look familiar to you?" Quinn asked.

I shook my head. At the top of the rise, the trees cleared and we looked into a small valley. A high noon sun touched a pile of field stones on the valley's far side—the remnants of my childhood home.

I shivered and not from the cold. I had a bad feeling about this place even though my rational mind knew there was nothing to fear from an old heap of stones.

For a moment, I heard my sister calling Bobbi. The nickname was the only thing I retained from that old life. I had no memory of the fire and only vague impressions of my first family. Emmett had only recently filled me in on the details.

A man named Edward Wallis set the fire and took me. He kept me for three weeks, dodging Paragon agents who pursued us. It felt strange to know these things happened to me and left nothing but a black hole in my mind. What did Edward Wallis do to me in those three weeks? Had it been so traumatizing I blocked it? Or did he simply feed me grilled cheese and dump me in front of the TV, actions so mundane they made no impression on my young mind? Surely, I was distraught, crying for my mother, scared, or tired from running for weeks on end. Something blocked those memories, and pulling away the obstruction wouldn't be pretty.

I rubbed the side of my head.

"I should have some kind of epiphany standing here, but I don't."

Quinn squeezed my arm. I tensed and he pulled his hand away.

Damn. Why did I keep the distance between us? Why couldn't I let things go back to normal?

"Let's make camp and we'll explore. Something is bound to come back to you." Quinn headed down the hill. I watched his retreating back, thinking this trip had many possibilities for disaster.

We set up the tent in the valley, as far from the ruins as possible. After a quick lunch of sandwiches and cold coffee, we began our search for the grimoire.

"It's probably not in the house," Quinn said. "Paragon agents went over it after the fire, but I think we should start there."

I agreed. The pile of broken stones called to me, and I couldn't do anything else until we searched it.

We stumbled over rocks and dips in the ground until we stood beside the crumbling chimney. A blackened hearth opened like a raw wound at its base. The house's foundation and part of one wall still stood. I studied these remains, not sure what we were looking for—an obvious clue, a sign pointing *this way to treasure,* or a fallen stone revealing a hiding place in the hearth. We found nothing.

Standing by what must have been the front door, I couldn't get over the bleakness of the place. Some stones showed charring but most were drab grey and brown, blending into the dirt. I stepped inside the foundation.

Something felt off. I couldn't sense any aether here, not even the ever-present whiff of wildlife and dormant foliage. I turned to see the rest of the foundation. A wide swath of earth circled it. No weeds grew through the stones. No vines crept up the chimney.

"Nothing's growing here. It's been over twenty years. The vegetation should be covering this site."

"Mage fire," Quinn said. "The house was torched with it. Nothing will grow here for several decades yet. I have the original Paragon photos from the day after the fire in my car, if you want to see them. The ground was black as coal around the house."

Henry taught me about mage fire, the blending of normal flame with galvanic fire, a truly dark art. A normal fireball could kill, but mage fire went beyond death. It consumed anything organic, leaving nothing behind, not even bone. The remains of my parents and sister were here, mingled with the dirt where they died.

I felt the eerie chill of unseen eyes watching us. Maybe the spirits of Hannah and Ben Cole guarded this place.

My legs were suddenly restless. "Let's scout the site."

Quinn watched me. In the afternoon light, a scowl overshadowed his eyes. He wanted to shield me from the discomfort of poking into my sad past, but he didn't know how. I didn't either.

"Are you up to this?" he asked.

"I'm fine. I just need to move a bit."

We tramped around the valley, stumbling upon a small shed overgrown with vines. Quinn tried to open the door, but the rotten wood broke off in his hand. He peered inside.

"Might be worth a closer look. I'll need the axe from the car."

While I waited for him, I circled the shed. My feet sunk into the ground, still wet from spring thaw, and I stepped over a tumble of stones that might have once been a wall.

An image flashed in my mind. Someone crouched in a garden, wearing a floppy straw hat. The face turned to me, a solid handsome face. Yes, I remembered the garden, my father's pride and joy. I tried to imagine neat rows of vegetables growing here. Emmett said my parents set up this home away from all civilization, hoping Koro's agents wouldn't find us. I guessed that meant we grew much of our food.

A large wooden cross stood at the far end of the garden, tall enough to poke through the brush grown up around it. As I stared, another memory tugged at me. The crooked man.

"What is it?"

I flinched at Quinn's voice.

"Sorry. This place makes me jumpy."

"Are you remembering?"

"Bits and pieces. My father loved to garden. That is Ben Cole loved to garden." I frowned. I had three fathers. One I barely remembered, one who raised me, and one who wanted to kill me. Lucky girl.

"A scarecrow hung there." I pointed to the rotting post. "We called him the crooked man."

"Do you think that's what Siranda meant?"

"I don't know. It's a children's song. 'There was a crooked man who walked a crooked mile. He found a crooked crow's nest upon a crooked pile.'"

He frowned. "I know the rhyme, but that's not how it goes."

A heavy step in the trees beyond the clearing startled us. Branches cracked. A flash of white made me jerk backward into Quinn.

"Just a deer." He steadied me with a sure hand, then hoisted the camp axe over his shoulder. "I'm going to tear down the shed."

As I followed him across the soggy ground, I couldn't shake the feeling that someone watched us from the woods.

Quinn sheared away the brambles around the shed door, pulled a board loose and handed it to me. A quick smile and he turned back for another. After a minute, he shrugged off his jacket and I took a bit of guilty pleasure watching his shoulders bunch with each strike, his movements fluid and efficient. His body was made for manual labor with long limbs and lean muscle.

Seeing Quinn warmed by exercise, I could easily forget how sick he was. It didn't seem possible this vibrant man could have a fatal illness. So far, Quinn hadn't mentioned it. He pretended he was a hard-ass who didn't need things like medicine or rest. Those were for mere mortals. But Quinn wasn't immortal. Mawr would eventually kill him. Emmett had explained it all to me. The disease ate magic like an invisible parasite. Quinn could keep pumping himself full of aether but eventually, the disease would catch up to him, and he would waste away to nothing. Or one giant misuse of magic could push him over the edge.

He's endangering himself for me.

Quinn had been holding a board out for a long minute.

"You went somewhere far away. Was the weather nice?" He smiled tiredly.

"Just a little worry and self-recrimination to pass the time." I dropped the board on the pile.

"You shouldn't be so hard on yourself." His hand rested on the cockroach talisman at his throat.

"And you shouldn't be working so hard."

"I'll be fine. Exercise and fresh air are exactly what the doctor ordered."

I doubted that. I took the axe from him, and he didn't resist. My first strike skimmed off the boards and I nearly cut off a toe. Quinn watched me with a grin. Gods, I hated feeling like some inept...*girl* around him.

"It's harder than it looks. Pull your grip back on the handle and use the leverage to maximize your strike." I did as he suggested, and the next board cracked away from the wall.

Fifteen minutes later, I was sweaty in the chill air, but we pulled down enough brambles and rotted wood to push inside the rickety structure.

It was empty. If the shed held any secrets, they were buried under the dirt floor.

"Should we dig it up?" I asked.

"Maybe. But let's get the bellwether out here first. I want to check the foundation of the house with it too."

Bellwethers were rare artifacts used to detect trace amounts of magic. The coven had one and only the threat of Koro had persuaded Jane and the Council of Thirteen to let us borrow it.

He turned away, but I caught his sleeve.

"I'm sorry." The words erupted from me. We'd been studiously ignoring the rift between us, but the pressures of the day—the long drive, forced memories and proximity to Quinn—were all too much to handle. Something had to give.

His eyebrow teased upward. "For what?"

"For going AWOL last November. I didn't mean to cut you out of my life. It wasn't fair to you. But the longer I waited to call, the more awkward I felt when I picked up the phone."

"I get it." He squeezed my fingers, his grip warming a line straight to my heart. "You were scared."

Wait, what?

"No..."

"It's okay. You have every right to be scared."

"I'm not scared."

Quinn squeezed my hand again and turned toward camp while I struggled to find a better rejoinder. Lord and Lady, having the last word wasn't fun when you sounded like an obstinate child.

I loaded up with an armful of cut boards, dumped them in camp and went back for more. The exercise did nothing to burn through my agitation. Why did my thoughts freeze around him? Would we ever get back to that easy relationship we'd once enjoyed?

A whistle startled me. Quinn stood on the low rise leading to the ruins, waving his arms. He'd found something.

CPERCEPTION

Bobbi looked pissed. Quinn could see it in the set of her shoulders and pinch of skin between her brows as she advanced across the uneven ground. Anger suited her. The flushed cheeks and slightly messed hair were damned sexy. He doubted she'd thank him for that insight. Somehow, he was responsible for her anger, but the finer points of his crime escaped him.

"You found something?" She wouldn't look him in the eye. That was fine. He could wait her out.

"It's a cellar." He brushed aside a spill of rock debris covering a pair of metal doors with bent handles. Bobbi's expression loosened from displeasure to uncertainty.

"You remember something."

She shook her head. "Nothing concrete. Just a feeling. Has the bellwether detected anything?"

"No."

The relic leaned like a walking stick against the stone foundation. Made of aether-conducting ash and topped by a silver dragon's head, the bellwether smoked continually as it detected aether in the environment. The trick was reading the smoke, and so far it only leaked pale white threads, its baseline reaction.

"Stay here and I'll check it out." He was trying to be kind, but Bobbi's eyes hardened again.

"No, I'm coming."

Somehow, he knew she'd say that.

Rust clogged the door hinges, and they worked at it for several minutes before the left side finally swung open. Stone steps led into blackness. He grabbed the bellwether and headed down.

The damp chill settled over him as soon as they reached the hard-packed dirt floor. Quinn could stand in the center of the small room, but the ceiling sloped to rough walls. He turned, looking for any sign of a hiding place. The bare room held only an old metal shelf unit, now empty and bent. He waved the bellwether around, starting at the floor and working up the walls.

"How does that thing work anyway?" Bobbi asked.

"It's a sensate compass. The smoke will change colors for different kinds of magic. And aether repels it to give a sense of direction."

"Doesn't seem very precise." Bobbi's forehead crinkled like it did when she concentrated. "Why isn't it reacting to our aether then?"

"I keyed it to us in the activation spell. Otherwise, the user's aether would taint all the readings."

He continued with his probing. Bobbi stood still, her eyes far away. A shiver rippled through her shoulders. Quinn wanted to ask what she was thinking, but that way lay dragons. She saw him watching and frowned.

"I spent a lot of time down here. I can feel it. Like the damp and dark are part of my bones."

"Maybe you took refuge here during the fire?" He didn't want to put her through this, but something needed to jar her memory if they were ever to find the book.

"No, but I remember hiding down here another time. Mom told us to be quiet, but Bethany wouldn't stop crying." Bobbi shrugged. "That's all I got."

The door slammed shut with a screech and a bang. Darkness crashed down on them.

Quinn turned and bumped into Bobbi. He gripped her shoulders, steadying himself more than her. Slowly, his eyes adjusted, taking in the crack of light seeping through the uneven doors. He strode to the steps and pushed upward with all his strength, but the doors held.

"Something's blocking us in."

Several long minutes passed while they waited in the dark for an attack that never came. Bobbi watched the door, hugging herself against chill or fear.

"It'll be all right," Quinn said.

"You don't have to do that."

"What?"

"Reassure me. I don't need your platitudes. This is bad. I can deal with it."

Quinn reached for his cockroach talisman.

Lord and Lady, save me from women with something to prove. He normally found Bobbi's feistiness alluring. But right now, they needed to work together to get out of this cellar.

"I don't know how I pissed you off, but let's table it for later. You're right. This is bad. Apart from the fact that we're trapped in here, we know we're not alone. So are you going to help me or are you going to ride out your peeve?"

Even in the dark, he could see Bobbi's belligerence wilt. Crap. If anyone had earned the right to be belligerent, it was Bobbi.

"I'm sorry. I didn't mean to sound harsh. Would you believe me if I said I'm scared too?"

Bobbi nodded, her eyes wide in the dim light.

"Good. My aether is too depleted to be effective, but you can open the door. I'll guide you. It'll be good battle practice."

"That sounds ominous."

"It is. I know you've got decent ward armor. Time to go on offense."

Bobbi was shaking her head before he finished.

"I can't do it. Henry's been trying to show me, but I can't make it work. And last time, with the demon…"

"You can." He cupped her face with his hands, forcing her to meet his eyes. "An aether strike is much like a ward. You just need to redirect the power. I can show you if you let me."

That request wasn't as straightforward as it seemed. Fain squashed Bobbi's aether, violated her at her deepest core. He wasn't sure she was ready to let someone into that sanctuary again. Maybe she never would be.

"Okay," she said.

"Good. Take my hand." Her fingers slipped into his. "We don't know what's waiting on the other side. So be ready for anything. I'll guide you through the spell, but you need to let me in."

Her hand trembled. Her eyes held his, and he felt the weight of her unspoken demand: *tread lightly.*

"Pull a ward around yourself," he said. Aether encircled her. "Do you know how to concentrate the ward on one spot?"

"Yes." She spoke through gritted teeth.

"Do it. Pull the ward into a hotspot in front of you. Then push it out with all your force toward the doors."

Her aether swirled, hot spice tingling across his skin. He squeezed her fingers. Aether started to pool but she lashed out too soon, and the strike failed. Bobbi's shoulders slumped.

"It's okay. You didn't focus it tight enough. Try again. This time, wait for my signal before you launch it."

Again her aether surrounded them. Tentatively, he reached out with his magic and herded hers in a gentle nudge. She tensed. He pulled back, but she got the idea and narrowed her aether like an arrow pointing at the doors.

"That's right. Now let it fly."

Aether lashed from her. The doors exploded, spilling light into the cellar. Quinn shot up the stairs, knife poised for attack.

He squinted into the late afternoon sun, turned and jumped at a shadow. Bobbi followed, and they checked the ruins.

They were alone.

Shards of a thick branch lay beside the crumpled doors. Someone had jammed it through the handles to lock them in the cellar.

"We're being watched," Bobbi said quietly.

Quinn nodded. "We'd better set wards around camp."

Scission

They set wards in a fifty-foot circle around the tent. Ward work came easily to Quinn, but his energy flagged and he let Bobbi make the last check of the perimeter.

"You're using too much magic." She sat in a camp chair beside him.

"I'm fine."

He wasn't. He ran on borrowed aether, but he'd be damned if he'd let this illness beat him. Not today.

They built a campfire, ate a simple dinner as the sun set, then listened to damp wood crack and pop as it burned. The flickering flames mesmerized Quinn, lulling him into a near doze.

Bobbi fidgeted. She crossed and uncrossed her legs, fiddled with the metal tab on her can of cola and squirmed in her chair. She thrust a long stick into the heart of the coals and watched the tip turn bright orange.

Something rustled in the underbrush and she jerked around. Her burning stick knocked another branch from the fire, and it fell with a shower of sparks. She stamped on the embers even after the sparks died.

"Easy," Quinn said. "You don't get extra points for pounding it into oblivion."

"Am I the only one who feels a dozen pairs of eyes watching us from the shadows?"

"Probably more. These woods are home to a lot of critters—raccoons, opossums, weasels. Maybe even a bear or two."

"Way to make me feel safe. Is this the part where you tell me they're more afraid of me than I am of them?"

"Except the bears. They don't fear much but a shotgun."

"Terrific."

"Don't worry. We'll lock all the food in the jeep. They won't bother us tonight."

Neither of them mentioned the other things that could be watching from the shadows. A horde of minor demons had erupted from the rift. Paragon agents were tracking them down, but they had no idea how many escaped.

And someone had locked them in the cellar. Only fatigue kept Quinn from jumping at shadows too.

They listened to the crackle of fire again. Bobbi seemed to have overcome her earlier pique, though he still didn't know what he'd done to anger her. Once they'd enjoyed an easy camaraderie. They could talk for hours about anything and nothing. Now they swayed between hot and cold. One minute he could almost imagine that William Fain never came between them. The next, Bobbi tucked her aether around her like a cocoon, shutting him out.

Something moved beside the tent. Bobbi yelped and jumped up, knocking her chair into the fire. The stench of burned nylon filled the air and Quinn reached for the smoldering chair. The raccoon, who'd been boldly sniffing for crumbs from dinner, glared at her before stalking back into the trees.

Quinn laughed. He couldn't help it. Bobbi glared at him, one hand holding her stick like a weapon.

"Scared of a little raccoon? He's certainly not scared of you."

Bobbi's eyes flashed. She threw down the stick.

"Fine, I'm scared. Scared of a raccoon and shadows in the dark. Scared of going to sleep at night, of waking up in the morning. Scared that anyone I meet in the street could be working for Koro. I'm scared all the time and it's exhausting. But you know what scares me the most? You."

Quinn's grin died.

"Me? Why? You still think I'll soothe you when you're not looking." They would never move past that.

"No. I'm afraid you can't possibly want me now that you know who, or what, my father is. That's why I never called you. So I wouldn't have to see the look in your eye when you told me we're over."

She stood defiantly before him, arms crossed to hold emotions in or to keep him out. It amounted to the same thing. He pulled her arms loose, leaned in and covered her lips with his. She wouldn't relax under his touch, but she didn't pull away. He parted her lips with his tongue, seeking the softness within. She trembled and he pulled her against him. His hands spanned the entire breadth of her back, as if trying to hold all the pieces of her together. Her shoulders unhitched, and she kissed him back. It wasn't a simple kiss. It was a forging, a new road blazing over the old. Her fingers sought out familiar haunts on his body, the touch igniting passion, and he fought the urge to crush her against him. He pulled away and smoothed back her hair.

"I don't care about Koro." His face lingered inches from hers. "At least not as he pertains to your lineage. And it's not like I don't come with baggage."

Bobbi shook her head, but he kept going.

"Look, I'm not saying we jump into a relationship right now. I'm saying that when you're ready, I'll be here."

She peered at him, her eyes eager, and nodded.

The setting sun had taken what little warmth the day offered. He let Bobbi change first while he doused the embers and bear-proofed the remains of dinner. Away from the campfire, the cold and damp immediately settled on him. Inside the tent, he found her standing before their unrolled sleeping bags, wearing loose cotton pants and a long-sleeved shirt.

"It's so cold." She rubbed her arms.

"Get in, and I'll put a warming spell on the bag." She slid into her bed, and Quinn laid his hands flat on the nylon bag. Warming spells were simple and took little aether, but the edges of his vision darkened as he forced his magic into the threads.

"That should help. Wake me in the night if it wears off."

Bobbi smiled and her shivering eased. He changed into similar loose clothes and slipped into his bag. He didn't have the energy to warm it, but he tucked himself against Bobbi. He was almost asleep with the comforting pressure of her back against his when she spoke.

"Are you still awake?"

He mumbled a reply.

"Do you think whoever is out there will attack tonight?"

"No. They can't get past the wards. They'll wait for daylight when we're moving around in the open."

"But why did they lock us in the cellar? It makes no sense."

It really didn't, and Quinn had no answer.

"I just want you to know that it was never about you. I mean, I trust you. I always did. The reason I never called…" Her voice fell away. He was wide awake now, waiting for her to speak her piece. Whatever words followed wouldn't change anything. She was it, the one he waited for all his life. He'd known that for months. She might not want a relationship, but that didn't change his feelings.

"It was about me not trusting myself. I've always been the girl who got things done. Now I'm the one who fails, the bumbling idiot who blows things up and loses herself…" Her voice caught. He turned, pulled her close, and pressed his face into her hair.

"You are none of those things. You're the bravest person I know. And a strong witch. It will all come together. And I can't wait to be there to see it."

She let out a small, stilted sob.

Some time later, her breathing eased and he fell asleep surrounded by her aether.

PASSION

Something woke me. I lay in the dark listening for the scrape of a foot or scratch of a claw—something to let me know what disturbed my sleep. The night was eerily silent. No frogs or crickets chirped this early in the year. No wind tousled the bare branches.

My unzipped sleeping bag let my heat stash escape. I was cold to the bone. Quinn's warming spell must have worn off. I didn't want to wake him. He tried to hide it, but he was tired and over-extended in the aether department. And I didn't dare try an unknown spell. My track record wasn't stellar. I'd probably set the tent on fire.

I re-zipped the bag and hunkered down inside, hoping to regain the lost warmth.

A branch cracked outside.

I sat up, staring at the tent wall glowing faintly in the dying moonlight.

"Bobbi?" Quinn said groggily.

"I heard something."

Another small sound came from outside. A shuffle of leaves? Or just my tense imagination? A rustle, this one closer, then the sound faded as if moving off.

"Probably your raccoon friend," Quinn said.

I nodded and shivered.

"You're cold. Let me warm your sleeping bag again."

"No. You've done too much magic today." I thought he'd protest or downplay his illness like he always did. Instead, he grinned.

"I guess we'll have to warm up the old-fashioned way."

"I don't think that would be a good idea." Sleeping next to him with wads of sleeping bag between us had been hard enough. I wasn't sure what my treacherous hormones would do if we were trapped together in the same bag.

"You wouldn't deny a sick old man a bit of warmth on a cold night, would you? Strictly an energy-sharing arrangement." He faked a cough. His eyebrow quirked up. Gods, I'd missed that look.

"Of course."

In the tight space, we somehow reformatted the sleeping arrangements by zipping the two bags together into a double-sized bed. I snuggled into it, my back pressed against Quinn's chest. His left arm draped across my hips. I squirmed to get comfortable, and his erection nudged my back. I tensed.

"I'm sorry." He scooted backward. "You just feel so good, and it's been so long since I held you."

"It's okay. I'm not made of glass."

"I don't want you to think I would ever pressure you."

"I don't know. Something is putting an awful lot of pressure on me."

He shifted and the pressure in question only slid across my butt.

"You know what I mean. You have every reason to need your space. I won't invade it. Not mentally, at least."

"Maybe I'd welcome a little invasion." Suddenly I had no good reason to keep Quinn at arm's length. The feel of his kiss lingered on my lips, and I couldn't deny that I wanted more.

I turned awkwardly in the confines of our bed.

"I asked you for time and space to think. You gave me more than I needed really. I've come to terms…" My voice broke and I gave a shaky laugh. "Well, maybe not. I don't know if I'll ever accept what happened. But what William did to me—what he tried to do to me—had nothing to do with sex or romance. I don't think he even liked me. He wanted power, and my blood was his key to it. When I look at you, I don't see him. When you touch me," I lifted his hand to rest it on my hip again, "I don't think of him."

Our lips were a bare inch apart. Darkness cloaked us, boosting my courage. I leaned in and kissed him. He tasted of campfire smoke and a salty-sweetness that was all Quinn. His lips parted and his hand tightened on my hip. His tongue tasted mine, sending shots of desire through me. I felt myself warming, loosening, and I squirmed against him again.

"We're wearing too many clothes," he said gruffly.

"Mmm. But they're terrifically loose."

His hand slipped under my shirt. With a light graze of his finger, he circled my nipple, then gently squeezed my breast. I sucked in my breath and his mouth crushed against mine again. Fingers worked down my stomach and under my waistband, trailing heat behind them.

For a fleeting moment, panic flared in my chest. Quinn stopped. His gaze lingered on mine, looking for permission to go on.

In the weeks we dated, we'd come to this point before, but never more. By some unspoken agreement, we decided to prolong our courtship, to enjoy the teasing foreplay of first dates. Then William Fain taught me to seize every moment because it might be my last. I wouldn't let him destroy this now.

I wriggled out of my sweatpants.

"Your turn." I tugged at the waistband of his pants, pulling them down. In the small space, the fabric snagged on his erection.

"I think I've caught a big one. Should I throw it back?"

He let out an animal groan. "Don't you dare."

My hand gripped his cock, fingers barely circling its breadth.

Lord and Lady, what glories you make.

I freed him from the confines of his pants. In the cramped space we had little room to maneuver. He slid between my legs, not penetrating, but dragging his length against the swollen pressure there. I gasped, then stretched into the feeling, letting him stroke me, wetting us both. I rolled to straddle him. The blanket fell away and I tore off my shirt. I didn't feel the cold, not with Quinn's hands exploring my chest, stomach and hips.

"So beautiful," he whispered. His aether circled me, licking at the edges of my magic. I leaned down to kiss him, savoring the mix of our lips and tongues. Then I rose on my knees and let the tip of his cock nudge me, enjoying the exquisite tease. Quinn gripped my hips, spanning them with hands that shook with the need to pull me closer.

"Are you ready for this?" He seemed to glow in the dim light and desire burned in his eyes.

I nodded, unable to speak. And slowly—so achingly slow—I lowered myself, filling every sense with Quinn.

Later, we had the presence of mind to dress quickly and conserve whatever heat our bodies produced. Tucked into the crook of his shoulder, I enjoyed the feel of his fingers running through my hair.

"I hope that didn't exhaust you too much," I said.

"It was exactly what I needed." I could hear the smile in his voice.

I had so many things I wanted to tell him now that we'd broken our silence in the most spectacular way. I wanted to talk about William and ask how Quinn had known I was in danger. I wanted to talk about my family, Paragon and Koro. But now was not the time for any of that. Now was the time to connect on a primal level, letting our aether mingle and work out all the kinks.

A shadow spread across the tent wall, the silhouette of a great winged beast about to pounce.

DETECTION

Quinn rolled and sat up. The shadow grew, filling the tent wall. Wings stretched from square shoulders topped by a bulbous head. The creature raised a long hand, fingers tipped in claws to rake the nylon.

He grabbed his knife, never far from his side, slashed the wall and bolted outside. Crashing sounds followed a high scream as the attacker escaped into the woods. He ran after it. Dirt, sticks and leaves clung to his bare feet. He stopped when a rock lodged under his toe.

Bobbi caught up to him as he limped and swore.

"How did it get through the ward?"

"I don't know. It wasn't human. I saw a long tail disappear into the trees. Really long." He gripped her hand and they stood like two warriors facing an army in the darkness.

They'd get no more sleep tonight.

Morning greeted them with fog.

"We might as well wait for the sun to burn that off." Quinn poured them each a second cup of coffee. Bobbi clasped her mug, warming her face in the steam.

"Is there anything better than coffee brewed in an old-fashioned percolator over a campfire?"

She looked haggard, more so than one sleepless night could account for. The stress of the past few days—all hells, the past six months—wore on her, leaving dark circles under her eyes. Nothing could truly diminish her beauty though. It wasn't a veneer laid over her skin but a light from within. Quinn wished he could ease her somehow. They needed to hurry up an find the grimoire.

Time to bring out the big guns.

"Since we have time to kill, I could help you remember."

Bobbi lifted her eyes from the fire. "Remember?"

"You had flashes of memory yesterday. It's all there, locked in your head. I don't know if someone blocked those memories on purpose or if time has simply faded them…"

"Or maybe I blocked them myself because they're too horrible to remember."

"Or there's that." He let her work through those options for a moment. "But we might need those memories to find the grimoire. I can help. That's all I'm saying."

"With what, hypnosis?"

"Sort of. More like a seeking spell, but I'd have to couple it with soother magic. It's the only way I can guide you."

Bobbi sat back, shaking her head. It was too soon. He'd pushed too hard.

"I'm sorry. I should have known that one night of sex wasn't enough to ease your concerns—even life-altering, really great, getting-a-hard-on-just-thinking-about-it sex." Quinn grinned and nudged her with his knee.

Bobbi let out a harsh laugh.

"Fine. Let's do it." Her mouth set in grim determination.

"I know how you feel about soothing. We can find another way."

"This was your idea, and now you want to back out of it? Just do it."

"It's not that easy. It's not something I do to you. You have to be on board one-hundred percent. You have to trust me. I'll be inside your head. I may see things you'd rather keep private." Things he'd rather not see, like her memories of Fain.

She reached for his hand and squeezed. "I trust you." Their eyes met. Her smile trembled a bit.

Quinn unpacked his weaver kit from the trunk.

"You've probably been learning mostly connate magic." He felt oddly reluctant to mention Henry. "But a finding spell is traditionally weaver magic."

"I didn't know you were a weaver too."

"Any witch can be a weaver. The magic comes from the spell—the props and incantation. You just need to follow the recipe. Finding spells are fairly common. I should have everything we need." He dumped a pile of stones from a cloth bag, selected two moonstones and handed them to her. "Hold these, one in each hand." They lay in the flat of her palm as she examined the smooth opalescent stones. He closed her fingers around them.

"Hold them firmly. These are your anchors."

Next, he took out a short silver candle and anointed it with oil.

"Mmm. What's that scent?" Bobbi asked.

"Honeysuckle." He tapped another drop from the bottle and smeared it down each of her temples. Then he sorted through a pencil case and pulled out a fat purple marker. Bobbi eyed it suspiciously.

"You're not going to draw a mustache on me, are you?"

He grinned. "It's washable. But no, not a mustache. An eye." He drew a purple oval on her forehead. "That's your third eye, the one that can look forward or back." He lit the candle. "Stare at the flame. Try not to blink."

Bobbi gazed into the flame. Her expression went slack.

He intoned the traditional words, "Bound by light, ask the right. Bound by light, bring the sight." A tiny light separated from the candle wick. Bobbi's eyes widened in surprise.

"This is a seeker. It's going to search your mind for the memories, and I'll be along for the ride." He took a third moonstone, passed it through the flame and pressed it to the mark on her forehead. The seeker bounced with energy.

"When your physical eyes feel tired and dry, let them close and your third eye will open."

Bobbi let her eyes drift shut. Quinn took a moment to draw aether from his roach talisman. Emmett's injector was ready in his pack too, in case this spell went wild.

"I'm going to soothe you now. Just a bit. Think of it as a mild sedative, okay?" He waited for her permission. She had to be an active participant, or this would never work.

She nodded. The light ball thrust through the stone into her head. Bobbi gasped, but Quinn took the edge off her distress. He lowered the moonstone. Her face composed, but he could feel her fear like a snake coiled to strike. He pushed a little more calming aether.

The seeker drifted through the miasma of her memories. Quinn closed his eyes to block out the physical world and concentrated on the images of Bobbi's mind. Light and shadow swirled, coalescing into brief glimpses of thoughts that faded before he could grasp them.

He resisted the urge to rifle through her thoughts. It would be so good to know, for once, what she was thinking. But this spell always unnerved him. It was such an utter baring of the soul. If he stepped clumsily, he could damage her psyche for good.

Then one sharp image pushed forth. Desire hit him along with her most recent memories of two bodies tangled together in the dark, his face masked by shadow.

Oh. She thought he smelled good and damn…that's what it felt like to be a horny woman? Good to know.

Move on! Bobbi's voice rang sharply as if she'd spoken aloud.

Fine. He left those memories reluctantly, knowing he'd never get another chance to see himself through Bobbi's eyes.

"Focus on a memory of your parents or your sister. Even a place or an object that has significance."

The images swirled, formless now with only skittish clouds of color in the darkness of her mind. She was spinning out of control again.

"I can't find any!" Her breathing increased sharply.

"You're okay." Calm flowed out with his words and Bobbi's anxiety slowed. "What about yesterday. Did anything spark a memory?"

He heard a small child calling "Bobbi! Bobbi!" The ruins appeared as they stood now, but the sky was all wrong. Day turned to night then sped into day. Clouds raced by as stars left streaks in the sky. The sun rose and set, moon following like a comet. Bobbi was turning back time, visualizing the thread of her life spinning backward, until the image froze on her childhood home, standing solid against a night sky.

Her mind erupted in fire. Darkness. Heat. Flame. They stood at the center of an inferno. Screams pierced the night. The image blurred and they stood in a long hallway choked by smoke.

Hell, no. They'd fallen into Bobbi's memory of the fire that killed her family. She whimpered beside him, and he crushed the image with a blast of soothing magic. She flinched as if he'd hit her.

Damn. He didn't want to do that. She'd been battered by soother magic before. He wanted to ease her back into it, not bludgeon her with it.

Are you okay to go on? He spoke through the seeker, not ready to bring them back to the physical world. The shift could be jarring. He felt her agreement.

Try another memory. Something farther back. Lord and Lady, he hoped she chose something happier.

A scene emerged from the blackness of her mind. Wildflowers swayed in the wind. A child ran through the shining flower heads with airplane arms.

Bobbi look at me! I'm flying! She squealed and ran off.

Colors billowed and ebbed, revealing and hiding a blond woman. She smiled and touched his face. No, Bobbi's face. This was her memory, not his.

"Sing it again, baby."

A child's voice joined hers.

"There was a crooked man who walked a crooked mile. He found a crooked crow's nest upon a crooked pile. He crossed a crooked bridge and swam a crooked stream. And slept in his cave in a deep crooked dream."

"That's right. I'm so proud of you! Now remember…" The woman touched her forehead with two fingers, right on the spot of her third eye.

Bobbi jerked her memories from his grasp. He opened his eyes to find her staring grimly at the receding fog.

"I know where the book is."

EXCURSION

We called him the crooked man."

I stared at the rotting post beside the old garden. In my mind's eye, a scarecrow hung limply on a crossbar, hay-stuffed head painted with a smiling face so he would frighten birds and not my little sister.

"He was the trail marker."

"Are you sure?" Quinn watched me intently. The fog had burned off. In the morning sun, the shadows under his eyes gave him a haunted look. I nodded and gripped his fingers, glad for the anchor as memories returned.

"Repeat it. You must not forget." My mother's voice echoed in my head, then my tiny voice answered. *"There was a crooked man…"*

"That's why I know a different version of the rhyme. It was my mother's way of teaching me the path to our special place." I closed my eyes and tried to recapture more fleeting memories. "I remember a clearing that butts up against a tall bluff. We used to picnic there. It's close enough for a child to walk to from the house." I pressed the memory for more details before it slipped away. "And a cave. We pretended it was a castle. That way." I pointed to a small opening in the trees beside the overgrown garden.

Quinn shrugged. "Well, I'm up for a hike." He looked up for a nap, but he would never agree to let me check it out alone, not after the strange visitor at our site last night. He activated the bellwether while I packed a small bag.

As soon as we slipped into the woods on a path that was little more than a deer trail, I felt my first connection to this land. Quinn's finding spell unlocked my memories, and they came spilling over me now. I could see my little sister skipping up the path ahead of us, blond ponytail bouncing, childish voice counting steps for the sheer joy of hearing her own voice. My mother pointed out plants, explaining their uses in medicine and ritual. Sometimes my father would join us, looking for the perfect piece of deadwood to whittle into a toy.

All these images lay over the bare spring trees as I looked for a landmark matching the second line of the verse.

He found a crooked crow's nest upon a crooked pile. A crooked pile could mean anything. And the bird's nest wouldn't have survived the last twenty years. But I had no doubt we headed in the right direction.

I stopped and held out a bottle of water. Quinn needed rest.

"They're alive in these woods," I said. He took a sip and handed back the water with a quizzical look. "My family. I can feel them all around us. Even if we don't find the grimoire, I'm glad we did the finding spell. Thank you."

Quinn tipped an imaginary hat.

We continued on as the path widened. It was soft underfoot, littered with a thick pad of dead needles as it twisted through tall pines. The angle steepened enough to make my hamstrings burn. The next part roughened even more. A natural staircase of mossy boulders led straight up. I paused to let Quinn catch up, stretching my legs to give him a moment's pause. He leaned on the bellwether like a walking stick. So far, the artifact hadn't so much as belched.

"You think we're headed the right way?" he asked.

"I'm sure of it. I remember this place. The first time I climbed these stone steps, I turned back to yell down at my parents. 'Look Mommy! I climbed a whole mountain!' I might have been part billy goat." I smiled at the memory. I'd been so proud. Bethany needed help from Dad, but I climbed all by myself. As an adult, the climb didn't disappoint. I was panting by the time I reached the top.

Behind me, the stone steps seemed to drop into the bowels of the earth. Ahead, a rock ledge opened onto a magnificent view. The valley spread before us, grey and brown trees just starting to sprout green.

Stepping back from the view, I dug in the underbrush beside the ledge until I found a rock about the size of my fist and placed it at the base of a pile of stones as tall as me.

"The stone pile," I said. "There's no nest. I remember now. Dad said this was as tall as a crow's nest on a ship." It wasn't that tall, but to my child's view, it had been huge. "We used to pretend we were pirates, exploring the seas." My eyes blurred with sudden tears. The memory seemed like a story from someone else's life, someone who'd grown up carefree and secure in the knowledge that her family would always be there for her.

Quinn squeezed my hand. "Remembering is a double edged gift."

I nodded through my tears. On one hand, I was thrilled to have some connection to my family. On the other, I now knew how much I'd lost.

"This way." I pulled him back into the trees. The path widened as it joined a hiking trail. We wouldn't see many hikers this time of year, but I couldn't shake the feeling that we were being followed. No matter which way we turned, I felt eyes on my back. The bellwether remained inert, but my aether tingled.

The crooked bridge was easier to spot, a narrow wooden crossing over a creek. We followed the stream for a while as it slithered through the trees.

"We have to cross over it again, but I'm not sure where," I said.

"It'll come to you." Quinn's confidence in me was comforting and unsettling. We walked in silence until nerves and frustration stopped me. The path seemed endless, and one bend looked much like another.

"The rhyme says 'swam a crooked stream,' but this creek isn't more than ankle deep. Maybe we need to find a place where it deepens?" I handed Quinn a bottle of water. The day grew hot and the bare trees offered little shade.

"Maybe the water level was higher when you were a kid? Or it could be an exaggeration for the poem's sake." The bellwether was unhelpfully quiet. "Your aether knows where it's going. Trust it."

We kept walking. The path narrowed and the trees thickened. We lost sight of the creek bed but could still hear it burbling over rocks.

Something crashed in the woods to our right. We stopped. I waited for the telltale white flash of a deer. Quinn touched my shoulder, then pointed to the bellwether. A thin stream of red smoke trailed off its end. Red meant demon aether.

Quinn pointed into the dense underbrush and I nodded. We left the trail. Brambles tore at my jeans. The ground dropped away in soft, spongy mud and I slid down the bank to the creek. The crashing sound came again from the far side of the water. Quinn held up the bellwether, which let out a constant red smolder now. Whatever taunted us, it had a significant aether signature, and it seemed to be leading us rather than running away or attacking. We followed the faint crashing sounds.

Like lambs to the slaughter.

We crossed the stream by hopping from rock to rock then climbed the opposite bank. My hands and knees were muddy by the time we reached the top. I caught my breath standing on a rise in a small clearing. Ahead of us a granite bluff blocked the path and a sharp moment of déjà vu hit me.

I'd been here before.

DECEPTION

Bobbi looked like she'd been punched in the gut.

"This was our special place." She swayed and Quinn steadied her. "We had picnics here and pretended to be brave explorers." She marched to the stone bluff and pushed aside a mess of brambles to reveal the opening of a cave, big enough for a stooped man to enter.

Quinn eyed the dense forest while she cleared the bushes with her knife. He held the bellwether like a club, ready to take on anything that popped out of the trees.

With the last bramble hacked away, Bobbi rested against the wall.

"We have to look inside," Quinn said, "but that'll leave us vulnerable to an attack."

"I could go in while you stand guard."

"No."

He pulled her against him and kissed her, lips parting with rough need, tongue a questing touch that left aether tingling in his veins. Her fingers trailed up his shoulders, twining in the hair at the nape of his neck. With a burst of need, he wanted all of her touching all of him. Instead, he let her go.

She put the top of her head against his chest and stared at the ground like a shy teen. He rubbed her arms and back, needing the contact more than he wanted to admit.

"No matter what we find in there, I want to know that we're okay." He pushed her back gently, forcing her to look up at him. The finding spell had been rough. He hoped it wouldn't destroy the intimacy they'd tentatively built up.

"We're good." Her smile wavered, but it was sincere.

Armed with a flashlight, Bobbi headed into the dark fissure. Quinn followed with the bellwether leaking smoke in a pale stream.

The cave was empty, but Bobbi seemed to see more than bare rock walls.

"We once spent an entire afternoon in here, waiting out a thunderstorm. Dad told us stories to keep us calm."

Quinn walked the cave's perimeter, waving the bellwether up and down the walls. It suddenly bloomed red.

"Here." He knelt. A pile of rocks had been artfully laid to blend seamlessly with the wall. He dug at a stone and pushed it aside to reveal a hollow in the ground.

"There's something inside." He pulled out a canvas wrapped bundle, too small and bulky to be a book.

They hadn't found the grimoire, but it was…something. Even without the bellwether's sign, Quinn could tell it had great power. Its aether sizzled.

"Take it outside." Bobbi coughed. Smoke filled the small cave now.

Back in the daylight, Quinn handed her the bundle and planted the bellwether in the ground like a torch. Bobbi unfolded the cloth wrapping to reveal a small silver statue of a horse with a sharp horn protruding from its brow. It should have been whimsical, except a rusty brown substance covered the horn.

"That's blood," Quinn said. "If your mother left it for you, it's probably keyed to you."

"It's always about the blood, isn't it?" She sighed, then looked to Quinn for approval. When he nodded, she stuck her finger with the horn.

There are moments in time that seem to hold more weight than others, moments where forces converge, the gods look up from their great game of chess, and the universe holds its breath. This was one of those moments.

Then the universe exhaled and all hell broke loose.

The silver horse exploded in a ball of light leaving a huge leather-bound book in Bobbi's hands.

A creature shot into the clearing, its thin body topped by a bulbous head with enormous black eyes. Leathery wings spread from its back, waving frantically.

"Divine lady! Run now! Take your treasure, most holy one, and go! Go! Go! Before the dark one comes!"

A spear of lightning exploded against the cliff.

The creature shrieked and disappeared into the trees, trailing a long sinewy tail.

Another bolt hit the wall, and a woman stepped from the trees.

Quinn pulled Bobbi behind him and threw up a ward.

"Tanya!" Bobbi said.

"Who?" Quinn evaluated the new threat.

Dark curly hair framed a round face, her mouth set in a grim line. She stood with good balance, knees slightly bent and hands raised in the classic mage pose.

"She's a nurse for Gavin's mother," Bobbi said.

"Among other things." Tanya's smile didn't reach her eyes. She jerked her hands and currents of electricity flew from her fingers, zapping Quinn's ward. The impact shuddered through him. Bobbi tried to pull him away, but with the cliff at their backs, they had nowhere to go.

"But you're not even a real witch," Bobbi said.

"Please. Do you think those pathetic wannabes at the library are my real coven?" Tanya's sneer transformed her pleasant face into something ugly. "I use them as a power source. Simple hens don't even feel it when I drain them."

Quinn remembered Bobbi's story about reaching out to a modern coven that met at the public library, but right now he was more concerned with keeping them alive. He strained to hold the simple ward spell.

The witch squared her shoulders and raised her arms. Blue currents streamed from her fingertips, clashing with his defenses. He could feel the heat melting his aether like wax.

Gods, he hated galvanic mages.

Given enough time, Tanya would burn through his ward. Behind him, Bobbi gripped his shoulders. Aether leaked into him from her touch, but not fast enough to make up for what he fed into the ward. He groped for the roach talisman and sucked it dry, then pulled a penknife from his pocket. It wasn't much, but mages were an arrogant breed. Tanya might be too confident in her ward to guard against any other kind of attack. Quinn had no such preconceptions. He'd learned magic and fighting on the streets of Haiti. He flicked open the knife and flung it. Tanya screamed and grabbed her left shoulder. The barrage of electric fire stopped.

"You cut me!" Tanya stared at her bloody hand in horror.

Quinn's ward was failing. Behind him, Bobbi mumbled an incantation, trying to call up a ward. She stumbled over her words and began again.

"Can't even get a simple spell right. What a pathetic fool." Tanya smiled, not a happy expression. "You don't deserve that book. It should be mine. He entrusted it to me!"

She raised her hands again. Electric sparks clustered at her fingertips, then she let them go, thrusting white-hot fire straight at his chest.

Quinn's ward crumbled. Pain seared him, locked his muscles tight and he fell into darkness.

CPRESERVATION

Quinn dropped like a stone. His limbs seized. He stiffened, eyes showing white, and he lay still.

He's dead. The thought froze me. I looked at his handsome face, now slack and pale. He couldn't be dead. Not now. Not when I'd found my way back to him.

His chest rose and fell. Not dead. But close to it.

A deep growl brought me back. Tanya screamed. Lost in shock, I hadn't noticed the new battle taking place right in front of me. The imp-like creature returned and flung itself on Tanya. It bit her ankle, worrying it like a dog with a bone. Its flailing wings battered her. Tanya fell and rolled down an incline out of my view, taking the creature with her.

I jumped at the reprieve and tossed the grimoire and the flashlight into the cave, then grabbed Quinn under the arms and hauled. He was heavier than he looked, and I managed to drag him only a few feet before my fingers slipped.

Behind me Tanya swore. The imp growled. Magic flashed in lightning bursts. I didn't stop to watch but pulled Quinn another foot. The bellwether had gone wild with all the aether discharge and filled the air with smoke. I coughed and pulled. We crossed the threshold of the cave and I slumped Quinn against the cool wall, hiding him in shadow.

Another scream tore through the air, high pitched and inhuman. The imp was dead or hurt. That bothered me more than it should have. The creature had to be a demon. It probably came through the rift and somehow followed us from the coven. But it also tried to warn me.

I mumbled the spell to bring up a ward. Need supercharged my magic, and a thin film of aether stretched across the cave's entrance.

Thank you, Henry, for making me practice until my nose bled.

Warding the entire cave entrance proved more difficult than calling up a personal shield. I pushed as much aether as I could muster into it. I would protect Quinn and the grimoire. Tanya wouldn't be getting either of them.

She limped into sight, her pant leg torn. A blotch of red seeped through her shirt where Quinn's knife had struck. Smoke wafted in front of her face, obscuring and revealing a snarling expression. She grabbed the bellwether and tossed it into the trees, heedless of the damage it might cause to the dead foliage. Raising her hands, she tested my ward with the tips of her fingers. It rewarded her with a nasty zing of aether.

She smiled. "You've progressed in your studies since we first met."

I glared at her.

"You seemed like such a nice person back then. I would've never guessed you'd get caught up with Jane Smith and her precious coven. They're not the good witches they pretend to be, you know." She stepped back. Electricity gathered at her fingertips. "But then, who knew you'd turn out to be the daughter of a demon." Her grin said, *yes I know all your secrets.*

I had to keep her talking. My ward spell needed time to ramp up to full efficiency, a flaw that I'd been working to fix.

"And you seemed so sane when we first met. Who knew you were really a psychopath."

Good one, Bobbi. Antagonize the murdering witch.

Tanya narrowed her eyes. "Why haven't you attacked me yet? Your boyfriend at least had the presence of mind to throw a knife. But I expected a better offense from the witches of the famous Hidden Coven. Is it because you can't attack me or you won't?" She seemed genuinely curious.

I wouldn't tell her about Quinn's illness. And she didn't need to know my limitations.

"I may be new at this witch thing, but I make a mean ward. You won't get the grimoire."

"Let's just see about that." She lashed electrical fire like a whip. I cringed as her aether clashed with mine, but I got a taste of the dark magic tainting it. That meant a blood sacrifice. And I knew which demon she'd prostrated herself to.

"Koro won't thank you for hurting me." I gritted my teeth as she launched another attack. The onslaught of magic over-heated the air inside the cave.

"You think he has fatherly concern for you?" Tanya barked a laugh. Sweat dripped down her nose.

"Not so much, but Dad has big plans for me."

Tanya hurled more lightning at my ward, and I fed it more aether. She let her attack drop away, her face red with exertion. Her aether couldn't hurt her, but the heat had to be uncomfortable.

"The divine one has given me free rein as long as I bring him that book." Tanya's curls clung to her damp face. She smiled. "He doesn't need you anymore. He's got me."

The sparkle in her eye turned maniacal. "Thank you for unlocking it, by the way. You saved me a lot of hassle."

I glanced at the ancient book lit only by the dying flashlight. I shouldn't have been so keen to break the glamor my mother put on it.

"I won't let you have it."

Tanya struck again. Seconds ticked by while her burning aether lashed mine. She stopped, breathing hard.

"You won't last."

"I seem to be holding my own." I'd sparred with Henry for hours. I could outlast her aether reserves. And then what? We'd fight it out like a couple of brawlers? I hoped Quinn would wake up before then. I unsheathed the hunting knife at my waist. Unlike Tanya's ward, mine would block an attack from any weapon, but if she broke through my ward, the knife would be my last defense.

Tanya bowed her head. Wind blustered through the trees behind her. When she raised her eyes, they burned red. She channeled demon magic. Her lips moved in a rhythmic chant. She raised her arms above her head. Blue fire spread from hand to hand, roiling in ethereal waves.

No, no, no.

That wasn't the regular zing of galvanic magic. And it wasn't firebug magic either. It was mage fire, the flame that melted bones to ash. Only the most accomplished witches could produce the blue flame, or those blessed with dark aether from a stronger being. The fire might come from Tanya's hand, but the power behind it was Koro's.

It would burn through my ward like paper, then it would fill the small cave with flame, destroying everything it touched.

She spread her hands, letting the blue fire flow between her fingers.

"You wouldn't dare," I said. "The grimoire will burn too. You won't risk your prize."

"Gods, you are a dumb bitch." Tanya shook her head. "The book is written in Koro's blood. It's protected by his aether. Mage fire can't hurt it."

I glanced back at Quinn. I could shield him for a few moments, but then my body would collapse and burn. And Tanya wouldn't leave Quinn alive.

She pressed her hands against my ward. Fire spread over it. A screech like sonic nails across a chalkboard left me clutching my ears. Heat blasted me. Under the mage fire onslaught, the ward turned blue and blurry like an antique glass window. Tiny cracks spread across the glass.

Tanya snarled and renewed her efforts. The screaming fire filled all my senses, blinding, deafening and scorching. The sensations triggered the last of my blocked memories, and I was suddenly six years old again, standing in the center of a blue firestorm.

DOMINION

My sister's screams woke me.

Our room was filled with smoke, the heat unbearable. A wall of blue fire separated our beds. Bethany pressed against her headboard, clutching her stuffed rabbit. Flames leaped at her like striking snakes.

I didn't know what to do. Never in my life had I experienced such crippling fear. Up until now, my worst nightmare had been a splinter Dad removed from my foot. My innocent mind couldn't wrap itself around the enormity of the danger I faced.

I couldn't save Bethany. Only Mom and Dad could do that. Mom and Dad who saved us from every hurt and sickness. They would know what to do. I ran to their room and jerked to a stop at the door. A moment stretched into eternity while I gaped at their bed, now a blue pyre for their blackened bodies.

"Mom!" I threw myself on the blazing bed, not believing or understanding that they were beyond saving. Not caring if I burned away in the flames.

But I didn't. Blue fire rolled over me, tasting my flesh and moving on to more palatable prey. The curtain lit like a wick. I crouched in the center of the room, arms wrapped around my knees, hiding my face.

Eventually, my sister stopped screaming.

The fire finally burned down. As the sun rose, two strong hands pulled me from the charred remains of our house.

The memory hurt like cut glass in my lungs. I didn't want it, didn't want the burden it thrust upon me, but I welcomed the knowledge it brought.

Tanya's face twisted with demented focus. She glared at me through the cracking ward. Blue fire lashed from her fingertips.

The hilt of my knife slipped in my sweaty palm. I gripped it, poised for an underhand strike. Tanya took a deep breath, fueling herself for the last blast of aether.

I let my ward drop.

Fire blew the hair back from my face and turned the world blue. I plunged my knife into Tanya's gut, driving it up under her ribs, just as Henry taught me.

Her lips parted in a silent "Oh!" Surprise doused her spell, and the cave fell into smoky darkness. I stared into her bulging eyes.

"You forgot this dumb bitch is also made with Koro's blood. Mage fire can't hurt me."

I pulled the knife back, and she slumped to the ground, blood pooling around her. When her eyes turned vacant, I dropped the knife, not bothering to check her pulse. I was done with Tanya and her bizarre crusade. Quinn needed me.

I fumbled in the backpack for Emmett's medicine, yanked off the cap and plunged the needle into Quinn's thigh. He didn't even flinch.

Come on, come on.

His pale face beaded with clammy sweat. I watched in horror as his chest rose and fell, stopped, then shakily rose again.

Quinn was dying.

Tears welled in my eyes and I forced them back. I'd wasted enough time on self-pity, time I could have spent with Quinn. Time I would never get back.

"I love you." My fingers grazed over his stubbly chin. He couldn't hear me, but I didn't care. I kissed his lips. They were warm and unyielding.

I loved him. It was that simple. Nothing else mattered. Not Jane's disapproving looks or the threat of Koro hanging over us. Not even the devastating illness that would take him from me. I loved Quinn and I would lose him. I was still that scared kid, waiting in the dark and knowing no one would come.

A small hand gripped my shoulder. I turned to see the imp peering at me. "Is divine mate dead?"

Divine mate? Wouldn't Quinn love that title.

"Not yet."

The imp nodded and scuttled around the cave to Quinn's other side. It placed two gnarled hands on Quinn's chest. The snake-like tail slid under the small of his back and wrapped around his stomach.

"What are you doing?" I tried to yank the tail off, but it hugged Quinn in a vice grip.

"Please, most holy one. Let me help. I heal, yes?"

I sat back on my heels. "You can do that?"

"Perhaps. Most beatific one must be easy now. I will try."

The imp's hands glowed orange, and I felt aether wash over Quinn.

"Divine mate has illness in every part of his being." The creature scrunched its snub nose. A pointy tongue poked from the corner of thin lips. Its body shook with some effort I could only guess at. Quinn's back arched as his muscles seized. Then he lay flat, his breathing calm and even.

The imp slumped back, its body noticeably shrunken. It looked at me with huge eyes ringed in thick lashes, and I realized it was a female.

"He will live, for now. But I cannot take away all illness. My healing not strong enough."

I nodded. Quinn rested comfortably. I couldn't expect more.

I offered a bottle of water to the imp. She grabbed it, drained the bottle, and wiped a hand across her mouth. The leathery wings perked up.

"What's your name?"

"Trezn Sogb, most supernal one." She bowed. "It is hard name in this world. It means…" she scrunched her face in concentration, "smelly plant with blades. You would call it Rosie, yes?"

"Thank you, Rosie. For helping him."

She straightened and puffed out her skinny chest. "I serve divine angel. I save her from servant of bad ones." She pointed to Tanya's corpse. "Bad servant follow you, most holy angel. I follow her. I never let harm come to divine one."

Understanding dawned on me. "You're the one who locked us in the cellar, but why?"

"Bad servant mustn't find book written in dark blood." She scuttled to the grimoire and hefted it onto her shoulders. "Please, we destroy it now, yes?"

I squeezed her knobby hand with bark-dry skin. "I don't think we can. It's immune to mage fire. But I promise we'll hide it and keep it safe from the bad ones." She placed the book in my lap with solemn reverence.

"Why do you keep calling me divine?"

Rosie's eyes gleamed with zeal.

"You are most holy one that my mother spoke of many, many years ago. We are ruled by holy ones…bad holy ones. They eat pain. My pain. Family's pain. All pain good to bad holy ones. But Mother spoke of great holy ones who live in other worlds. They come if I pray. So I pray. And you, serene one, answered. I smell your divine blood, most grandest of holy ones." She sniffed my arm.

"My blood. You mean my demon blood." She came through the rift and latched onto me because I smelled familiar.

"Yes, demons. Divine ones. And you are my blessed one, most sacred of celestial beings. Supernal essence of heart, godliest demon in order of…"

"Okay, I got it. That's enough. Just call me Bobbi."

"Bobbi?" Her nose crinkled in distaste, curling her upper lip to reveal razor sharp teeth. "As you wish, most divine Bobbi. I serve you, yes?"

Sigh. I didn't want a servant.

"We'll see. For now, you can help me dig a grave."

COMPLICATION

Gavin studied the people gathered in Jane's living room. It was too quiet for a space filled with eight witches and one small demon. A fire spat and popped in the hearth adding stuffiness more than warmth. Spell work wasn't his forte, and Gavin wished he could leave. Jane made it clear that she expected them all to pitch in with this most important and delicate task.

She sat at the large round table with Myra and Grant, the coven elders. Myra read from the grimoire, turning the ancient pages with care as if they might bite her. Grant's chin had long since fallen to his chest, and he snored softly. One wisp of hair fluttered around his wrinkled and sun-spotted head. Abilene and Henry took up the seats at the far end of the table. Behind them, Quinn rested on the couch, his head propped in Bobbi's lap. The imp perched on a stool by Bobbi's feet, a look of joyful ease on her face. Rosie was one of the many complications caused by recent events.

Jane's patch on the rift was a temporary fix at best. The elder witches had been studying the grimoire for hours, searching for a spell to permanently close it. The book wasn't giving up its secrets easily.

Jane sighed and leaned back in her chair.

"Most of these spells are just triggers." She took off her glasses and rubbed a hand over her eyes.

Advanced witches often hid their most potent spells under other spells, the way old masters painted over canvases. The newer spells acted like keys to reveal the hidden ones. Trigger spells could be nasty pieces of work, and poor execution could leave a witch maimed or dead. They weeded out weak magic users and assured that only a true adept could access the real spells in the grimoire.

"This could take weeks," Myra said with pursed lips. She was one of the original Thirteen, the witches who founded the Hidden Coven and built the core. Her mastery over magic was second only to Jane's. "We need to get more people on it."

"No," Jane said. "The fewer people involved the better. Koro has eyes everywhere, maybe even inside the coven."

Gavin felt a sting of guilt. Tanya was his mother's nurse. They all thought Stacy was insane. She claimed to talk to Koro, and the doctors insisted she only relived months of torture endured over two decades ago. But what if Koro actually was talking to her? Gavin didn't know what he'd do about that complication. Moving her to another facility wouldn't help. Maybe it was time to bring Stacy home.

"None of us will be leaving this room until we at least figure out which spells are triggers," Jane said.

Gavin sighed. This was going to be a long night.

"I'll make more coffee," Quinn said. He stood and walked out of the room. Gavin couldn't help smiling at the way Bobbi's eyes followed him. It had been a long time coming, but those two had finally reconnected. He tried not to think of the dark cloud on the horizon, the one matching the grey circles under Quinn's eyes. He barely made it home from their trip into the Adirondacks. From what Gavin could gather, only some healing intervention by the imp kept him alive.

His eyes roamed back to Rosie again. Could it be that not all demons were evil? Or that demon realms were inhabited mostly by innocent creatures like Rosie, ruled over by the malevolent ones like Koro? These ideas shifted Gavin's entire world view, and they would keep him awake many nights in the future while he pondered their implications.

Yes, this room was full of complications tonight. Complications and possibilities. Gavin's gaze snagged on Henry, sitting quietly with Abilene. With his head bowed over a page of translation, Henry's dark curls fell into his eyes. His lips pursed with thought. Abilene said something and Henry chuckled, his whole expression changing. Abilene flushed.

It seemed his little sister had a crush on the Paragon knight. He could easily forget how young she was. Jane groomed her for leadership of the coven, and most of the time Abilene acted wise beyond her years. But seeing her flirt with a handsome man, she looked like nothing more than an awkward teen.

Henry saw him watching and winked. A slow smile spread across his face, and it was Gavin's turn to fight off a blush. He knew exactly what Henry was thinking.

How soon can we duck out of this meeting and steal a few private moments together?

Poor Abilene. Someone would have to burst her bubble, but it wouldn't be Gavin.

A bright orange light flared up from the grimoire, and everyone jumped back. With screeching fireworks, the light exploded over their heads and rained sparks. Grant woke with a snort as Henry swatted a spark on his shoulder before it set his shirt on fire.

Jane smiled grimly. "It seems we found the first trigger."

Kororaeth followed the slave over fiery sands. Amstarth Desert was not his favorite place. Though the heat of the seven suns could not harm him, the desert was too bright, too endless and open for his liking.

"This way, great one. This way." The disgusting creature urged him on. Koro despised imps. Oh, they could be useful as fodder for dark magic, and they made decent house slaves, but the constant groveling wore on him. He would have dismissed the imp's claims of finding a rift, but he'd seeded this desert with dimensional snares himself nearly half a century ago.

He stopped and grabbed the imp by its skinny neck, pulling its face up to his eye.

His lip curled in a snarl. "You tell the truth, or I will kill you, kill your clan and burn them for fuel."

"No, no! Great one, I tell only truth. Always truth!" The creature squirmed, trying to bow even though its feet dangled four feet above the ground.

Koro bared his teeth and let it drop.

"My patience wears thin, imp."

"Yes, great one. I take you now." It scampered away again, clambering over a giant mound of rock in the shape of a scull with horns, then up another dune.

Koro followed, his senses tingling now.

Once he roamed at will between worlds, feasting on the delicacy of human blood and magic. But a godling with grandiose aspirations doomed him to live cut off from that nourishment for all eternity. The desire for that meaty aether drove him now. His whole purpose focused on finding a way back into the world of human witches to taste it again. All his plans, all his dealing and scheming directed him toward that one goal.

"Here it is, great one. I told you, yes? I told you I bring you to the gate." The disgusting imp bounced with excitement.

They stood in a valley of sand between two natural stone pillars. The wind blew over the remains of a tent. Scattered armor and other gear lay half buried, as if a camp had been hastily fled.

The air felt different, weightier. That is what drew him here all those years ago. In this place, the veil between worlds thinned. He'd planted his magic snare and let it sit. Humans were greedy for power. They looked for it everywhere. In books, plants and rocks. Even in the heart of their world. Eventually, some weak human would stumble on his bait of pure aether and not be able to resist it. In this way, he'd been recruiting vassals for thousands of years. Rifts had opened before, but they had never been stable. He'd barely snatched four females into his realm before the last one slammed shut. He longed for a portal anchored enough to allow him to cross over into the human world.

He pulled back his thick lips, taking the scent into glands in his jowls.

Yes. It tasted of human aether, spicy and delicate all at once. He sniffed again and smiled. That wasn't the scent of any human. That was the reek of his kin.

He'd hooked his bastard daughter.

His beards bristled with desire, and his phallus stood erect, a mighty monument to his vigor. He had not forgotten how that puny bitch denied him his last attempt to manifest in their world. He would make her pay. This time she would come to him. This time he would drain every drop of her blood to break out of his prison and return to the land where humans ran fat and free, ripe fruit for his taking.

"I smell humans, but where is the rift?" His voice boomed like mountains colliding. The imp cringed.

"It is here, great one. Right here." He pointed to the empty air. "Look! Look! They try to close it with their feeble magic. But it is here!" He prostrated himself in the sand.

Koro stroked his lower beard, contemplating the emptiness before him. It shimmered with heat coming off the sand. He reached one massive hand and sliced the air. His black claw snagged on something and his lips spread in a hideous smile full of jagged teeth. He pulled the claw away and a tiny thread of the universe came with it.

The witches tried to repair the rift, but it was only patched. In time, he would unravel it.

"I please the great one?" The imp looked up from his servile posture.

"Yes." Koro reached down and pulled off the creature's head. He drank hot blood pumping from its neck and tossed away the corpse. Blood soaked his skin and hair. It was only imp blood, nothing like the ichor from the veins of a human witch.

He sat on the burning sand and stroked himself.

Soon.

Book 4

BELLWETHER MAGIC

ENFORCEMENT

Rosie wiggled her butt like a cat ready to pounce. She leaped from the creek's edge and landed on the opposite bank—some twenty feet away—with a graceful flutter of stunted imp wings.

She turned with a shy smile.

"Your turn, most beatific one."

I slogged through the icy knee-high water to the other side, grumbling about show-offs, and we headed up a muddy hill.

The air misted, not rain nor fog, but a clinging hybrid of the two that seeped into my clothes and dripped from my hair. It dampened sound and filled the space between trees with ghostly elegance, leaving ample cover for our prey.

I had no idea how Rosie tracked through this numbing weather. Up another muddy slope, past a giant wheel of roots from an upended tree, she followed a path I couldn't see.

Rosie came through the dimensional rift that my blundering magic opened a few months back. Attracted to the scent of my demon blood, she followed me like a rescue puppy but, in truth, she rescued me. At least, she rescued me from a life without Quinn. Her healing magic brought him back from the brink of death after my father's latest attempt to kill me.

Thoughts of Quinn tangled my emotions. There was desire—he was one good-looking male specimen—and a good dose of worry, since his illness had no cure. And love. I finally and freely admitted the depth of my feelings for him.

But today, Quinn mostly ticked me off.

Which was why I now slogged through the rain hunting imps instead of back in the relative warmth of my cottage at the coven.

We sparred this morning and not with swords or magic. With words, the most hurtful of all weapons. While he hadn't actually said the rash of imps infesting the forest was my fault, any deaths or damage they caused were on my head. The Paragon knights rounded up most of the beasties and I decided it was my job to hunt down the last stragglers. Quinn didn't agree.

And then he did the unthinkable. He tried to soothe me, to sway my emotions with magic so I wouldn't leave. In the months since William Fain's attack, I learned to protect myself against such magic, and Quinn's was a half-hearted attempt at best. I saw right away he regretted it, but his petty trick fired my rage. More words were flung about. Accusations of weakness and mistrust. I yelled. He yelled. I yelled some more. He forbade me from going hunting alone.

I went anyway.

It seemed like a good idea at the time. Now I wasn't so sure. Rosie and I had scoured the forest for hours with no sightings of the last band of imps. We knew they hid out here somewhere because the Paragon sentries spotted them on their nightly rounds, but every time they tried to make contact, the imps fled.

"Are you sure you know where you're going?" I asked. Rosie stopped and held one finger to her nose. Her fingers had extra knuckles and looked more like weathered twigs than appendages.

"I smell them, most divine super being. Blood. Death stink. Unwashed *impzadzl.*" She sniffed the air and pointed up another muddy hill.

All I smelled was spring rot, but if Rosie said the imps were close, I believed her.

Weariness and rain dampened my anger, and I wanted to set things straight with Quinn. It was time to wrap up this little escapade. I'd put off using my magic as long as possible, but now I called it and surrounded myself in a warm cloud of aether. The chill instantly left my bones. Trudging over the mushy ground, my thoughts turned dark as the spell fouled my mood even more than the weather. Lately, using my magic brought this black taint like a fog of dissatisfaction that muddied my emotions. It was becoming harder to ignore.

In the two months since returning with my mother's grimoire, I'd taken up residence in the Hidden Coven and begun magic training in earnest with the witches to guide me. Except there were no other magic users like me. No one in the coven could properly train me. My power came from demon blood. Simple spells exploded in my hands, while dark magics, like connecting to the coven's hungry core, came with ease and left my mood dark and sour.

Maybe when I drank the aether of that berserker demon, it poisoned me.

Or maybe my demon heritage caused it. Either way, I hoped the murkiness was a temporary side-effect, something I would overcome as I mastered my talents. For now, it only added to my dismal mood.

Rosie stopped at the fresh carcass of a pig-like animal. The imps weren't the only creatures to come through the rift, but they were the most sentient. The imps hunted the other beasts for food. Perhaps they didn't like the taste of our pigs and pheasants. That meant fewer beasts for our hunters to round up, but I was more concerned with finding the imps before they migrated into the general population.

The carcass was gutted, its soft internal organs gone along with the thick slabs of muscle. Bony legs, tusks and skull were left for scavengers. Rosie knelt and touched the rib bones still red with blood.

"Not long ago. They eat." She nudged a pile of smaller bones beside the dead beast. They were gnawed clean. "They ate much. Slow like…*zerbogs*." When I looked confused at the imp word, she made a vague gesture at the ground. "Squishy beast, big shell. Eat leaves and children."

"Snails?" I didn't know of any snail that could eat a child, but Rosie's world was far different from ours.

"Snail. Maybe. It slow?"

I nodded. Rosie's grasp of our language came mostly from serving humans captured by Koro. Possibly hundreds or thousands of captives, my mother among them. That thought darkened my already black mood and I shut it down.

I glanced at the sky, barely visible through the canopy. It was hard to tell in the mist, but it had to be late afternoon.

"Can we catch up to them?"

Rosie stuck one gnarled finger in her ear and scratched. The gesture made her seem child-like, except for the razor-sharp teeth protruding from her mouth even when it closed. She relaxed and listened. Her leathery wings opened and shut with the beat of aether flowing through her veins.

A loud snap broke the silence. Rosie spun, but I was already staring at an imp with a nocked arrow pointed at my chest. A dozen more emerged from the mist, pointing crudely made spears with fire-hardened tips. I dropped my warming spell and started spinning a ward.

"Move." One imp prodded me with a spear. Since he stood only two-feet high, he hit the back of my knee. The jab startled me, and I lost the threads of my spell. Rosie snarled.

"It's okay," I said. "Let's see what they want."

"They want food. They eat you, most holy one." Rosie stepped between me and the larger imp with the bow. She snapped a few words at him in their mother tongue. The imp growled. Rosie lunged at the bow, but he jerked back. Two others tried to grab her.

A dozen spear tips held me still while Rosie thrashed and cursed in a mixture of English and imp tongue.

"Stupid…impzadzl…Get off!" Rosie's tail lashed out. A shriek told me she hit her mark.

"Fenryn, you die!" She pointed at the imp with the bow and arrow. He seemed to be in charge of this band of rogues. "You assault holy one?" She pointed at me.

"Not holy," Fenryn said. He was taller than Rosie but younger. The gold triangle tattooed to his forehead was brighter, his face less like worn leather, and his flattened nose had been broken more than once. Like the other male imps, he was tailless.

"Stupid." Rosie's tail swatted Fenryn on the back of his head. "No brains. Smell. She most supernal celestial holy beatific one. Even broke nose knows."

The spears dipped as imps dropped to their knees, heads pressed into the wet earth.

Fenryn stood his ground though he let his bow drop. Either his mashed nose wasn't sensitive enough to detect my demon heritage, or he didn't care.

"Bring," he snapped. "Horg choose."

DISAGREEMENT

Quinn watched Bobbi walk away.

He'd screwed up. He didn't need to see the stiffness in her back to understand. The hurt in her eyes had told him everything.

He stood under darkening clouds long after she disappeared into the forest, wanting to go after her and knowing he couldn't. Already, his legs trembled from standing so long. The mawr was kicking his ass today, but even if he was perfectly fit, Bobbi wouldn't welcome his company.

How had he been so stupid? He let a simple argument get the best of him. No, he didn't want Bobbi going into the forest with alien beasts running around, but she wouldn't listen to reason. She was hellbent on fixing this mess as if the safety of the entire coven rested on her shoulders.

It didn't. He was the security chief. It was his job to make sure the coven stayed safe, stayed hidden. He'd failed, and now he was failing at this relationship thing.

The sky opened and dumped cold rain on him.

Perfect. She was out there with only an imp to guard her and she'd get soaked. He cursed his weak body for holding him back. Then he cursed his bad judgment.

When the argument got out of hand, he'd soothed her.

Lord and Lady, what was I thinking?

William Fain once held Bobbi in his sway for days using soother magic. He tried to rape her as Koro's proxy. Quinn witnessed the devastating effect of Fain's assault and watched with pride as she climbed out of the depression and fear that followed. She learned to wield a sword, a knife and her magic so no one could ever soothe her again. And then the attack came from the one person she should trust the most.

The sight of her eyes widening in shock as she broke through his aether and realized what he'd done was one nightmare he would take to the grave. He rubbed rain from his eyes with a shaking hand. Thankfully, that grave wasn't far off.

Let the gods damn him.

He could reason all he wanted—mawr left his judgment impaired or exhaustion made him want to end the argument—but those were excuses, and unforgivable. Still, he would beg her forgiveness when she returned.

A shout came from the imp yard. He dragged a hand through his wet hair and went to see what the problem was.

One of his guards found him as he burst through the trees at the head of a clearing.

"What's going on?"

"Rioting," the guard said. "Can't tell why. They're a strange lot."

Quinn had ordered a temporary fence set up around three old cottages to house the imps that the knights had rounded up. The creatures couldn't be kept prisoner forever, but until he knew exactly where their loyalties lay, he wasn't taking any chances.

Several imps beat on the fence with large sticks. As he watched, a gang of the little creatures heaved against a post, and it gave way in the soft ground. The imps cheered and rushed through the gap only to stop short when they saw Quinn and the guard.

"We no criminal!" cried the imp in the lead. "No fence!"

"You are our guests." Quinn held out placating hands. "The fence keeps you safe."

Grumbles rose from the pack of imps.

"Other beasts hunt in those woods," Quinn continued, "beasts that came through the rift like you. We don't have enough guards to protect you."

"Impzadzl protect impzadzl." The imp pounded a fist against his bony chest.

Quinn was weary. He wanted to go home, get out of the rain, and sleep. Instead, he stoked what little aether he had left and wove a binding spell to keep the imps contained.

"Go back to your cottages and we'll discuss it." He tried to sound reasonable. The imps muttered and wandered away from the enclosure. The spell was taking longer to shape than it should. He needed to keep them together until then.

Thunder rumbled. Several imps spooked and ran for the trees.

"No!" Quinn shouted. He cast his spell like a net, trying to contain the fleeing imps but didn't have the power to make it work. They scattered even as the tattered ends of his spell fell away, leaving him gasping for air.

He doubled over as pain shot through his gut.

"Get Paragon…Get Henry," he said through clenched teeth. "Tell him to round up the imps. And fix the fence!" The guard was already running for help.

Quinn sunk to his knees on the cold, wet ground.

JUDGMENT

Rosie snarled, and I held her back.

"It's all right." I wanted to meet this Horg guy. If we convinced this last band of rogues to return to the coven, at least part of my mess would be taken care of. Then I just needed to fix the gaping hole in dimensions. No biggie.

I let the imps lead me, walking in the middle of the spear-bearers while Rosie dashed around, knocking spears aside if they got too close.

Fenryn brought us to a small campsite huddled against a rock outcropping. A shallow cave provided the only shelter, and here stood the biggest imp of the lot. Nearly three-feet tall—a good head above the others—he leaned on a thick spear at the cave opening. A small fire burned at his feet and a female imp fed it sticks.

Rosie tugged on my jacket. I leaned over to hear her whispered warning.

"That Horg, most divine holy one. Make him believe or killing start."

I didn't know if Horg was a name or a title, but the way she dropped her eyes to this new imp made me think he had power. Fenryn whispered in his ear—no doubt informing him of my claim to fame—and Horg watched me. There was intelligence in his gaze, but also a good dose of animosity.

Make him believe, Rosie had said. My aether was demon-laced. Most of the imps sensed it but apparently not all. Rosie wanted me to convince them I was what they called a holy one, the demons who ruled their world and enslaved them.

I didn't want to enslave anyone.

I bowed to Horg. He frowned but nodded slightly. A good start.

Someone thrust a plate of crispy meat into my hand. I remembered the dead pig creature.

"No, thanks. I'm good." The server-imp thrust the rough wooden plate harder and accompanied it by the prod of a spear. I took the meat. It stank like sewage.

They'd moved several large rocks into place around the fire pit. Imps are strong for their size. I sat and balanced the plate on my knee. Horg sat on a taller rock so our eyes were level.

He ate in silence, feeding charred bits of meat to the female at his feet. She was pale and underfed with the twitchiness of a beaten dog.

Horg seemed willing to wait until the food was consumed before opening discussions. I studied the situation while pretending to eat the disgusting meat. By the piles of discarded bones, they'd been settled here for some time. I sized up the rest of the group, about a dozen males but only the one sickly female.

"What's wrong with her?" I whispered to Rosie.

"Blood whore." Her lip curled and a low growl came from her throat. I wondered if Rosie's disdain came from a moral compunction against prostitution or if the term meant something worse. Before I could ask, Horg threw down his plate.

"You not demon. Not holy one." He flicked his fingers at me in a dismissive gesture.

Rosie puffed herself up, ready to defend my celestial reputation. Fenryn primed his bow again. This time the arrow pointed at Rosie. I held her back with one hand on her bony shoulder and addressed Horg.

"I am not holy in this world, but I carry the blood of the one you call Kororaeth."

Several imps sucked in their breath. Others muttered or made quick signs with their hands.

"We impzadzl free." Horg stood and pounded a fist against his chest. His tattered shirt fell open to reveal a chunky stone, sparkly like fool's gold on a cord around his neck.

"Here we not follow. Here we go as we go." He waved a fist toward the woods.

Horg's English was worse than Rosie's, but his sentiment was clear. He wouldn't be bossed around anymore. So far, "we go as we go" meant only as far as the forests around the coven, but if they kept going, they'd end up in a populated region. The coven's ward kept out humans, not animals. And since Rosie had followed me to my old house in the Adirondaks, we could assume it didn't affect the imps either.

Magic was seeping into the world, leaking from bloated ley-lines. I could let the imps go. Sooner or later, the growing magic would force mundanes to confront other supernatural creatures as they came out of hiding or from whatever stasis kept them safe these past centuries. But my world—the one I left behind in Ashlet with its quaint main street and nosy neighbors—wasn't ready for Horg and his rogue imps yet. I worried less for Ashlet's citizens than for the imps. They would be killed or detained for further study the moment they were discovered. Somehow, I had to convince them to come back to the coven.

"The witches won't hurt you." I hoped I wasn't lying. "Out there, others of my kind won't understand you. They'll be afraid. They will attack you."

"Not fear humans!" He tugged at the stone on his necklace.

"You should fear them. They'll lock you up and cut you open just to learn what you are."

Horg sneered. "You not holy. You stupid. Coward. Horg not fear."

I took a deep breath. My aether seethed blackly inside me and I fought through its angry bite. I needed diplomacy, not threats.

Rosie stepped forward and slapped Horg across the face. Fenryn let go. His arrow slammed into her chest, flinging her ten feet before she dropped like a rag doll.

I ran to her side. Fear and anger sparked my aether, and I easily called up a ward to surround us. Rosie lay limp, eyes closed, an arrow stuck in her chest just below the left shoulder. A black stain spread from the wound. I didn't know what to do, where to touch. My aether reached out, but I couldn't heal the way Rosie did. I couldn't do anything! My magic was useless. Anger boiled in me, churning the aether like a typhoon.

Then Rosie opened her eyes. She gasped and yanked out the arrow, leaving a ragged tear of skin and black oozing blood but no further damage.

I took a deep calming breath.

The imp heart, it seemed, was not in their chest. Good to know.

Watching Rosie rant and curse calmed my aether down to a simmer. She marched to Fenryn and yanked the weapon from his shaking hands.

"I no mean hurt!" He raised his hands like a shield and begged. "Please! I no mean…"

Rosie clubbed him over the head with the bow and tossed it in the fire with a growl. Fenryn toppled, unconscious before he hit the ground. She spit on him.

I wanted to be Rosie when I grew up.

Horg watched the drama, making no effort to intervene. I followed his lead and pretended the interruption never happened. Rosie's wound was already healing, and she sat at my heel to guard my back.

"Humans don't like change," I said to Horg. "They fear things they don't understand. They will hunt and kill you. You say you don't fear them, but can you keep everyone safe?" I looked pointedly at the rest of the imps. Many looked scared, but that fear might have been for Rosie's snarl. "I offer you a safe place at the coven."

Horg squinted suspiciously at me.

"You let us into your sanctuary?"

"Yes. We already have several impzadzl with us. We are caring for them. "

He took a long moment to consider my words.

"No."

He turned away in dismissal.

The rain and cold wore on me. The endless trek through the woods exhausted me. My heart hurt from my argument with Quinn, and Rosie's wound frayed my nerves.

I was done.

No band of imps would push my buttons any further.

I drew my blade and sliced across my forearm. Churned up aether burst from the wound. The imps nearest me instantly dropped and pressed their faces to the ground.

I ignored them and turned back to Horg.

I needed him to see me, the real me. And if he saw the darkness clouding my aether too? Well, that might convince him to listen to my orders, at least until all the imps were safely back at the coven.

The magic came readily to my fingertips. I needed to use it. Yes. Need. It filled me. The need to taste the darkness. It pulsed through my veins, bringing strength and black euphoria.

Blood dripped down my arm to my fingertips and I flung it at Horg. He flinched as if burned and dropped his eyes. Several imps took a step backward. Someone gasped. Blood splashed the female imp. She licked it off her lips and keened like a wounded animal. Only Rosie's quick reactions kept her grasping hands away from me.

My eyes felt hot and wet and I knew they'd be glowing. Power raised every hair on my body as I puffed up like an angry wolf. Darkness hovered on the edges of my mind, promising violence.

"Hear me, Horg!" Power thundered through my voice. "You will obey, or I will burn you, burn your clan and spread the ashes to the wind!" I flung my aether at the fire and it roared into the sky, an instant bonfire. I pointed at Horg but turned my head, meeting the eyes of every imp who dared me. One by one, they fell to their knees. Only then did I turn to Horg. His face twisted in fury, but he knelt in the dirt and choked out, "Holy one."

"Bring them!" I said.

Rosie smirked and grabbed a fallen spear to prod the imps into compliance.

I let my magic fizzle. Dissatisfaction grumbled in my stomach as it always did when I called the aether but didn't let it out to play. I snatched the spear from Horg's grip and jabbed him until he fell in line with the others. His lip curled into a snarl, but he dragged his female along without protest.

Ailment

It was after dark when I left the imps with Gavin and his vestals. He would make sure they cared for the new arrivals.

The misty rain ended on the walk home, and my hair dried in fuzzy curls around my face like a dandelion gone to seed. I hesitated to knock on Quinn's door. Should I go home and change first? I tried to smooth down my hair. To hell with it. I wasn't here for a romantic tryst. I was here to clear the air.

I knocked.

"Come in." Quinn's voice came quietly through the door. I opened it and found him lying on the couch in the middle of his main room. A faded blanket lay over him and he looked small under it.

I stepped through the door and took a deep breath. It was now or never.

"I want to talk about this morning."

His dark eyes acknowledged me with a slow blink.

"We both said nasty things. Well, I said nasty things. And you let me believe some others."

He stared at me with his trademark dark intensity.

"I screwed up." I had to get it all out before I lost my nerve. "I opened a gods-damned rift. But I've been thinking, I couldn't have done it on my own. I mean, I mess up the simplest spells. There has to be something else going on here. I just can't figure out what."

I rubbed my tired eyes.

"Look, all I want to say is that I'm doing my best to make things right. I needed to find those imps today before they crossed the ward. I'm trying to clean up my mess and I'd appreciate your support. Instead, you treat me like a glass flower, afraid I'll break if I step the wrong way."

Quinn rolled his eyes at me.

No, wait. That was no sardonic expression. His eyes showed only white.

His limbs convulsed, knocking the blanket on the floor. He was having another seizure!

I dropped to his side and grabbed his hands. They were cold. He was on the brink, barely holding on, while I ranted like a loon.

Lord and Lady!

I willed my aether into him, but I had no healing power. I held him until his shaking finally slowed. He opened his eyes and slurred, "Get Abi. Not…not Jane."

I ran. The ground was wet and slick. I skidded around a bend and made for Jane's house, hoping to find Abilene first. One look at my face and Jane would know something was wrong. Luckily, Abilene was just getting home, and I met her in the front yard.

"It's Quinn," I said breathlessly. "You need to come." Her eyes widened, and she pointed back down the road.

"Go! I need my supplies. I'll meet you there."

I needed Rosie too, but she was with the imps at the far end of the coven. And she'd been shot today. I couldn't ask her to spare aether for healing another.

Quinn was shivering when I got back. I pulled the blanket off his bed and laid it over him. He gripped the faded material like a lifeline.

"My father made this…f-for me." His teeth chattered. "He w-was a great weaver."

"It's beautiful." I tucked the blanket around him, turned to his small kitchen and set the kettle to boil.

"Do you have a hot water bottle," I asked.

"B-bathroom."

I rummaged under the sink until I found the rubber bottle, surprised at how steady my hands were.

Keep busy. Don't think about Quinn wasting away before your eyes.

The kettle whistled as Abilene blew in through the front door. I filled the hot water bottle and tucked it under the blankets by Quinn's feet. The wood stove—used to heat the entire cottage—had burned down to embers. I stoked it with fresh wood while Abilene examined Quinn.

She laid her hands on his chest. Magic swirled around them, but I couldn't see how she was using it.

"He needs an aether transfusion and fast," she said. "I gave him some yesterday. It should have been enough." She bit her lip, holding back worry.

Quinn's illness was progressing faster than we thought.

"I can't give him more. I'm too low. It would be dangerous. Do you mind?"

Did I mind? She wanted me to give Quinn my aether. No. I couldn't do that. I'd give him my life if I thought it would help, but my aether was tainted. I still felt the rank darkness that overcame me when I fought with Horg. I wouldn't infect Quinn with it.

"I can't." I stumbled over the words. Could I tell her the truth? Already, most witches in the coven avoided me. Abilene was the only one who never balked at my heritage. She would if I told her what lived inside me.

She watched me with a frown.

"Why not?"

"I just can't."

Her expression settled into one of Jane's—stern, commanding and impassive all at once.

"Well then, be useful at least and find someone who can." She turned away.

I left her fussing with Quinn's blankets and went to find an aether donor. In the village square, Henry, my former magic and martial arts trainer, spoke to several Paragon knights. I pulled him away and explained my need. He followed me back to Quinn's.

"Don't tell Jane," I whispered before we entered the cottage.

Henry smiled. "Not a problem. I try not to talk to Jane at all."

Quinn looked even worse. His face was wan, and his eyes seemed sunken to his soul. Under the blankets, his chest barely rose and fell, each breath a struggle to fill his lungs.

"What do you need?" Henry asked. Abilene shot me an angry glare, then pointed to the chair.

"Sit here. This will hurt."

Henry sat. "Do your worst."

From her bag, Abilene pulled a plastic box like a first aid kit. Inside, a long gray filament lay coiled. Something about it seemed familiar.

"This is a new procedure I've been working on." Abilene picked up the filament. It lay across her hands like a heavy piece of yarn.

"Is that what I think it is?" Henry eyed the thing with a scowl.

"It's a vampire slug." The yarn twitched as Abilene held it near Henry's arm. Lord and Lady, she was going to let it bite him!

"Just do it." Henry's jaw bulged as he gritted his teeth.

"It'll only hurt for a minute. The slug's venom will numb you."

"Terrific."

Abilene lifted the slug. One end split like jaws opening and clamped onto Henry's forearm. He flinched but otherwise held still.

"What's it doing?" I asked. "Drinking his blood?"

"Aether, not blood," Abilene said. "Now hush and let me concentrate."

She stretched the other end of the slug toward Quinn. It latched onto his throat just above the collarbone. He didn't move. Oiling her hands with a spicy scented oil, she ran them over the taut slug from where it attached to Henry, all along the slick gray body to Quinn. Its flesh glowed in the wake of her touch. Soon the creature pulsed with a steady orange light.

"There. Are you okay, Henry?" Abilene asked. He nodded but said nothing. A vein strained at his throat.

Quinn's color improved. The change was immediate. His breathing returned to normal and he seemed restful.

"Amazing," I said.

Abilene beamed.

"It's based on the original theory the Thirteen used to build the core."

That's why the vampire slug looked familiar. It was a smaller version of the core's thirsty tentacles.

"I finessed the spell so it's portable. It has many possible applications. I've been thinking of patenting it with the High Coven. With the magic flux and all, we might need a lot more in the way of magic medicine in the future…"

Abilene rambled on about the possibilities for her spell. I turned to find Quinn watching me, his eyes hooded and dark. Suddenly, our little spat this morning seemed less than pointless.

"I'm sorry," I said, gripping his hand.

"Me too." He smiled. "Stay with me?"

"Always." I sat on the floor beside the couch and laid my head on his shoulder, watching Henry's aether pump into him through the slug.

Half an hour later, Abilene announced that Henry could stand no more. She unlatched the slug, now grown fat on his aether, and packed away her gear.

She offered to help get Quinn to bed, but he resisted her fussing and stood on his own.

"Thank you," he said. "Both of you. I feel better." He shook Henry's hand and walked them to the door.

"You'll take care of him?" Abilene glared at me, still mad that I hadn't offered up my aether.

"Of course. I'll stay the night."

"Make sure you rest," Abilene scolded Quinn. He kissed her on the forehead, then gently pushed her out the door.

I made tea.

Quinn sat at the kitchen table, his mug warming his hands. I sat across from him.

"We should talk," I said.

Impediment

When Bobbi came to live at the coven, Quinn cleaned out an extra cottage, so she had her own space even though she spent most of her time at his place. He enjoyed having her stay with him, but his illness was progressing faster than he expected. There were times he craved privacy—times when he didn't want anyone fussing over him like a dying man.

He fiddled with his mug, thinking this was one of those times.

"You're right. We should talk." He rubbed a hand over his face. How could he explain why he'd committed the ultimate betrayal and soothed her? Why did he do it? Because he was weak. They all knew that.

Quinn is sick. Quinn is dying. Quinn looks like warmed over pot roast.

He heard them talking. Or rather he heard them stop talking when he entered a room as if their words might crack the fragile shell that held him together.

He wasn't weak. Yes, his body was dissolving like a sand castle in the rain, but the fire inside still burned. The fire to *know* things.

And Bobbi was the most unknowable thing. She watched him with those inscrutable eyes, hiding her magic from the world and from him. She thought she hid the darkness inside her. But he'd experienced the true might of her aether. She couldn't hide it from him when they made love. It didn't scare him. Only losing her scared him. That was the worst part of this damned illness. He was losing bits of himself everyday.

Already he'd passed off most of his duties to Henry. He no longer wielded magic with any assurance. Soon he'd need help for the simplest things. Someone would have to feed him, bathe him. Wipe his ass.

The thought horrified him.

Bobbi would do it. And every time she wiped drool off his face, he'd lose a little more of her. Of himself.

"After what Fain did to you…" He tried to come at the problem from the back door. "I didn't consider that at all. This morning, I mean. I didn't want to fight with you. I'm sorry." He was making a mess of this apology.

Bobbi shook her head. "It doesn't matter."

She didn't look angry anymore. Good. He wouldn't play the pity card on purpose, but at least the damned mawr had some usefulness. It was hard to stay angry when they had so little time left.

"You know what I really need? I need to get into bed and feel your naked skin pressed up against mine." He smiled. "It would do a lot to heal me."

Bobbi smiled back. "Are you trying to seduce me?"

"Maybe."

"Seems like an awful waste of poor Henry's hard-earned aether."

"You can share yours with me then." His hand slipped up her thigh, but she pulled away.

"You don't like to share?" he asked.

She stood and turned to the sink, fiddling with the cups, washing them, placing them in the drying rack and wiping her hands on a dish towel before turning back to him.

"Come on." He pulled her across the room to the bed.

She stumbled into him and they fell laughing onto the covers. He pinned her and rested on his elbows, looking down at her face. He took her all in, from the peak of her hair to the dark blue eyes, and full curve of mouth.

"You're so beautiful."

Dear Lord and Lady, did that lame line just come out of his mouth?

Bobbi smiled. It didn't light up her face. It was a smile to reassure. She was here. She was on board, no matter how feeble he might be.

Slipping off her shirt, she lay beside him, skin to skin. She filled his senses: her scent, the soft touch of hair on his shoulder, her aether mingling with his like shadow and fog.

The feel of her surrounding him made him hard.

Welcome old friend.

He wasn't dead yet.

He traced her lip with a thumb, then pushed it inside. She sucked, dragging teeth along the pad of his thumb. Direct hit to his groin. He kissed her, willing her to let go and forget the day of arguments and illness. She responded, but she was tense. He lingered in the kiss, tasting her with tentative touches of his tongue, not stopping until she melted against him.

He tugged her on top of him. She stretched, and he enjoyed his body against hers, inch for inch.

"Sir, I believe you were at death's door a few hours ago," she said with mock severity. "Tell me you have only rest on your mind."

"I'll rest with the dead when I'm ready. But for now…" He flipped her and pinned her arms above her head to begin work on the sensitive hollows at her throat.

"You have pep for a dead guy," she said. He laughed, tickling her neck with his breath. She squirmed. This was their thing. They refused to let his illness have any hold on them. If they laughed in its face, it could only take his body, not his soul.

Bobbi wiggled to kick off her shoes and pants while Quinn stripped. He pushed aside her white lacy bra, eager for the flesh underneath. He straddled her and leaned in for a kiss before moving down, his tongue circling her nipple, drinking fire off her skin. Her back arched as she ground against him.

"Easy now. I'm not done yet." He turned his attention to the other breast. She arched again.

Quinn hummed and continued to lick and nip. His lips tugged at her ear, then bit her shoulder, the soft flesh of her inner arm and the swell of her breast.

"What's that song?" Her voice came breathy and faint.

"Just an old song. *The arm bone's connected to the shoulder bone…*" He kissed her arm and shoulder. "*The neck bone's connected to the rib bone.*" More kisses trailed from her neck to chest, then he went back to tug at her nipple, now standing at attention. She made a small animal sound.

"*The nipple bone's connected to the…*oh, look." He grinned and planted more kisses down her stomach. "Looks like the nipple bone's directly connected right here." His tongue found the nub in her fur and he sucked it.

She cried out. It was a beautiful sound. He circled with his tongue, feeling her excitement grow. Her hands fisted in his hair, her body arched, and he drank it all in until she throbbed with release.

She fell bonelessly back on the bed, and he crawled up her body, his erection so hard, the grating of her skin against his almost set him off. She smiled and kissed him, all previous tension gone. One hand snaked down to grip him, ready to guide him inside her.

That's when the world went black. The edges of his vision darkened, then closed on him. Light came back quickly but left him shaking. And weak. So gods damnable weak.

"Fuck." He fell back on the covers, shivering like a hypothermia victim, all romantic thoughts forgotten. Bobbi touched his face, and he jerked away. He couldn't deal with the pity shining in her eyes. Not now.

"Are you okay?"

"Fine," he said through teeth gritted against the chattering.

"Can I get you something? Tea?"

Why did she think tea would solve every problem?

"Just leave me alone."

She sucked in a breath as if he'd slapped her, and he shrank into himself even more.

What an ass he was, spiraling out of control, letting self-pity and weakness steer him in an unbreakable loop.

"Lord and Lady, I'm a selfish ass," Bobbi said.

He couldn't help a grin. "I was just thinking the same about myself."

"No. Even this morning, I understand what happened. I shouldn't have been so upset."

"My fault—"

She laid a hand over his lips. "No faults. Not between us. Not anymore."

She covered him in blankets, though the night wasn't cold and slipped in beside him, warming him with her body. After a while, the shaking stilled.

"I'm sorry," he said. "Aether transfusions give me a bit of a high. Make me overly optimistic."

"It's okay. I should have made you rest."

"I'm tired of resting."

"I know."

Resting wouldn't help. They both knew it. No amount of sleep would replenish the aether that mawr stole from him.

FOMENT

I didn't sleep well. In my dreams, shadowy figures chased me through a shifting forest. Trees stepped into my path and tripped me as I ran. Fog wrapped ghostly arms around my wrists and tried to pull me down into the murk. I didn't need a shrink to tell me I was reliving yesterday's hunt for the imps, but it felt bigger than that. The shadows tasted of my aether, and once I turned and saw myself standing there. Me watching me run. I was stalked by my own magic.

I woke feeling uneasy. Quinn was already gone. Coffee, usually a cure for all morning ills, only added to the acid roiling in my stomach. I clutched my mug and stood on Quinn's front porch. The rain passed overnight, leaving the world scrubbed raw.

Someone called to me and the bright morning sun sliced across my eyes as I turned. Gavin trotted up the path.

"How is he?" He nodded toward Quinn's cottage.

"Much better. Already up and on the job. Your man has potent aether."

Gavin smiled. "He does."

Henry and Gavin didn't hide their romance, but neither did they advertise it. Henry was intensely private, and I wouldn't offend him by prying.

Rosie yawned and stretched her wings. Apparently, she returned during the night and slept on the front porch. Seeing her, Gavin seemed to remember his original intent for the visit.

"You need to talk to the imps," he said. "They won't listen to us."

"The new group won't integrate with the others," Gavin said. "They refuse to sleep in the cottages, and they won't eat anything made by human hands." He explained that their odd behavior affected the imps already living in the compound, and now all of them slept on the cold ground, ignoring the vestals' attempts to bring food and comfort. And worse, they were tearing apart the cottages and burning furniture.

"I thought you and Rosie might make them listen to reason." Gavin rubbed his face. He looked tired and more rumpled than usual.

"What do they want?"

He shrugged. "I have no idea."

"Well, let's go find out."

We emerged from the forest trail where three large guest cottages stood in the clearing surrounded by a wood fence. Plastic mesh blocked a large gap in the fence.

"What happened there?" I asked.

Gavin shrugged. "They tried to escape yesterday. Broke through and ran off. We've got more guards posted."

Keeping the imps segregated made me uncomfortable. The fence wouldn't keep them in, but it sure made our position on their status clear.

I marked the guards walking the compound's perimeter, all Paragon knights. When had Quinn let them supplant the coven's security detail?

We stepped inside the yard and I smelled smoke. In the center of the clearing, a pile of wooden chairs burned. An imp slowly turned a spit with a blackened carcass. Two dozen more imps sat around the fire drinking from earthenware mugs.

Another group sat on the porch of a cottage. That's when my gaze snagged on the damage. The second cottage was missing a wall. I peered right inside to the empty room. As I took in the sight, an imp pried off another board and carried it to the fire pit.

"They took offense at the extra guards and started burning anything they can carry away," Gavin said.

"They stupid ungrateful, *hoogstzn*." Rosie huffed. *Hoogstzn* probably wasn't a compliment. "Most beatific one should toss them into pit of burning oil." Apparently, that was an acceptable punishment on her world.

"Let's see what's going on before we start deep-frying people."

She harrumphed. "Holy idol of celestial grace is most merciful."

Rosie's honorifics were becoming more elaborate. And more tiresome. I didn't want to be her god or anyone else's, but arguing with her was useless. She believed I was holy like the demons who ruled her old world, and she would serve me as such. That didn't mean I accepted her servitude. In fact, I tried not to command her to do anything. Asking and commanding were fine distinctions, but at least my conscience was eased.

"Bobbi." The quiet call caught my attention. Henry broke away from the other knights and headed toward us.

"What is that?" I asked, pointing at the barbecue.

"A boar, sort of. It came through the rift and tore up the forest. The imps asked to hunt it."

"And you let them?"

"We followed, of course," Henry said. "Damned good trackers those little guys. And tough too. It took near twenty of them to take down that beast, but they did it. Not a coward among them." He seemed pleased that the creatures he guarded were capable of such violence. Henry always did like a good fight.

Another imp left the fire to pull a piece of siding off the cottage and toss it into the flames. The remains of a sofa and table already burned in the fire pit. They'd stripped everything flammable.

"If they keep tearing the cottages apart, they won't have any place to live," I said.

"We tried explaining," Henry said. "They don't seem to care. We hoped you and your, uh…sidekick here could talk sense into them."

"Maybe." Rosie listened to me, but despite Horg's willingness to follow me back to the coven yesterday, I wasn't sure he would take my instructions.

I surveyed the scene in the harsh morning light. The imps on the porch were all occupied with tasks. One sharpened a blade with a whetstone, another wove a net, while a third ground a pestle into a large mortar. Something odd struck me. These imps were all female, easy to recognize by the long tails curled at their feet. The knife wielder's tail thrummed the porch boards in a beat to her whetting.

I glanced toward the others. All tailless males, except for the female at Horg's side. She sat with shoulders hunched as if trying to make herself unnoticeable. Her thin tail wrapped around her chest like a blanket.

Horg wasted no time setting himself up as king of this little colony. His gaze settled on us and he snarled. Rosie lifted a lip and snarled right back.

"Why don't you like him?" I asked.

"*Kehaziuf.*" Rosie spat in the dirt and translated. "Servant of bad Holy One."

"Weren't you all servants? I thought you had no choice."

"Horg like it." She bared her sharp little teeth.

So, Horg was not so much a slave as a fellow conspirator.

"And what's with her?" I nodded toward the female imp at the fire. "You called her a blood whore. What does that mean?"

Rosie sniffed. "She sell sex for blood of holy ones."

"What? You mean she drank from the demons?"

Ew.

Rosie nodded and smiled smugly. "She addicted. No holy one. No drink."

Well, that explained why the thin female's eyes followed my every move. She was going through withdrawal and I was the only source of her fix.

"How often do they go hunting?" I asked Henry.

"Not often, but we can't let them out again. That Horg guy stirred things up. The bonfire is his doing. But he doesn't do much for himself. Seems to like to watch the others work."

After a life of servitude, I bet he enjoyed his new lordship.

"You'll keep an eye on them, right?" I asked.

Henry nodded. "They can't get through the ward anymore. Jane and the Thirteen tweaked it to block them. But as you can see," he pointed to the stripped lodge, "there's a lot of other mischief they can get up to."

I approached Horg's little band of merry imps and they fell silent. Not that they were chatty before. The lone imp turning the spit kept his arm moving, but the others sat meekly with their heads bowed. Only Horg dared to meet my eye.

His female friend watched me with hunger in her reddened eyes. Drool slipped from her mouth, but she didn't wipe it away.

"Can we chat for a moment in private?" I wanted to get Horg away from his minions, hoping to appeal to his better nature if he didn't have an audience to play for.

"Talk here."

Fine.

"You need to stop tearing down the cottages for firewood."

Horg sipped his drink, thick fingers nearly eclipsing the small cup. His low brow shaded deep-set eyes, but I read intelligence in them.

"No."

I took a deep breath. No use getting frustrated. The language barrier alone was enough to cause misunderstandings.

"There's plenty of good wood in the forest to burn. Use that."

"No."

"Why not?"

"Not burn."

"You mean you can't burn it or it won't burn?"

"No." Horg didn't seem to have any expression besides a multipurpose scowl.

"Right. Let's make something clear." I marched to the tree line. It didn't take me long to find a thick deadwood branch in the forest littered with post-winter debris. They had no excuse for burning the house.

When I returned to the fire with my branch, the imps instantly forgot their meekness and jumped to their feet. Horg's jaw unhinged like a snake's and he let out a roar.

"It will burn. I assure you." I tried to keep my voice even. Diplomacy was never my strong suit, and these guys pissed me off. Aether boiled in my veins, getting ready for an attack. I reached the branch toward the fire pit and suddenly a dozen spears pointed at my chest. Horg didn't move.

"Not burn."

"Okay, no burning." I let the branch drop to the ground. The spears lowered.

Rosie brushed past the weapons. She jabbed a finger at Horg and yelled in their language. Horg stood and towered over her, but Rosie didn't back down. Her tail swished, and the other imps jumped out of its way. The five females rose from their tasks on the porch, all eyes focused on this new confrontation.

Horg and Rosie screamed at each other. Spittle flew from his mouth, flecking her face. She stomped her foot. He shook a fist. Finally, the big imp had enough. He backhanded Rosie across the cheek, hard enough that she flew backward and landed only inches from the fire. The other imps gasped.

The females entered the circle like grim reapers on the hunt. One by one, they drove a fist into Horg's face. Each blow cracked like thunder. Horg held his ground. He didn't block the punches, but neither did he cower. After each of the five laid a blow, he wiped black blood from the corner of his mouth and nodded.

The females retreated without a word.

I had a lot to learn about imp justice, but I liked it.

I helped Rosie up.

"Are you okay?"

She glared at Horg. "He hit like…butterfly." That was probably a worse insult in her mother tongue.

"Why are they burning the houses?"

"They ignorant fearful impzadzl." Rosie rubbed the dark mark left from

Horg's strike. I waited for more. "Horg say wood not dead, most holy one. He say forest spirits live in wood found under their protection. Burning brings curse."

I sorted that in my head. "Don't forest spirits live in living wood like trees?" I asked.

"Dead trees have dead spirits. Live spirits take anger if burned, most holy one." She bowed her head as if worried the news would displease me.

"I see." Horg didn't want to risk angering the forest spirits by burning their dead. "But they burned wood in their camp yesterday."

"There is special…" Rosie searched for the word, "special chanting?"

"A spell?" I asked.

"No magic. Blessing. Special words release dead spirits from wood before burning."

Horg pointed angrily at Henry. "Soldiers not let blessing for dead."

More was going on here than a misunderstanding. I pulled Henry, Gavin and Rosie away from the others to confer.

"Is this true?" I asked Henry. "Did you stop them from practicing these death rites?"

He shrugged. "Didn't seem like a good idea to let them continue. They might call it a blessing, but they were chanting in a circle. Looked an awful lot like spell-work. And there's no telling what these little buggers can conjure."

"So, no chanting," I said.

"Not on my watch." Henry was adamant, and I saw his point. Without understanding their language we'd have no idea what their chanting meant. They might summon a wraith or a minor demon, and we'd be helpless to intervene until it was too late.

"What about the wood from the cottages? Doesn't that hold spirits?" I asked Rosie.

"Cottage wood very dead. Spirits far away and no risk to impzadzl."

"So, if I bring them really dead wood from another place, they'll leave off burning down our cottages?"

"Maybe." Rosie shrugged. "Horg intensely stupid."

I glanced at the imp lord who sat back on his rock, no worse for the beating he took. He didn't seem stupid to me.

"Is there anyone in this camp you trust?" I asked. "Anyone you're sure isn't under Horg's sway?"

Rosie pointed to the five females on the porch and three others.

"Tell them to perform the rites under your supervision." Rosie nodded deep enough to be a bow.

I turned to Henry. "Set up a ward in a space big enough to contain their rites."

"Outside the fence," Henry said. "I don't want Horg anywhere near it."

I agreed with his precautions. Walking back to Horg, I ignored the hunger in the blood whore's eyes as she scanned my every movement.

"We will let you perform your spirit rites," I said. Horg brightened. "But I choose who does it." Horg scowled. I let a bit of demon shine from my eyes. The blood whore whined. "You will do this, or I will separate you from the others. And you will learn the true difference between a guest and a prisoner."

Horg considered for a long moment.

"Yes, holy one." His words were polite, but the hate in his eyes told another story.

RESENTMENT

With the midsummer festival only a week away, Jane's house was full of witches making preparations. Quinn let himself in through the kitchen where two witches argued over a recipe for mooncakes. Others were busy making flower crowns and sewing gowns. Novice witches traditionally joined the coven at the sabbats. It was a busy time, one that would normally keep the head of security running from dawn to dusk. But today, Quinn was at odds.

The screen door slammed behind him. A young woman came in carrying baskets of dried herbs and left them on the table. She smiled shyly at Quinn and disappeared out the door again. He headed toward the great room to find his mother.

Bobbi's voice stopped him in the hall, and he peered inside the room. She stood beside the round wooden table while Jane fussed with a floral arrangement, removing stalks and trimming them with scissors before putting them back. His mother, always the perfectionist.

Despite their night of rest, Bobbi looked tired.

"We need to make some decisions about the imps," Bobbi said.

Jane wave a hand as if Bobbi's concern was nothing more than smoke in her eyes.

"The imps are being cared for."

"For now. But they won't live happily ever after in your little cabins surrounded by a fence. They aren't prisoners and we can't treat them as such."

"You're suggesting we let them go into the wild?" Jane raised an eyebrow. Quinn saw Abi in the expression. Did Bobbi see him in there too? The thought unsettled him.

"Maybe. I don't know," Bobbi said.

Not a good answer. Bringing problems without solutions wasn't the way to get what you wanted from Jane.

"Gavin said they're settling in," Jane said. "They seem docile."

"Not anymore. They're burning the cottages piece by piece."

Jane continued to arrange flowers. Bobbi looked worried. Quinn hadn't heard about the burning cottages. He'd ask her about it later. Or maybe he'd ask Henry, who wouldn't spare Quinn the details, worrying for his health.

"I sorted them out for now, but promise me you'll keep watch on them," Bobbi said.

"You want me to guard the imps who aren't prisoners?" Jane twisted words to suit her.

"A watch is not a guard. It's information." Bobbi's tone turned exasperated. "We need to understand their intentions before they do something drastic."

"Wouldn't your pet imp be a better spy?"

Bobbi shook her head. "They segregated the females from the pack. I'm not sure if that's custom or only to keep Rosie away. But one imp stands above the others. Horg. He seems to be their leader."

"Should we kill him?"

Bobbi gaped. The simple question shouldn't have shocked her. Jane would do it. If Horg became a problem—if Horg even hinted at being a problem—she'd kill him.

"We don't need to be that drastic," Bobbi said grimly. "Just have him watched."

"Most people bring their security concerns to me," Quinn said from the doorway. "You know, the head security guy."

Bobbi flinched and looked guilty. His mother turned dark eyes on him, as if she'd known he was listening.

"The vestals are watching Horg," Quinn said. "And I've managed to convince a few imps to report to me too." Which Bobbi would know if she'd come to him with this problem. The sweet—if stunted—romance from last night had done little to bridge the gap between them.

"I would like to speak to my mother," he said. Bobbi nodded and left. Quinn waited until she was out of earshot.

"There was a security briefing about the festival this morning and no one alerted me." Quinn took the scissors from her hand and replaced the flower she held, forcing Jane to give him her full attention.

"You were indisposed." Her lips pinched. So that's what this was about.

"Abi told you about last night."

Jane nodded. *Damn the hells.* He'd asked her not to say anything. His little sister couldn't keep a secret.

"You'd think a son would tell his mother when he almost dies."

The guilt trip. Jane didn't pull out this weapon often, but when she did, she was a master at it.

"I didn't almost die."

"That's not what I heard." Another stab.

"Did you tell Abi she'd go to bed without her supper if she didn't spill the details? She's not a child, Mother. Stop treating her like one. And I'm not a child either."

"Then stop acting like one."

"Me? I'm just trying to do my job. You're the one acting infantile."

Jane grabbed the scissors, snipped a stem and placed another flower.

He saw no point in trading insults. Jane was immune to them, and it wouldn't get him what he wanted, which was to not lose everything important all at once.

"I'm sorry. I should have told you. But that's no reason to exclude me from the festival details. I'm still head of security. I need to know what's going on."

"You're weak." Her words flashed like a knife strike. "It's time to stop pretending. You can no longer be effective in your job. I've given all security concerns to Henry, and Gavin is taking care of the festival."

Quinn stared. She couldn't be serious. First, he failed to make love to his girlfriend; now he was losing his job. If this damned mawr was going to kill him, he wished it would happen soon.

"Fine." He turned away from his mother.

"Quinn wait."

But he had nothing left to say.

EXPERIMENT

I left Quinn with Jane. He looked angry, and I couldn't blame him. Men put so much importance on the act of love. The moments we spent together—not talking or making love, but just being—those were the ones I'd remember long after he was gone. I pushed my palms into my hot eyes and ducked outside, hoping no one would see me so near to tears.

The council meeting would begin soon. I composed myself and went to find Abilene, hoping to catch a few moments alone with her before the meeting started. We met every day, trying to sort out the grimoire Quinn and I brought back from my family's burned out home. Somewhere in its pages, we hoped to find a permanent fix to the hole I'd torn in dimensions. Jane patched the rift and Paragon knights guarded it. So far, nothing else had come through, but it was only a matter of time.

And the grimoire was tricky. Every page could be a trap. Spells were layered over older spells to catch unwary novice witches. I was a very novice witch, but the book was written in demon blood, possibly my father's blood, and so the council deemed me necessary to the process of unlocking its secrets. The group consisted of Jane, Grant and Myra, the only three witches left from the original Thirteen who founded the coven, plus Abilene, Quinn, Gavin, and Henry. With the return of warm weather, we met in the garden. After one trigger spell set Jane's living room curtains on fire, we all felt better taking it outside.

Henry and Gavin were sparring with wooden staffs when I arrived. Their mock fight was more for exercise than battle training, and the intensity that locked their gazes came from an altogether different source. Henry was sweating, his face a deep red. I'd trained with him many times. It took more than light sparring to make him sweat. Had we taken too much aether from him yesterday? Probably. But Henry was strong and healthy. He'd bounce back quickly.

I plopped down next to Abilene who watched them from the patio, arms crossed on the table and head resting on her wrists.

"All the good ones are gay," she said.

"Or your brother."

"Or both." She turned without lifting her head. "You look as tired as I feel."

"Long night."

"Did Quinn keep you up? Is he okay?"

"No, and yes." I didn't want to say more. Quinn wouldn't thank me for airing our personal problems, but I needed Abilene's advice. She was young, not even twenty, but wise beyond her years. On my first visit to the coven, she became my mentor. I went to her for advice about all things magic, but she was also Quinn's sister and Jane's daughter. I couldn't be sure she wouldn't run to them with my confessed sins.

"I'm sorry I couldn't help more with him yesterday."

"It's all right."

No, it really wasn't. Her offhand manner told me she was still disappointed.

"I was afraid of making things worse," I said. She rolled her head along her arms and frowned.

"What do you mean?"

Here goes nothing. I took a breath and spat it out.

"Is it possible my magic is changing me?"

Abilene sat up.

"Changing you how?"

"I'm not sure. Yesterday, I called my aether to control the imps, and I felt different."

When I didn't say more, she prodded. "Different how?"

I watched Henry fake a strike at Gavin, then duck under his return swing, so Gavin's arm circled him. They stood frozen for a moment. Henry pushed away with an evil grin and swung his staff again. Gavin barely raised his in time to parry. The fact that Gavin let Henry touch him so freely told me their relationship had progressed far beyond flirtation.

"Bobbi, tell me what's going on." Abilene said, pulling my attention back.

I shrugged. "I got angry. Really angry." I remembered the unfiltered rage. I wanted to kill Horg for defying me. "Maybe I'm imagining it, but it feels like my aether is tainted."

"Tell me what happened."

I told her about the hunt and the imp encounter. To her credit, Abilene didn't try to sell me platitudes about being over-tired or stressed.

"Is this the first time?"

"No." I thought back to other magic trials, battles to the death with a berserker demon and my standoff with Tanya, Koro's latest agent to strike at me. I'd been furious during those attacks, but who wouldn't be? How did I separate my normal temper with the taint of my magic?

"It might have happened before, but it's getting worse."

"Is this why you didn't want to give your aether to Quinn?"

"Yes."

Abilene thought for a long moment.

"Your magic is different," she said cautiously. "We don't really understand it. You have abilities we recognize." I was a sensate like Abilene. We sensed magic and detected its source. I had other abilities like a resistance to mage-fire and in extreme cases, I could draw aether from another living being. I used this killing magic only twice, on a wraith and a minor demon, and I kept that secret to myself.

"But there's a lot we don't know about your magic, too." Abilene's eyes shifted away from mine. "No one has ever studied demon magic up close."

"No one who ever lived to tell the tale, you mean."

"Right."

"But is it possible that using my magic is corrupting me somehow? Should I be looking behind me for a sprouting tail?"

"I don't think you should worry. But if you want, I can research it."

"Thank you." I wanted to say more, but Quinn joined us, sitting not beside me, but on the far side of the table. He opened a tech magazine and read. Abilene noticed his seat choice and raised an eyebrow in an expression that was Quinn's clone.

He glanced up, saw me watching and scowled. I winked and blew him a kiss. He scowled again. Oh, boy. Something got his goat this morning. I'd sort him out after the meeting. Life, I discovered, was too short to stay mad at the ones you loved. As soon as this meeting ended, I'd ease the crease from between his brows, whether or not he wanted my fussing.

Jane came through the kitchen door carrying a cloth wrapped bundle. Myra followed with Grant leaning heavily on her arm. The three witches sat. Henry and Gavin joined us, puffing from their workout. Jane laid the bundle on the table and unwrapped the book like a prized artifact. Why did she bother? It's not like anything could destroy it. We'd tried to rip out pages, burn them, cut them, shred them. Nothing. Water beaded off it like it was made of wax. I suspected even acid would fizzle out uselessly on it. The grimoire was written in Koro's blood and made to last.

Jane flipped through the heavy pages. They shifted with a slithering sound that made me squirm.

"What's on the menu today?" Gavin asked when Jane stopped at a particular page.

Abilene peered over her mother's arm and said, "Looks pretty straightforward. It's a binding spell." She read off the ingredients. "A poppet stuffed with bloodroot, broom and chamomile. One white taper. One black taper. Salted water."

"A binding spell?" I said. "Can we use it to close the rift?"

Abilene shook her head. "I don't think so. It's something you would use to keep another witch from doing you harm." She read on in a dramatic voice, matching the text's flowery writing. "Now thy heart be bound not against mine. Now thine intent be purified…basic stuff."

"It's another trigger," Myra said.

Grant bobbed his agreement. "We should cast it to be certain." His voice quavered with age, and he pointed at the page with one gnarled finger. "Sometimes a spell is just a spell."

"No. We can't waste time casting every spell in the book," Jane said, then turned to me. "Give me your hand."

Stupidly, I held it out. I should have known better. Faster than a snake strike, Jane whipped out the athame she kept on her belt and sliced across my forearm.

"Mother!" Quinn jerked up, his chair falling to the flagstones. Jane held my wrist in a vise-grip and pulled until my arm hovered over the book. We all waited in silent horror as my blood stretched and fell. It beaded and rolled across the page. Then the book trembled and sucked the blood into the parchment.

Thunder clapped in the blue sky. A branch of flame shot from the page and circled my throat. It strangled and burned. I struggled, gasping for air, but the phantom fire held me tight, slowly pulling me closer to the book that sat unmoving on the table. The others shouted, but I couldn't make out words through the roaring in my ears. My vision pricked with blackness as I lost the fight for breath.

A white flash stung my eyes, and I fell, gasping for sweet air.

INDUCEMENT

Fire leaped from the book and circled Bobbi's throat.

"Bobbi!" Quinn jumped over the table. He grabbed her, not caring if he burned his hands.

"Mother! Do something!" He shook Bobbi. The fire didn't burn, but her eyes bulged as she fought for air.

Jane spat a power word. The demonic flames sputtered and disappeared, leaving Bobbi limp in his arms. She was so pale, so fragile looking. A blue vein pulsed at her temple. Her eyes opened to slits but showed only white.

Rosie appeared and pressed her hands to Bobbi's chest. Jane knelt on the grass and reached for Bobbi, but the imp growled and snapped her sharp teeth.

"She's fine," Jane said placidly. Rosie growled again. Quinn had little sensate magic, but even he picked up the deep throb of Rosie's healing. Her hands seemed to glow, but that might have been a trick of the light.

"Mother, stand back." His growl was almost as fierce as Rosie's. What had Jane been thinking? Bobbi's magic was unstable. And blood magic was always risky, even without the demon connection. He would take a strip off Jane later in private.

Bobbi's eyes fluttered.

"What the f—"

He leaned down and cut off her curse with a kiss. Everyone watched and he didn't care. Her aether buzzed across his lips. He rested his forehead against hers and breathed in her scent, like ripe apples, summer grass and something entirely unique that was Bobbi.

Mine.

"I thought I lost you again."

"Now you know what it feels like," she said.

"We're all dying. Some of us are just better at it than others."

She shoved him without force, smiling weakly. He kissed her again.

Jane cleared her throat. Quinn sat back on his heels but didn't let go of Bobbi's hand that dripped blood onto his sleeve.

"I'm taking her home." He pinned Jane with a glare. "Then you and I are going to have a chat." Jane pursed her lips but nodded once.

Rosie pranced nervously at Bobbi's side as he helped her up. He was glad she could walk because he didn't have the strength to carry her. She leaned heavily on him, and Abi scooted under her other shoulder to pick up the slack. The three of them shuffled along like a six-legged beast. Rosie darted ahead to open the door.

"I'm fine." Bobbi's expression was grim as she slumped at the kitchen table. Abi put the kettle on.

"You're not fine." He pulled grass from her loose ponytail and tucked a stray lock behind her ear before examining the wound on her arm. Her pulse raced under his touch.

"Can you get the first aid kit?" she asked, and Quinn nearly kicked himself for being so slow-witted.

"Of course." He found bandages, gauze and hydrogen peroxide under the sink in her small bathroom. Abi poured tea as he cleaned and wrapped Bobbi's wound.

"Do you have any idea what happened?" Abi asked.

"What happened is our mother sliced open her vein, and the grimoire fed on her like a bloodsucker," Quinn said.

"Did she know it would react like that?" Abi's eyes were big. Quinn didn't want to trash their mother in front of her. Jane had many faults, but she was also Abi's hero. He wouldn't be the one to shatter that image.

"I suspected something would happen," Jane said from the doorway, "but I had no idea it would be so dramatic."

Rosie bared her teeth. Her eyes tracked Jane as she crossed the room and laid the grimoire open on the table. Bobbi crossed her arms and set her lips in a thin line.

She was pissed and he didn't blame her. What Jane did was inexcusable. Witches didn't harm others. Stealing blood was a slippery slope that ended in addiction to dark magics. But Jane knew that slope well. His mother had lived through some horrible things: her kidnapping by Koro, the deaths of her first child and husband. She hardened under the strain like a sword under the blacksmith's hammer. The result left her with a sharp mind and little regard for the feelings of others.

"I've been looking for a way to override the triggers," Jane said. "There are over three hundred spells in this book. If we unlock each one, it will take far too much time."

"So, I'm supposed to bleed all over it and hope that cracks the triggers?" Bobbi said.

Jane pointed at the book.

"Look what you uncovered."

Quinn peered at the page. The simple binding spell had vanished, revealing another spell underneath.

"*Laktentem Konversi*," Bobbi read. "That's not Latin, but it sounds similar."

Abi leaned over to see. "It's possible someone tried to transcribe it phonetically from Latin. You find that a lot in the old spell books."

"That's what I think," Jane said. "It would roughly translate to *backward suckling*."

"I don't get it," Bobbi said, but Quinn had a bad feeling.

"Converso usually means a blocking or counterspell." Abi's voice took on her excitement. "Something to reverse what has been badly done."

"Yes." Jane showed her teeth in what she passed for a smile. "It's a counter spell to a sucking curse…"

"No." Quinn stood up and leaned over the table, forcing his mother to meet his eye. "There is no cure for mawr. You know that."

"But there is." She tapped the book. "It's all laid out here. Simple really. The only stumbling block is this line." She read the words carefully. "Anoint the fire with the blood of the holy unholy." She looked at Bobbi. "That would be you."

More blood. Jane would bleed Bobbi dry on the smallest chance it would cure him.

Bobbi scowled.

"No." Quinn put steel in his voice.

Jane lifted her chin. "Yes."

"Don't I get a say in this?" Bobbi asked.

"No," Quinn and Jane said at the same time.

Bobbi turned away, fists clenched at her sides. Blood soaked through the fresh bandage on her arm. She looked out the window, far away from him. Quinn wanted to go to her, to pull her into his arms and reassure her…of what? He had no platitudes to make things better.

Abi read over the spell ingredients.

"We need four twigs—oak, willow, hazel and elm—a few tapers, and oh, wait. I'm not sure what this means. A source to the mother?" She paused and looked at Jane. "This looks dangerous. Quinn's right. We need more information before we try anything rash."

"We have no time for research," Jane snapped. "Look at him. He's a walking corpse."

"But you saw what a drop of Bobbi's blood did to the book. What if it backfires? It could kill one of them. Or both."

Jane would risk it. Quinn saw it in the set of her shoulders and her grim expression. He was dead if they did nothing, and Bobbi was a reasonable sacrifice if it meant saving him.

"We'll set up wards to protect the village," she said.

"No." Quinn slammed his fist on the table, making the teacups rattle. "I won't allow it!"

"You have no say in this!" Jane yelled right back. "I rule this coven."

"Enough!" Bobbi snarled from across the room. A wave of aether washed over Quinn. Bobbi was leaking magic at an astonishing rate. He'd seen her angry before and she certainly had reason now. But this felt wrong. Like Bobbi wasn't truly in the driver's seat. She glared at them all, then turned and stalked out.

Quinn moved to follow her, but Abi stopped him.

"Let her cool down." She bit her lip with uncertainty. Quinn stared after Bobbi and was glad to see Rosie trailing behind her.

Jane tapped the open grimoire.

"Can we at least discuss the spell?" she asked. "If it's too dangerous, I'll back off. I promise. But we shouldn't give up so easily. You can't give up." She gripped his arm.

He looked from her hand to her pleading eyes. Jane almost never touched him. She wanted him to live. He couldn't fault her for that.

"Fine." He sagged into the chair. "But if this spell puts Bobbi or anyone else at risk, we call it quits. Understood?"

"Understood."

REALIGNMENT

I seethed. The cobblestones hurt my feet as I pounded through the village square. I passed a witch carrying a basket. She smiled, then gasped when my black aether hit her. Fear stoked her eyes, and she cringed as I strode by.

Magic coursed through me, making me strong—strong enough to defy the mistress of the coven.

More witches cringed from my path. I didn't care.

They'd all been afraid of me since the berserker demon broke through the ward. Those who hadn't seen me kill it heard the tale from others. I opened the rift. I was the beacon for my demon father. My crimes were innumerable.

I once longed to find a coven to teach me, a safe space to learn about this strange and wonderful power growing in me. But my power was dark, not wonderful, and the coven was not the haven I hoped for.

Rage built in me, fueling the darkness, and as the aether burned, it fueled greater rage. I ran without purpose. My feet knew where to go. I ran until I came face to face with the rift. Then I stopped, panting and sweating in the warm afternoon. Two Paragon knights watched the empty training yard from the tree line. Jane's patch held, but the rift's energy shivered across all my senses.

The guards watched me.

They must hate me too. Forced to stand all day, watching a blank spot in the air just in case a demon burst through. What a boring job.

My fault. My fault. My fault. Guilt nattered at me like a bad mantra.

I lay on the warm grass and stared at the rift. It buzzed like a swarm of gnats. I closed my eyes, shutting out everything but my connection to the Great Mother.

A small hand slipped into mine.

"I take it from you, great one," Rosie said.

I hesitated, but the weight of the dark aether was too much. I gave her everything I had. Rosie's tiny body went rigid. She acted as my conduit, funneling my rage and power into Mother Earth. The ground undulated beneath me as She accepted it all, and the anger bled away.

The sun hid behind a cloud and the temperature dropped to a comfortable degree. I lay against the spinning planet, wondering at the path that brought me here.

Without the rage, I had only despair. Quinn had contracted mawr through a curse put on him many years ago. The curse was only the vehicle for infection. Once mawr took hold, it was always fatal. He was dying and I couldn't help. Or could I? Jane and Abilene seemed convinced that my blood was the key to his cure. They might be grasping at straws, but what if they weren't? What if my blood could heal him and he was too stubborn to let me try because trying might put the whole coven at risk?

My mind circled these arguments until they twisted into a tangle of unknowable futures. Somehow, I had to pluck one thread from this snarl.

"Are you done with your little snit?"

Jane peered down at me.

"Fuck off." I didn't want to fight, and every conversation with Jane was a battle. Rosie growled.

I closed my eyes, hoping Jane would get the idea and leave. After several silent minutes, I opened them again. She studied the space where the rift hung invisible.

Curiosity got the better of me. I sat up.

"What's it like?" I asked.

Jane looked confused.

"Through the rift, I mean. You've been there?"

"Yes." She pursed her lips. I thought she'd say no more, but she continued. "It's hot. Much hotter than here. And the air buzzes with aether all the time. It's…unsettling."

Yes, I sensed the alien aether leaking through the badly patched rift.

"And my father?"

"He's a monster."

"I meant, what does he do there?"

Jane laughed harshly. "I wasn't exactly privy to his business." Her eyes drifted to some horizon I couldn't see. Rosie watched as if ready to pounce.

"He lives in a castle of sorts," Jane said, "not like any castle you've ever seen, but fortified. And he's very driven. He has one purpose and he won't stop until he succeeds."

"Why is he so desperate to come here?" I never understood that. In his world, Koro was King. He had hundreds of servants like Rosie tending him. Why would he leave his sanctuary for our world where magic was so much more limited?

"For us," Jane said. "Human aether is an addiction for him, and witches even more so. I'm not sure, but I think something in our magic keeps him young."

"I thought demons were immortal?"

Jane shook her head. "Long lived, but not immortal."

I stood and held my hands out.

"I'm drawn to it," I said. "Even if the imps hadn't told me Koro lives there, I would know. But what are the odds that my screwup opened a rift directly to him? Aren't there infinite worlds?"

"It wasn't a coincidence," Jane said. "I think it was a trap."

I narrowed my eyes at her. Jane was awfully chatty. She never gave up information so easily. She wanted something and I would take the advantage.

"What do you mean, a trap?"

"Agnes was the real expert on portals." Jane sighed. Agnes was one of the original Thirteen, but she died many years ago.

"I looked through her research. It would be nearly impossible for you to open a portal on purpose to a specific realm, let alone by accident. Koro set snares."

"Like rabbit snares?"

"Yes, but this trap grabs your aether and pulls it through to his realm, effectively opening the door. He's done it before. That's how he took us all those years ago. It can only be done in places where the veil between worlds is thin. Like this yard. It's one reason we train here. The earth's aether is close to the surface, easy for new witches to latch onto. But it takes someone with knowledge of how realms bump up against each other to find this spot."

"Would Koro have this knowledge?"

"Most definitely. And I think he set the snare to trap humans with his blood. There are probably more of you in this realm than we know."

More of his spawn. More babies bred from captive and abused women.

Jane's expression was unreadable, her eyes blue flint.

I remembered those horrifying moments when William Fain's soporific spell wore off and I woke to face Koro in his body. I couldn't even imagine the horrors in Jane's memory.

After a moment, she shook herself and said, "I want you to cure my son."

Whoa. Keep calm and change the topic.

"I want to help him too, but he's a stubborn man." I ended that thought before adding, *it runs in the family.*

"For now," Jane said.

"What does that mean?"

"It means there will come a time when Quinn can no longer choose for himself. And I expect you to back me when that happens."

Ah. Jane came here, pretended to commiserate and gave me information I wanted. That was the lure. Quinn was the hook.

Before this, the problem and possibility of Quinn's cure had choked me with indecision. Jane's blatant manipulation suddenly cleared the way. I chose my words carefully.

"I will respect Quinn's wishes."

"You would let him die?"

"I would let him choose."

"Stupid." Jane spat the word. "You're both stupid and selfish."

Selfish? How was Quinn's choice selfish? It was his body. His life. If he chose not to endanger anyone else to save it, I would respect his wishes, no matter how my heart ached. I tried to order my thoughts into an argument to punch through Jane's resistance.

Karl, one of Quinn's guards-in-training, ran into the yard.

"Mistress, Gavin says to come immediately. It's the seer."

CPRONOUNCEMENT

Twenty years ago, thirteen witches founded the coven and built the magical reactor to fuel their shielding spell. Within this bubble, they were free to pursue magic, protected from their enemies.

Until Koro set his sights on breaking the ward.

That night seemed a lifetime ago to me, but only a year had passed. I'd been so naive. When the magic failed, I thrust myself between the ward and the core like a wedge and held them stable until others came to the rescue.

It nearly killed me.

The core liked my blood and it never let me forget it. Its hungry magic sought me out as I entered the clearing with the two tall cairns, but I was no longer a neo-witch. I slapped the core's seeking away with my aether. Despite the sucker-punch Jane landed on me by spilling my blood, I felt strong. And still a little angry. The core's magic retreated without further assault.

Several people stood outside the second cairn, and I was shocked to see them huddled protectively around the seer who stood blinking in the sunlight. I'd never seen Siranda anywhere but crouched in the corner of her one-room house, drawing pictographs on the walls in magic. She was taller than I thought. Long hanks of greasy hair hung over her face with skin so pale it was almost translucent. She wore only a loose white tunic because she fussed with tight-fitting clothes. The vestals who kept her clean and fed often found her naked, her clothes ripped and thrown off in a fit of pique. The tunic was a compromise, but it did nothing to hide her jutting collar and shoulder bones.

"She won't go back inside," Gavin said in greeting. Quinn and Abilene stood by his side. This event was odd enough for an audience, and a dozen vestals watched from the cottages nearly hidden in the trees.

Siranda hummed a tuneless song, swaying to the music. She met my eyes and grinned as if a secret passed between us.

You kill me! The only words the seer ever spoke to me.

I shivered.

"What happened?" Jane asked.

"There's a message." Gavin pointed into the cairn.

Jane and Abilene poked their heads inside.

"Fuck." Jane's curse startled me more than Siranda's odd behavior. Jane didn't swear. Not ever. She stalked away, not giving us another glance. Abilene smiled, shrugged apologetically, and followed her mother.

"Might be a good time for a bath," Gavin said, and he gently led Siranda toward the cottages.

Quinn let me go in first but followed close behind. The room tasted stale like a tomb with the faint odor of sickness from Siranda's long isolation. The walls and ceiling usually pulsed with red and purple pictographs, products of Siranda's seeings. I'd seen her create them with magic that sprouted from her fingertips. Today, all the images were pushed aside like Scrabble tiles shoved from the board. On the clean slate, one message throbbed in red ink.

I WOULD SPEAK.

"What does it mean?" I whispered.

Quinn shook his head and pulled me back into the sunshine.

"It means we're in big trouble," he said. "It's a message from the Lady."

"The Lady? You mean…" I couldn't wrap my mind around that.

"The goddess."

"Does she do that a lot—talk through Siranda?"

"Only once." His eyes were grim. "Right before a plague decimated her last coven."

EMBODIMENT

With midsummer less than a week away, festival preparations were in high gear. Most witches would perform the sabbat in family units, but the celebration wouldn't really start until Jane opened the ritual circle. In the training yard, four massive deadwood piles sat at the cardinal points, waiting to be lit.

Quinn wasn't here to inspect the midsummer preparations. As of this afternoon, the yard became ground zero for Jane's plan to contact the Lady. Everything else was put on hold. Half a dozen witches spent an hour laying another ward around the yard. Quinn walked its perimeter with the bellwether, evaluating its strength. Jane had handed off his duties, but she couldn't stop him from double-checking their work.

The silver dragon head atop the bellwether spewed smoke in different colors as it sensed aether. For a witch like him with subpar sensate abilities, it was an invaluable tool. He finished pacing the ward and set the bellwether staff into the ground beside the rift. Its smoke turned burned a murky orange in response to the aether leaking through the patch.

He turned to find Bobbi inspecting the pile of stones marking the berserker demon's grave. She frowned, and he knew she was reliving the battle, giving life to the fear and guilt it brought. Rosie, never far from Bobbi's side, bared her teeth as he approached, but didn't intervene when he rubbed Bobbi's tense shoulders.

"Time to take the weight of the world off these." She snuggled against him and he wrapped his arms around her.

We have so little time. It was a useless thought that brought no comfort and only poisoned the time they had left. With some effort, he shoved it away.

He glanced at the angle of the sun, barely visible through the trees and guessed it was an hour before sunset. The others would arrive soon.

"Is it safe to perform the spell here?" Bobbi asked. The question nagged him too.

"I don't know. Can you feel anything coming from that grave?"

She closed her eyes and concentrated on the mound hiding the berserker demon's corpse.

"No. Nothing. It's deader than dead." Then she turned. "But I feel that." She pointed at the rift. "It makes my aether tingle."

They walked toward it and Bobbi held up both hands.

"There's heat. Like warm wind blowing off the desert. I can almost taste it." She shivered.

"What are you doing?" Jane said as she approached with Abi.

Bobbi lowered her hands. "Just testing the patch."

"Worried my spell won't hold?"

"Of course not." Bobbi looked contrite, but she didn't back down. Good for her. "I'm worried about how this ritual will affect the rift. We should do it somewhere else."

"This is the spot closest to the ley-line," Jane said. "And the Lady will want to see the rift for herself."

Quinn shook his head.

Abi set down a round rug woven with protection runes. Jane unpacked a basket. She laid the items for her altar around the rug, including the heavy grimoire.

"Bobbi's right," Quinn said. "Didn't you say contacting the Lady requires an empty vessel?"

"Siranda will be the vessel. She's our best choice, and the Lady has spoken through her."

That was a bad idea on so many levels.

"We have a strong circle here," Abi said. "Nothing unwanted will get through. Now stop fussing."

She pushed him gently away to finish laying out the altar. Quinn wasn't convinced. A strong circle meant nothing when the rift was inside it.

They needed more protection.

Gavin arrived, leading Siranda by the hand. Henry followed, dressed in full battle gear with a sword at his hip. He met Quinn's eye with a stark gaze. He was worried too. Quinn pulled him aside, and they conferred quietly.

"Can you spare some knights? We need more firepower here."

"Agreed," Henry said. "She's still hell-bent on this plan?"

Hell bent. Hopefully those words weren't prophetic.

"Yes."

"Then we need backup for sure." Henry left to gather more troops.

Quinn scouted the yard for weaknesses. It all came down to the rift.

Gavin tugged on Siranda until she stood on the rug. She danced a bit, shaking her legs and whining like a dog wanting to go out. Someone had tied sandals to her feet, and she didn't like them. She raised a foot and shook it, trying to dislodge the shoe.

"Fine," Gavin said. "Give me your foot." He unbuckled the sandals, and she sighed with something close to happiness as her toes dug into the rug. Gavin stowed the shoes in a pack, removed a shawl and wrapped it around her shoulders. Siranda showed no indication she appreciated the warmth, but Gavin smiled and patted her shoulder.

"You're very good with her," Bobbi said.

"I've had a lot of practice."

"How's your mother?"

Gavin shrugged. "Quieter now that Tanya is out of the picture. I might move her here, into one of the spare cottages."

Tanya was his mother's nurse at the Riverview Psychiatric Care Facility. Quinn was never sure if Koro reached out to Tanya because she was the caregiver to a woman he tortured and impregnated, or if Tanya was already under Koro's sway when she took the nursing job. Either way, Tanya used her connection to Gavin and the coven to try to steal the grimoire left for Bobbi. She nearly killed Quinn in the process, and Gavin couldn't forgive himself.

Quinn saw the self-recrimination in his eyes every time his brother looked at him. He wished he had something reassuring to say. It wasn't Gavin's fault. No one could predict where Koro would attack next.

Henry returned with the knights. They circled the yard and stood at parade rest, hands loose at their sides but ready to draw weapons. Henry carried a sword belt and handed it to Bobbi.

Jane glared at Henry. He shrugged and raised his hands.

"What? Better safe than sorry."

Bobbi smiled and buckled the sword to her waist.

While the others set up, Quinn drifted over to the rift and watched the bellwether leak pale red smoke.

"Don't you think your crude attempt to classify the Lady's magic will offend her?" Jane asked from behind him.

"It's not for the Lady," Quinn said. If a demon possessed Siranda during this ritual, Bobbi, Abi and the other sensates would know immediately, but Quinn wouldn't let his limitations become a liability. Jane was adamant about this foolish spell, but he would monitor it with every tool in his possession.

"I want to be sure we're talking to the Lady, and not a demon sneaking through the rift," Quinn said.

"The rift is closed," Jane said.

He pointed at the thin stream of red smoke. "It's only patched."

"You doubt my ability to keep the coven safe?"

"The chances of Koro breaking through our layers of protection are slim to none, but you of all people should know demons revel in slim chances."

Jane stepped closer and lowered her voice for his ears only.

"How many times in a witch's life is she invited to speak to the Lady? Once. If she's lucky. And apart from the great honor, we need the Lady's help to survive this mess. If we don't try, we've already failed. Everyone will be watching. They have faith in us. In me. But if they think my family doubts me, we'll have dissension in the ranks. I need you to get on board with the plan or get out of my way." She met his eyes, unblinking. "Now, do I have your cooperation?"

Quinn hesitated but nodded slowly.

"Good. There's Myra," Jane said. "We're almost ready to start. Make yourself useful and set guards to keep the spectators at a distance."

Feeling like a scolded boy, Quinn gathered the junior guards to do Jane's bidding.

Myra arrived with two helpers to carry her baskets of magic goodies. They set up the second altar on the other side of Siranda. Myra laid down another rune-woven rug and prodded Siranda until she sat on it with legs crossed. The seer ignored the rest of the preparations and swayed to music only she could hear.

"So, how will this work?" Bobbi asked. She looked worried. Quinn took her hand and she squeezed it.

"It's really cool,"Abi said. "Mom and Myra are going to weave their spells in tandem. I've only read about this before." Her face lit with excitement and Quinn smiled at his sister's enthusiasm. Too young to realize she wasn't invincible, Abi saw only the chance to expand her arcane knowledge.

"Basically, Mom will call the Lady, while Myra draws Siranda's soul from her body and stores it in that." She pointed to a round earthenware jar with runes etched on its side and topped by a cork.

"But she'll die!" Bobbi said.

"Only for a moment." Abi waved her hand as if the detail made little difference. "A body can't live without a soul for long, so they'll time it carefully. Siranda's body will be vacant for only a split second, then the Lady will take over."

Quinn frowned. A split second was a lifetime of opportunity for a demon. Half the battle of possession was ousting the mortal soul. And they were offering up an empty vessel. It was pure demon bait.

"And when we're done? How do we get Siranda back in her body?" Bobbi asked.

"Simple. We just open the jar. Siranda's soul will naturally seek out her body." Abi finished with a pleased smile.

Bobbi turned to him. "Do we have enough backup?" At least she understood the gravity of this situation.

"If Koro breaks through the rift, there isn't enough backup in the world to stop him," Gavin said grimly.

Bobbi shivered and Quinn pulled her tight against him. Jane was right. They needed solidarity.

"It'll be all right." He tried to sound convincing. "And the Lady will have answers to help us."

"I hope so."

The Paragon knights were ready, and a crowd stood around the field's perimeter.

One of Myra's helpers walked in a large circle around the seer and the two witches with their altars. She held a heavy sack with a hole in one corner and spilled a line of salt. Abi followed on the outside, stopping to light candles at four points. Inside the circle, Jane bowed over a lit candle, pricked her forearm with her athame and pierced the earth with the blade. She repeated this at the other three candles, then let her robe fall over the wounds. She walked back to her altar, turning her back on the rift as if it were nothing. Quinn locked his eyes on the patch of empty air, waiting for some *thing* to burst through.

Myra lit a bundle of dried herbs and blew on it until the smoke swirled around Siranda's head. Its savory fumes mixed with the bellwether's until the seer was almost lost in the haze. Jane raised her blade to the sky, now near dark, and intoned the prayer.

"Hail, Lord and Lady. We have built our temple in your honor. We have prepared the way for you. Hear our call!"

Magic sizzled around the circle. The evening fell silent.

Myra blew on the bundle of herbs. Siranda seemed amused and tried to catch the wispy trails of smoke. Then Myra chanted, and the spell caught. The smoke reacted as if snared in a fine net. Sweat dripped down Myra's face. This magic was too much for the old witch. Someone else should have taken the lead. Quinn stepped forward to stop her as the smoke coalesced into a wind funnel, seizing Siranda in its grip. The seer tensed. Her back arched, eyes bulged and mouth hung open in a silent scream. The smoke plunged into her head and out the other side, swirling and twisting through the air until it streamed into the ceramic pot. Myra plugged it with the cork before crumpling to the ground. Abi stepped forward to help the old witch but stopped. No one could break the protective circle until the spell ended.

Jane glanced at Myra gasping for air but didn't move to help her.

"Hail!" she called again. "Lady hear our call. We come as bidden. Hear our call!" Her robe fell away to reveal the arm streaked with blood.

Lightning lit the sky and suddenly the yard plunged into darkness.

WONDERMENT

Only the council witches stood near the circle highlighted by the candles. Beyond us stood a larger circle of onlookers and knights, and then the forest—all lost in shadow. I gripped Quinn's hand as the air became thick with magic.

The seer stood, her expression no longer vacant and her whole body glowing with an inner light. Skinny, bedraggled Siranda was gone. In her place stood an ethereal beauty. The Lady moved with grace and feral strength.

She looked at Jane, then at Myra who lay dazed on the ground. Her eyes met each of us gathered outside the circle. Gavin sucked in a breath. Abilene wept silently. The Lady's gaze lingered on Quinn, who looked pale as a ghost, and she frowned.

Then her eyes fell on me. They burned with blue fire and I couldn't turn away. Her lip curled into a slight smile, but she said nothing before returning her attention to Jane.

"Lady." The mistress bowed low. Blood from her arm dripped onto her white robe. The Lady, in Siranda's form, took Jane's arm and kissed the red streaks. The blood faded as if the cuts had never been.

"Blood is the key," the Lady said. Her quiet voice thrilled me like the opening notes of an aria.

"The key?" Jane frowned. "To closing the rift?"

"Keys open and keys close." Her words surrounded us as if they came from the trees, the sky and the ground.

"I don't understand." Jane's face showed no confusion. Was she being deliberately obtuse, forcing the Lady to make her wishes clear?

I didn't see her move, but suddenly the Lady stood before the rift. She held her hands up to the power coming through the gap. The rift's outline crackled with blue veins of energy.

Behind the Lady, something moved in the shadows. A beast paced, its form indistinct and menacing.

"There are no accidents," she said. "Not even this gate. The one named Kororaeth set a trap." She turned and smiled at me. *Yes*, she seemed to say, *you fell into that trap.* "But even his actions were fated. The worlds needed to breathe. One to another, the way lovers share intimate breath."

She smiled at the shadowy beast. It pawed the ground. I couldn't see its true form, only that it was massive.

"We need to close the rift," Jane said.

"Do you?" The Lady smiled. "Close it and you will be running forever. Open it and you become the hunter. Gateways between two worlds are a gift. I can give you the power to make the gift permanent. Spill the blood of one who is of both worlds across the threshold and the door will stay open permanently. The worlds will be as one."

"Isn't that dangerous?" Abilene said. The Lady ignored the interruption, focusing entirely on Jane.

"You think we should take the fight to Koro," Jane said.

"I can give you the key to open and the key to close, but you must choose the right path. Open it and the worlds will join as one. Magic will be born anew here. Or choose to close it and your world will remain as it is, locked in its circle of limitations. But hear this," her voice rose, and a gust of wind followed it, "You must choose." She held her hands to the rift and tore downward with one fingernail. The rift blazed open with a nerve-shredding screech. "The gate is unstable. As it stands, the worlds will not rest easily together."

Red light from the otherworldly desert shone through the gate and clashed with the blue glow emanating from the Lady.

Jane looked shaken. "I understand."

I was glad she did because the whole discussion spun me.

Jane knelt, and the Lady placed her hands on her head as if in blessing. Jane stiffened. The veins on her neck stood out in harsh relief. Her eyes fluttered but didn't open. The shadow beast huffed like an angry stallion. The Lady released her grip and Jane sagged sideways.

Abilene rushed to her mother's side but stopped short of breaking the circle of salt.

The Lady stepped over the rune woven rug, picked up the grimoire and flipped through its heavy pages. She stopped and tore one out. Even with a blade, we couldn't cut the pages, but the Lady simply yanked it from the binding. As an afterthought, she looked piercingly at Quinn, then ripped out another page and handed both to Jane.

"You have what you need. I will take this abomination somewhere it can do no more damage." She slipped the enormous book into the folds of Siranda's tunic and it disappeared.

"Thank you." Jane held the parchments as if they were made of spun sugar.

"I would speak to the children of the demon," the Lady said. "Bring them before me."

Quinn let my hand go. I hadn't even realized he was squeezing it. I moved toward Gavin who waited at the edge of the circle. We two, the children of Koro.

"Come, come." The Lady held out her hand. I looked at the circle of salt, standing like a barrier of stone between us. Jane's circles were strong. I couldn't break it if I wanted to. The Lady smiled, and all Rosie's superlatives came to my mind: beatific, supernal, celestial, divine. The Lady deserved all these labels and more, even wearing Siranda's scruffy mortal coil. Her true face glowed from within these human trappings. It radiated serenity as she reached across the salt and drew us into the circle.

Aether sizzled through me as I crossed the barrier, and then I felt only the Lady's warm embrace. She hugged me, then Gavin. His eyes glowed with the rapture seizing my heart too. The Lady was pure love. I experienced it in every pore and muscle. Her love fed my heart and coursed through my veins.

Me, the daughter of a demon. The incompetent witch who opened rifts and screwed up spells. She loved me.

"Yes, child. I do." I heard the words in my head but didn't see her lips move. "It is not easy to be the tree uprooted by the hurricane. Neither is it easy to be the hurricane. You are the children of greatness. Terrible greatness." I would have wept at her words, but her touch filled me with joy.

"I cannot carry your burdens for you. I have greatness to bear too. Instead, I give you a choice. Your father will never stop seeking you. You are his blood, his key into this world. I can hide you from him, cleanse your blood of its demon greatness, if you will. He will no longer be able to find you, but there is a cost." Her eyes darkened as if storm clouds rolled in their depths.

"Your magic is caught up in your blood. Hiding you from your father will dampen that magic. You may be left with some or none at all. This I cannot predict. Do you accept my gift?"

She turned to Gavin first. His expression glowed in her reflected glory.

"My magic is dedicated to the Lady," he said. "As long as I have breath, so is my life dedicated to caring for her children. I accept." She took his face in her hands and peered into his eyes, then nodded as if satisfied with what she saw there. She kissed him. Light burst from the meeting of their lips and suffused Gavin, head to toe. The Lady continued to press her lips to Gavin's. Not a sexual gesture. It was pure power. The light surrounding him pulsed as she drew on Gavin's magic. She pulled away and the light faded. The Lady reached into her mouth and withdrew a small bead, black and shining like onyx.

"Is that my magic?" Gavin looked at it in wonder

"Not all. Only the parts given to you by your father." She tucked the bead into her tunic and it disappeared like the grimoire.

"Thank you." He bowed his head. She turned to me.

"Do you accept?"

Panic welled in me. Clean blood, free of my father's taint. Such a gift! No more looking over my shoulder for agents of the demon. No more fearing the darkness inside me. I remembered the foul wraith I killed and the berserker demon whose aether I guzzled like sweet tea. I thought of the rage that crept into my mind when I stood up to Horg and exploded from me when Jane drew my blood. All marks of my father's power.

But I just discovered my magic. Was I ready to give it up? How much came from my father? Would I still sense aether around me? Could I throw fire magic? What other powers were at my disposal that I hadn't tapped into yet?

The Lady saw my indecision and smiled. I knew what I had to do. My demon blood meant my father could find me, but it also meant I could find him.

And kill him.

If we were going to take the fight to Koro, I would need all the greatness—dark and light—inside me.

I shook my head.

The Lady smiled. "You are the hurricane." She kissed me too, a mother's kiss. A blessing and nothing more.

"For you then, I have another gift." She gave me a flat, smooth stone with a hole at its center. A hag stone.

"Look through it," she commanded.

I held the stone to my eye. Through its hole, the scene around us brightened. The Lady sparkled with pure energy. Behind her the stalking creature came into my view. No longer a shadow, he stood tall and proud in a circle of light. A horned beast as big as a moose, but more delicate and regal in his bearing, with a glorious rack of silver antlers. The Lord of the Hunt paced around the circle, stopping to paw the ground before the rift. The Lady smiled fondly at him.

"Without the light, there is no shadow." She touched my chest and my heart thundered against her hand. "You live in darkness as if that is the only place for you. I would tell you to step from the shadows, but I see you are not ready. When the time comes, this stone will bring you into the light of my blessing. Use it only under the most dire circumstances for its power is not infinite."

I nodded and clutched my talisman.

The Lady sat on the stool. Her beauty faded and suddenly she became the seer again. Jane reached toward the clay jar to release Siranda's aether.

The bellwether belched red smoke.

A shrill cry leaped from the trees and the imps attacked.

ENGAGEMENT

Quinn spun to face a horde of raging imps—many more imps than those from the compound. Where did they all come from? Horg must have pretended to surrender, in order to get near the coven and bring in this larger army.

The knights stood their ground, but small quick bodies washed over them, around them, even ducking through their legs. Several died on the ends of Paragon swords, but they kept coming, screaming like banshees and brandishing sharpened sticks.

The witches gathered to view the Lady's rite jumped into the fight. Quinn held back. They didn't need his weak aether in this battle nor his shaking sword arm; they needed his strategy. He eyed the yard. Who were the imps targeting? The witches? The seer? The rift? Abi and Bobbi were safe at his back, but Jane and Myra were vulnerable. Jane's ward circle was broken, the salt smeared as the imps stormed over the altars.

Horg screamed a war cry and ran for Siranda. From around his neck, he pulled out the cord with a stone dangling from it—a stone that now glowed deep red. Leaping like a martial artist in a Kung Fu movie, he bellowed and landed on Siranda, smashing the stone on her head.

Magic exploded, a crash of power so strong, it brought Quinn to his knees.

The bellwether bloomed with blood red smoke.

A demon.

Siranda rose with the stealth of a wraith, eyes burning red, mouth hanging open unnaturally wide. She roared and spittle flew from her lips.

Siranda wasn't home.

The imps timed the attack with precision. The chaos left Siranda an empty vessel, easy pickings for possession. The demon had been riding Horg's talisman, inert until the imp called it forth.

Damn the devils! No one else noticed Siranda's takeover.

The battle raged on. Small and fast, the imps took a surprising amount of damage before they went down. He had to stop Siranda before the demon that rode her flexed its muscles.

She picked up the altar, carefully prepared by Myra and threw it.

Quinn lunged at her. Four small bodies tackled him. He fought off grasping hands. Someone bit his calf and he grunted, kicking the offender away. Grappling through this sea of bodies, he lurched towards the seer.

Horg stepped in his way. Blood smeared his face and chest. His eyes gleamed with mania. He raised Jane's ritual athame that dripped blood. Quinn kicked his wrist. Horg hissed and dropped the knife. Quinn caught it before it hit the ground, and with a deft swipe, plunged it into Horg's chest. Jane's athame was honed by years of anointing, and it cut through anything. He dragged it down the imp's chest, slicing through bone, organs and flesh. Not knowing where their damned hearts were, he would slice the creature to shreds if he had to. He pulled back the blade, ready for another thrust.

Horg fell, his eyes cloudy.

The beast wearing Siranda's skin roared again and Quinn spun. Red smoke from the bellwether wreathed her face. A knight lunged at her with a drawn sword, but she sidestepped the blows with eerie grace, ducked inside his reach to grab the knife at his belt. He trapped her arms against her, while a second knight tried to disarm her. She closed her eyes, lowered her head and intoned a dark prayer. When she opened her eyes again, they were black.

She tipped back her head and screamed. The noise screeched through Quinn's mind like hot nails. The knights holding her flew backward, crashed into two more rushing to help, and they all landed in a tangle beside Bobbi who fought with another pack of imps.

The Siranda-beast raised her blade and smiled.

Blood of one who is of both worlds. The Lady's words. Blood that would straddle the gate between two worlds. Blood that would bind their worlds together forever.

She's going to kill herself. He knew it like the truth of his own heart, but he was too far away to intervene.

"Bobbi! Stop her!" he screamed as more imps attacked him. Bobbi turned and gaped.

Too late. Siranda dragged the blade across her throat.

Magic burst through the field followed by screams. My first thought was for the core because the magic beat like the pulse of a heart. Then I had no time for speculation.

An imp jumped on my back. Teeth sunk into my shoulder. I fell and rolled. The creature screamed and I leaped away.

Horg's blood whore snarled and lunged again, her teeth red with my blood. My shoulder burned. I raised my sword, but Rosie jumped on the weaker female and broke her neck with one snap.

She nodded. "Holy one."

I nodded back. All my muscles quivered with spent adrenaline. Then more imps jumped us. Rosie's tail slashed back and forth, the bony edge cutting down bodies like a scythe through hay. I stood with my sword at the ready, letting her guard my back as I sought the source of the strange magic.

The ward held. But someone had unleashed a magical wallop.

"Bobbi!" Quinn yelled. I spun. Standing at the far end of the yard, he fought off a tangle of imps. Between us, Siranda stood holding a knife. Paragon knights lay like broken dolls at her feet. Her grin looked big enough to split her skull.

"Stop her!" He yelled, sparing a breath to make me see what I should have already seen.

Something was wrong with Siranda.

She tilted her head back and dragged the knife from ear to ear.

Lord and Lady.

Blood spurted and Siranda smiled. She dropped the blade and lurched forward. Two steps from the rift, she staggered as blood loss caught up with her.

The Lady's warning pounded in my head.

Blood of both worlds. I thought she meant me and my demon blood. But I wasn't the only demon here tonight.

Siranda—whatever possessed Siranda—sacrificed her body to anoint the rift. Her blood anchored the ground on this side. If she pulled herself through the rift to bleed on the other side, it would create an unbreakable link. Koro would finally have his open invitation to the coven.

The demon pitched forward with the echo of shots fired. Damn! I looked around. A knight fired a handgun into the melee. Idiot! In this mess, he would hit someone else. Even I knew you couldn't take out a demon with bullets.

The demon barely flinched from the wound, but the momentum of the hits drove it forward. It fell and crawled on. Blood covered its hands, face and chest and soaked the ground. It should be dead, but it doggedly dragged Siranda's carcass toward the rift.

My magic boiled. Dark magic fueled by fury, not fear. I would not let that demon plunge my world into war. Aether flowed from my fingers into my blade.

I ran, jumped over bodies and landed in the clear. The Siranda-creature thrust a bloody arm through the rift. In the same moment, I plunged my sword into its back. The demon shrieked and fell slack. Its lifeless body sagged forward, half in our world, half in the other.

The ground shook. Magic tore through me like my veins were ripped open. I fell, gasping for breath. Other witches were down, dead or unconscious. Someone screamed as the anchor between two worlds slammed into place.

Then the night fell silent.

Siranda slumped in the gate with my sword in her back.

You kill me!

The first words the seer ever spoke to me howled through the yard like a wailing ghost. Or maybe it was only the manifestation of my guilt.

ℭPAYMENT

The bellwether lay broken among the remains of Myra's altar. I picked up the pieces. The silver dragon head streamed pink smoke, reacting to the residual demon aether in the air. A gust of hot aether-laced wind tossed the smoke, blowing in from the desert through the rift.

Not a rift. It was no longer a tear in dimensions. It was a gate. Open now for all eternity, for better or worse.

I gazed through the door to the alien world. Sand dunes rippled off to the horizon, so yellow they looked drenched in melted butter. A blazing red sun hung in the cloudless sky. It seemed achingly empty.

The Lady offered us a choice. Open the gate, let magic from the other world into ours and take the fight to Koro. Or close the rift and hide. At least until Koro found another selfish human to sponsor him. Neither option appealed to me, but the demon piloting Siranda's body took away the choice. The gate was open, and we'd have to deal.

For now, no one waited to burst through from the other side. Maybe Koro didn't even know about it. Unlikely. We posted four guards to watch the alien desert. Jane would allow no one to step through. Not until the council conferred.

As I sorted through the debris left by the fight, I wondered what the gate would mean for the rest of humanity.

Our ley-lines were swelling, leaking magic back into the world. Soon the growing magic would wake a response in people. Paragon officials were investigating this phenomenon. Would we see a surge of magic users, people whose talent lay silent for generations until magic levels rose enough to trigger it? Would we see a return of mythical creatures dormant for thousands of years?

Now alien aether streamed through the gate, adding to this mix. I didn't understand the Lady's conviction. How would our worlds be better off joined?

It seemed like bad politics to me. No doubt scholars of all disciplines would debate the question long and hard. But I had to deal with its reality now.

I collected the remains of Myra's altar and found the broken jar that had housed Siranda's soul. At least she was finally free of the mortal bindings that never seemed to fit her. Her body lay under a shroud. She would be mourned and celebrated as a true daughter of the coven.

Three others were seriously wounded and two knights unconscious. Whatever magic the demon-possessed Siranda used to concuss them was effective, but the medics thought they would recover.

My shoulder ached from the blood-whore's bite, but my shirt was stiff with dried blood, so I left the medics to care for the more seriously wounded.

Dozens of imp corpses burned at the far end of the yard. Horg had been hiding a larger force in the woods all this time.

And I let him into the coven.

Not all imps had fallen under Horg's sway. After the attack, Rosie returned to the compound and brought back nine imps who refused to fight for Horg, including all the segregated females. They sat quietly to one side while Jane and the others debated their fate.

Horg's band—or the few left—were bound and gagged and sitting in the stirred-up dirt under the watchful glares of Paragon knights.

Jane motioned for a knight to remove one of the imp's gags. It was Fenryn, the bow-wielding imp who brought us to Horg's camp in the forest.

"Why did you attack us?" Jane asked. Fenryn spat at her feet. Jane questioned him some more, but he gripped a wound on his arm and refused to speak.

Rosie stepped forward and bared her teeth. Fenryn flinched away.

"Horg would bring bad holy ones," he blurted, eyeing Rosie warily.

"Bring them here?" Jane asked.

Fenryn started to wail, a high keening sound that grated my nerves.

"Answer me!" Jane snapped. Fenryn rocked and cried.

Jane motioned to Rosie. "Get him to speak."

I gritted my teeth. I didn't like Jane bossing her around, but Rosie complied. She wrapped her tail around Fenryn's throat and squeezed. His leathery face turned purple. One captive whimpered. Rosie didn't let up.

Unnoticed by the others, the imps who stood with Rosie slipped away into the forest.

Rosie let Fenryn drop to the ground gasping for air and turned her attention to a smaller imp. This one also blubbered as Rosie's tail circled his throat, but I made no sense of his words.

"Ask how they communicated with the other side," Quinn said. He would feel the sting of this attack. Security was his responsibility. Even if his illness meant he offloaded most of that responsibility to the knights, he would agonize over today's loss. I snaked my arm around his waist. He bled from several cuts and trembled from exhaustion. I leaned into him to take some of his weight, hoping he'd think I was only looking for comfort.

Rosie let the imp drop and grabbed another. He shrieked and babbled.

"He cry for mother," Rosie said with disgust.

The imps weren't talking. We left them with the guards and moved to the other side of the yard to discuss their future in private.

"What should we do with them?" Abilene asked. Even before this fiasco, the imps were a problem. The division in their ranks added a complication.

Nine imps stood with Rosie. Six remained from Horg's little army. I rubbed at the tired spot between my eyes. I should have seen this coming. Horg had gathered a force around him. I thought it was for his protection, or at worst, so they might mount an escape.

"It never occurred to me they could be in contact with the other side," I said. Quinn squeezed my hand and pulled me toward him.

"None of us saw this coming." He kissed the side of my head. "Not your fault."

"We'll send them back through the gate," Myra said. She'd been knocked out in the fight, but she was tough. I imagined the old witch tossing imps through the rift with her bare hands.

"No," Jane said. "They know too much about our defenses. We send them through and they'll run right to Koro."

Gavin arrived on the tail end of the inquisition after seeing to the wounded.

"My vestals can't keep watch over them indefinitely and the knights will be stuck here guarding the rift," he said.

"We can't keep them, and we can't send them back. That's perfect." Abilene paced with a rare show of impatience, immediately quelled by a glare from Jane.

Rosie's imps returned, their arms bulging with stones.

"What's this?" Gavin stepped in front of them but the imps streamed past with their heavy loads.

"This problem not yours," Rosie said. "These are dead." She waved at the prisoners. Her tail thumped the ground in a signal. Across the yard, her little band unleashed their missiles. The first stone hit one of the rebel imps between the eyes. He shrieked and fell.

"No!" I yelled, already running, but it was over before I reached them. The rebels lay dead under a heap of rock. Rosie thumped her tail again and the remaining imps sat quietly, the blood lust gone from their eyes.

Rosie bowed at my feet.

"Most beatific one, I give death in payment."

Payment. For Siranda's life. As if one negated the other. Her long fingers clasped my foot.

"Please, holy blessed one, do not send us back."

I stared at the little imp. Her tail swished in the grass. She pressed her face into the dirt, fully expecting me to punish her for the crimes of her people.

"It's all right, Rosie. You can get up." She scrambled to her feet. "Can you take the others back to camp and keep them there for now?" Rosie barked a command in her native tongue and the imps disappeared into the trees.

Quinn jerked his head toward two young guards. "Follow them. See they stay put." The guards nodded and left.

"Well, it seems your little friend has saved us some trouble," Jane said. "Can we trust her?"

I almost shook my head to say I didn't know. But I did. Rosie would never betray me. Her undying loyalty had been a burden. Now I saw it for the blessing it was.

"You can trust her. She'll keep the others in line."

The crowd dispersed, some to have their wounds bandaged, others to clear away the wreckage of the spell used to contact the Lady. Every able knight stood at attention around the gate, but so far only the desert wind came through—the wind and a constant stream of alien aether.

"I should go lie down," Quinn said. "Do you mind?"

I looked at his pale face, eyes sunken into dark circles and tried not to crumble under a wave of loss.

"Do you need me to see you home?" I kept my voice perfectly neutral. Quinn wouldn't thank me for pitying him.

"Not tonight." He winked. "I need sleep more than anything."

I nodded. We both knew I wasn't flirting. I watched him limp away, my heart aching. How many more battles could his body handle?

Gavin stood with Henry, examining the gate. I approached, wary of intruding on their private conversation, but caught only the tail end of their plans to erect a ward around the gate.

"Can I talk to you?" I asked Gavin. He nodded. I met Henry's eyes, silently asking him for privacy.

"Good fight." He squeezed Gavin's shoulder and left.

I turned to the gate and peered into the gap. The sky darkened on the other side, dunes turning purple in the fading light.

"I wonder if their days are the same length as ours," Gavin said. "I'll spend some time here gathering information, I think."

"Why did you let her take your magic?" I asked.

Gavin froze. I pulled out the stone the Lady gave me and ran a finger along its smooth edge.

"We don't know if she took all of it," Gavin finally said. "I haven't tried to use it yet." He shoved his hands in his pockets. "In truth, I'm afraid to. I don't feel any different, but losing my magic will be like losing a limb."

"Will it be worth it? To be free of Koro's influence?"

Gavin shrugged. "He hasn't been after me the way he's been after you, but yes. If our father's blood can be washed from my veins, any loss of limb is worth it."

He patted my shoulder and walked away, leaving me in the sunset glow of the alien world.

Adjustment

Quinn made it as far as his front porch. Exhaustion crumpled his legs under him as he sank into a chair with a weariness that reached right into his heart. Everything had been taken from him this week. He could no longer do his job. His body betrayed him. He couldn't trust it to stand up to the simplest task. Throughout the battle, he'd been less worried about taking a hit than passing out and becoming a burden to the other fighters. Things should not have come to this point. If he'd been doing his job these last weeks, Horg would never have been near the ritual with his demon talisman. Siranda would be alive and there wouldn't be a fucking hole in their world.

Gods, he needed a drink. But he was too tired to stand. Too tired to even go to bed. He would just sleep here. Or sit and stare at the sky until the sun rose.

Except Bobbi would find him in the morning, and he'd have to face the pity in her eyes again. Oh, she tried to hide it, but every time she looked at him, she was counting the hours they had left together.

He was losing her too. Shame and anger warred for space in his thoughts.

"Hey." Her voice came from the darkness. There was no light here, no street lamps or glow from the cottage window. Nothing but the rising moon to reveal her standing by his porch, and even then, he could see the damnable concern on her beautiful face.

"I thought you were going to bed," she said.

"Wanted a drink first."

Bobbi looked at his empty hands, then went inside and brought back two bottles of beer. He took his and drank. Bobbi sat on the other chair and pretended to find interest in the night sky.

"So, what are you really doing out here?"

"Pity party." He grunted and sipped his beer.

"Huh. Can I join?"

He risked a glance at her. Torn shirt and a bandage snaking up from shoulder to neck. Dirt and blood streaked her face, but she smiled.

Lord and Lady, nothing brings this amazing woman down.

"You hurt?" He nodded at the bandage.

"An imp bite. Those little buggers fight dirty."

"They've got a brutal sense of justice too."

Bobbi nodded and brought the bottle to her lips.

Watching Rosie's imps stone the rebels brought their new situation into sharp focus. The world on the other side of the gate was not like theirs. Law and morality would no longer be the subjects of debate for policy-makers and theologians. They would become the anchors holding them together, the personal compass they would all have to follow in the face of terrible things to come.

"Did Jane and Gavin get the ward up?" he asked. In the past, he would have never left the site unsecured.

Bobbi nodded. "A temporary one. Abilene is working on a way to fuel the new ward from the magic coming through the gate. Sort of the way the core pulls aether from the ley-line. It's all very complicated, and she's excited about it."

"I bet."

They watched the stars float by.

"Are we going to do this all night?" Bobbi asked.

"Do what?"

"Talk about trivialities and ignore the real problem."

"You think the possible invasion from a demon realm is trivial?"

"You know what I mean."

The exasperation in her tone was satisfying.

"Actually, I would like to talk to you about something that's been bothering me," he said.

She laughed bitterly. "Just one thing? Would that be the murders? The betrayals? The impending doom?"

"I'm worried about you."

Bobbi fiddled with the hag stone, turning it over and over in her hands.

"I'm fine."

"You made some odd choices in the battle earlier."

When she said nothing, he prodded again.

"You didn't use your magic to stop Siranda—"

"Not Siranda," she said sharply.

"Not Siranda," he agreed. "The thing using her body. You could have stopped it with magic, but you chose the sword instead."

He turned to her, tipped her chin up with one finger, forcing her to meet his gaze.

"Are you afraid to use your magic?"

"And what if I am? So far, magic hasn't done me much good. Are you forgetting about how I nearly killed myself on a simple fire spell? Or how about the time I tore a hole in our world?"

Her eyes blazed with anger, but he saw fear too. She still held something back.

"You also saved me from a wraith," he said. "I haven't forgotten. And you stopped Tanya from getting the grimoire. Your magic did that."

The last year was a whirlwind of ups and downs. Bobbi nearly died at her father's hands twice. They battled demons together and found comfort when they could, all the while, his strength eroding as Bobbi's magic grew.

"Tell me what you're afraid of."

Bobbi's thumb circled the hag stone relentlessly.

"You know what Jane will propose, don't you?" he asked.

She nodded. Soon Koro would find the open gate and step through into their world. They couldn't let that happen. They needed to take the fight to him.

"How can you face him if you're afraid to use your magic?"

"You don't understand."

"Make me understand."

She stared at the rising moon for a long moment.

"When I use my magic," she started hesitantly, "I feel different. I become different. Like there's another being inside me, waiting to get out. An angry being. It scares me."

She wouldn't look at him.

"Has this been going on long?"

I shrugged. "I guess so. But it's getting worse. There's a darkness inside me. When I use magic, it takes over. I can't stop it. Abilene is looking into it, to see if I might be taking on aspects of my father."

Now she shot him a quick glance and he saw shame burning on her cheeks.

"You weren't going to tell me."

She shook her head. Of course not. She hoped to keep it from him until it no longer mattered. Until he was too far gone to face what she was turning into. Her lack of trust hurt, but he was helpless in this fight and that hurt more.

"You should have told me."

"Maybe."

They sat for a long time listening to the wind rush through the trees. She would go through the gate to that forbidding land and he couldn't help her.

"If you can't use magic, how will you kill Koro?" he asked.

Bobbi shivered.

"When the time comes, I'll unleash everything I have at him," she said. "It'll be a one-time shot, but I have to try."

"You don't plan on coming back."

She turned and cupped his face in her hand.

"There won't be anything to come back to."

He kissed her, a tentative gesture. But as soon as his lips touched hers, the fire ignited in him.

Bobbi pushed away, rose and pulled on his hand.

"Come to bed."

"Why? So, we can lie side by side like brother and sister?"

"Yes. If that's what you want."

It wasn't. He wanted so much more. He wanted to pick up a sword and crash through that gate, find the bloody demon who threatened his coven and cut off his head. He wanted to bring Siranda back from the dead. Prove the Lady wrong and find a spell to close the gate. Make his people—his family—safe.

He wanted to make love to this woman.

And suddenly that was the most important of his desires. For once, his broken body complied. Blood-boiling aether ran through his veins.

She tugged on his hand. He rose but didn't let her pull him inside. Instead, he kissed her. It wasn't gentle or kind. He pushed her up against the wall and claimed her. She tasted of fire. Her lips melted under his, fingers tangled in his hair, pulling him deeper. Their bodies ground together at chest, hip and knee.

She made his aether sing and he was no longer the dying man. He was pure passion, needing her right now.

She grabbed his face in her hands, stopping the kiss, and searched his eyes.

No! Please don't say it. Don't ask if I'm okay.

"I love you," she said.

Then her mouth trailed down his jaw, nipping, sucking and kissing. Every touch of her lips fueled his desire.

"Gods, I want you right here on the porch."

Bobbi arched a look at him. "Beds are over-rated anyway."

MOMENT

The entire coven came out to watch Siranda's shrouded body burn. The rites for her passing were solemn as befitted the station of a seer. A few vestals wept. They had tended Siranda's daily needs for years, not an easy job with her resistance to any kind of personal hygiene. But still, the vestals mourned.

Quinn didn't. Not that he had hard feelings towards Siranda. He'd pitied her. They couldn't have forced her to leave her cave-like home, but he was never comfortable with the arrangement. The coven benefited from her prophecies and kept her fed and clean, but some of the witches were altogether too proud of their seer, the way an old king would be proud of an exotic animal caged in his menagerie.

Certainly, her life was never easy. He watched the rising smoke and hoped she finally found peace. Bobbi gripped his hand. Her other hand lingered on the hag stone threaded on a leather cord around her neck. Her eyes were far away.

He knew exactly what she was thinking. She killed Siranda just as the seer once prophesied. But like all prophecies, this one held only a kernel of truth. Bobbi may have struck the blow that killed the seer's mortal coil, but the imps set the demon on her and broke the jar holding her soul. Once that was loose, no one could save her.

Bobbi wouldn't see it that way. She held the weight of the world on her shoulders. Daughter of a demon, instigator of the rift threatening their world and holy one to the band of murderous imps that somehow became her responsibility.

The Lady confirmed Jane's suspicions; Koro trapped Bobbi's aether, forcing the rift to open. That knowledge did little to ease her conscience. He wished he could help bear her burdens.

Jane intoned the final lament for Siranda's soul. Quinn squeezed Bobbi's fingers, and she smiled at him. Even in her exhausted state—neither slept much last night—she took his breath away. He wanted to nab her, carry her away like a caveman with his stolen bride and hide from the rest of the world. The need hit him like a visceral instinct. No use explaining to his instinct that they would have time for love and lust later. Instinct saw through lies. His time was running out. Her time was questionable. They had only now.

The lament's last notes faded, and the witches dispersed. Only the vestals remained to tend Siranda one last time.

"Council meets in an hour," Jane said.

Quinn tightened his grip on Bobbi's hand. The council meeting marked the end of their free time together.

"Come with me," he said.

Quinn pulled me by the hand so hard, I tripped into him. He swept me into his arms and kept moving.

"Where are we going?" I asked.

"Away." The glint in his eye was pure determination.

He set me down beside a stream. The rest of the world vanished behind trees and the sound of rushing water.

He kissed me hard and I felt myself respond. Kissing Quinn was like sky-diving and sitting at home before a warm fire all rolled into one. A mix of excitement and comfort. He kissed me long and deep, then pulled away, his hands twisting in my hair.

"Don't go through that gate."

"I have to."

A muscle pulsed at his jaw, hands ran from my hair, to my neck and down. He pulled off his shirt, then mine, and I lay back on the grassy bank. His eyes pinned me in place as he undressed me. When I lay naked, they roamed across my body, heating my skin with their intensity.

I was ready for him and I arched like a cat to prove it. We had no time for foreplay, no time for niceties. We had only now, this one moment to say everything that needed saying. And there were no words.

He gripped my hips as I unzipped his pants and set him free. He lifted me and sank deep. My pleasure spiked. I ran hands along the hard ridges of his back, wanting to pull all of him inside me. His fingers were everywhere, and my skin flared with fire in their wake. His body fit against mine like we'd been carved from the same rock. I met his thrusts, hot, slick and wet, wanting more. Faster. Harder. Lost in the rhythm of our need, A wave of ecstasy cascaded over me, drenching me, stretching me until I was nothing but pure sensation. I came down from this high grasping his shoulders as he tensed and finished.

He collapsed beside me and I savored the weight of his body against mine, savored every last second of this feeling. This was it. This was all we would ever get. Tomorrow I would leave for an alien world and he'd be gone when I returned.

If I returned.

I breathed him in, kissed his shoulder, neck and the salty tears that touched the corners of his eyes. He was feeling it too. These moments were precious because they were our last.

"I love you." His words were hot against my ear. I wanted to say it back to him. To brand him with my own "I love you," but words stuck in my throat. All the words. Everything I'd ever wanted to say to him but couldn't. He stroked the hair away from my face and smiled sadly.

"It's okay. I know."

He kissed me again, sealing his love inside me with the touch of his lips.

As the afternoon light faded, I lay against his chest, listening to the steady beat of his heart, wondering if I would ever hear it again.

Commitment

I sat quietly in the corner of Jane's living room, holding Quinn's hand tightly in mine. Last night we'd finally broken through the wall of crap mounting between us. Amazing how sex—really good sex—could do that. We made love again in the forest like wild animals, after a funeral, no less. And the abandon felt right, like letting go of all our restraints. A big "Fuck you" to all the problems waiting to tear us apart.

Now we were back in the real world, listening to Jane argue with Gavin, then Gavin argue with Abilene. Then Jane argued with Abilene. Henry threw in his two cents of dissent too. Myra, bruised from yesterday's fight, sat fuming and rattling her teacup while Grant snoozed in the rocking chair, oblivious to it all.

"We have to go through the gate," Jane said. "Why can't you see that?" Her normal unflappable calm was definitely flapped. With unwashed hair and clothes unchanged since yesterday morning, she looked like a harridan.

"I agree," Gavin said, "but we need more time. Henry called Paragon—"

"We don't have time!" Abilene said. "Koro might already be on his way. He set that trap for Bobbi. Didn't you hear the Lady?"

"He probably set hundreds or thousands of traps," Myra said. "Certainly, he can't monitor them all."

"Are you willing to bet our lives on it?" Jane asked.

Things went downhill from there.

I was sick of the bickering, the stalling and the futility of it all.

"I'm going through."

No one heard me. I stood up, my body aching from the battle and a mostly sleepless night.

"I'm going through the gate." They stopped squabbling and finally looked at me. "You can all sit here and dither about the details, but I'm going. Today."

Quinn rose and squeezed my hand. It would be hard for him to see me go, but I could have kissed him for his support when I needed it most.

"I'm going too."

Wait, what? I turned to face him. He couldn't be serious. He smiled and raised that wicked brow.

The squabble broke out again, this time with Quinn's health—or lack thereof—at the core.

Jane slammed her open palm on the table.

"You can't be serious. You won't make it a mile into the desert before you topple from sheer exhaustion."

"I'm going." Quinn set his stubborn expression in place. I agreed with Jane on this one. I didn't want to leave him—especially since he might not survive until I got back—but he couldn't help me with this task. At worst, his illness would hold me back. I was trying to find a tactful way to say this when Abilene cut through the noise.

"What if we could cure him?" she said, looking pointedly at Jane.

"No!" Quinn barked. "We had this conversation before, Abi. It's too dangerous."

"More dangerous than sending Bobbi into a demon realm alone?" Abilene said with a sweet smile? Oh, she was good.

"Look, I've been researching this Konversi spell. It's simple. You said you'd try it."

"I said I didn't mind if you looked into it." Quinn's eyes flashed danger signs. "I didn't say I'd go ahead with it."

"We should," I said. Quinn looked at me incredulously. "I'm serious. I'd rather have you with me than sitting around here worrying about me. But let's face it, you come with me, you'll slow me down. And that's the best-case scenario."

Harsh words, but worth it if they knocked Quinn out of his complacency.

He ran one finger down my cheek and I leaned in to his touch. The rest of the room—the witches, the fights, the fear—all faded to nothing.

"It's too dangerous. You could die," he said softly.

A hysterical laugh bubbled up from the depth of my gut.

"I'm going to confront an honest-to-gods demon on his own turf. How much more dangerous can it get?" I grabbed his hand and pressed it to my chest. "I want you with me, but I need you whole."

He stared for a long minute. I took in every detail of his face, the black brows, the way his hair dipped over his forehead, the slight laugh lines around his eyes that would deepen as he got older.

Lord and Lady, I wanted him to have the chance to live long and make great laugh lines.

He pressed his forehead against mine and whispered, "Okay."

Treatment

Quinn and I waited outside the core's cairn as the sun set. Tree branches thrashed overhead. The wind whipped and died and whipped again. The lulls in between gusts felt like the Lady holding her breath. In the distance, sheet lightning sparked silently.

Abilene and Gavin prepared all day. The Konversi spell to break Quinn's curse wasn't complicated, but it required long meditation on Gavin's part. Now we would find out how much magic the Lady left him.

The darkness deepened as Abilene set up inside the cairn. I wished we could wait for sunrise, but time was running out. We needed to get through the gate before Koro discovered it was open.

A hundred feet away, Siranda's old home stood empty and dark, the magic of her seeings faded from its walls. The coven brought the structure over from Romania, stone by stone, to honor the seer. Would they tear it down, or let it stand as a monument? I supposed the Thirteen would make that decision.

Gavin and Jane emerged from the trees. Henry and two knights followed. I didn't want to take anyone away from guarding the gate, but this could go wrong in so many ways, and I appreciated the extra muscle.

Gavin held up a poppet, a small stuffed rag doll, then hugged his brother.

I'd never heard the whole story of how Quinn contracted mawr, but he'd been in Haiti with Gavin when a voodoo priest cursed him. They searched for days and almost caught the priest in a chase through the twisting alleys of a slum. Only Gavin had seen his face. So today, he was given the task of meditating over the poppet, imbuing it with this vague memory.

"I've got your back," Gavin said. Quinn clutched the poppet and thumped him on the shoulder. Gavin rigidly accepted the embrace.

Quinn turned to his mother next. She wore her full Mistress of the Coven regalia: shimmering white robe, pale wood staff and hair shining like a silver crown. I thought Jane would have last-minute advice or admonishments, but she held Quinn's face in her hands and said, "I love you."

Quinn ducked his head and kissed her cheek.

Two vestals came down from the cottages. Two more sat inside the cairn, feeding aether to the core, but we needed extra hands on deck. After my last encounter with the core, I wanted trained vestals ready to take over if necessary. Gavin explained our strategy to them while we waited for Abilene to finish her preparations.

Quinn leaned against the stone wall. He looked relaxed, but I knew he didn't like this plan. I couldn't blame him. So much could go wrong, but only one thing needed to go right. We had to cure him. I had Koro to thank for giving me this chance. Quinn would never agree to the risk if I wasn't going through that gate. His stubbornness came up against the one argument he couldn't refute. I needed him at my side when I faced my father.

He didn't like it. That was obvious by the rigid cut of his shoulders and fists clenched at his sides. He saw the look on my face and opened his arms. I pressed my cheek against his chest, listening to the slow beat of his heart. He hugged me fiercely.

Abilene came out of the cairn with one of the core's vestals. She was a young witch, no more than twenty, but the vestals were always young. Supporting the link between the core and the ley-line was exhausting work, and vestals burned out early. This one looked scared as Abilene and Gavin conferred quietly.

Quinn kissed the top of my head. I turned to tell him I loved him, but he held a finger to my lips.

"Anything you say will sound like goodbye." Then he replaced the finger with a long, lingering kiss.

"We're ready." Abilene interrupted us.

I entered the cairn first with Rosie at my heel. The second vestal sat cross-legged in the center of the room with the core's purple veins attached to her throat like leeches. More tentacles reached for us. Rosie swatted them away with a growl and a tail swish. Gavin, Abilene and Quinn came in. Jane waited at the door with her staff planted firmly in the ground, our last defense if everything went sour.

Above us, the core hung from the ceiling, pulsing like the heart of a giant beast.

I studied Abilene's spell presentation. In the middle of the room, a black candle—anointed with my blood—sat in a box lined with broken shards of mirror. The box sat on a mound of black salt. Four twigs were laid in a square around the mound. These would be the hazel, oak, elm and willow. Quinn dropped the poppet into the box, so the mirrors reflected on it.

"What if you can't break the curse?" I asked Abilene.

"Then pump him full of aether and we abort the mission." Her tone was confident, but she looked so young. The dim light of the glowing core accented her dark hair and eyes, leaving her face a pale oval in the shadows.

No one spoke, as if the silence held off the inevitable.

"Let's get on with it," Quinn said. "We've gone over every contingency." Abilene lit the candle.

Quinn stripped off his shirt and sat in front of the one remaining vestal, another young witch with dark circles under her eyes. She plucked the sucking tentacles from her skin and guided them to his throat. He jerked as they latched on. Veins stood rigid on his neck.

"Don't go too far," Gavin said to the vestal as she rose and slipped outside. Even with one less body, the space was tight, the air stale and heavy.

Quinn collapsed backward, pillows catching his fall. Every muscle in his body clenched. The core's bite wasn't pleasant. I remembered how it felt, like a thousand tiny teeth tearing away bits of your soul. It should only last a moment, until the ley-line's aether stream connected to the hungry machine. But Quinn wasn't connecting to the ley-line. He would let the core drink his aether dry, drawing the mawr with it. And in that moment, when his body emptied of all magic, Abilene would break the curse put on him years ago, so it couldn't reignite the disease. Then Rosie would revive him, pumping aether back into his body before his soul left it for good.

My job was to make sure the core let him go when they needed it too. Gavin stood behind me with his hunting knife, ready to sever the tentacles if they refused to obey, but that was a last resort. The core was a delicate machine, part organic and part magic. It would regrow lost tentacles, but the ward would be vulnerable until it did.

"How long will this take?" Quinn said through gritted teeth.

"Not long," Abilene said.

I watched the man I love die. As the core sucked away his aether, he grew pale, his eyes shrank into his skull and his shoulders slumped.

Foreboding suddenly gripped me. These were our last moments together!

I wanted to lean in and kiss him, to lay my head in the hollow under his chin and breathe in his scent. But I had to trust in the plan. I clutched his icy fingers. My sensate sight told me his aether was nearly dry. He started to shake, from cold or shock. His fingers clenched mine and went slack. He thrust backward, seizing as the core took the last of his aether.

"Now!" yelled Gavin.

"Not yet," Abilene sprinkled something over the candle and the flame burst upward.

Quinn's eyes rolled to white and his back arched.

What was Abilene waiting for?

She sprinkled more powder and spoke the incantation in bastardized Latin. Quinn writhed, and the tentacles twisted with him, not letting go of their prey. Abilene's voice rose, and she shouted the last words of the spell.

Nothing happened. The room went deathly silent except for the scratching of Quinn's feet against the floor.

"It's not working!" Abilene said. She gathered the four sticks and held them over the flame, shouting the incantation again and cracking all four twigs at once.

The curse broke. I felt it! Like a breath of clean air after almost drowning, the magic zinged through me and disappeared.

"It's done." Abilene crumpled over her altar. Gavin rushed to put out the candle before it set her hair ablaze.

Quinn lay still. The core's tentacles unlatched from his throat with a sickening slurp. They twitched in the air, looking for a new source of aether. Thunder rumbled in the distance. Or maybe it was the ward cracking without the core to fuel it.

None of that mattered now.

"Rosie, quickly!"

The imp jumped into action. Her gnarled hands glowed as she pressed them into his bare chest. Quinn bucked as if he'd been zapped by a defibrillator. His eyes didn't open. Rosie pressed harder. The air was charged with expectation.

Rosie grunted and shifted her weight. Her hands glowed bright red, but Quinn didn't move. The imp sat back, breathing hard.

"Most beatific, supernal one…"

"Rosie! Just tell me!"

She hung her head. "I cannot do this thing. Divine mate gone."

No!

I looked around at the stunned faces. No answers. The tentacles flailed about. I grabbed one and shoved it at Quinn's chest.

The core was a battery, wasn't it? An aether store, just waiting to be tapped? But the tentacle wouldn't latch onto Quinn. He had nothing left to give.

"Try again!" I snapped at Rosie. She pressed her hands to Quinn.

The tentacle wavered above this new source. I grabbed it and shot my aether into it the same way I stoked my sword with fire.

"Take him!" I snarled. The tentacle jerked and latched on to Quinn's pale throat.

I reached above and pressed my hands into the giant pulsing core. It gave way like thick gelatin. I poured my will into it, commanding it to reverse the flow, taking aether from the ward and pushing it back into Quinn.

The core bucked and tried to squirm from my grasp, but I held on. The familiar darkness clouded my mind.

How do you like it, you aether-sucking monster? Not so fun when it's done to you, is it?

The darkness was pushing me beyond my limits. I would give up every-thing, even my soul, to save Quinn. I gritted my teeth against the pain caused by the core's desperate backlash. Someone behind me screamed.

The ward cracked, a sound like the sky breaking, but I didn't care. The gate was open. There was nothing left to protect. Only Quinn.

But Quinn didn't move. His lips were blue.

"No!" I called for more aether—more darkness—and it came willingly, suffusing every pore, every vessel in my body. I poured everything into Quinn.

He didn't move.

A terrible weight of silence fell over the room. It pounded in my head, driving out all sanity. The rage held me firmly in its grasp, pushing me to let it out.

I scrambled outside. Lightning scored the night sky. My aether responded with blue electricity tingling at my fingertips. I let go a blast of rage-fueled magic. It shot from my hands and smashed Siranda's cairn. Rock shards flew in every direction.

Quinn was gone.

Gone!

I screamed. Blue fire burst from me again. The stone cairn tumbled like building blocks.

Another blast and trees burst into flame.

Rage turned hysterical. I wanted to laugh at the ridiculousness of it all. I was going to face a demon—my father!—and for what? To come home and live my life in peace?

There was no peace. There was only blue fire coursing through my veins. I let go another blast into the sky, hoping I could burn the stars.

From behind me, someone yelled meaningless words. I blasted the forest again.

"Bobbi stop!"

Warm arms gripped me. I struggled to be free. The dark aether needed to vent or I would explode!

"Bobbi, it's me!"

His scent stopped me. Woodsy and warm, it hit my hindbrain when nothing else would.

Quinn.

Fire fizzled out on my fingertips.

I lay on the ground, looking up through hazy shadows at his face. His beautiful, worried, alive and breathing face.

"You're okay!"

"I am. You have to stop now." He kissed my tear-stained cheeks. I gripped his arms, feeling life and aether flowing and wanted desperately to believe.

"I thought you were gone."

"I know."

Fear and relief overwhelmed me, and I fell against him.

He stroked my hair and held me until I stopped shaking.

"How can I face Koro like this?" I said. "The darkness took me. I couldn't stop it."

"But you did."

"Only because you came."

"I will always come for you."

Above us, the ward crackled and flamed, burning away the last connection to the broken core.

ᴄDEPLOYMENT

The whole team assembled on the grassy field before the gate. The midsummer festival was two days away, but already four great bonfires burned.

"We'll keep them lit until you come home," Abilene said, hugging Quinn. "They'll help you find your way back."

Quinn wiped the tears on her face.

He was a picture of health, skin slightly bronzed, shoulders bulked out again and dark eyes alert. The core more than revived him, it revitalized him. The cost was the ward. Myra nearly had a coronary when she learned what I'd done to their magical machine. As one of the original Thirteen who built it to protect the coven twenty years ago, she took the destruction personally.

I thought the loss was a good thing. We could no longer hide from Koro and we shouldn't hide from the world. But one triumph at a time.

Henry chose a knight to come with us, a lean, angry-looking woman named Sybil. He wanted to bring a dozen guards, but we all agreed a small party would be most effective. At the moment, he stood at the edge of the yard, saying his goodbyes to Gavin.

Regret tugged at me as Gavin's face crumpled. Henry whispered into his ear and they embraced. Yesterday, that was me, ready to say goodbye to Quinn, not knowing if I'd ever see him again. Now we stood together at the gate, about to step through to an alien world. For better or worse, we had comfort in each other.

Rosie sat at my feet, her long tail wrapped around my ankles. She also chose another to accompany us. Erita was a battered looking imp with one milky eye and a truncated tail. She'd survived for decades as a courier for Koro and knew the red desert intimately. Both imps stared through the gate with solemn gazes. The wind picked up on the other side, blowing sand in dense

"

clouds. Every now and again, the alien wind buffeted us, bringing spicy scents of the unknown.

"Want to wait for calmer seas?" Quinn asked.

"We've waited too long." I took his hand, needing his skin against mine. "I'm surprised Koro hasn't already come through."

Quinn frowned. "Bothers me too."

"Maybe he doesn't know it's open?" That didn't seem right. Two months ago, before we patched it, dozens of alien creatures came through. Now? Nothing.

"Something's blocking his passage to the gate?" More plausible, but that answer only brought up more questions. What kept him away? Where would the gate lead us?

"I guess there's only one way to find out." Before we stepped forward, a voice stopped us.

"I'm coming too."

Jane carried a large bag on her shoulder.

"Mother, you can't be serious." Quinn blocked her.

"Get out of my way." Jane laced her voice with command. I took a step back, but Quinn was undeterred.

"I'm coming and you can't stop me." Jane glared at her son. "An excuse you've used on me a dozen times in your life." Quinn glared back, then his eyes softened. He lowered his voice.

"How can you even think of going back there?"

Jane survived unbelievable horrors on that world. Going back could break her.

"I know Koro. I know how he thinks, and I know the inside of his castle. How many of you can say that?"

She had a point. Even Rosie, one of his servants, never saw his inner rooms. Jane's experience could mean the difference between success and failure.

"You can't go!" Abilene threw herself into her mother's arms. Jane hugged her and petted her long black hair. I'd never seen Jane be remotely affectionate before. It was unsettling.

"Abilene, my heart. You'll be fine. If I don't come back—"

"Mom! No!"

Jane held up a hand for quiet. Abilene sniffled.

"If I don't come back, you will make a fine mistress. You're ready. Myra and Grant will help you. Listen to your heart and listen to the Lady."

Tears streaked Abilene's face. She hugged Jane once more then stood back. Gavin put his arm around her shoulder, his eyes glassy from holding back tears.

"Shall we go?" Jane hefted her pack. Henry took it from her and added it to the weight he already carried.

Quinn grabbed my hand and together we stepped through the gate.

Book 5

GONE MAGIC

Invaded

A zing of aether ran along my skin as I stepped through the rift. I emerged onto a plateau overlooking a vast red desert. Two huge standing stones flanked the rift like guardians. Hot wind tossed sand against them and tugged at my hair and clothes. The air tasted of alien magic—spicy and exotic. I shivered despite the heat.

The light fell differently here. It was too yellow, like butter melting down the horizon. I looked back at my world, now just a doorway filled with green leaves and blue sky. The cool colors already made me nostalgic.

As the others stepped through the gate, we stood silent and uneasy. We were seven in all, our little band of…what? Soldiers? Vigilantes? Heroes, definitely. Whether we found our target and killed the demon Kororaeth or not, we were all heroes.

After Quinn came Jane. I didn't want her along on this trip, but no one said no to the Mistress of the Hidden Coven. Next came the imps—Rosie, my self-appointed protector and Erita, our guide. Last to come through were two Paragon knights, Henry, my former magic trainer and Sybil, his chosen guard.

Standing on a rocky outcropping with the glowing gate at our backs, I hoped we looked impressive to whatever spies Koro had set to watch.

There had to be spies. The veil between our worlds thinned here, making it the ideal place for Koro to set his snare. I'd foolishly sprung it, opening the portal. He wouldn't waste all that time and aether only to let us walk into his world unannounced.

I peered over the edge of the plateau. About a hundred paces away, a piece of white fabric flapped in the wind. It was a tent, broken and half-buried in the sand. Now that I recognized it, other bits of the abandoned camp became obvious. The wheel of a cart rested against a rock. Pots, tools and bits of armor lay discarded and partially buried in the flowing sand. Someone, many someones, had been here recently, but for now, we were alone.

"That was too easy," I said. "There should be more…I don't know. More something."

"You expected fireworks?" Henry asked.

"I expected something. Or someone."

"Be glad we have no welcoming party." Quinn also scanned the horizon with a grim expression. "Looks like the imps camped here before coming through the rift."

"But why would they abandon it?" I asked. "It makes no sense, if they were sent here to guard it."

The wind scuffed across the rock plateau. Intermittent puffs of sand billowed up from the dunes like dervishes.

Henry and Sybil circled our base of stone, guns pointing into the rolling dunes.

We waited.

All was silent but for the restless sand.

"Where are they?" Quinn didn't whisper exactly, but his voice slipped into the sighing wind.

"Something's not right." Henry's gaze never stopped moving.

The wind picked up, reshaping dunes to mimic great beasts moving across the desert. The constantly shifting sand could easily mask an army.

"We need to move out," Henry said after several tense minutes.

Erita pointed into the desert and mumbled in the imp tongue.

"This way, most blessed one." Rosie tugged my hand. I had no idea how Erita could tell the right direction in this featureless place, but she moved off with purpose and I followed. Quinn stopped to help his mother down the first steep dune. I turned to the side and slid. Sand filled my boots.

We stepped over the remains of the camp, including several skeletons gleaming in the sunlight. One was humanoid.

"Step where I step," Erita said. "Sand has teeth."

I nodded, not wanting to know if she meant literal teeth.

We walked in a single file with Erita and Rosie in the lead. The ground shifted randomly under my feet, and I fell on my knees more than once. We climbed up dunes and slid down the other sides. Sand-laced wind slashed at exposed skin, and we bundled up in scarves. The heat sucked every bit of moisture from my skin.

Henry stepped aside to look behind us and sank to his knees in quicksand. Dropping his pack, he braced himself with his rifle's butt. The sand pulled him deeper. Within seconds he sank to his waist.

"Take my hand!" With my feet planted at the edge of the quicksand, I reached for him. Quinn grabbed me around the waist and we hauled Henry back to solid ground. He emptied sand from his boots and pockets, his rapid breathing the only indication of the near-death encounter.

Erita pushed through us to stand over him. She was small, even for an imp, with one milky eye. Her stubby tail quivered like an arrow. She glared at Henry with her one good eye and spoke in gruffly accented English.

"I say step where I step."

Henry nodded. "Yes, ma'am."

We all took a moment to drink from our canteens. We were an hour into the journey that would bring me face to face with my demon father, and I already felt lost.

The landscape didn't change. Quinn saw no sign of Koro or his minions. Occasionally, small creatures darted across the sand, too fast for him to see more than snake-like shadows. He took a cue from the imps who ignored them. Sybil, Henry's choice of Paragon muscle, was twitchy with her gun. Every time the sand stirred, she swung her rifle to meet the danger.

"You're going to wear yourself out," Quinn said. "We've got a long road ahead of us. You might want to tone down the paranoia."

Sybil glared at him but didn't loosen the hold on her gun. Quinn fought the urge to reprimand her. As the coven's chief of security, he expected blind obedience, but Sybil's first loyalty was to Paragon not the coven. He'd keep an eye on her before her trigger-happy finger got them into trouble.

Jane called for frequent rests.

"I knew she'd slow us down," Bobbi said as they rationed water from a canteen.

"She's not stopping for herself." Quinn kept his voice low. "She thinks I'm fragile."

"Are you?" She watched him with a steady gaze. The wind pulled at a loose lock of hair and whipped it about her face.

Lord and Lady but he loved this woman.

He pulled her to him and whispered in her ear. "You fixed me up good. We've got this."

They stole two precious minutes of contact, but her frame never relaxed.

"You okay?" he asked.

She shook her head and smiled dryly.

"I love that sound. Your beating heart."

Not long ago, his heart had nearly stopped as the mawr attacked his aether and drained his life. Bobbi cured him. No one else had the sheer power to do it. She didn't see it that way, of course. Bobbi only thought of how her cure almost finished him off. But he knew the truth. She was the strongest witch he knew. And though she worried her magic was tainted with darkness, he could see the pure light shining from her eyes every time she looked at him.

He pushed her scarf aside and kissed her.

"I'm glad you're here with me," she said.

"Me too." He grinned. "No place I'd rather be."

No matter what the next few hours or days brought, he'd rather face them with Bobbi than spend his days without her.

Erita fidgeted with impatience, ready to move on. They walked through the draining heat. The landscape never changed. Once, a line of elephantine beasts appeared on the horizon. They took no notice of the humans, and they trudged on.

"How long are the days in this place?" Quinn asked Rosie. He desperately wanted the red sun to set and give them a reprieve from the heat. The imp shrugged.

"As long as needed."

Rosie's English had improved by leaps and bounds. She was being deliberately obtuse.

On the next rise, Erita stopped and pointed.

"There."

Another henge of stones jutted from the desert, barely silhouetted against the dying light.

"We go there. Stop for…" Her last word was unrecognizable. She looked at Rosie for translation.

"We stop for storm," she said.

"What storm?" Henry asked. "The sky is perfectly clear." He was right. The wind died hours ago. Quinn looked up at unfamiliar stars just starting to fleck the sky. Erita didn't answer.

Distances were deceiving in the desert. Just because they could see the henge on the horizon didn't mean it was close. They walked on as the sky darkened and the wind picked up. Soon the blowing sand was thick enough to choke on, and Quinn lost sight of the standing stones. Henry pulled a rope from his pack and linked them in a chain. Erita danced from foot to foot while he secured them.

"We run," she said. They stumbled and slid over the ever-changing landscape. Quinn tightened the scarf across his face, but the sand found its way inside, chafing and choking.

"We won't make it!" he yelled over the roar of the wind.

"We must!" Rosie yelled back. "Sand devours all!"

Quinn ran. Ahead, he could barely make out Jane and Bobbi stumbling down yet another shifting mountain. The blowing sand swirled like a curtain. He pressed on. One step. One slide on loose ground. Another step. Always forward. Always battling the biting wind.

When the henge finally reared up in front of him, Quinn could barely breathe. He staggered into the circle of stones to find Jane seated in a lotus position, eyes closed as if in meditation.

She opened her eyes and said, "Is everyone inside the stones?"

He nodded.

Jane clapped her hands once. The sound echoed like thunder and a ward sprang up around the stones.

Inside their little tent of magic the wind died. Outside, it blew with monstrous force. Within minutes, a drift of sand piled against the invisible ward.

"We'd better get some sleep," Henry said. "We'll have to dig our way out tomorrow."

WAKENED

The storm blocked all light from the sky. We sat in our bubble, listening to sand scour the ward.

Hours passed.

We ate sparingly from our rations. Quinn produced glow sticks from his pack and lit our small cave in green light. Jane was already asleep. The long walk and strain of calling a ward big enough to cover us had worn her out. The rest of us took turns sleeping, with Sybil on first watch.

Quinn and I took thin blankets from our packs and made our bed against one of the standing stones. It wasn't private or comfortable, but I could feel sleep pulling me down as soon as I nestled against Quinn's chest.

Later—hours or minutes—something woke me. A scuffing sound of shoes on the sandy rock. Sybil stirred Henry to take over the watch. Staring into the blackness, I listened to them shuffle around until they settled. The night fell silent again.

Quinn's arm was a comforting weight across my chest, but I could no longer sleep. Every time I closed my eyes, my father's face loomed over me as it had when he possessed William Fain. How much worse would it be to look upon his true face? Red eyes mocked me under his bulging brow. Thick wet lips spread like a wound across his face as he forced himself on me. His teeth found my neck in a kiss to steal my aether and my life…

I sat up gasping and pulling at my collar. The darkness was a physical presence filling my lungs. I needed to get out!

But I couldn't. We were locked in a ward under who knew how much sand, but we were safe. The storm made us safe. Eventually, my breathing calmed.

I thought I was over the whole William Fain affair. The nightmares hadn't shown up in months. But in the darkness, he felt so real.

My agitation hadn't bothered Quinn. He murmured but didn't wake. That was good. He might have been cured of the mawr, but his body had taken a beating over the last few months, and this trip wasn't doing anything for his recovery. I let him sleep.

A light flicked on as I rose. Henry nodded to me from across the cave as I quietly joined him. Rosie and Erita were curled like kittens nearby, one of them snoring in soft grunts. I stepped around them and sat next to Henry.

"You should sleep," he said. "I'll wake you in a couple of hours for your turn."

"Can't. I'm too restless."

He handed me a flask. I took a sip and liquid fire burned down my throat.

"What the hell is that?" I sputtered and gave it back.

"Courage." Henry grinned.

Above us, the storm slashed at Jane's protective bubble.

"How long do you think it will last?" I took another swig of courage.

"I don't know. I thought the wind was slowing, but that could be wishful thinking. I've been listening to it for so long, it almost sounds like voices."

I knew what he meant. The sand sloughing across the ward sounded like the gods arguing in harsh whispers.

"Is a watch really necessary?" I asked. "Nothing would be out in that storm."

"Precisely when you should expect an attack."

We listened to the angry gods while I brooded about my nightmare.

"Koro lured me here. He's been trying to trap one of us for a long time. One of his offspring, I mean."

Henry nodded but didn't answer. He was good at letting me wrestle through a problem on my own.

William Fain was the first of Koro's agents to attack me. As a being of pure aether, Koro couldn't survive in our world. At least not until the ley-lines flooded it with enough magic to sustain him.

So Koro sought entry another way. The gate was only his first step in his plan. During our council meetings, we debated this point many times. Myra argued that he would simply burn up if he tried to come through in his true form. Jane's prediction was more ominous. She believed his very existence in our world would destabilize the laws of nature and cause catastrophes on an epic scale. I didn't know which theory to believe. Either way, with the gate open, he would have no trouble sending minor demons through, like the berserker. Those could wreak havoc all on their own.

Koro's magic might be too strong for him to survive in our world, but some loophole of physics meant he could rebirth himself into that world if he could find a vessel strong enough to bear his demon essence.

So he seeded traps to lure unsuspecting females. He trapped Jane and my mother this way and impregnated them.

I was the culmination of those plans.

I was the vessel that could birth a demon.

If he caught me at home again, he could push his way into our world through my womb. If he caught me here, he might simply possess me. I wouldn't wait around for either fate. I would fight him on my terms.

I took the hag stone from my pocket and ran a thumb around its smooth edge. The Lady gave it to me when she spoke through Siranda's form. Looking through the stone's natural hole heightened my sensate abilities. But more importantly, the Lady told me that in my greatest need, I could use it—only once—to call her. Judging that greatest need was all relative. Did a smothering sand storm qualify? What about getting lost in an endless desert?

Henry watched me, waiting patiently for me to finish my thought.

"Before I met you, Koro possessed a man name William Fain and tried to impregnate me." The words fell like sharp stones in the darkness. He probably knew this story, but I needed to say it more than he needed to hear it.

"Jane said he could be reborn in our dimension, but he needed a strong host. One with demon blood. Me."

I shivered, thinking about how close Fain had been to raping me. Henry handed me the flask and I drank. Liquid courage would have to do until I found the real thing.

"He lured me here for some reason. I don't know why he wasn't waiting for us or why he hasn't sent soldiers already."

"That's been bothering me too." Henry lifted the flask for another sip.

"When we find him…" I played out the possibilities in my mind. None of them ended well. Even if I managed to kill Koro, I wouldn't walk away unscathed. "He might possess me, use me for his schemes to break into our world."

After a long pause Henry asked, "How do you plan to kill him?"

That question was loaded with traps. How much should I tell him? About the darkness that crept over me every time I used my magic? About my special abilities to siphon magic from others, a uniquely demonic talent feared by most witches? I hadn't even told Quinn all of it. No one truly knew what I was capable of, not even me.

Henry laid a warm hand on my arm.

"You don't have to tell me."

But I did. I needed him for one crucial task.

"I can drink aether," I said quietly. "Human aether, demon aether, it doesn't matter."

Henry's eyes widened. "The berserker…"

"Yes, I weakened him enough to kill. It's also how Koro kills. It's his reason for wanting into our world, so he can drink human aether freely. I don't know, maybe it gets him high."

"What does it do to you?"

I shrugged. "Gives me one hell of a headache to start."

"Is that all?" He prodded me with the toe of his boot.

"No." I covered my face in my hands as if I could hold back the confession. "It feels really good, you know? Like a drug. But dark. It's like getting the high and the downer all at the same time. But it doesn't matter. I'm not going to drink any humans. Just Koro."

"That's your plan to kill him? Bleed off his aether before he does the same to you?"

"It sounds ridiculous when you say it, but yes. That's the basic plan."

"And how will you get close enough to pull this off without being killed outright?"

"I didn't say it was a fully formed plan." I grabbed the flask, took a sip and wiped the back of my hand across my mouth.

"Right. Well, just tell me where I fit in, and I'll have your back."

Irrational tears burned my eyes. He would have my back. And so would Quinn and Rosie. I knew I could count on these three, if no one else. But I had a job for Henry alone.

"When we get to that point…" I took a deep breath and started again. "When I face my father, and if I fail, I need you to kill me before he uses my body for whatever he has in mind."

"Kill you? I can't—"

"You must! Quinn won't and I don't dare ask Jane." The mistress of the coven might find my death a little too convenient. This was a last-ditch plan only, one that I could only entrust to Henry. And even then, he'd have to get through Quinn and Rosie to deal that final blow.

"I can't let Koro have me, and not just because I'm afraid of what he'll do to me." I was. Terribly, obsessively afraid. "But worse is what he can do with me. If he finds a way to survive in our world, life as we know it is dead. So I ask, will you kill me?"

Henry nodded slowly. "Let's make sure it doesn't come to that end."

"That's the plan."

BURIED

Quinn woke to silence. The storm had finally blown itself out. They'd left all electronics on the other side of the gate, and their only timekeeper was a mechanical watch Jane wore on a chain around her neck. By her reckoning, they'd lost thirty-six hours to the storm.

Only one small gap at the top of the ward let in sunlight. The sand nearly buried them.

"This is going to be a tricky exit," Jane said, studying the problem. If she let the ward drop, the sand would spill into the cave and suffocate them in seconds.

"Can you dissolve one section of the ward?" Henry asked. "We might survive that much sand coming in. And we could climb out."

Jane shook her head. "The ward has been standing too long. Its web of aether is too finely meshed for me to break it apart without losing the whole thing."

"What about Abilene's drill offense?" Bobbi asked. During practice sessions, while Bobbi had struggled to keep an active ward, Quinn and Abilene bombarded her with spells. Abilene excelled at a sort of aether drill that relentlessly ground away at a small part of the ward while he distracted Bobbi with fire bombs.

"It might work," Quinn said. "If we drill a hole up high enough."

One of the standing stones lay on its side, giving them a large step up. Henry and Bobbi took turns drilling through the ward while Quinn and Sybil cleared away sand as it fell in. After a few minutes, Bobbi stepped off the rock. Her hand shook as she wiped sweat from her forehead.

Quinn pulled her aside. "You okay?"

"No. I think someone else should take over."

Sybil stepped onto the rock and continued the spell that had so far made only a dent in the ward.

Jane watched with pinched lips. She wanted to say something about Bobbi slacking off, no doubt, but Quinn instinctively understood. Magic was stronger here and alien. None of them could predict how even simple spells would react. And Bobbi feared more than a magic backfire. Nothing he said could convince her that her aether wasn't tainted.

"Can you help me clear the sand," he asked.

Bobbi nodded but wouldn't look him in the eye.

Half an hour later, they had a tunnel to the surface made up of loose sand. Sybil stood on Henry's shoulders to stabilize it with a petrification spell. Good to know they had a geomage on hand. Manipulating rock, sand and sediment was a specialized skill. It might come in handy if they needed to burrow into Koro's castle.

Quinn nodded his thanks to Sybil and climbed through the hole. When they all emerged, squinting like mole rats, Jane let the ward drop and the sand sank around the standing stones until they were no more than steps in the dune.

"How long until sunset?" Henry asked.

Erita studied the sky, her one good eye squinting. She spoke in the imp tongue.

"Four hours," Rosie translated.

"How far to the next resting spot?"

"Longer," Erita said.

They hefted their packs and headed out.

In the second hour trekking over the slipping sand, thirst warred with boredom in Quinn's thoughts. He worried about Jane, who plowed along using her staff like a walking stick. She was stubborn enough not to complain, but she had to be tired. He begged for frequent rest stops, turning the tables on her mothering by pretending his recent illness forced the need.

Jane never spoke of the time she'd been held captive and tortured on this world. During a restless summer between high school and college, she and three other young women found a grimoire. Unknowingly, they fulfilled the perfect conditions of an odd spell, and they cast it in a place where the veil between worlds was thin. The spell pulled them through a crack in dimensions to Koro's world. He kept them for months—Jane, Molly, and Bobbi and Gavin's mothers, Hannah and Stacy. When he finally returned them home, they were all pregnant. Of those babies, only Gavin and Bobbi survived. Molly miscarried. Jane buried her stillborn son in the cemetery where William Fain tried to work his dark spell.

Quinn wondered what Jane must be thinking as they pushed closer to Koro's den. Was she afraid? Angry? Only her eyes showed from behind her scarf and they gave away nothing. But he couldn't deny this was as much her fight as Bobbi's.

"Is the sun giving you deep thoughts," Bobbi asked.

Quinn smiled with humor he didn't feel.

"Nope. Just wondering how much more sand I can fit in my boots. He's the one with the deep thoughts." He jerked a thumb at Henry who scribbled in a journal as they walked. "I think the sun has cooked his brain and turned him into a philosopher."

"Very funny," Henry said. "I'm making a map, sort of. It's surprising how many landmarks I've spotted."

He was right. The desert appeared empty at first glance, but they'd passed several outcroppings of rock, many with standing stones like the ones they'd sheltered at.

"This way, if we lose our guide," Henry glanced at Erita, "we might have a chance of finding our way back."

Rosie and Erita shared a look and cackled.

"Stupid human," Erita said.

Henry paused in his writing and glanced up. "Why?"

"Desert alive," Rosie said. "Sand come and go. Rock rise and fall. Desert never the same two days together."

Henry lowered his journal.

"You mean all these notes are useless? How do you know we're going the right way?"

Erita tapped her nose.

"Odor it."

Henry looked to Bobbi and she shrugged.

Rosie spoke to Erita briefly, then translated.

"She say home of grand holy one make odor she can follow."

Henry still didn't follow and Bobbi translated Rosie's translation.

"The imps won't say Koro's name aloud." Rosie and Erita winced. "I think she's saying his castle leaks aether and she can sense it."

"Can you?" Quinn asked.

Bobbi closed her eyes and quested outward. Quinn's weak sensate abilities could feel nothing.

"The desert isn't as dead as it seems," she said. "I feel pockets of hidden life, and a tug of aether from a stronger source—strong but far away." She opened her eyes and pointed ahead. "That way. It could be Koro—" the imps winced again—"or it could be another demon."

Erita sniffed her.

"It odor like you."

"It smells like me?" Erita nodded. "Then it's probably him."

That satisfied Henry and he put his notebook away.

The sun set in a dazzling wash of purple and red. They stopped to eat and admire it. Once again, a herd of elephantine beasts walked the horizon line.

"What are those?" Quinn asked.

"You call them…broodbone," Rosie said. No doubt the name was a bad translation from her tongue.

"No good eat," Erita said. "But dangerous."

They looked peaceful, plodding along in a line, silhouetted by the sun, but Quinn was happy to admire them from afar.

They walked through the darkness, grateful for the cooler temperature. The desert came alive at night. A small moon chased a larger one across the sky. Red and yellow serpents were camouflaged against the sand until they zipped right between Quinn's feet. Several species of night birds prowled for smaller prey and a large lizard lumbered by, completely oblivious to their presence even when Erita slapped it with her tail. She proved to be a great resource about the local fauna, and by the time the sky lightened toward dawn, she'd caught five smaller lizards for breakfast. Sybil proudly held up two more spiked on the end of an arrow.

They stopped at another odd rock formation, this one a mound of boulders stacked one on top of the other like a giant's game. The imps ate two lizards raw, devouring everything but the skulls. Henry and Quinn roasted the rest with quick blasts of fire.

"You'd think that the ones who haven't recently been near death could step up and do the cooking," Jane said with a bland gaze at Bobbi.

"Mother, don't start," Quinn said. Jane raised an eyebrow at him. They were all simmering in the heat. Before this was over Bobbi and Jane would boil over. Jane knew something was wrong with Bobbi's magic, and she'd keep pushing until she found out what. Quinn just hoped that when Jane pushed too far, he'd be there to intervene.

He picked bits of charred meat off his lizard and choked them down with water. No one spoke. As soon as the sun topped the horizon, the heat became stifling. They slept in the shadow of the rocks. Too hot for close contact, Bobbi lay beside him with her head resting on her pack. When the sun shifted, Quinn nudged her groggily to move out of its scorching rays. Then he dozed again.

Several other creatures hid from the daylight in and around the stones. Quinn jolted awake when something crab-like skittered across his chest.

"What the hell was that?"

Bobbi opened a bleary eye.

"If it didn't bite and it didn't nest, just ignore it." She shifted the pack under her head and went back to sleep. Some help she was.

He woke again at dusk feeling sluggish and hot.

They ate and drank the ever-smaller reserve of water in silence.

Then they walked.

Sheltered

I was ready to fall down and let the sand devour me when Rosie tugged on my hand.

"Come, most beatific one. We rest at *Rahrahee*."

I mumbled acknowledgment and kept walking. That's all there was now. One foot forward, calf muscles tight and screaming, trying to keep every step steady on the shifting sand. Then the next foot. Constant pain. Constant thirst. So tired, I barely noticed the change when the ground hardened. I looked up, stunned to find us entering a small forest.

Rahrahee was an oasis.

In the pre-dawn light, the colors were muted, but already I could see this forest was remarkable. Tall, thick-trunked trees topped in massive fleshy leaves like mushrooms grew here. White hair-thin vines hung from the mushroom heads, swaying oddly in the windless air. More vines and smaller shrubs tangled in the spaces beneath the trees. As the light grew, every plant, tree and vine shone with a different hue. The clamor of color made me dizzy.

Erita led us down a well-marked path. This place was used often, probably a standard rest stop for desert dwellers and those foolish enough to try crossing the arid expanse. The imp led us to a camp at the center of a clearing. We drank from a well and filled our canteens. Erita disappeared into the bush and came back, arms laden with purple fruit.

"Zima!" she proclaimed proudly. The zima fruit was pulpy and sour but also juicy and filling. We ate and slept as the sun rose.

In the late afternoon I woke feeling, if not refreshed, at least human again. My leg muscles protested when I rose, but a few light stretches loosened them.

"Where are you going?" Quinn yawned and tried to pull me back down.

"Get up, lazybones. I want to explore before we leave." I won the tug-of-war and he grudgingly stood up.

Henry was on watch and he warned us not to stray too far. We followed the path into the trees. A drowsy afternoon hush lay over everything, the creatures and insects all waiting out the stifling heat.

"We might be the first humans to ever see these freaky trees." Quinn reached up and one of the hairy vines tickled his palm. He jerked his hand away.

"Does it hurt?" I asked.

"No. Just reminds me of the core's tentacles." He smiled wryly, then turned serious. "While we have a moment to ourselves, we need to talk."

"Never the words a girl wants to hear."

"I'm serious. We need to talk about what's coming."

Death is coming. Death, pain and oblivion. I didn't want to discuss it. Not yet. Maybe not ever.

"Aren't these trees amazing?" I asked, trying to distract him.

Quinn frowned. "I mean it. We need to make plans."

"No."

"No?" He arched that damned eyebrow.

"There are no plans to make. We find Koro. We fight him. He has all the advantages. We have none."

Except he doesn't know I can drink his aether.

"We need a plan." Quinn's expression was resolute. He wasn't letting go of this. "How exactly will you fight him? You're too afraid to use your magic."

"When the time comes, I won't hold back. I promise." I'd have no choice. The darkness would propel me forward.

"How can you be so sure?" He grabbed my hands. "I see you resisting your magic all the time. How do you know you're even capable of letting it all go?"

"Because I have to." I swallowed around the lump in my chest. "I have only one shot at this. I will kill that beast or die trying. I have nothing to lose."

Quinn looked hurt. "You have me."

Tears blurred my eyes. How could I make him understand?

"When this is done, you won't want me," I said. "You think I don't have a plan, but I do. When I face Koro, the darkness will consume me. Even if we live through it, there won't be anything left of me. I will always be a danger to you and the coven. When this is done," my heart felt like jagged ice in my chest, "I'll be dead or I'll be gone."

For several long seconds, he said nothing but simply processed my words. He seemed to come to a decision, and gently wiped the tears from my cheeks.

"So we have this moment," he said. "That's it?"

I nodded.

"Then we'd better enjoy it."

I stood on my toes and kissed him.

"Gods, I miss you." He pressed his forehead against mine, then kissed the corners of my eyes, the tip of my nose and finally my lips. I knew exactly what he meant. For days, we'd been constantly together, and yet not. Every night we fell into exhausted sleep, with no privacy for any kind of intimacy even if we'd had the energy for it.

The rough living looked good on Quinn. His hair was messed and fell across his forehead in a black wave. The scar above his eye from his fight with William Fain gave him a rakish look. I ran my hands up the hard, lean lines of muscle on his arms. His skin was hot and tanned. He was so alive.

Tears burned my eyes, but I held them back. I wouldn't spoil this perfect moment. Mawr had almost taken Quinn from me. Against the odds, we'd healed him, but I hadn't rejoiced in that good fortune yet. I couldn't imagine a future with him. Our togetherness was only a respite. In another few hours or days, we'd face my father and I'd lose him anyway.

But we had this moment.

His dark blue eyes shone with a hint of mischief as he slipped hands under my shirt. He pulled me against him, our damp shirts and damp bodies mashing together. He kissed my neck, his hands searching for more skin. A sigh of released need escaped me. I arched backward, confident he'd hold me upright as he continued…

A screech from above startled us apart.

A creature hung from one of the vines and chittered. About the size of a cat, it glared at us from golf ball-sized eyes. It hung from long multi-jointed limbs and was covered in fur like the husk of a coconut. It chirped unhappily at our intrusion.

When a second creature joined in the scolding, we backed away.

"Okay!" Quinn held up his hands in surrender. "We're leaving. You might give a guy some privacy with his girl." The creatures screeched and something landed by our feet with a splat and an intense stench.

"Oh, gods!" I laughed and gagged at the same time. Quinn grabbed my arm, and we stumbled up the path out of their target range.

"Please tell me that wasn't what I think it was."

"Yep. Shit. What a way to ruin a romance."

We grinned like kids who narrowly escaped detention and walked on. I was happy just to be with him in this moment, holding hands and pretending we were a normal couple. A normal couple on a stroll in an alien wilderness.

The path wound through the trees. I assumed it would come out at the desert, but we never made it that far. A secondary path branched from our trail, almost unnoticeable in the dense underbrush. We would have walked right by it, except strange aether tugged at me as we passed.

Magic.

Something down that path emitted strong magic.

"Let's go this way." I pointed into the bushes.

Quinn looked skeptical.

"I feel something."

He nodded and we turned down the path. That was one of the things I loved about Quinn. He didn't need to analyze a problem from all angles. He trusted me to make a decision. Thinking about the poo flinging beasts, I hoped I wasn't leading him into something worse.

Branches slashed at us as we pushed through. I almost turned back when the vegetation became too thick. Quinn cut away a snarl of vines and we kept going.

"It's getting stronger." The aether called to me now. We cut through more underbrush and came up against the trunk of a massive tree, its hairy vines floating high above us. But the tree wasn't the thing that drew my attention and shocked me to my core.

Another gate shimmered in the shadows.

EXPOSED

Quinn stared at the gate.

"Where do you think it goes?" Henry asked.

They'd gone back to the camp for the others and now stood in the dense underbrush, staring at the second rift leading to an unknown world.

"Not home," Quinn said. Even his weak sensate skills could tell the aether coming through that gate was alien.

The implications were staggering.

Koro spent years—centuries, maybe—seeding snares in places of power, hoping one of his offspring might trigger the trap and open a gateway. It worked, but how much harder would it be to find an open gate to another realm? On some level, Quinn always knew it was possible. Infinite worlds existed beyond theirs, but reaching them was a statistical improbability.

Now they were faced with the reality. A permanent gate existed between their world and this one. And this gate meant their world was open to other realms too. Open and vulnerable.

Sybil unslung her rifle and pointed it into the rift.

"Put that away." Quinn pushed the barrel down. In his experience, nothing good ever came from pointing guns at the unknown. Sybil glanced at Henry who nodded, then let the gun drop.

Jane stepped forward and peered through the rift. The gate stood five feet high, edges glistening like melting frost. The nearly opaque doorway shifted with shadows from the world beyond.

"Should we go through it?" Henry asked.

"We can't afford to be side-tracked." Jane dismissed it and turned away. "We must push on to Koro's castle." The imps winced.

"But how can we just leave it?" Sybil asked.

"It'll be here when we come back," Jane said. No one qualified that with *if we come back.* "Besides, we don't know what's waiting through there. It could be a trap."

Warily, they turned their backs on the gate and returned to camp.

Something shoved Quinn into the trees.

"What the hell—"

He landed on one knee and pain spiked up his leg. A grey figure dashed past them and disappeared into the shadows of the forest.

"Did that come through the rift?" Henry asked, his sword already out.

"I don't know," Quinn said. "I think so."

Sybil ran after it. They waited until shots rang in the distance and a cloud of squawking birds erupted from the trees.

Quinn stood and pulled his knife, feeling useless and twitchy. Bobbi gazed back toward the gate with huge eyes.

"Come on." He took her arm and steered her away. "Lets get back to camp."

Hours later, Quinn eyed the trail leading away from camp, expecting someone or something to burst from the shadows. Sybil had returned with no news of the strange invader. The figure had eluded her.

Now they waited out the worst of the heat in edgy silence.

Jane sat in a meditative trance. Erita slept, but Rosie sat at Bobbi's feet, gazing at her idol with innocent admiration. Bobbi petted her absently. She stared at the hag stone given to her by the Lady, turning it over and over in her hand. Her eyes had a hollow, scared look that worried Quinn. Seeing the second gate had rocked her too.

Henry scribbled in his journal and Sybil cleaned her guns obsessively.

They couldn't escape the sand and it must have been terrible on the guns. Every time he shifted, sand grated against Quinn's skin. It was in his socks, his shirt and his underwear. He could feel it grinding in his teeth, and they didn't have enough water to wash the grit away.

He watched Sybil stroke the barrel of her rifle with a soft cloth. She'd already cleaned that gun. Now her fussing was just busy work.

"Why the guns?" Bobbi asked. "You know you can't kill Koro with that, right?"

In the coven, the knights stuck to traditional weapons—swords, knives and bows. Firearms didn't work well against magical beings like demons.

Sybil had only two expressions, scowling concentration or scowling disgruntlement. Now she frowned as if Bobbi had insulted her best friend.

"Other things in this world might take a bullet nicely," she said. "Things that have probably never seen a gun. Call it the element of surprise."

"Fine. Just keep it pointed away from me," Bobbi said.

"It's unloaded."

"I don't care. Guns make me nervous."

"Says the girl who killed a wraith." Sybil showed her teeth.

Two days into the trip and their group had already dissolved into bickering. Though they huddled together for protection, each of them was alone with their thoughts. If he encountered this problem with his guards at home, Quinn would put them to battle training. Nothing brought a group together like a good physical workout. But here, in this harsh landscape with so few reserves, they had to preserve their energy for the real fight, the one that could jump at them from any shadow.

Time to change the subject.

"Do you know what came through the rift?" Quinn asked Rosie.

"Ska'in." Rosie made a sign with her fingers like a ward against a curse. "Fire rippers. "

That didn't sound good.

"Are they dangerous?" Henry asked.

"Much dangerous. But secret too. Ska'in no bother."

"Did it come from another world?" Quinn asked.

"Maybe." Rosie shrugged again. "Ska'in from Saka."

"Where's Saka?" asked Quinn. Getting information from the imp was like pulling secrets from a CIA spy.

Rosie bared her teeth and rolled her eyes. He'd been around her enough to recognize her expression when someone said something stupid.

"This Saka." She thumped her tail on the ground.

"This world is called Saka?" asked Bobbi.

"Yes. Blessed holy one has world with a name, yes?"

"We call it Earth," said Bobbi.

"Human peoples name world for dirt?" Rosie sniggered. "Saka mean all." She waved her arms and her tail as if to encompass the entirety of the world. "Ska'in first peoples of Saka."

If these Ska'in were natives, they might know where to find more gates, and more importantly, how to use them.

Bobbi might not be willing to plot their assault on Koro past getting there and smashing heads, but Quinn had always been a planner. Until now, he had no tools to work with. Bobbi and possibly Jane might have some tricks with which to battle a demon, but his magic was more limited.

Now he had the first glimmer of a plan. If only he could get his hands on a Ska'in.

CRUSHED

As the sun went down, the oasis woke. A cacophony of screeches filled the air, some right overhead, others answering from far away. Our packs were heavy with fruit. We filled our bellies with as much water as we could hold and moved out with more energy than the previous nights. The imps danced with nervous energy.

The oasis might have been a haven from the scorching heat, but I couldn't shake the feeling that something watched us from the trees. Maybe the mysterious Ska'in or maybe something more malevolent. I felt better when the horizon lay bare ahead and behind us.

According to Erita, we would reach the edge of the desert that night. The thought of leaving the sand behind put a boost in my step. Already, the ground was more firm, and we started to see outcroppings of scraggly bushes.

I still wondered why we hadn't met another soul along the way.

"Is the desert usually this empty?" I asked Erita.

She glared at me. "Desert full of sand."

"I meant, is it usual not to meet other people? You traveled this way before, right? And Rahrahee has obviously been visited by many people. Why haven't we seen any?"

"Yes. It wrong. No people." Erita lifted her chin and sniffed. "I stink battle." She swished her stubby tail with agitation.

"She means she smells blood, most beatific one," translated Rosie.

"I got it."

I sent out my magic, trying to sense what she did. What did a battle feel like in the aether world? Death, I supposed. Upheaval. If those were ahead, then Erita's senses were better than mine. I smelled only sand.

Less than an hour into our journey, thunder rumbled. I glanced up at the clear sky. The sound rolled on like a revving engine, coming closer. And fast.

Erita whistled. Her one good eye was wide and erratic.

"Find hide! Find now!"

But there was no place to hide. The landscape was barren.

"Who's coming?" asked Henry, but Erita fled.

"Rosie!" I shouted over the growing noise. "What's happening?"

"Broodbone! Run!"

The ground shook in tune to the thunder and we scattered.

"This way!" Quinn grabbed my arm and we ran. Ahead, Jane stumbled in the dark. Quinn slung her over his shoulder in a fireman's lift. Jane squawked but he ignored her. Behind us, gunshots echoed over the thunder.

"Here!" I pointed to rocks jutting from the sand. Quinn dropped Jane onto them and jumped up, pulling me behind him. It wasn't much of a hiding spot. We crouched on top of the platform, peering into the dark.

And then the beasts were on us. They stampeded, swerving around our little haven, so close I could have touched one. Bigger than buffalo, they had wide flat faces and three-pronged brows. Some time, millions of years ago, a triceratops came through a gate to this world. Or maybe our world was the destination? These thoughts filled me as I watched the beasts rage past. They kicked up a sand cloud that forced us to pull scarves over our noses. And still they streamed on. How many in this herd? Hundreds? Thousands?

"Where are the others?" I shouted and coughed.

Quinn shrugged and pointed into the mass of running beasts. I hoped they'd made it to safety.

One of the broodbone screamed and fell. It was immediately lost under the hooves of the endless stampede. Another beast clipped the rocks, nearly sending Jane sprawling. Quinn grabbed her by the shirt and yanked her back. She collapsed, coughing onto the rock.

Quinn held Jane's shoulder with one hand and gripped my arm with the other. Through the dust, I met his gaze and held it as the world around us went mad.

The flow of bodies eventually thinned and stopped. When the thunder of hooves died, we were left in a silent cloud of stirred up dust.

The imps stumbled out of the darkness. We jumped down from our perch.

"Divine one! You live!" Rosie wrapped her skinny arms around my knees. I hugged her fiercely. Erita watched us with an expression half-way between awe and disgust. I pulled her into the hug too.

"Stay here while I find the others," Quinn said.

"I'm coming with you."

Rosie would have followed too, but I made her stay behind with Jane.

We found Henry first. He'd teleported away, but his odd magic could only take him short distances, and he hadn't made it out of the stampede. He took refuge in a small stand of bushes. The beasts mostly ran around it, but one tried to jump the bushes and landed on Henry's ankle, snapping the bone.

We helped him back to the others and left him in Rosie's care for healing.

There was no sign of Sybil.

"We may need to wait until daylight to find her," Quinn said.

We'd hung on to our packs, but Jane's supplies were scattered and crushed. Only the canteen remained intact. I drank deeply, resisting the urge to rinse and spit the grit from my mouth.

In the distance, I could hear Henry calling for Sybil even as Rosie healed him. I quested out with my aether and tasted Sybil's signature magic. Having spent the last five days with her, it was familiar. Even the dust couldn't mask it. I followed another trail of debris and found her trampled pack, but that wasn't the source. I walked on, already knowing what I'd find. Her aether had the sharp taste of death.

Beyond a small gully, a mound of boulders rose from the sand. Sybil hadn't made it to that haven. She lay face-down in the dirt, her body a mangled heap of bloody cloth. A crossbow lay a dozen feet away, broken beyond repair.

"Gods damn," Quinn said from behind me. I hadn't moved. Couldn't move. He crouched and rolled the body over. Her face was a red mash. A rifle lay beneath her. How much time did she waste shooting into the dark instead of running?

"I'll get a shovel," Quinn said. I nodded and sank to the ground.

MOURNED

We can't leave her here," Henry was adamant. They stood around Sybil's grave, exposed on the open plain. Quinn wanted this business done, but Henry wasn't budging.

"She was my first student when I joined Paragon." Tears streaked through the dust on his cheeks. "I won't leave her."

"We can't bring her with us." Quinn tried to sound reasonable. He soothed with his words. The gleam in Henry's eye suggested he wasn't thinking rationally. Quinn squeezed his shoulder, letting his magic ease Henry's panic. It was all he could offer.

Bobbi's eyes widened and she turned away. She still had this knee-jerk reaction to soothing magic, but Quinn knew a little soothing could be a kindness, and they needed Henry's focus. Grief would have to wait.

Henry took the time to wrap Sybil in the spare clothes from her pack and laid her broken bow and rifle beside her. His rifle was also crushed in the stampede, and they piled it beside the grave with the rest of the ruined supplies.

Jane sang the funeral rites, calling the Lady to watch over their fallen sister. Would Sybil's spirit find its way to the Lady from this strange land? Quinn had no idea, but they couldn't suspend their journey. Too much was at stake.

But when he lifted the first shovelful of sand, Henry stood between him and the body.

"I lost knights under my command before," he said, "but I never left anyone behind."

Quinn glanced at his mother, hoping Jane would pull rank. But Jane was lost in her thoughts and didn't react.

"Erita, can you find this place again?" Bobbi asked. The imp nodded. She took Henry's trembling hands in hers. "We have to leave her for now. But we'll come back. I promise."

"She can't stay in this alien place. We have to take her home." His eyes were wide and lost.

"I know."

They covered Sybil in sand, but the barren desert offered no rocks for a cairn.

"The scavengers will dig her up." Henry was one step away from hysterics.

"We could ward the grave," Bobbi said.

Quinn agreed. But Henry was too weak from healing his broken leg. He turned to Jane who pointedly looked at Bobbi. Gods damn the woman. She would force the issue of Bobbi's reluctance with magic eventually.

Quinn sucked in a breath and steadied his aether. A ward was a simple spell. He'd been doing them since grade school, but this was his first complex magic since recovering from mawr. Cooking a few lizards didn't count since that involved drawing magic from the environment. The ward would have to come from his own well of aether.

When Bobbi reversed the flow of magic from the core and refilled his empty well, she saved his life. But no one knew if the drastic cure had fundamentally changed him. Time to find out.

Bobbi squeezed his hand, giving him moral support even if she could do little to boost him magically. He laid hands on the mound of sand and pushed magic into and around the grains. He instinctively sought the shape of the body and shrouded it in magic. The mound shimmered with a new ward, and he sat back on his heels, satisfied with the job.

"Still got it," he said, more relieved than he cared to admit.

Bobbi smiled. "You sure do."

They left the grave site and followed the trampled ground left by the stampede. Broken shrubs and the occasional broodbone carcass were the only landmarks. Scavengers circled overhead, their shrill cries breaking the silence.

The sun rose and they turned onto a new path, looking for a place to shelter from the heat. The ground hardened. They no longer fought with the sand for every step forward, but the sun still beat them down. Quinn's skin felt tight across his face. His tongue stuck to the roof of his mouth.

Henry limped. Rosie had treated his ankle, but the injury and healing sapped his aether. The rest of them weren't in much better shape. They needed rest—for the body and spirit—but they'd find none until this business was finished.

As the heat rose, an unholy stench filled the air. Their scarves did nothing to mask it.

"Is there a city around here?" Quinn asked Erita.

"One city. Holy city," she said. "Much far." She pointed to a smudge of mountain on the horizon. That would be Koro's digs. Too far for the reek to be city waste.

The wind shifted, blasting them with the foul smell.

"What is that?" Bobbi held her hand to her nose.

"Death," Jane said. She seemed unaffected.

The path dipped down, then up again. Quinn's legs burned as he climbed. Exhausted as he was, his mind couldn't stop sorting through their options. They needed to find shelter from the sun soon. A city or village would be best, a place where they could learn about Koro's business and set up a plan of attack. Unlike Bobbi, he wasn't willing to storm the demon's castle with nothing but his magic.

And the fact that they hadn't encountered any natives bothered him, but not long after, they did.

And they were all dead.

ℭBATTLED

At the top of the hill Quinn stared down at the carnage. The battlefield was a scrubby plain on the edge of the desert. Broken corpses festered in the rising heat. Swords lay beside fallen warriors. Knives stuck from chests and eyes wherever he looked. Blood had dried in brown stains beneath the bodies, and flying insects covered their faces.

Bobbi turned and vomited while Rosie fussed at her side.

"Must be a hundred bodies," Henry said quietly.

Quinn nodded. "At least."

He felt uneasy, as if someone watched them from the end of a long scope, but they seemed to be alone with the dead except for a flock of birds with long vicious beaks. These feasted on sightless eyes and other soft flesh.

They were alone but for how long?

"We need to move," he said.

Henry crouched by two combatants. Their arms were locked like lovers. Both had multiple arrows sticking from their backs as if the archer hadn't discriminated friend from foe.

"I recognize these guys." Henry pointed to a dead imp. He was similar in appearance to Rosie and the other imps but taller and bulkier. "But who are these?"

The second body was short and burly. At first glance, he seemed dark skinned, but on closer inspection, he was covered in fine brown fur. His armor, made from enameled metal and painted in bright colors, was shattered against his mangled body.

Bobbi recovered from her nausea, though she looked a bit green as she approached.

"Do you know them?" Henry asked Rosie.

"I see one," Rosie's tail thumped the ground. "Much long ago. Pelags.

Servants of far away holy one, kin to…" Her voice trailed off and she pinched her lips before saying the demon's name.

"They're servants to another demon, you mean? Like Koro?" The imps winced and Rosie nodded.

"Don't seem like kin. They're fighting each other," Henry said.

"Bad holy ones have bad families," Rosie said.

They studied the scene, looking for understanding. Why were these soldiers fighting here, in the middle of nowhere? Were there more? Quinn scanned the horizon. The morning was quiet except for the scavengers.

"At least we know what spooked the broodbone," Jane said.

"And why Koro hasn't sent out a welcoming party," Henry said. "He's preoccupied with this cousin of his."

"Maybe. We can't take anything for granted," Quinn said.

"Koro wouldn't let another demon distract him." Jane's hard blue eyes fixed on the mountains where their target waited. "He has one purpose only. To get into our world."

Quinn agreed, but from the state of these soldiers, it didn't look like Koro's kin came for Thanksgiving dinner.

They moved out reluctantly. Leaving that many dead unburied and unconsecrated left Quinn with a nagging unease. He sensed a miasma of aether above the field. The dead leaked magic and left an aether stench more lethal than the physical rot. Someone with the knowledge to harness that aether could do some real damage.

The desert, with its shifting sands and changeless horizon had lulled them into complacency. But now they walked on solid ground. The stampede and the battlefield jerked everyone back to reality. They were alone in an alien world, with no one to help them and dangers they couldn't anticipate.

Henry shot a lizard that scavenged the bodies. They walked on until they found a small grove of trees and cooked it. The sun was already high enough to make them lethargic. They ate and waited out the worst of the day's heat. Quinn was anxious to move on, but now wary of other travelers on the road. If Koro and this new demon were at odds, he didn't want to get caught in the crossfire.

Jane paced around the small camp while Henry cleaned his weapons with methodical concentration that had more to do with burning off anger than any need for cleanliness.

So far, the insect life had been scarce, but in the shade of the trees, swarms of small white gnats floated around their heads. At first Quinn thought they were pollen or cottony seeds until they started to sting. Any bit of moisture attracted them.

"Ouch!" Bobbi swatted a nasty biter and covered her face with a scarf. Erita pulled a pile of broodbone dung from her pack and lit it on fire. The earthy smoke repelled enough of the bugs that they could breathe without inhaling them.

They settled in for a long hot afternoon, all except for Jane who paced with restless energy.

"Why are we just sitting here?" she asked.

From the nest she'd dug in the cool ground, Erita opened her one good eye.

"Road not safe." She turned over and fell back to sleep. The imps could sleep anywhere, under any conditions. Quinn envied their easy retreat from the realities of the journey. When they left the desert behind, with its moisture sucking heat, the temperature dropped a bit, but they now feared wandering soldiers.

"We're wasting time!" Jane snapped.

"Mother, sit down," Quinn said. "Save your energy for tonight. We're moving as fast as is prudent."

"Always the security chief." Jane turned and paced some more.

"Why are you so eager to put yourself in Koro's way?" Henry asked as he sharpened an impeccably sharp knife. It was a good question. "Bobbi's the only one who actually has a chance of killing him."

Jane swung around, her eyes blazing.

"I will kill the demon. That is the only purpose left to me. I will kill him or die in the attempt."

She sat back against a tree trunk. Her gaze raked across each of them. The afternoon was silent except for the ceaseless burr of insects and the gentle stropping of Henry's whetstone against his blade.

Jane never spoke of Koro. Quinn had learned the story in bits and pieces over the years. His father excused Jane many times, citing her experiences with the demon for her behavior. But Jane always seemed rock solid, and Quinn never bought those excuses.

Perhaps it was the stress, the heat or the boredom. Perhaps she knew this was a one way trip. But something set her off. Like cracking open a long-sealed tomb, Jane began to speak.

REMEMBERED

"Koro locked us in a cell with no food and only water from a stagnant pool," Jane said.

Lord and Lady, she's going to tell us the story of my conception. I wasn't sure I wanted to hear it, afraid the true telling would overshadow the few memories I had of my mother. Quinn's grim expression said he didn't want to hear this either, but Jane was relentless. The words leaked out like pus from an infected wound.

"The water made us sick. Stacy threw up so many times, I thought it would kill her. Hannah and Molly huddled in a corner, shaking from fatigue and illness."

Jane looked at me as if I reflected my mother's weakness.

"I thought Koro had forgotten us, left us to die. Later, I wished he had. But a servant finally came. One of these creatures." She waved at Rosie and Erita, who listened reluctantly, wincing every time Jane spoke the demon's name.

"We were bathed and cared for. Their food didn't sit well in our unsettled stomachs, but they forced us to eat. Stacy couldn't keep it down and they scolded her for messing up the fine gowns they dressed us in. At this point, we had no idea where we were or who kept us captive. Even among these strange creatures, we didn't realize that we'd come to another world. How could we?" She paused. "They say not knowing is the worst kind of fear. It's not.

"When they brought us to Koro, I saw the true face of evil. You cannot imagine his…ugliness. It isn't skin deep. It's a thing you feel. Like black tar on your soul. He fills the room with hate, lust and anger."

Jane paused again and I remembered to breathe.

"Stacy screamed and he hit her. No. That's too gentle for what he did. His fist broke her nose and cheek and sent her slamming into a wall twenty feet away. She looked like a broken doll. I thought she was dead. And then she whimpered feebly like a baby. I stood between her and the beast. He laughed." She laughed too, a harsh grating sound. "And I suppose I was funny to him. How could one small woman defy him? But I did. I screamed at him to leave Stacy alone. He grabbed me by the hair and threw me down. Then he raped me."

Her fists pounded on her raised knees as if keeping time with her thoughts.

"I should tell you that Koro is not human. He might have been once, I don't know. But he is a brute, massive across the shoulder with hands that can break your skull. And he's deformed. His manhood, I mean. We are not compatible as mates. But that didn't stop him from trying. I bled for days."

Lord and Lady. I closed my eyes wishing I could block the sound of her voice, but it only brought the images of her torment into my mind's eye.

"He eventually stopped his…attentions, when he could not impregnate us. But he found another way. With magic and a proxy, he finally planted his seed in all of us." She waved a hand at me, the result.

I felt sick. How could I be this creature's daughter? If Koro used a human proxy to beget me, I might not have his blood in my veins in the true sense, but his aether ran with mine.

Quinn gripped my fingers hard. He leaned in and whispered, "I love you."

In that moment, I adored him. He knew me so well. I squeezed his hand and tried to smile.

"I'm telling you this not for your pity or to make you fear Koro," Jane said. "Those are useless emotions here. But I want you to understand what we face. Not a berserker. Not a half-demon crazed with rage. Koro is strong but cunning. His magic is beyond anything we can imagine." Jane squinted into the brightness beyond our hiding spot but her gaze turned inward.

Henry cleared his throat. The knife he'd been cleaning lay forgotten in his lap. "I have no argument to keep you from attempting this kill. It is your right." He bowed slightly toward Jane. "But what makes you think you can do it?"

Jane reached into her pack and pulled out a wooden case about a foot-and-a-half long. Inside lay a short silver spear, honed to a point at one end and etched all over with runes.

"The Lady gave me the spell to create this. It came from the grimoire. This is the reason Koro was desperate to keep the book from us. It's the only weapon that might kill him."

She held the spear up with a triumphant glint in her eye as if she had already done the deed.

"You should give it to me," I said quietly. "I have the best chance of striking a killing blow."

Jane jumped to her feet, waving the spear above her head. "Did you not hear me? He mutilated me!" The outburst caused a flock of birds to erupt from the trees with raucous caws. "He impregnated me with a monstrous child. Do you know why baby Justin died? Because I killed him! I took one look at the demon I had borne and I strangled him!"

Molly had accused Jane of killing her baby as we stood over his grave. At the time, I'd been appalled to think Jane could murder an innocent newborn. Now I wasn't so sure. What would we see if we dug up his tiny body? Was he even human? Was I?

"Maybe you have the most cause," I chose my words carefully. "But I am what Koro wants. I'm the one who can get close enough to use that spear."

Jane's lip curled in a sneer. "And what makes you think you could do it? You, who can't even produce a simple ward. You're afraid of your own magic. You'll never be half the witch I am. The Lady knew it too. She gave me the spell to create this!" She raised the spear above her head.

"Mother, stop this!" Quinn stood between us, rigid in the shoulders and legs as if ready to spring. If Jane launched herself at me, he would stop her. I would never ask him to make that choice.

I laid a hand on his arm, but my words were for Jane. "It's fine. You're right. I am a bumbling witch. I made the rift and broke the ward. But I also killed a berserker and a wraith. Have you never asked yourself how I did that?"

Jane stared at me, her eyes dark with fury. Then the light dawned.

"You!" A hand went to her mouth. "You siphoned them!"

"Yes." I let that admission sink in. "I am the daughter of a demon. And like the demon, I can kill by draining a body of its aether."

Jane looked ready to kill me where I stood.

"That's why Koro wants me so badly," I said. "I am the vessel strong enough to bear him in our world. Should he possess me, I can feed for him. But that is also the way I will kill him."

Jane's glare turned calculating. Quinn looked as if I'd punched him in the stomach. He might have suspected what my dark powers meant, but speaking my plans aloud made them real. I wasn't coming back from this fight.

I turned to Jane. "You can try to toss that spear at him from a distance or you can give it to me and when I get close enough, I'll drive it right into his heart while I drain his aether dry. Not even Koro could survive that." I held out my hand for the spear.

We stared at each other for a long moment.

"You have no right to anything that is mine." Jane pointed the spear at Quinn, then turned and walked to the far end of the clearing.

"Don't listen to her," Quinn said.

"She's not wrong."

He folded me in his arms, and I could feel myself trembling.

He kissed me next to my ear and said, "Let her have the spear. For what it's worth, we're all in this together." He pushed me back to look directly in my eyes. "When the time comes, I'll be right at your side. You know that, right?"

I nodded, not trusting my voice.

While we waited for the sun to set, we sat listening to the quiet stropping of Henry sharpening his blades.

SCAVENGED

Near sunset, Quinn roused me from a half-sleep.

"Look." He pointed toward the setting sun. In the distance, a line of travelers crested a hill, silhouetted against the dying light. They walked in single file with a steady but ground-eating gait. Hooded robes hid their faces. I couldn't tell how tall they were, but I got an impression of lithe power and long limbs. Letting my aether reach out, I tested them for magic. One of the travelers stopped and stared at our little camp hidden in the trees. I reeled in my aether but not before tasting their odd magic. It was powerful but tightly contained like fire inside a kettle. The stranger stared for a moment longer and then followed his troupe.

"Ska'in," Rosie hissed beside me.

"The same as the one that came through the rift?" I asked. She nodded.

"We should go after them," Quinn said. "They could help us."

"No!" Rosie gripped my arm. "Please, most blessed holy one, we not speak to them. Ska'in like…private."

Rosie was truly agitated. She knew this world better than us, so we waited for the travelers to pass, then collected our gear and began our nightly trek.

Keeping off the main roads, we followed a footpath winding through scrubby landscape. Without the fear of quicksand, we could finally walk in pairs, though Jane preferred to march ahead and Henry brought up the rear, taking it slow on his injured foot.

"I think we should have contacted those Ska'in," Quinn said as he helped me over a slippery rock formation.

"Rosie seemed pretty adamant," I said. "I think we should listen to her." When he didn't respond, I prodded. "She did call them fire rippers. I don't think that's because they like to sing campfire songs."

"No, I get it. But maybe Rosie has only encountered them in her service to

Koro. Maybe the Ska'in would be receptive to meeting outsiders. If they can travel through the gates, they must be used to strangers. And we need allies."

"Or maybe they'll kill us on sight. We have no way of knowing."

Quinn grunted an agreement.

The ground began to rise and fall. Small stands of stunted trees with purplish-grey leaves popped up from the hard-packed earth. We couldn't see far in any direction. If the flora had been more lush, it would have reminded me of home and the rolling hills of Pennsylvania.

Erita seemed to follow an abstract path, taking us from one hidden spring to another. At each, we rested and refilled our canteens.

We came across more fallen warriors, some were pierced by arrows in the back as if they'd been running away, others cut down by swords. They were alone or in twos and threes—the stragglers of a bigger army. The air again reeked of death, and carrion birds were busy in the darkness.

Near dawn, we crested a hill and looked out over a mile-wide canyon. Thousands of corpses littered the dusty field.

My flimsy scarf did nothing to block the stench of putrefaction. I gagged but forced myself not to vomit up any precious water.

As the sun rose, the devastation and gore were unbearable to look at. Ugly grey birds flocked overhead, cawing and fighting, though enough meat lay decaying in the sun for all.

I suddenly needed the affirmation of human touch. I leaned my back against Quinn's chest. He wrapped his arms around me, but still I didn't feel safe.

Henry seemed to sag at the sight of so much death. He was one of the most indomitable men I knew, but my former teacher was running on empty. I didn't know how much more of this horrible place he could take.

Jane stared at the carnage with flinty eyes.

"Look! Most divine holiness. Look! City!" Rosie tugged my shirt in her excitement.

In the distance, the sun gleamed on the towers of a great castle. My father's home. We were close, but we had to cross the battlefield to get there.

We wound down the path. Loose rock skidded under my feet and Quinn caught my arm before I fell.

At the bottom of the hill, we surveyed the ground but found no easy route through the massacre.

"Shut down your sensate ability," Jane said. "Don't try to touch the magic here. There's too much. It will overwhelm you."

I nodded, already getting the gist of what she meant. Without a soul to contain it, aether leaked from a corpse for hours or days after death. Like the last battlefield, a cloud of aether hung over this one. But this field was much bigger. A hundred bodies had created a buzz of magic. Here, thousands upon thousands of bodies rotted in the sun. Their aether hung like a pall of smog over the valley. Despite Jane's warning, I couldn't resist testing its potency. I reached for it. The aether derived from the life force of all those dead soldiers tasted of anger, pain and confusion. It hungered for the life denied to them, and tried to latch onto me.

I reeled my aether back and locked it down tight, fighting the darkness inside me that recognized real power.

Jane watched me with an I-told-you-so smirk. I wanted to remind her that she'd once been a young untested witch too. How could I learn, if I didn't try? But then I remembered how Jane's first attempt at magic landed her in Koro's dungeon, and I held my tongue.

Walking through acres of corpses was a nightmare I could never have imagined. In every direction, I met sightless eyes. I saw bloated tongues and gaping wounds crusted over in the sun. The scavengers weren't shy. They tore off bits of flesh right beneath our gazes. A light wind blew some scrap of fabric and I jumped. Quinn's expression was closed, but he looked at every face we passed as if committing them to memory.

There were equal numbers of imps and pelags. The fighting must have been bitter, but no signs pointed to a victor. Were the remaining pelags now besieging Koro's castle? Was that why my father hadn't come out to greet us yet?

"I've got a live one here," Henry called from ahead. Beside him, a young imp struggled to breathe. His chest rose and fell, stopped, then rose in another painful breath. Blood dried on his face and stained his shirt. He wore no armor.

"Can you speak?" Henry knelt and wiped away blood with his scarf. The imp's eyes fluttered but didn't open. "Tell us what happened here. Why are you fighting?" The imp was too weak to answer.

"Can you heal him?" I asked Rosie. She pulled aside the soldier's torn shirt. His intestines spilled from a hole in his stomach and lay desiccating in the dirt.

Rosie shook her head. Henry pulled his knife and slit the imp's throat. After one final chest heave, he lay still.

We moved on. The castle and the mountains seemed impossibly far away.

The killing field was endless. I became immune to the rank smell, but wore my scarf over my face to protect against the hordes of biting insects.

Movement caught my eye, and this time it wasn't the wind. Someone scavenged among the dead.

"Hey!" I called. He froze and looked up. I met dark eyes set in a small gaunt face. He was skinny and dirty, dressed in nothing but ragged short pants.

It was a human boy.

He grabbed whatever treasure he'd found on the body, turned and ran.

"Wait!" But the boy sprinted around the bodies like a gazelle.

"We have to go after him!" I said. Quinn was already moving.

"Follow him," Henry said. "I can't run."

I nodded. "Rosie, you and Erita stay with them and follow at your own pace. Can you do that?"

"Yes, most divine one. I follow you always."

Satisfied the imps could track us, I ran after Quinn.

REUNITED

The boy's trail was easy to follow at first. His bare feet left distinctive prints in the dirt. Quinn tracked him to the far end of the valley, where it narrowed before squeezing through two mountains. Here, the ground became rocky. He lost the tracks, but the kid could only have gone one way.

He stopped to wait for Bobbi to catch up.

"He's gone through there," he pointed to the slit in the mountain.

Bobbi caught her breath. He handed her his canteen and she drank only a sip. "We have to follow him."

Quinn agreed. Of all the creatures he imagined in this place, a human child was not one of them.

They climbed over razor-sharp rocks as their eyes adjusted to the deep shadows. Quinn slipped and threw down a hand to stop his fall. Sharp stone tore his palm. This path wasn't a road. If anything, it looked like someone built up the rocks as a barrier, perhaps one of Koro's defenses.

"Are you okay?" Bobbi grabbed his injured hand. "You're bleeding. Let me wrap it."

"Forget it. We can't lose that kid." He bound the wound with his scarf as they moved on.

The pass narrowed sharply, and Quinn turned sideways to squeeze through. Overhead, only a slash of reddish sky could be seen. After a tense moment wedged in the rock, the pass widened.

On the other side, they faced a small clearing. No visible trails led from the pass. Quinn examined the grass-like ground cover for tracks.

"Nothing. It looks like he just vanished. Can you sense him?"

"I can try."

Bobbi stood with her head tilted back, sun bathing her face in a yellow glow. Her hair was limp and uncombed. A small cut leaked blood on her cheek and her lips were dry and cracked. It didn't matter. Her beauty glowed past the dirt and grime. It outshone the worry and fear and even the darkness she believed grew inside her. She might be the spawn of a demon, but when he looked at her, he saw only a true daughter of the Lady's grace.

She opened her eyes, smiled and pointed into the grasslands.

"He went that way."

They ran across the clearing and found a small path, no bigger than an animal trail, hidden from casual view by a shaggy bush with spiky thorns. Bobbi tore off a bit of her scarf and tied it to a thorn so Henry and the others could follow.

The path led into a dense forest. Trees with smooth opalescent bark grew to heights that would rival the California redwood forests. Grey-green leaves blocked the sun high above. A soft moss grew underfoot, spongy to walk on and noise dampening. The effect was eerie silence, and Quinn felt like he walked on hallowed ground.

They followed the aether trail through the trees, stopping when they smelled smoke.

"Do you think they're burning bodies?" Bobbi asked.

Quinn frowned. "Smells more like cooking fires."

They continued with more caution until the trees ended and they stood outside a ragged village. Huddled around a central well, huts were cobbled together from deadwood, mud, and bits of cloth. A road led away from the village and back into the mountains. They were coming at it from the far end and no one noticed their approach until they were almost at the village center. A thin old man sat with his back against the stone well. The hands in his lap shook with palsy. His glassy eyes turned to them, and a drop of drool leaked down his chin.

A grey-haired woman appeared carrying a bowl. She stopped abruptly when she saw the strangers.

"Who are you?"

"We're travelers," Quinn said. "From far away. We mean you no harm."

The man reached for the bowl and gobbled a rice-like grain, using his shaking fingers as a shovel. The woman looked them up and down. Her deeply tanned face was covered in fine wrinkles. She wore a collection of rags tied around waist, shoulders and head, leaving most of her skin bare.

She circled warily, assessing them like livestock.

"You dress oddly." Her words were strangely formal. "What linen can this be?" She fingered Quinn's backpack.

"It's nylon," he said.

"Nigh-lon." Her lips puckered. "From far away, for certain. What is it you wish from us? We have no food to spare."

"We don't want food." Quinn hesitated. What exactly did they want? To know how a group of humans came to be living on an alien world? That question might be considered impudent.

"We want information," he said. "We wish to know more of the two armies who lie dead in the valley past the mountain."

A group of children, all underfed and poorly dressed, ran out to see the strangers. The boy they'd followed pointed and whispered to another girl.

"Find Leofrick," snapped the old woman. One of the children ran off without a word and returned with two old men and another woman, all armed with spears.

"You will lay down your weapons," said one of the men. He looked like he could barely hold up his spear. The others were similarly wasted, with hollowed eyes and sunburned skin. Not much of a guard. Were these the strongest this village could put forward?

Bobbi shared a look with Quinn. They could easily take these people down, but he unsheathed his knife and dropped it in the dirt. Bobbi unbuckled her belt and let her sword fall too.

The relief on their captors' faces was almost comical.

"You are human," said the old man who seemed to be in charge.

Quinn nodded. "We didn't know there were other men and women living here. We are not your enemies."

The man stared at them for a long moment. A muscle twitched below his eye. Finally, he motioned for the spears to be lowered.

"I am Leofrick," he said. "Welcome to what remains of our village."

Leofrick led them to a hut at the far end of town. As they walked the one street, older children watched from open doorways and younger ones followed in a gang. They were all thin and hollow eyed, dirty and mostly naked. Quinn saw no other adults.

The grey-haired woman walked beside Leofrick. He introduced her as his wife, Beatrice. At their hut, she went to an outdoor cooking hearth and scooped up two more bowls of the mush. She handed them to Quinn and Bobbi with a look of resignation.

Quinn didn't want to eat the last of their food, but he didn't want to insult her either. He took a few of the hard traveling cakes from his bag. They'd left most of their food with Henry and the others, but he could offer this small token.

"Please accept these as our contribution to your hospitality." He opened the plastic bag and showed her the cakes. Beatrice frowned and crinkled the plastic.

"Thanks to you." She wrapped the cakes in a cloth and slipped the bag into the folds of her ragged dress.

The bland mush had never even been in the same room with salt, sugar or spice. Quinn ate it mechanically.

They sat on a log near the fire. Leofrick squatted beside the hearth with his own bowl. He wore only short pants made from a coarse grey material. He looked to be in his fifties, with skin tanned a deep ruddy brown and grey streaked through his red hair and beard.

He said nothing until he finished eating. Food was more important than words. The gang of children lingered nearby. Even the toddlers looked old in an odd way. These people had hard lives and it showed in every grimy line on their faces.

While he ate, Quinn surreptitiously studied the group. An older girl nattered incoherently and the others ignored her. One boy piggybacked another and not for fun. The passenger's legs were wasted sticks of flesh, likely unable to hold his weight.

Once Quinn saw them, other infirmities were obvious. The facial tics, the palsied hands. One child walked with the aid of a crutch. Starvation, illness or both had taken a hard toll on these people.

"You are from Earth," Leofrick pulled his attention back. Bobbi was still choking down her gruel in small bites.

"Yes," Quinn said. A ripple of whispers went through the watching crowd.

"How came you here?"

"We came through a rift, a gate from our world."

He thought he'd have to explain this in more detail, but Leofrick nodded.

"Did the fire rippers bring you or the demon?"

"Neither. I opened the gate," Bobbi said. "It was an accident."

Leofrick's eyes widened and he tensed, either to run or to attack.

"You are not demon?" he asked in a low voice.

"We are human," Quinn said. "Like you. The demon tricked us to open the gate." He didn't even glance at Bobbi. He wouldn't give away her heritage. Clearly, living in the shadow of Koro's castle made these people jumpy.

"How did you end up here?" he asked. "Did you come through a gate too?"

"I was born here. All the children of Ruth were so born." Leofrick stretched his legs and sighed. He rubbed thigh muscles that trembled from the effort of squatting.

Children of Ruth? That had the ring of a religious denomination, the way one said child of Christ or followers of Buddha.

Before Quinn could ask about the reference, the air split with an aetheric screech and a fire ripper stepped through a gate from another world.

CHRONICLED

Two more fire rippers came through the gate before the first one closed it with some alien magic. They stood in the rigid pose of guards on duty. Taller and slimmer than humans, they moved with a wiry strength. I recognized their brand of aether. These were definitely the same beings we spotted on our journey.

Up close, the Ska'in were striking, with pearly blue and orange scales and large dark eyes under protruding brows. One of the guards breathed deeply, flaring the tiny slits of his nostrils as if taking our measure by scent. They wore grayish robes that shimmered like their scaled skin, but the first one's robe was edged in a deep orange fabric. A sign of seniority?

"We greet you, human warrior." His gravelly voice intoned the English words perfectly as he nodded to Quinn. "Demon," he hissed at me. Quinn tensed and stepped closer.

Leofrick jerked around to stare at me.

Damn and double damn. Announcing my demonic heritage wouldn't earn me any trust points with these people.

But the fire ripper was already moving on.

"We know of your plans to attack Koro in his house. We come to aid you."

"How could you know our plans?" Quinn asked. "We're not even sure what we're doing."

"We are Ska'in," he said, as if that explained everything.

"You've been spying on us," I said.

"Take no offense." The Ska'in bowed. "I am called Benjin. These are my brothers, Tal and Karnet." The other Ska'in bowed slightly. "We have watched humans for many years and helped the children of Ruth break the chains of the demon." He bowed to Leofrick, then turned his attention back to Quinn and me. "This human-demon has power to open gates. Her blood sings." He reached toward me with a three-fingered hand. Long nails capped each finger and he lightly grazed my cheek.

Quinn stepped between me and the Ska'in.

"Don't touch her."

Benjin's huge eyes turned to Quinn.

"Settle, human. The Ska'in do no harm. We have never met another who can open gates like us. Other than the dark one who stole our lands. Have you come to steal from us?"

I shook my head.

"Then we have no quarrel with you."

"What do you really want?" Quinn narrowed his eyes.

"We come to aid in your quest," Benjin said. "We have much to discuss and plans to make, but we shall wait for your compatriots to arrive."

That wasn't good enough. I had questions. A lot of questions.

"But how…"

Benjin held up a hand to stall me.

"Soon," he said, then he put his long arm around Leofrick's shoulder and the two walked out of earshot. I watched them, looking for signs of aggression, but they seemed well acquainted, friendly even.

Beatrice's mush sat like a hard stone in my gut. She scattered the children with a sharp word and we were left alone to wait.

"Did Rosie tell you they could open rifts?" Quinn asked. We sat in the relative coolness on the shaded side of the hut, sipping water that tasted of stewed weeds.

"No. But maybe that's what the 'fire ripper' name refers to," I said. Certainly I would have a chat with Rosie. She couldn't tell me everything about every creature inhabiting Saka, but surely a being able to walk between worlds deserved a mention.

Leofrick sent out scouts and the others arrived at sundown, surrounded by excited children.

Rosie took one look at the Ska'in and thrust herself in front of me, snarling and snapping her tail. My brave protector.

"It's okay, Rosie." I patted the imp. "Benjin won't hurt us." I hoped that was true.

"Be at peace, imp." Benjin's words were terse, but his mouth stretched into what might have been a smile. "We are no longer enemies. Not as long as you walk with the people of the Lady."

"How do you know about the Lady?" Jane asked sharply.

"You have many questions," Benjin said. "I will answer them all."

Two of the older children hauled wood from a nearby pile and built a fire to chase away the swarms of insects that came out as the sun set. Beatrice brought out a small jug and a collection of earthenware cups. She poured a drop of liquid into each and passed them around.

Benjin held his cup in a salute.

"We welcome this first union between the people of the Lady, the children of Ruth, the Ska'in of Saka and the Impzadzl." He tipped his head toward Rosie and Erita, who scowled back. "May our union ride on gentle winds."

Benjin sucked back the drink as did Leofrick and Beatrice. Henry was the first of us to give it a try. His face showed no reaction when he swallowed, but his eyes watered. I sniffed the brew. It smelled vaguely like vodka. What the hells. I tossed it back and it burned a brisk path down my throat.

Immediately, the world became brighter, the night sounds crisper. The drink boosted my senses. Aether burned brightly from every being around our campfire.

"What is this stuff?" I asked.

"You would call it aether tonic, I think. We call it *spidz*," Benjin said.

"How do you speak our language so well?" This spidz was warming me, making me bold.

"We are travelers," Benjin said. "Many times, over many of your centuries, we visited and studied your world."

"Why?"

"We watch and learn."

"Yes, but for what purpose?"

"Knowledge is purpose."

That line of questioning got me nowhere. I sat back and enjoyed the subtle hues of aether coming off the Ska'in. They glowed yellow to red, with a deep blue core like the campfire flames.

"Did you bring Leofrick and his people here?" Quinn asked.

"No. The Ska'in do not interfere. Ruth and Abbot came through a gate. Many generations past. Abbot was a sorcerer who thought he could control Kororaeth. He made a deal with the demon. A deal that went bad."

Most deals with demons did. It was the reason sorcerous magic was notoriously unstable. It came from harnessing the aether of a demon. Those ties were intricate and hard to maintain, and the demons always looked for ways to twist them to their advantage. Sorcerers didn't have long life expectancies.

"They came to find power," said Benjin. "Instead, they found slavery. These are their descendants." He gestured to the group of children listening at the edge of the firelight. Leofrick nodded along as if he'd heard this tale many times before.

"Koro enslaved them?" Henry asked. "For what purpose? To work his fields?"

Leofrick took up the tale. "Not right away. At first we were bred for food. Many years ago, he tried to breed us with other demons, and even himself."

I glanced at Jane. Her flat expression gave nothing away.

"When you say food, do you mean he eats aether?" I asked.

Leofrick nodded. "Though sometimes he fed his dogs with human meat."

Lord and Lady. How long had these poor people suffered here?

Gates to our world were usually unstable, lasting just long enough to pull an unsuspecting soul into this world. Koro had been seeding such traps for years, centuries perhaps. As I listened to Benjin tell of the first humans to inhabit this world, I realized Jane and her friends were possibly the only ones Koro ever sent back. Ruth and Abbott weren't so lucky.

Only the crackle of the fire broke the silence while we all sorted this story.

"You said Koro bred with humans," Jane finally said. "Did he succeed."

"Some, but we are too frail to produce the soldiers he wants." Leofrick shrugged. Benjin laid a comforting hand on his shoulder, a gesture that spoke of a deep understanding and shared trauma.

"When his plans failed, Kororaeth kept the children of Ruth to satisfy his craving for aether. Humans, it seems, have aether as sweet as the ichor of the gods." He smiled sadly. "The demon is addicted to them."

I looked around at the worn faces. How long had Koro been feeding from them?

"But we are sick," Leofrick said. "A sickness in the blood. Nearly half our adults become afflicted."

"Bah!" Beatrice said with a dismissive wave. "We sicken and die because we are frail. How can anyone live on gruel?"

"Perhaps." Leofrick didn't look convinced. "But even before we lost our food rations, people sickened."

"You haven't always lived like this?" I didn't mean to sound impolite. I had no idea what hardships they endured.

"No." Leofrick rubbed at the twitch on his eye. "Once we had guards. We were forced to work the fields for long hours every day. But at least we had food.

Now the guards are gone, but so is the food. We scraped together the grain left in the fields to rot after the armies trampled through. But it is not enough."

"The guards left when the armies came?" Quinn asked.

Leofrick nodded. "At first we rejoiced to see the enemy of Koro attack. But the war has brought us no reprieve."

"Who is Koro's enemy?" I asked.

"Athag," said Benjin. Rosie and Erita chirped unhappily and made a sign to ward off evil.

"Some say he is Kororaeth's brother or cousin," continued Benjin. "Perhaps this is true. He came through a gate from another world."

More gates. I thought of the door to our world standing open on that sandy hill. We were vulnerable. Only a few witches and Paragon knights stood between a demon horde and all of humanity. And the worst part? No one, not even the coven, knew of the danger. We had to finish this and return to warn them.

"Can you open a gate to Koro's castle?" I asked.

"Why would you willingly go into the house of a monster?" Benjin's alien eyes hid his emotions. Was he afraid of Koro or only curious?

"Because I am the only one who can kill the monster."

Benjin shook his head. "There is no killing. Kororaeth is a demon. His death is not for us to take."

"Because you won't or because you can't?" I asked.

"For the Ska'in, there is no difference." Benjin spread his fingers wide in a gesture that might have meant submission.

I huffed out a breath. These Ska'in liked to talk in circles.

"Settle, human. We may not kill, but we will take you to your father's house."

REKINDLED

The quiet discussion continued around the fire long into the night. The children wandered off or fell asleep where they sat. No one moved to put them to bed. The rest of us made plans to confront Koro.

"The demon cannot be killed," Benjin said.

Jane scoffed. "Not true. I have it on the Lady's authority that this will kill him." She held up the spear that was never out of her reach these days. It glinted blood red in the firelight.

"No insult to the Lady," Benjin bowed to her, "but she is mistaken. The demons are first elements. They are aether. Our only hope is to weaken them enough to trap them. My brothers and I," he nodded toward Tal and Karnet who rarely spoke, "have searched the worlds over to find the perfect prison. One from which the demons may never escape. We will exile them there."

Jane said nothing, but her grip on the spear didn't loosen.

"But how do we get into the castle?" Quinn asked. "There are two armies standing at the gates. Do you plan to fight your way in?"

"The Ska'in do not fight."

"A tunnel runs from the dungeons into the forest," Leofrick said. "It's about a day's walk from here. Most of the servants have scattered, but we must watch for soldiers."

"Can't you open a door to the inner castle?" Quinn turned to Benjin and quirked his eyebrow. The expression didn't have the same effect on the Ska'in as it did on me. He simply spread his long-fingered hands.

"Kororaeth wards his castle heavily. We must use stealth instead, but once behind the wards, our magic will aid us."

"How, exactly?" Quinn wanted to know. And the discussion turned to all the eventualities we might encounter.

Jane was unusually silent. Like her daughter, Abilene, Jane normally lusted after any new arcane knowledge. But the mistress of the Hidden Coven sat watching the small campfire as if mesmerized by the flames. Ever the Paragon knight, Henry managed to slip in queries about Ska'in politics, magic and history. Instead of being affronted by the inquisition, Benjin patiently answered his questions.

The spidz had long since worn off and I felt restless. I rose and wandered to the edge of the village. Away from the fire, my eyes grew accustomed to the dark. I pulled the hag stone from my shirt. It hung on a leather cord, long enough that I could easily hold it to my eye. Through the hole at its center, the night took on an eerie glow, almost as if I were looking through night vision goggles.

It wasn't that the scene seemed better lit when viewed through the stone, but I could see the essence of every object. A boulder was no longer a black shadow against other shadows. It became the spirit of stone—the aching eons of history as it was pushed from the land, worn down by rain, broken from a mountain crag and rolled to this resting place. All that experience shone from its core.

Everything falling under the hag stone's gaze shone with life. Aether hummed up the tree trunks into the veins of the leaves. Deadwood smoldered with the aether of rot, an extension of life. I could even feel the life blood flow of water seeping to the well at the village center.

The Lady promised this stone would guide me, let me see the world as it really was. In my greatest need, I could use it once to call on her aid. I didn't know how the Lady's magic could reach this alien world. Maybe all worlds were one. Maybe the Lady lived in all things. It didn't matter. In a few hours I would face off against my father, a demon with the power to rip out my soul. I desperately wanted to call in my chip and have the Lady by my side right now.

"Leofrick says not to wander too far," Quinn said from behind me. "The forest around the village isn't safe."

I nodded. Nothing was safe on this world.

"You should go back," I said. "They're making plans to storm the castle. Isn't that what you wanted?"

"And you have nothing to add to the plans?"

I shrugged. What could I add without revealing my true dark nature to Leofrick and the Ska'in. Who would run into battle with me once they knew I could drink their aether like the beast we were hunting?

"I have only one plan. But I'll let you guys work out how to get me in front of him."

"And then what? You'll sacrifice yourself to save the rest of us?" His tone was bitter. "I'm not on board."

"It's not your choice."

He ground out an angry noise, and glanced at my fingers, now twined in the hag stone's cord.

"Thinking of using that?"

"Yes. Maybe…I don't know."

His hands closed over mine. "Not yet. The Lady can't do anything tonight and neither can we."

I waited for the inevitable "chin up" lecture, ready to lash back at him. I couldn't take a pep talk right now. My nerves were raw with anticipation. My legs felt ready to run off without me. I jumped at the sound of a night critter moving through the underbrush.

"Hey." Quinn rubbed my arms up and down and I felt as if he sloughed off my skin. I shivered.

"Come here." He pulled me close, enveloping me in his scent and the thrilling comfort of him against me, so hard and soft at the same time. His hands caressed my hair, slipping under my collar for the sensitive skin at my nape.

"You have that look," I said.

"What look?" His thumb circled my nipple through the fabric of my shirt.

"That 'we can never be alone and we're all about to die, so I mean to have you' look."

"Do I?" The arc of his eyebrow tugged at my lust.

"You do." I swallowed hard. "It's a good look."

I responded to his touch. My world was about to end, and gods be damned, I wanted this man. We slipped into the shadows. A massive tree provided all the cover we needed. He pressed me against its leeward side. My hands fumbled with the button of his pants even as he slipped off mine, fingers sliding along my thighs. His mouth found the hollow on my neck. He blazed up my throat to my lips, and we joined in a kiss that blotted out everything else. Our bodies, slick with sweat, pressed together against an alien tree while the voice of an alien race told stories around a campfire only a stone's throw away.

I wrapped my legs around his waist, clung to his shoulders, and he filled me. He pulled back and we locked eyes before he slowly pushed his entire length back in. A low growl came from his throat. Then need drove us. His thrusts came hard and fast and I met each one with urgency. Frenzy took over and I felt nothing but the swell of passion that overrode all my senses, coming to a crescendo. He seized inside me and time stood still. All the worlds fell away and there was only me and Quinn joined in body, aethers mingled as one. Then breath and life came back and we collapsed to the rough ground.

After a few moments, the sounds of night creatures returned. I lay wrapped around him, with no desire to move.

We had our moment—finally—but we deserved so much more.

Stationed

They rested the next day and headed out in the late afternoon. In the end, two men from the village and six teens—four boys and two girls—offered to come. Quinn pulled Leofrick aside.

"We don't want to put you all in danger," he said. "All we need is a guide."

"You will need more than that to get past the sentries. We have weapons. We can help." Leofrick looked even older in the harsh light. Quinn couldn't believe he'd survive a long march to the castle, let alone the battle. But Leofrick's mind was set. Quinn sighed.

"Show me what you've got."

Their weapons were swords and bows pilfered from the dead, sturdy enough, but he still didn't like it.

"The children should stay behind." He pointed to the boys and girls, some no older than twelve, who waited to join them.

"There are no children here," Leofrick said. "Only people with nothing to lose. We will come and hope you can fulfill your promise."

Quinn put his hand on his shoulder. "I can't guarantee we'll take down Koro. But if we return, I promise you safe passage back to Earth. You must all come home."

Leofrick looked at his people loitering in small groups, some too weak to stand.

"I don't know if they will go. Many are too ill, others are too stubborn. They will be hard to move."

"Let's get through one problem at a time," Quinn said. They might bring these people back to the coven, but he didn't think they would ever find a true home. They were the lost children, transported to this dismal place by a cunning demon and forced to breed for his pleasure. How could they move on from that?

The road leading from the village twisted around the mountain. When they started this journey, Quinn's legs had been wasted from the mawr. But they gained back some muscle in the past days with the constant walking. Even though the climb steepened, he felt strong and ready to face whatever they found at the end of the road.

Bobbi was unusually subdued, thinking about her intended sacrifice. Why was she so resolute about standing up to her father alone? He would never let that happen. The imps trotted sedately at her side. Rosie held Erita's hand. In the shifting shadows, they could be mistaken for children on their way to kindergarten. Henry's limp had eased after another bout of Rosie's healing, but the circles under his eyes were deeper. Jane walked alone. His mother kept her own counsel these days and added little to their planning.

Quinn walked beside Benjin and Leofrick, hoping to learn more about Koro. Perhaps they knew of some weakness they could exploit.

"How long have the armies been fighting?" he asked.

"Many suns," Benjin considered. "You would call it five months."

"A terrible storm came one night," said Leofrick. "A bright light unlike any we'd seen before tore open the sky. The next day, Athag's armies attacked."

They had also faced a storm after coming through the gate. Could the activation of such portals cause the weather to turn violent? They knew so little about this touchy magic.

"Our guards left us then," continued Leofrick. "We haven't seen them since."

Five months since they'd had regular food. Quinn glanced at the children carrying axes and swords. They didn't seem to be flagging at the effort of the hike.

They moved along a narrow path through the forest. The light failed quickly as the sun set, and the shadows provided perfect ambush sites. He felt eyes watching them.

A clatter of armor and voices announced soldiers ahead.

"Into the trees," hissed Leofrick.

Quinn glanced at the road behind them as the others ducked into the bush. Too late to hide their tracks. If the coming soldiers were observant they would see a large band of travelers had turned off the road right here. But he had no time to wipe out the trail.

He crouched under the low hanging fronds that filled the spaces beneath the trees. Bobbi pressed against his back and he could feel her trembling.

Moonlight crept through the canopy and reflected on the leafy underbrush, making the plants glow eerily. A light wind tossed the branches and the shadows shifted constantly.

The oncoming soldiers took no measures to hide. They spoke in low voices in an alien dialect. One of them stopped right in their path. Quinn tensed.

Had they found the tracks? No. A steady thrum of water hit the leaves. The soldier relieved himself, then moved off.

A crack of a branch stopped him. Someone in their party had given them away. The soldier turned back to the trees, peering into the shadows. One of the others called to him and he grunted a response. Thick fingers parted the leaves inches from Quinn's face. He held his breath and sent out a thin wisp of soothing.

You're not worried. Nothing here but shadows and grubs.

Quinn had no idea if soother magic even worked on imps. But the soldier paused and scratched under his helmet. Another call from ahead and another grunt, then the soldiers moved on.

Quinn listened to the creak of their armor until the night became silent again.

"How many?" Bobbi asked.

"Four at least. Maybe six. A scouting party, no doubt."

They returned to the road more subdued. All conversation ceased as they leaned into the darkness, ready to jump back into the trees at a moment's notice.

Hours before dawn, Benjin led the party off the main road. They tramped through the forest to a small clearing well out of earshot of any passing soldiers.

"We camp here," he said.

"Are we close?" Jane asked. The grind of the road had worn her down. With her hair matted and face covered in dust, she was no longer the regal mistress, but her eyes shone with determination. If Benjin pointed her in the right direction, she'd storm the castle by herself right then.

"There is a cave nearby. It leads into the lower section of the castle," Benjin said. "With the light, we will know better how the armies fare and can make our plans then."

"It doesn't matter how the armies fare," Jane said. "We're going in regardless."

"Mother, we're all tired." Quinn handed her his canteen. "Let's rest and take Benjin's advice. Tomorrow we'll be in a better position." Jane's lips pinched thinly as if she held back a curse. Then she took the canteen and wandered to the edge of the clearing.

"You should go talk to her." Bobbi nudged him. "I'm worried that she's going to do something rash."

Quinn agreed. Jane was on the edge, and if she went over, there was no telling what kind of damage she could do to herself and the others.

He found her standing in a small pool of light from one of the larger moons. It caught the etchings on the silver spear as she turned it over in her hands.

"You're not going to try to convince me to give this up again are you?" she asked without turning.

"Would it do any good?"

"No."

They stood together in awkward silence. Behind them the noises of a camp settling down for the night were less comforting than uneasy. Quinn didn't know what to say to his mother. He never did. Her mind worked on a completely different plane than his. She had never needed the strength of another. Not him, not his father or the other witches. But right now, standing in the dim light, holding onto her weapon like a lifeline, she seemed oddly vulnerable.

"You think I'm stubborn," she said. "You think I don't want to give her the spear because I'm greedy for the kill." She sighed and turned. Something suspiciously like tears glistened in her eyes. "You're only partly right. If Bobbi kills him, she won't come back from it." She pressed the spear in his hands, but didn't let go. Her fingers wrapped around his. She was giving him a choice.

"Let me do this. I have given you so little." She spoke over his protest. "Don't say it. The Lady knows I would never win any mothering awards. But I can do this. I can kill Koro and set you both free to live without his shadow hanging over you."

He pushed the spear back to her. She was giving him more than a choice. She was giving him the gift of a life with Bobbi.

"Thank you." He leaned down and kissed her cheek. She sniffed and nodded once, then turned back to her contemplation of the moon. He hoped that she was gathering the Lady's strength from its light.

Clashed

We stood on a plateau, surveying the valley as the sun rose over the tip of the mountain. Yesterday, we saw this same sight from the far end of the valley, with Koro's castle a distant glint of rock. This morning, the castle loomed beside us, a monstrous beast of white stone with rough-hewn towers cutting into the sky. It was hard to tell if they were natural formations or not.

In front of the castle's main yard, a wall ran from one mountain ridge to the other, effectively holding back the army camped in the valley. Only one gate led through the wall, a massive door of metal and stone. Above it, dozens of archers were poised to fend off any attempt to breach it. Hundreds of bodies were piled before the wall, along with discarded weapons, arrows and rocks. Several fires burned where pitch had been dropped on the invaders, and the morning stank of smoke and burned flesh.

But for now, all was quiet. Athag's army rested, filling the valley with their camp. On the wall, Koro's soldiers gazed down at their foes.

"Where is this back entrance to the castle?" Jane asked. "We should go now."

"No." Quinn's tone was determined. "We wait and watch. We need information before we run off half-cocked."

"This?" Jane flung an arm at the waiting armies. "What can you possibly gain from watching two armies posture at each other. We need to attack Koro while he's preoccupied."

"Exactly why we should wait! What better cover than war? Once Koro's focus is on battle, we can sneak in unnoticed."

"And then what? We face two demons instead of one?" Jane said.

"Maybe we'll get lucky, and they'll kill each other." I shrugged when Jane turned to glare at me. It was worth a shot. But clearly Jane didn't like the idea of anyone taking Koro's death from her.

"Hey guys?" Henry's calm voice broke through the argument. "Something's going on down there."

Movement rippled through Athag's army. Soldiers stirred from their cooking fires and picked up weapons. From our vantage point high on the cliff, they looked like toys. As they lined up to face the castle gate , they seemed haughty and proud, like a boy's idea of battle. I thought back to the field of dead. How many of these soldiers would be lifeless obstacles ground into the dirt by the end of this day?

What possible motive could Athag have to conquer Koro? Did it matter? I supposed it did. If Athag was a good ruler who saw the suffering of Koro's people and wanted to help, then the war had purpose. But could a demon be good? The pile of corpses at the wall proved that Athag had already attacked at least once and had little regard for life.

On the wall, Koro's soldiers stood ten deep, ready to repel grappling hooks or burn any ladders trying to mount their defenses.

A trumpet sounded. From the far end of the valley, a catapult launched its missile. The stone crashed against the wall, leaving no visible damage. Koro's archers loosed flaming arrows to set the catapult ablaze, but it sat just out of reach. Screams erupted as the arrows landed on men. The catapult lobbed more rocks with little effect except to crush soldiers trying to mount the wall.

Athag's army threw itself against the immovable gate. Soldiers died at its base and they fell from the walkway above. For the moment, Koro seemed to have the advantage, but he couldn't fight back without opening his gate.

The battle raged on.

"We need to go now!" Jane said. "You wanted a distraction? Well, there it is."

I had to agree.

"Wait," Quinn said. "Something's happening."

Jane scowled, but turned back to the spectacle below.

Something was happening. The sieging army parted like a wave, and a single figure strode through their ranks to stand before the wall.

Athag. He wore black armor that sucked the light from the sky. Spikes crowned his head, either his natural horns or a battle helmet. He lumbered with a rolling gait.

On the wall, another figure strode out, moving soldiers aside.

My first glimpse of my father. From our distance, all I saw was a black clad figure, much taller than the soldiers around him. I clamped down on my aether, fearful that even from afar he might sense me.

But my father had other worries.

"You can't win, cousin!" Athag's voice boomed as if amplified through a megaphone. "Come out now and I will spare your soldiers."

Right. Koro cared nothing for the lives of his soldiers. He wouldn't surrender.

"I have reserves for months," Koro called back. "Go home Athag. Or we will watch you all starve."

I felt magic boil seconds before Athag launched a firebomb at Koro. It smashed into the wall below him with a spectacular blast of blue flame that burned on bare rock.

Mage-fire!

Koro retaliated with an aether missile. Athag threw up a shield and magic skidded off him without harm. Nearby soldiers dropped by the dozens. Whatever magic Koro was packing, it killed efficiently.

Athag threw another mage-fire bomb. This one landed on top of the wall. Koro easily sidestepped it, but those around him weren't so lucky. Soldiers screamed and tried to put out the fire that would burn through bone.

Didn't Athag know mage-fire couldn't hurt Koro? Even with my diluted demon blood, it couldn't touch me.

In rapid succession, he launched more balls of the blue fire. His soldiers used the cover to throw up grappling hooks. And now it made sense. Athag wanted inside the castle. Mage-fire couldn't hurt Koro, but it did a good job of terrorizing his army.

Koro ignored the invaders and his sentries, all dead or cowering in fear. He seemed to grow taller, preparing for an attack.

"Look." Henry handed me binoculars. Through the lenses I saw Koro up close. Bald, with a thick grey hide, his eyes blazed with red hate below a bony brow. A lipless mouth spread wide, too wide. His thickly muscled arms reached up and strained as if he pulled aether right from the air. His mouth grew wider, bigger.

And he screamed.

The sound cut across the valley. Even at our distance, it brought us to our knees. A scream laced with aether. I dropped the binoculars and clutched my head. Fear—irrational, unnatural fear—rushed through me like a wave. I wanted to run, to lash out at anything, anyone who came near. My breath came in ragged gasps.

"STOP!" Athag's voice boomed and the fear left me.

Below, half his army had started to flee from Koro's fear-laced scream. Athag diffused it, but the army was in disarray.

"How can we fight that?" I asked. Quinn touched my cheek, his eyes dark.

"We don't fight him," Jane interrupted. "We are not medieval knights concerned with honor. We sneak inside and stab him in the back."

"She's right," Henry said. "We can't face off against either one of those creatures. Our only chance is stealth and surprise."

"Then we'd better do it right the first time," Quinn said. "We won't get a second chance. Leofrick, can you send scouts ahead to check out this back door? I want to make sure the way is clear."

Leofrick nodded and turned to speak to the children.

"Find a clear road to the tunnel, then send word back. Meet us at the old mill. You know the one?" The lead boy nodded and the children slipped like shadows between the trees.

This was it. Before the sun set again, I would face my father.

ᴄDEPLOYED

We waited beside the skeletal remains of an old water mill. A weed-choked stream—the first I'd seen on this world—flowed past it. Not far downstream it fell over a small bluff, filling the air with white noise. Good for us because it masked any sound we might make, but we had to strain to hear anyone coming up the path.

Suddenly, the sky lit with blue light that reflected off the odd opalescent trees. A delayed boom followed and the ground shook. The demons were lobbing magic again.

"We have to go now," Quinn said.

"The scouts aren't back yet." Leofrick gazed anxiously up the road. "It's too dangerous. We have no idea where the troops are."

I was more worried for the scouts. They were late. How could those children face off against armed soldiers?

"We must go now." Benjin rose from the stump where he sat. Another boom sounded.

We gathered our weapons and left the rest. Speed was now essential. If we beat Koro and evaded the armies, we could return for our packs. If not, a few canteens and flashlights wouldn't matter.

As we marched out of camp, I gripped the hag stone in my fist, willing whatever dormant power lay within it to inspire me.

Instead of heading up the road, we crossed the shallow stream and slipped into the trees. We were a force of twelve—humans, impzadzl, and Ska'in. By some tacit agreement, we kept Jane to the middle of the group. Leofrick and his gang saw her as a weak old woman. They had no idea of the power she could unleash.

Jane hung onto the Lady's spear like a lifeline. I thought of wrestling it from her, but in the end, I left her to it. If the Ska'in were right, the spear would make no difference.

Sounds of battle filtered through the trees. We followed a dry gully running parallel to the valley where the battle raged. Somewhere nearby, swords clashed, aether burned and soldiers died. Hearing the battle was worse than seeing its destruction. I jumped at shadows and expected an ambush at every bend in the trail. Either army could have scouts down here.

Rosie and Erita dashed up our line, ducked into the underbrush on either side and emerged ahead, only to repeat the process as we caught up. The third time they did this, I stopped Rosie.

"What are you doing?"

"Forest hide killers. I keep holy one safe." Her tail swished in agitation. I let her go. I could understand the restlessness and her need for action. Aether buzzed in my veins. I wanted to vent magical steam. But I dared not. I would need all my strength soon enough.

At the end of the gully, we began a slow descent that wound around Koro's mountain. The sounds of battle dimmed until they were a distant thunder—menacing but not urgent.

Benjin stopped and raised one bony hand, listening to the noises of the forest. After a long minute he turned to us.

"The entrance we seek is ahead. But I do not trust the forest," he said.

It was too quiet. Away from the burble of the waterfall and the clamor of battle, we should have heard more life—birds chirping, insects or the occasional crunch of leaf or twig under rodent feet. I heard none of that.

I could just make out the entrance to a cave nestled in an outcropping of rock about fifty yards ahead. Between the cave and our current hiding spot lay a clear glade, open to the sky.

Henry motioned that we should skirt the glade and stick to the shadows. Benjin led the way and, one by one, we followed. Henry and the three Ska'in reached the cave when a shout broke the silence.

A band of brown-pelted pelags streamed into the clearing, swords slashing at the underbrush.

"Run!" Quinn urged. He took Jane by the elbow and propelled her toward the cave before turning back to the fight.

I ran. Behind me, swords clashed. Someone screamed. Was that a child's cry? Had the scouts found us in time to get slaughtered?

An arrow clattered against the stones beside my head and I dropped to the ground. I got turned around and thrashed in the shadows, looking for the path.

"Blessed one, hurry!" Rosie's tail wrapped around my wrist and guided me forward. I fell into the cave, landing hard on the stone floor.

Quinn jumped in behind me. "Is everyone here?"

"No," Benjin said. "Leofrick and his men are still out there, but we must go."

"We can't leave them!" Henry said. I could see from his expression he'd left enough people behind already.

Leofrick ducked into the cave.

"Go!" Sweat, grime and blood slicked his hair back from his face. "My men will fall back to this spot. It's small enough that we can hold them off for a while."

Benjin spoke quietly to his brothers.

"Tal will stay too. Should you find yourselves surrounded with no way out, he can open a door back to the village." Leofrick nodded his thanks and the other two Ska'in moved deeper into the cave. Jane and Henry followed. But I hesitated.

"Go!" Leofrick urged again.

I kissed his cheek. "May the Lady's light find you in this dark place."

Leofrick smiled, though it didn't reach his eyes. Then I let Rosie and Quinn lead me away.

DETAINED

The tunnel dipped sharply as soon as they left the comforting light from the entrance. Underfoot, the dirt was packed hard and slick. Sudden darkness made them all clumsy. Jane stumbled and slid into Bobbi, who fell against Quinn. He braced against the rough wall as they found their footing again.

"You'd think they could put in stairs," Bobbi mumbled.

They groped toward a faint light. A lantern hung on the wall, illuminating the stark stone hallway enough that Quinn could see it wasn't a natural formation. It was excavated from the mountain.

Lanterns were placed at far intervals and they walked in and out of shadow, stopping often to listen into the gloom ahead.

"Someone uses these tunnels regularly," Quinn said. "Otherwise they wouldn't bother to light them."

"Maybe we should ward ourselves," Bobbi said.

"No!" Jane's command cut through the darkness. "He can sense magic this close to his base." None of them needed to ask who "he" was. "No magic or we lose our element of surprise."

Henry agreed with a nod and pulled his sword. Quinn thought Koro would be too busy fending off Athag's attack to bother with anything else, but Jane knew the demon better than anyone.

The narrow tunnel let them pass only in single file, Henry in the lead and the Ska'in bringing up the rear. Quinn already missed Leofrick and his gang. He hoped they made it out of those woods. Their new smaller group would be easier to slip past guards, but he felt defenseless and didn't like it. If they were attacked, he couldn't protect the entire group.

The steady descent leveled off and the ground hardened to stone.

They had no idea how the battle went above. If the demon mages still unleashed their magic bombs, they were too deep to feel the repercussions.

At the next lantern, a door made of thick wood blocked the tunnel. Henry pulled the handle and the door opened with a rasp of metal grating against stone.

"Stop," Henry hissed. From somewhere ahead came the sound of pounding feet. Many feet. A guard patrol? They waited for quiet, and then moved through the door cautiously.

On the other side the tunnel widened into a long dimly lit room. More doors lined one side. Massive rusted hinges suggested they'd be heavy to open. Each one had a small cutout window blocked by bars.

Behind him Jane choked out a gurgle like she'd been hit in the chest by an arrow. Quinn caught her as she crumpled to the floor. Henry and Bobbi turned with swords ready, looking for signs of attack. Frantically, Quinn searched Jane for a wound. Had she been struck by a dart? A magic assault? But she simply stared at the barred doors. A hand lifted to her mouth.

"You've been here before," Bobbi said, and Quinn felt like an idiot. Of course. Jane had been held captive in this mountain for months. Maybe in these very cells. His mother was so unbending that he sometimes forgot she was human. Seeing her undone by her memories unsettled him.

He had no chance to find words of comfort. A patrol of imps marched through the door at the opposite end of the hall and stopped short when they saw the group of humans, imps and fire rippers. The soldiers recovered quickly from their astonishment. The imp in the lead snarled a command. They raised weapons and fanned out.

Six of them against eight of us. Good odds.

And then the two Ska'in disappeared.

Damn the cowards. They'd vanished, leaving three armed fighters against six.

He assessed the guards. These weren't the small thin imps like Rosie. These were a bigger breed, bulky with muscle from swinging war axes and barely a head shorter than Quinn. They wore armor made of mottled leather like lizard skin. It would deflect a nick, but not a full on assault. He made mental notes of their weaknesses as the guards continued to move around the room, trying to cut off escape.

"Stay behind us," he said to Rosie and Erita. They huddled next to Jane where she slumped against the stone wall. Quinn pulled his sword free. Bobbi and Henry were already in fighting stance, one tall and dark, the other small and blond. Henry's teaching was obvious in her posture. They stood in perfectly mirrored positions like the yin and yang of battle.

One of the guards yelled and they attacked.

He met the first one with a clang as axe met sword. The imp's thick lips curled into a snarl as he pressed his advantage. Quinn braced himself. The imp was small but thickly muscled. And Quinn wasn't fully recovered from his illness. The soldier pressed him backward. Grunts and clangs of weapon hitting weapon told him the others had also engaged. An imp screamed behind him, but he didn't dare turn to look. His eyes locked on the one whose axe ground against his blade. Dirt and blood smeared his face. This wasn't his first battle today. Good. He'd be tired.

Quinn let his sword slide, hooked it under the curved end of the axe, then wrenched upward. The imp didn't let go, but his arm jerked up enough for Quinn to bring his blade around and slice into his side. After that, it was quick work. He slashed across the neck, dropping him in a splash of blood.

He turned to the next attack. Henry and Bobbi fought back-to-back, and even as he watched, Bobbi took down her opponent with a slick feint and undercut that slashed off half the imp's jaw. She turned to another.

Rosie hadn't listened to his command to stay safe. She danced around the fighting pairs, dashing in to bite the hamstring of a guard and darting out of his axe's range as he swung for her head. Erita lay unconscious or dead beside one of the fallen soldiers.

Jane fended off another attack. She'd pulled up a ward to protect herself. A furious guard chopped at her, but his axe never came within a foot of her head as it slammed against the invisible barrier. Quinn cut down at the vulnerable junction of shoulder and neck. He laced his blade with a touch of aether and it cut through the leather armor. The creature fell with a shriek, and Jane dropped her ward.

"You said no magic," he panted.

"He didn't leave me much choice." Jane gasped. "But we must hurry now. Koro will know we're coming."

The others had beaten back their assailants. Six imps lay dead or dying on the stone floor. Quinn took a moment to breathe and assess the damage.

Henry sat against a wall.

"You okay?" Quinn asked.

The knight waved a hand. "Fine."

Bobbi kicked off the last guard who died on her feet and ran to Rosie.

Beside her, Erita struggled to breathe. One of the guards lay dead nearby. Quinn couldn't even guess how the little imp took him down.

Rosie looked up with imploring eyes.

"She sleeps wrongly, most beatific one. I try healing, but I have no more."

Erita lay in a pool of blood, hers or the dead soldier's. Her chest rose and fell, the only sign of life.

"You stay with her," Bobbi said gently. "We'll come back for you."

Rosie looked from her friend to Bobbi and back again. Her tail lashed in agitation.

"I come with you, divine one. I help when you face bad holy one, but…" She clutched Erita's hand.

"I'll stay with the imp," Henry said. He rose and limped heavily toward her. "That last bugger took out my bad ankle. I'll only slow you down now."

He knelt beside Erita and took Rosie's hand in his.

"I'll take good care of your friend. Go take care of mine."

Rosie nodded and pressed the tip of her finger to Henry's forehead in a silent imp blessing.

LANCED

Our band of warriors was shrinking. Leofrick stayed to guard our backs. The Ska'in just disappeared. Now Henry and Erita could go no further. That was fine. None of them could help me in the end. I'd rather they all stayed away, but Quinn would never agree. And one look at the fierce determination on Jane's face told me she would move stone mountains to get at Koro.

She led us through the hall, stopping only once to peer through the barred window of a particular cell. She said nothing and, after a long moment, we moved on. I glanced into the empty cell. What did Jane's memories conjure there?

Quinn gripped my hand as we walked and I was glad for the contact. The muscles in my legs and arms shook as adrenaline fled my veins. The battle in the dungeon was swift and brutal. It left me strangely unsatisfied. Dark magic uncoiled inside me, brewing like a storm cloud.

Not yet. I pushed it back down. The magic in this world was easy to tap and soon I wouldn't be able to hold it back.

The Ska'in reappeared to take up the end of our train.

"Nice of you to join us now the battle is over." Quinn's eyes flashed with anger.

Benjin bowed stiffly.

"We are not warriors, human. This we explained already. We will aid you when we can." Quinn turned his back and we kept moving.

The dungeons ended at a steep staircase. Jane pressed her ear to the door at the top, one hand raised for us to be silent. We waited. Finally, she pushed the door and it opened on squealing hinges. The sound grated through the silence. Expecting an immediate attack, I rushed through the opening…and stopped.

We'd surfaced into a courtyard. Except for gusts of black smoke billowing from multiple fires, it was eerily still. Bodies lay in heaps. Hundreds of bodies stuck with spears and arrows. Sightless, decapitated and crushed bodies. Bodies pinned by stone missiles, burned, broken and leaking blood into the mud.

Nothing moved. Even the carrion birds hadn't found this gruesome scene yet. Faint moans indicated some still lived in the chaos.

We moved through the slaughter in a tight group.

"Where are the rest of the soldiers?" I asked, stepping over a severed arm.

"Gone. Or dead." Benjin stared at the tall tower at the far end of the yard. A boom sounded and light flared from the lower windows. "The demons will finish this battle and their minions fear the crossfire. They fled. We should too if we value our lives."

But none of us made a move to leave.

Another boom shook the air.

"That's magic." I could feel it in my teeth. Someone was flinging around a lot of aether.

"In the main hall." Jane glared at the tower. "Where he holds court." She brushed tangled hair away from her eyes and strode past the dead toward the hall.

Inside, I paused to let my eyes adjust to the gloom. At the end of the hall, two massive doors stood open, one crooked on its hinges. A collapsed wall buried the hall to the left. Through the doors, more debris littered the ground and two figures hung suspended in mid air. A nimbus of aether glowed around them. The demons faced off, each frozen in angry gestures as if locked in place by spells. Athag reached for Koro but stopped inches from his throat. Koro's arms curved back and down as if he'd been caught lobbing a softball. It would have been a comical sight except for the ferocious hate twisting their faces.

"They are spell-locked," Benjin said. "The first one to falter will be at the mercy of the other. We must hurry and set the trap before the magic wears out."

Already, I could see what he meant. Through sheer force of will, Athag's hands inched through the aether towards Koro's throat. He would eventually break the spell.

"We must send them to a prison world. One where magic is thin. They will not be able to escape." Benjin pointed to the ground below the floating demons and his brother Karnet set down his pack. They removed stones and small metal statues, setting them up in a large circle. The Ska'in still insisted the demons couldn't be killed. The circle would activate a spell to contain them.

A massive stone pillar stood at each corner of the grand hall. Etched stone-work on the ceiling had crumbled. Burn marks streaked the walls and all the windows were blown out. My feet crunched on broken stone and glass as I approached the suspended demons.

Athag had transformed. He no longer resembled anything human. Dark purple skin—nearly black—shone like chitin and his bloated body had the distinct aura of a cockroach, with a shell covering his back and neck. His arms ended in clawed appendages with razor-sharp edges, now only a few inches from Koro's throat. Bony shields protected his forearms and lower legs. Two whip-like protrusions on his skull were more antennae than horns, and he glared at Koro through glowing red slits.

Koro had changed too, though his transformation was less dramatic. His form was humanoid, but his bare head was grey with a skeletal brow. Two long tusks stuck from his lower jaw. The frozen position made his massive shoulders hunch. He wore a long brown robe made of animal hair. No, it couldn't be a robe. I looked closer. He wore his own body hair like a dress. It was tangled with dirt and debris like a Sasquatch rolled in mud.

I circled them, staring up with equal parts awe and revulsion. Dark aether clung to them, stinking of decay. Athag's clawed hand inched closer to Koro's throat. We didn't have much time, but I couldn't tear my eyes away.

Quinn stood close behind me. He didn't touch me, as if sensing my need to resolve the self-loathing that suddenly flooded through me.

"How is it possible that this…thing is my father?"

"He possessed a human male." Jane came to stand beside me, her expression flat and hard. "Your genes are wholly human. Only your aether is his. And that's all he needs to recreate himself in our world."

Quinn gripped my hand. "Don't do anything rash."

I felt a hysterical laugh bubble up in my chest. Rash? We were in another world, fighting a demon. How was that not rash? But I knew what he meant. We needed to assess, to gather our resources while Koro was otherwise occupied. Only then would we have even a slight chance of beating him.

Jane whipped out the small silver spear gifted to her by the Lady. She reared back. A look of pure hate twisted her face and she threw it.

"No!" screamed Benjin. The spear flew true and burst the bubble of aether. Now free, Athag lunged, as the spear hit Koro in the shoulder with enough force to shove him back. Both demons fell with a clatter of bone and chitin, scattering the relics the Ska'in had laid for their trap.

Koro roared. He tore the spear loose, spraying dark blood across the floor and stabbed it into Athag's eye. The other demon shrieked and lurched, grabbing for the spear with his claws. Koro rammed it home with an open-handed slap and Athag fell. I felt the magic of the spear blossom as it enveloped the demon in a blue light. Athag screamed. The light compressed, crushing him before it winked out. Athag's broken body lay still.

Then my father turned his gaze on us.

CONFRONTED

Mother!" Quinn yelled. What had she done? He reached for Jane but she yanked her arm away.

"I won't settle for trapping him," she snapped.

The arrogant woman! He wanted to strangle her! She ruined their one real chance of stopping the demon to stoke her overdeveloped sense of revenge.

Koro was free and Benjin's trap ruined.

The demon's eyes locked on Jane and he laughed, a sound that turned Quinn's bowels to water.

Jane had lost her only weapon, but she wasn't done. She lifted her hands. Aether tingled on her fingertips and she chanted. Her dirty face and tangled hair matched the rabid zeal in her eyes.

Quinn wanted to grab her, to pull her away and keep her safe, but the spell was too far gone. Her voice rose. Aether stirred the air, tossing hair about her head. If he tried to stop her now, the backlash of power could kill them both.

Koro watched. If Jane's escalating power worried him, he showed no sign.

"Kororaeth! Hear me! You have been judged by the Lord and the Lady. By their power, I sentence you to death!" Aether flew from Jane's fingers, struck Koro in the chest and spread across him like lightning. The demon convulsed. His eyes rolled back, mouth hung open in a silent scream. Veins bulged from his forehead as he fought the attack.

Then he shook it off like a dog shedding water.

His head snapped back and malevolent red eyes glared at Jane. With the flick of his hand, he let go a burst of magic. Quinn jerked Jane out of the way, and behind them a stone pillar shattered. Marble blocks crashed down where she stood only a moment before—crashed right through the floor in a cloud of dust and biting shards of rock. A hole gaped at their feet. A last stone dropped from the ceiling and the floor gave way. With Jane a dead weight in his arms, Quinn fell into the darkness, stones tumbling behind them.

From far above, Bobbi screamed his name, but he had no breath to answer her. He landed hard. Jane was ripped from his grip. He rolled down stone debris, bones jarring at each turn until he hit bottom and darkness fell on him like a shroud.

The ceiling fell. A stone column crashed through the floor. I watched in frozen horror as Quinn dragged Jane away, only to slip into the hole as it widened.

"Quinn!" My scream was lost as more rock thundered down sealing the hole. A wave of dust and debris surged over me and the hall fell silent.

Quinn was gone. Jane with him. Rosie lay dead or unconscious near the collapse. Blinking through the haze of dust, I found the two Ska'in standing against the remaining pillars. They threw off the dun robes and their skin took on the dappled hue of the stone, blending seamlessly with the background. Only their big black eyes stood out, watching but not offering any aid.

Benjin had explained the limitations of their beliefs and their magic, but their inaction still sucked. This was their planet. We came to fight for our world and I expected no less from them. Koro stole their land, enslaved their people, but though they watched me with enormous black eyes, they made no move to help.

A low sound came from behind the fallen rock.

I drew my sword and circled around to find Koro struggling to rise. His battle with Athag had taken a toll. His legs bent awkwardly underneath him. Blood soaked the long hair covering his chest. He grunted but it wasn't pain.

He was laughing.

"Your little army has deserted you, daughter." His heavily accented voice was thick and throaty. He pushed upward and leaned against a stone column.

"I hoped to separate you from your friends, but I became side-tracked." He waved at the still form of Athag. My sensate trigger felt aether pooling around him. He wasn't dead. The Ska'in said demons couldn't be killed, and they were right. Even the Lady's silver spear hadn't done the job.

"You knew we were coming?" My tongue felt like glue in my mouth.

"Of course, daughter. I tasted your magic as soon as you crossed into my land." A black tongue flicked over his thick lips. "I have been watching you. Such a long journey. You must be tired."

A tingle of aether nudged me. He was testing my wards. I slapped it away with my magic and he chuckled again.

"I'm fine, father. But you look a bit spent."

"Do you mean these?" He grinned and nodded toward his legs. Already they were straightening. He was healing himself. If I had any chance of winning, I had to attack now.

Part of me waited for rescue, for Quinn to fight his way out of the tunnels below or Henry to emerge, limping but defiant to fight at my side. None of that happened. I was alone. And it felt right. No one left to worry about. I could unleash the blackness inside my soul and only I would suffer for it. Me and Koro. I couldn't win, but I would take him down with me.

Quinn fought the darkness threatening to swallow him. How long had he been out? He coughed and nearly fainted again. His chest felt full of jagged glass. A broken rib for sure. Tentative inspection found the rest of him intact. He sat up, every muscle screaming at the insult. Rock dust fell away, leaving blood and bruises.

He lay halfway down a tumble of stone. Only a thin shaft of light came from the hole high above. The debris filled the space, floor to ceiling. Below lay darkness.

"Jane?" he called softly. No answer. He shifted. Stone shards slid beneath his feet and he stopped before the whole pile came tumbling down.

"Jane?" He called again. A low moan came from the shadows. As his eyes adjusted, he saw Jane face-down a few feet into the tunnel. The fall had flung her farther away from the debris, but he didn't like the way she lay. One arm was cocked at a bad angle.

A boom sounded from above. The rock pile shook and he slid on the cutting shards. Another boom.

Bobbi!

Above, she was facing her worst nightmare. No matter how much she tried to hide it, he knew she didn't expect to survive the battle. He'd promised to be at her side, to make the journey with her.

Indecision tore at him. He couldn't leave Jane to die. He glanced at the mountain of stone. Was it sturdy enough to climb?

Jane moaned—a wet gurgling sound—making the decision for him. His injured ribs screamed as he half fell, half slid down the rest of the rock pile and limped to his mother's side.

Gently, he turned her over. A contusion darkened the right side of her face. Blood matted hair to the back of her head, but in the dim light, he couldn't properly assess her injuries. He called up a witch light, a small glowing globe of aether. The simple spell was almost too much, and the edges of his vision darkened. He caught himself before he toppled sideways. The witch light bobbed and filled the tunnel with a shaky blue glow.

Jane's breathing was shallow. He took off his shirt and ripped it into strips, one to bind her broken arm to her side, the other to staunch the head wound. Her eyes fluttered open, but her gaze remained unfocused.

"Joshua?" Her voice quavered on his father's name.

"No, it's Quinn. I'm here."

"Quinn?" She tried to raise her wounded hand and cried out.

"Just rest."

A thundering crack came from above. Something crashed down to block the only light. Bobbi and Koro were battling it out. He could feel the massive burn of aether in the air.

Lord and Lady, take care of her.

Another crash. The rock pile was falling again, and he had no other thought but to get Jane to safety.

She cried out when he picked her up, but he ran. No time to worry about worsening her injuries. Rocks pelted the backs of his legs. Dust filled the small space, choking him as he ran with the witch light bobbing beside him.

I tossed a fire bomb at Koro. It broke over his skull, dripped flames onto his long pelt and flared. The demon snarled and slapped his chest, crushing the flame. The stench of burned hair stung my nose.

"Is that the best you have, little flea?"

No, I'd just begun.

I lashed out again, this time drawing water from the broken fountain. The drops flushed up and around Koro's shoulders like a mantle. As they fell, instead of drenching him, they hardened to ice. Koro flexed his shoulders trying to shrug off the trap, but I webbed magic through it to toughen the ice like Kevlar.

Koro strained. The ice shattered and melted before it hit the floor. His gaze rose to meet mine and he smiled like a proud father.

I hit him with everything I had. Abilene taught me bits and pieces of all different magics. I couldn't mold stone like Sybil, but I could raise enough aether to toss stone and we had a ready supply. I fired rock missiles one after another. Koro knocked most aside with ease. One grazed his shoulder, and he fell back against the pillar.

When I ran out of steam, a pile of stones covered him to the waist.

"Are you finished?" He pushed upward and rose on straight legs. While I played magic showdown, he'd healed himself.

"Your feeble tricks cannot harm me, little flea."

I called the wind. It tore through the hall, churning dust into whirling devils. I sharpened it like a spear and lobbed it at Koro.

Wind magic was old magic, mostly ignored by modern witches. After all, how much damage can wind really do?

It can topple buildings.

It can also steal breath.

My wind spear lanced Koro's throat and pushed back the breath he tried to exhale. I pressed it until his lungs burned. His already bulbous eyes bulged. Black lips hung open in a futile attempt to draw breath.

He pushed back against me. He was stronger, but tired. I was weak, but fueled by rage and desperation. We locked eyes, locked magic, and nothing in the hall moved.

Koro gasped. My wind spear broke, the loss of magic so jarring, I stumbled forward.

Koro held out his hand.

"You will do nicely, child. Come with me and we will achieve greatness."

My father reached for me. The father who tried to rape me. The one who sent assassins and tricked me into endangering my world. But he was my father and his eyes told me he would embrace my dark magic like no one else could.

I reached for his hand.

As our fingers touched, my other arm came down and I slashed him with my blade.

Koro deflected with his forearm, and the blade bounced off as if he wore metal armor. I kept hammering. His laughter boomed through the hall.

But my sword strikes weren't my only offense. Henry taught me to fight, but Quinn and Abilene taught me to fight dirty. The future mistress of the coven was as devious as her mother. And while I rained futile blows on Koro with my sword, my aether snuck under his defenses and drilled into his ward. A little flea burrowing under his skin. He didn't even notice as I hit the source of his magic.

And then I drank.

Quinn ran as far as he could, each breath a ripping pain. He feared his broken rib would puncture a lung. New injuries made themselves known. A hitch in his right ankle slowed him. Blood dripped into his eye from a wound on his forehead.

He had little magic left in reserve, but he put all of it into shutting down the pain. His only thought was to get Jane to safety. Find Rosie so she could heal her. And be at Bobbi's side as she faced her father.

The tunnel stretched into darkness, no doors, no turns, just a narrow shot through rough-hewn rock.

His crippled gait jostled Jane. She whimpered and cried in his arms, but he didn't slow.

His fuzzy mind focused on one goal.

"Stop," Jane whimpered. A weak hand clawed at his throat. His jog slowed to a walk. The witch light went out. He'd exhausted his aether and in his weakened state, he didn't dare dip into the near-empty well. Pain flared in his chest again. In the darkness, Jane's breathing was too loud. He laid her on the cold floor.

"Rest," she said. "Just need to rest. Then we'll go back."

He nodded, knowing she couldn't see him. He slid down the wall. They'd rest, then find a way back to Bobbi.

Koro backhanded me. Pain shot through my cheek. I crashed into the pile of stones and lay dazed. Blackness swirled at the edge of my vision. I pushed up and slipped on blood dripping from my arm. Shards of rock tore my shirt and skin as I clambered away.

I waited out the dizziness, knowing I had no time to waste. When my head stopped spinning, I searched for the line of connection to Koro's aether.

There. Like a fishhook, my aether had embedded in his. The line was thin but unbreakable. I pushed off stones slick with my blood and ignored the stabbing pains from my multiple injuries. It would all be over soon.

Koro waited for me. Perhaps he thought patience was a sign of strength. I was nothing but a minor annoyance, one he would soon squash. But I was attuned to his aether now and he couldn't fool me. He was weak. Weaker than he had ever been in all the eons of his existence.

Weak for a demon, but stronger than me.

I drew on the line connecting us. More dark magic seeped into me. Koro shivered, his long hairy body convulsing as I drank. His eyes widened in surprise.

Take that, dear father. You never expected your brat to have your talents, did you?

He smiled.

"Have it all, daughter. Drink of my power." I felt a surge of aether as he pushed it along the line to me. "You think you can hold my magic in your feeble human body? You can't. It will tear you apart from the inside."

I drank his black power. The more I drank, the more I wanted. It filled me with awe, in the old sense, as in fear of the divine.

I was divine.

Koro grinned and I grinned right back. The magic suffused me. Intoxicating. Exhilarating. No one could stop me. No one could hurt me.

"You are truly my daughter." Koro held out his hand again. "Join me. Forget your foolish dreams. We will conquer worlds together."

I stared at the bony grey fingers, wanting to take them. Wanting the power they would bring.

"You fear the darkness growing in you." Koro's voice soothed. "There is no fear. Only what you construct. Come to me. I will show you the freedom that comes in darkness."

A pained moan escaped my throat as I fought the urge to go to him. He nodded in appreciation. He understood me. The magic was stronger than anything else. I had no reason to resist.

Only a tiny spark inside me knew this was wrong, knew Koro wasn't offering liberty, but slavery. I clung to that spark, fanning it to life with memories of my family, my friends. Of Quinn with his one eyebrow quirked up, laughing at something I said…

"Come, daughter!" Koro's voice boomed. It was filled with command, just as when he terrified Athag's army into fleeing. My feet betrayed me, taking a step closer.

Lord and Lady help me be strong enough to resist!

The Lady! I dropped my useless sword and plunged my hand into my pocket, scrambling for my one final weapon.

The hag stone.

My fingers wrapped around its cool surface.

Koro saw me switch from indecision to action and he lunged. His massive hands closed on my throat. I didn't know if the Lady would hear me so far from home, but I gripped the stone and flung my plea outward with a burst of aether.

Lady! Come to me!

Koro laughed and squeezed out my life.

Quinn sat in the dark, listening to Jane's ragged breathing. The sound paused and he shook her. After an agonizing moment, she sucked in another breath.

This is bullshit. Sitting here like I've lost everything, when Bobbi is fighting for her life.

He shook off the haze of pain and exhaustion and pushed up, using the wall to pull himself to standing. The core may have cured his mawr, but he was a long way from full health. This whole trip, he'd fought to keep that fact hidden, but he could no longer deny it. He didn't dare try another witch light, but he found an old torch in a bracket on the wall and lit it with a puff of aether. The effort took more out of him than it should have. The torch sputtered to life. It wouldn't burn long. He needed to check Jane's injuries fast.

She was broken. Her hair, usually a perfect screen of silver, was crusted to her skull with blood, mud and dust. He lifted the makeshift bandage on her head and her eyes opened.

"You should have been more careful," she said.

Even now, she could give him nothing more than reproach. Her eyes were glassed, her words slurred.

"I told you to be more careful."

"Yes, you did." He wouldn't argue. Not now. He wasn't even sure if she spoke to him or some ghost only she could see. He rewrapped her head with the bandage already soaked with blood. His throat ached for water, and he wished for the first-aid kit, both lost under the rock fall.

Should he leave her and go for help? But who was left to help them? They were alone, trapped underground in an alien land. No one would come for them.

He'd let Jane rest a moment, but then they had to find a way out of the tunnels.

The torch flickered. When it went out they'd have only the comfort of each other in the darkness.

Jane was never good at comfort. Even when he was a small boy, she downplayed his hurts. If his skinned knee didn't pain her, it shouldn't bother him. A broken heart? No more real than the Loch Ness monster; there may have been sightings over the years, but they'd always proven to be hoaxes. That was how Jane thought.

He looked down to find her staring at him. The light of the torch cut across her face. Hard eyes pinned him, eyes no longer fogged over with confusion. Jane knew exactly where they were.

"I hated the smell of this place," she said. "Like cinnamon and blood. I couldn't ever stomach apple pie after."

After. She meant after she came home pregnant with a demon's child. After she escaped months of torture, starvation and rape.

She never spoke of those days to her family, perhaps believing she protected them from the thruth, but if he'd known, maybe he would have understood her aloofness, understood and forgiven her sooner. Instead, he only learned the full horror as an adult. And while his mature mind could forgive her, the years of growing up with an unloving and unlovable mother had already taken their toll.

She was right, though. The stone walls did have an odd spicy scent, made worse by the rock dust floating in the air.

"Are you comfortable," he asked. "Do you want to sit up?"

She shook her head, then gasped as if even this small motion hurt.

"You should have left me when you had the chance," she said, her voice a breathy rasp.

"Don't be—"

"You should have run. And left me." Her good hand clawed at his arm. "I would have left you."

He smiled and took her fingers in his.

"I know, Mom. It's okay."

She nodded and settled back. He petted her matted hair back into place. Tears and snot leaked down his face.

She coughed. In the dim light, the blood on her lips looked black. It bubbled as she pushed out one last breath.

Quinn stared at her. At her body.

That's all there was in the end. A shell leaking blood from lips that would never speak again.

She died in the place that broke her, far from home and her beloved coven.

He couldn't leave her here. He picked her up and ran, no longer worrying that his lumbering pace would hurt her.

Tested

I stood gasping for air on a grassy hill until I realized I could breathe. Touching my neck, I found it unbruised by Koro's assault. My heart pounded. I blinked at the odd sky. It was neither night nor day. The light was too even as if filtered through a white sheet.

Mushrooms ringed the hill I stood on, and tiny bell-shaped wildflowers pocked the ground. A fairy hill.

Massive trees of every kind surrounded the mound. Maple, oak, ash and pine towered over other trees I didn't recognize. White birch glinted in the darkness, and the breeze hinted at unseen fruit blossoms—apple, pear or cherry. Every trunk was tall and wide as if no axe had ever breached this place. The lowest branches soared high above my head. I had never seen such a forest. Then I realized where I stood.

Not a forest. The Forest. The primeval timberland that was the spirit of every forest to come after.

A raven cawed from the branch of a tall pine. I whirled around as more ravens landed, blanketing the branches with their black bodies. Their appearance filled me with foreboding.

"Shoo!" I waved my arms. The birds watched me with coal-black beads but didn't move.

The raven chides blackness. My adopted father Emmet liked to say that when us kids weren't getting along. It finally made sense to me. The ravens were judging me. And I got the feeling someone else watched through their eyes.

I squinted at the tree trunk below the ravens' roost. It had a face. Two dark eyes peered at me. I moved closer, my heart pounding. I knew that face. I recognized the huge black eyes. Benjin. His chameleon skin took on the ragged texture of bark as he stood against the trunk, so well camouflaged, he seemed to grow from the tree. His brother Karnet watched from a second trunk.

"How did you get here?" I asked. They didn't react.

"They come as witnesses only."

I spun to face the Lady.

Like the last time we met, she seemed larger than life, glowing with an inner light that filled the shadows beneath the trees. The ravens stirred and chirped. She calmed them with a smile and a gentle touch.

"Be still, my children. She means us no harm." The birds quieted but didn't leave off their vigil.

"Where am I?" I asked.

"You know already." The Lady's tone wasn't unkind. "Ask a truer question."

"How do I kill him?"

"The demon? That too you know."

I slumped. Defeat sapped the last of my energy.

"I have to give in to the darkness to win?"

The Lady smiled. Behind her the great horned stag paced through the trees, stopping to paw the ground.

"There is no winning. And no darkness."

I ripped my gaze from the sight of her majestic consort. The Lady's face was serene. She reached for my hand, and her touch filled me with unreasonable joy. I wanted to lose myself in the feeling, but that was as cowardly as giving into the darkness. I couldn't live within the Lady's light forever. Eventually, I would return to my world of shadows.

That thought jolted me back to reality.

"We have to hurry! I don't know what this place is, but Koro will kill the others if I don't return."

"You never left."

Two figures appeared before us. Like a translucent hologram, the image flickered. Koro and me locked together in our final fight. His unearthly face twisted in rage, mine red and gasping for air.

My hand lifted to my throat.

"But that means…" I was only here in spirit and Koro still held my body in a death grip. How long did I have before he choked the life from me? Would I even know? Or would my body fail while I was trapped in this spirit world?

"Stop spinning unwanted tales." The Lady smiled and tapped my head with one finger. "It is always so busy up here. Learn to stand still in the moment."

"Right," I grumbled. "Your body isn't being strangled by a demon as we speak."

"Time passes differently in the Forest. Only the batting of a bird's wing will pass before you return."

The ground shook, and I remembered the broodbone stampede, but the thundering announced a chaos of a different kind.

The ravens surged upward as a herd of beasts crashed through the trees. Horses, elk, mules and even some kind of giant goat, all were black as night. Their hooves tore up the ground and their braying calls ran like cold water down my spine. The riders wore costumes from another era—silks and brocades in every hue. And they weren't human. Some had horns. Others were monstrous or beautiful, but all were terrifying. Black hounds with flashing yellow eyes wove around the hunters. They snarled and fought each other, eager to start the hunt.

In the distance, the Lady's consort stood proudly on the top of a rise. His rack of antlers glowed silver in the odd light. He snorted and pawed the ground, his posture saying, *catch me if you can.*

A horn blew. The great Lord galloped away. Hounds howled. Horses reared and the hunt was on. I held my breath, certain they would crash into the trees, but the mismatched steeds slipped gracefully between trunks.

And then they were gone.

My heart thundered in my chest. I had just witnessed the Wild Hunt.

"How do they make you feel?" the Lady asked.

"Afraid."

"Yes. They are frightening. Ugly even, but also…"

"But also beautiful." They were graceful in their wild abandon, fierce and alive in a way I had never been.

"That's why I brought you here." The Lady tipped my chin with one finger. Reluctantly, I tore my eyes from the Hunt. She watched me with a patient smile. "To show you beauty in darkness."

She called out in a song I didn't recognize and the ravens returned, settling on the branches overhead and preening their ruffled feathers. The lady held out her hand. One bird flew to perch on her fingers. She held it inches from my face. The bird looked at me as if my eyes were tasty grapes.

"Do not look away," the Lady said. "See the way its feathers blend black on black. Isn't it beautiful?"

The raven's feathers were blue-black and lustrous. They were beautiful, but I sensed the Lady wanted me to see something more.

The bird flew up, banked left and swooped for my head. The Lady gripped my arm before I ducked. The raven's wing swished past my face. As it flew away, light glinted off its body like the facets of a jewel.

"It is not truly black, is it."

I shook my head.

"Now look." She touched my brow, shading my eyes with her hand. I was transported again, this time to the top of a sand dune looking out over the restless desert on Saka. Wind whipped hair about my face. Beside me, the Lady stood tall and proud, her gossamer gown untouched by the elements.

"Look." She pointed to the desert. The sun wheeled across the sky and dropped below the horizon, filling the desert with shadow.

"It is dark but also beautiful."

"Yes."

In the gloom, the shifting dunes were black, red and purple, like the velvet cape of a king. The sun rose, painting the landscape in gold. Sand creatures skittered over the dunes, leaving zig-zag trails like the brush of an artist. When the racing sun fell again, the darkness only highlighted the absent light.

"Without darkness, there is no light," I said.

"No." Her voice was stern. "Go deeper."

A flock of blackbirds filled the sky. They didn't belong in this alien landscape, but the murmuration felt right in this vision, and I wondered how I could ever have thought them evil.

In a blink, we were back in the Forest. The last stragglers of the Wild Hunt ran between the trees. The horns and braying of the dogs dwindled to a distant cry. Only the Horned Lord remained, his antlers filling the space between two trees while he waited for his Lady.

"The Hunt is neither good nor evil. Neither is magic." The Lady smiled and touched the side of my head. "It is only what you perceive it to be."

The ravens left in one great swirl of black beauty. I watched them until the last of their glinting forms disappeared above the trees and turned to the Lady.

"So you mean…"

She pressed a finger to my lips.

"Forget meaning. Just be."

She touched her lips to my forehead.

I blinked and was back in Koro's hall.

His grip tightened on my throat. The hag stone crumbled to ash in my hand. I flung it into his eyes. He jerked away. It was enough to loosen his hold. I stumbled back and put a pile of debris between us while Koro palmed ash from his eyes.

"Little bitch," he said, then slashed me with his clawed hands. His reach was too short and he missed by inches, but I felt a burn of aether across my chest. Blood welled through my shirt.

"I don't need to touch you to kill you." He smiled.

I pulled on the line of aether I'd hooked into him while we fought. In his arrogance, he never believed I could be a real threat. Now I drank deep.

His eyes widened when he felt me siphon off the last of his aether. He pulled back, trying to shut me down. I gulped magic, filling my well with his darkness, no longer afraid of it. The bitter magic was power, pure as the light of the sun.

Koro balked. In a panic, he threw a quick mage-fire bomb at me, but it rolled off like water.

I bared my teeth. "Like father like daughter. Mage-fire doesn't hurt me."

He twisted, trying to break free from my trap, but I'd snared him thoroughly, and the stream of aether leaving his well wouldn't slow no matter how he strained body or will.

I drank until his bony face hollowed to a husk, and I drank more.

His eyes glazed, then shriveled to dry nuts. The hair on his chest hung limp as his body shrank. Clawed hands twitched and he toppled.

I took it all until I felt like an overfilled pool, ready to burst. The hall brightened, every fallen stone and carved pillar came into sharp relief. In the distance, weapons clashed as the two armies fled. I could sense the movements of vermin in the walls, oblivious to the wars around them as they hurried on with their tiny lives.

Aether filled me. It seeped from my pores. I had the power to topple towers, to bend the will of thousands. To kill.

A hysterical laugh gurgled in my throat. At my fingertips, I had the power of the gods.

"Bobbi, you have to let it go."

I turned to see a man wearing nothing but ragged pants. Dirt and blood were smeared across his bare chest. Bruises and wounds mottled his skin. In my new-found greatness, I could feel the blood coursing through his veins, see his heart pumping with sturdy fear.

Yes, fear me. That was good. All men should fear me. All would bow down to me.

MASTERED

Y ou have to stop." Quinn kept his tone reasonable. Bobbi's expression scared him. Her eyes were…full. Not angry, but brimming with power. It rippled over her skin. She was a charged bolt of lightning, ready to rip through the sky.

"Bobbi, it's over. You have to let it go." He held out his hands, placating but not touching.

Her lip curled in a snarl. He froze. Blue light crackled on her fingertips. His heart thudded in his chest and she cocked her head, listening to it. The smile that spread her lips started feral, but as she laid a hand on his chest, it wavered.

Her eyes beseeched him.

"Quinn? Help me."

He circled her in his arms, feeling aether tremble through bone and muscle.

I breathed in his scent like a blind and deaf animal taking comfort in the one thing that still made sense. Aether ripped through my veins. It wasn't dark or light—the Lady cured me of that fallacy—but it seared like wildfire. I couldn't contain it.

Already, I could feel the power leaking from me. I longed to let it go in one burst, anticipating the exquisite relief that would bring.

It would also level the castle and everyone inside it.

"Let us help you, most glorious one." Rosie touched my hand and flinched as aether crackled up her arm. "That is our purpose. Why holy ones keep impzadzl. You are not first to drink too much."

I giggled. Like I'd drunk too much booze and not the entire wealth of a demon. It would be one hell of a hangover.

Quinn took my other hand. The aether simmered over both of them, wanting to add their power to the well. I held it back. We could form a chain, channel the magic back into the ground, like when I recklessly joined with the core so many months ago. I'd done it to save the coven and protect the precious ward so we could continue to hide from Koro.

We could no longer hide.

The coven's ward had fallen. I opened a portal to this world and we'd already found a door to another. How many worlds were now open to ours? How many more Koros were out there, waiting for the opportunity to feed on human magic? My father may have used me, baited me, but I fell for his traps.

And I continued to endanger my family and my race.

I dropped Quinn and Rosie's hands. There was no letting go of this power. I had to make it mine.

"No!" Quinn saw the resolve in my eyes. I leaned in and let my lips sizzle across his. Then I sat on the ruined floor among the shards of glass and stone, the mud, blood and debris, and I turned inward.

Magic filled me to excess. My aether flowed steadily in my veins. Koro's aether didn't fit. It clanged in discordance with mine and threatened to overload all my senses. I needed to assimilate it. I tried to squeeze it to my will, but Koro's magic rolled off like oil through water.

Dimly, I could hear Quinn yelling and Rosie crying, but I was too far inside my own awareness. They seemed like distant memories.

The two magics were at odds. I could never forge them into one.

Maybe I didn't need to. Maybe I was looking at this problem the wrong way. I was a vessel. The problem wasn't about merging. It was about filling. A switch flicked in my psyche, and Koro's aether suddenly mixed with mine like sand filling the spaces in a jar of stones.

The fear left me. I wouldn't explode. I wouldn't tear the castle down with excess magic. I felt heavy, weighted with energy, but also light, as if I could fly off on the next breeze. I probably could. My magic was potent now, stronger than any I'd seen. But when I opened my eyes and saw Quinn's concern and heard Rosie's lament, I decided to leave flying lessons for another time.

"We are not done here," said Benjin. The fire rippers stepped away from the wall.

I turned my ire on them.

"You hid when the fighting started," I said. "I should strike you down where you stand." I could do it too. Aether itched at my skin, ready to do my bidding.

"You could." Benjin nodded and held his hands wide. "But I said we are not fighters. As Koro learned easily when he took our land. Will you follow his lead?"

I cursed the magic inside me that leapt in response to his challenge. For the rest of my life, I would need to battle the urge to solve my problems with a spit of fire and aether.

"No." I suddenly felt overwhelmingly tired. "I am not my father. Tell me what you want from me."

"Nothing, Lady." He smiled. "You have done enough. We will finish. The demons are not dead. They cannot die. Even now, they draw magic from air and stone. It may be years before they are strong enough to even draw breath, but we cannot leave them here."

Karnet reorganized his altar with Athag at the center. Quinn helped them drag Koro's shriveled body next to it, then the fire rippers sealed the circle, staying within its boundary.

"Step back, all of you," Benjin said. "The land we will send them to is anti-magic. They will be unable to replenish their aether and will stay in this stasis indefinitely. But the effect upon this world will be immediate and devastating. We will work fast and the ward," he pointed to the circle, "should keep it from sucking too much aether from the air."

"But that means…" Before I finished, Karnet said a word that ripped through the air, and a portal opened.

The fire rippers were fast. They lugged the bodies through the hole. I saw them fall into darkness even as the portal slammed shut with a sonic boom. Benjin and Karnet slumped to the side and their ward fell. I ran into the circle, ready to heal them with all the aether at my disposal.

"It is too late, divine Lady," Rosie said. "They are gone."

I looked down at the withered husks of the Ska'in and knew she was right.

RETURNED

Quinn told Tal his brothers were dead. The Ska'in spread his hands in a gesture of distress or simple acceptance.

"He didn't seem surprised," Henry said as they watched him walk away.

"They planned it all along." Quinn was ashamed that he ever thought the fire rippers cowardly. "They knew that opening that gate would kill them. That's why they set up the ward."

Tal wouldn't be gone for long. He'd gather others of his kind to round up the pelags and send the intruders home, then meet them at the gate. He promised to close it, cutting off Earth's access to Saka and the infinite other worlds linked to it.

Henry, Bobbi and Quinn debated it for only a moment. They all agreed humans weren't ready to deal with such open access to other magic and people.

Leofrick survived his fight, but he refused to return with them, as did most of the children of Ruth.

"We have a new life here," he said. "We no longer need to fear Koro. I have no idea what will become of us, but it will be our choice."

Three of the older children chose to return, and Leofrick gave them his blessing.

The trip back through the desert took longer. A cart pulled by an ox that resembled a smaller, shaggy broodbone carried their few supplies and Jane's shrouded body.

Erita led them first to the gully where Sybil's grave was still warded. Gently, they put her beside Jane and continued on at the slow pace of the ox.

Bobbi was different. The new light shining from her eyes worried him. When he touched her, he could feel power surging beneath her skin. Rosie's fawning turned to silent reverence. And when Bobbi smiled at her she could barely contain her exuberance.

But it wasn't just the magic that made her different. She spoke with level authority. Her smiles never quavered the way the old Bobbi's did. When she kissed him, it was with a new assurance.

Quinn watched her for days, assessing this new confidence, until it hit him. She was happy.

He'd known Bobbi for over a year and he'd never seen her truly happy. Oh, she had moments of joy—when they made love, when she worked on Emmett's farm or quietly at her wool shop. But since he met her, she'd been on the run from one agent of Koro or another. She had no peace. And always, at the back of her mind she feared she wasn't strong enough, wasn't witch enough to prevail over the forces aligned against them. Those fears had been laid to rest.

He had no idea what she would do with her new-found power, but he suspected it would be great.

Their last night in the desert, they left the others to camp in private. They made love on the sand still hot from the setting sun. When they returned to the coven there would be plans to make and funerals to attend. But for now, they took simple pleasure in watching the alien stars fill the sky.

She lay with her head on his chest, their limbs entwined. He leaned down and kissed the top of her head. It was hard to feel where one of them left off and the other began.

"I'm sorry about Jane," Bobbi said. "But I think she never meant to come back."

Quinn stroked the hollow of her lower back, now cooling in the evening air.

"Abilene will need our help," he said. "She's very young to run a coven."

"I might be more of a hindrance than anything else."

Quinn frowned. "Stop it. Don't let Jane's shadow change you. You have power unlike any other, and you showed that you can master it." He thought she was over these bouts of self-deprecation.

Bobbi rose up to lean on one elbow.

"That's not what I mean. The Lady spoke to me. I can see her as clear as day. I understand so many things that were a mystery to me before. I have the power to affect real change now, and I'm not afraid to use it. I'm not afraid of anything."

Her smile felt like warm rain in the summer.

She lay back against him, her voice softer now. "Abilene still has her mysteries. And she should. She needs to find her own way to the Lady."

"What are your plans then?"

"I don't know. I guess I have a shop to run." She laughed softly. "That life in Ashlet seems impossibly far away. Maybe I'll leave it to Molly. I've always wanted to travel. And maybe there are more mysteries for me to uncover."

"I'm sure we could find some, if you'd like company."

The kiss she gave him said all he needed to know.

They found the gate the next day. As promised, Tal waited for them beside the standing stones.

Rosie and Erita hugged, cried and babbled in their tongue. Rosie refused to leave Bobbi, and Erita wanted to stay on Saka.

"You world much green," she sniffed. No one tried to convince Rosie to join her. She'd found her Divine One and wouldn't leave her side again.

Bobbi surprised everyone by hugging Tal. The Ska'in stood rigidly through the ordeal, but his mouth widened in a reptilian fire ripper grin.

"Thank you for closing the gate," Quinn said to him. "Though I'm sorry our people won't meet again."

Tal bowed. "Ride a soft wind, child of the Lady."

Quinn waited for the others to step through. Then he took Bobbi's hand and together they went home.

The cool blues and greens of the Pennsylvania forest disoriented me. After the harsh red sun of Saka, my home felt foreign.

A guard was posted at the gate, and as soon as we came through, the entire coven rushed out to greet us.

Henry limped into Gavin's arms, neither bothering to hide his tears.

"No!" Abilene screamed when she saw the two shrouded bodies on the cart. Quinn caught her and she pounded fists against his chest.

The three children of Ruth stood paralyzed with fear until a bevy of witches encircled them with welcoming smiles.

I saw it all—the joy, rage, sadness and fear—and not just as emotions playing across the actors' faces. I saw the magic behind it. Emotion was just another sort of power, a manifestation of aether. And the Lady taught me that all magic—light, dark, bitter or sweet—was beautiful.

I looked back as Tal kept his promise, and the gate winked out of existence.

"Well, I'm glad that's done," Henry said, holding Gavin's hands like a life-saver.

"Yes," I said. "Me too."

But already, I was tracing the fire ripper's aether signature, discovering how Tal had unraveled the gate between worlds and gleaning the intricate weave that would restore it.

Yes, many mysteries still awaited and I was looking forward to them all.

Dear Reader,

I hope you enjoyed reading *Hidden Coven* as much as I enjoyed writing it. Two years ago, I started a story about a bumbling witch named Bobbi who I just knew could do great things. I didn't expect her to take me to another world, but I'm very glad you were along for the ride.

Interacting with readers is one of the best parts of being a writer, and I'd love to hear from you. Feel free to email me at info@kimmcdougall.com and let me know what you thought of *Hidden Coven*. Or subscribe to my newsletter to get updates on new releases at https://kimmcdougall.com/Readers-Group.

Did you know that every time a reader leaves a review, the author gets a free unicorn? Okay, that's not true, but wouldn't it be great if it was? But seriously, reviews make the publishing world go round. You don't need to be a professional reviewer; a simple rating and a few words will help me get my books in front of more readers.

So if you enjoyed *Hidden Coven* please https://kimmcdougall.com/review-hidden-coven to leave a review at your favorite retailer and make this author's day.

Thank you,

Kim McDougall

What to Read Next

Critter wrangler rule #2: When scary things run away, something scarier is coming.

Someone is killing dragons. And the killings point to a civil war brewing among the fae.

When Kyra Greene finds an abandoned baby dragon, she doesn't want to bring him home. But until she can hunt down his thunder and stop the dragon killers, she's on babysitting duty.

As a pest controller with a soft heart, Kyra already has an apartment full of rescues, including a basilisk who thinks he's a turkey, a banshee nanny, and a pygmy kraken. She might take care of them, but they also fill her need for family. And when that family is threatened, she'll risk everything to save them. She'll even join forces with the handsome and irritating captain of the city's vigilante Guardians, who never fails to show up at her most undignified moments.

Along with a quirky cast of misfits and unruly critters, Kyra leaves the safety of Montreal Ward and travels through the dangerous Inbetween—the land beyond the protected city states, where magic is the only rule of law. Can she reunite the lost dragon with his thunder and stop a new and sinister force from invading their home?

With over 2500 five-star reviews, see why readers are calling *Dragons Don't Eat Meat* a laugh-out-loud adventure with delightfully evil critters and a slow-burn romance.

Dragons Don't Eat Meat is the first book in the Valkyrie Bestiary Series. Get it at your favorite retailer at <u>https://kimmcdougall.com/dragons-don-t-eat-meat</u>.

About the Author

If Kim McDougall could have one magical super-power, it would be to talk to animals. Or maybe to shift into animal form. Definitely, fantastical critters and magic often feature in her stories. So until she can change into a griffin and fly away, she writes dark paranormal action and romance tales, from her home in Central Ontario.

Visit Kim Online at **KimMcDougall.com**.

Other places you can follow Kim McDougall Books:

- Facebook: https://www.facebook.com/KimMcDougallBooks
- Instagram: https://www.instagram.com/kimmcdougallbook
- Amazon: https://www.amazon.com/-/e/B002C7CI2M
- Bookbub: https://www.bookbub.com/authors/kim-mcdougall
- Goodreads: https://www.goodreads.com/author/show/1432797.Kim_McDougall

Also By Kim McDougall

Valkyrie Bestiary Novels
Dragons Don't Eat Meat
Dervishes Don't Dance
Hell Hounds Don't Heel
Grimalkins Don't Purr
Kelpies Don't Fly
Ghouls Don't Scamper
Devils Don't Lie

Valkyrie Bestiary Novellas
The Last Door to Underhill
The Girl Who Cried Banshee
Three Half Goats Gruff
Oh, Come All Ye Dragons

The Hidden Coven Series
Inborn Magic
Soothed by Magic
Trigger Magic
Bellwether Magic
Gone Magic

Writing as Eliza Crowe
The Shifted Dreams Series
Pick Your Monster
Lost Rogues